Never Mind the Laptops

Never Mind the Laptops

✦

Kids, Computers, and the
Transformation of Learning

Bob Johnstone

iUniverse, Inc.
New York Lincoln Shanghai

Never Mind the Laptops
Kids, Computers, and the Transformation of Learning

iUniverse, Inc.

For information address:
iUniverse, Inc.
2021 Pine Lake Road, Suite 100
Lincoln, NE 68512
www.iuniverse.com

ISBN: 0-595-28842-1 (pbk)
ISBN: 0-595-65897-0 (cloth)

Printed in the United States of America

To Michael Bessie

Contents

Part III   MARVELLOUS MELBOURNE

Part IV   BOOMERANG

INTRODUCTION

At my two-room primary school in rural Scotland, I learned to write on a wood-frame slate tablet. (Paper was scarce in those post-war days.) Today, my children type their—often Internet-researched—homework assignments on a laptop computer. In less than a lifetime, we have gone from the most primitive to the most advanced technology.

As computers have advanced, an epic struggle has been raging to apply technology to transform learning. The struggle continues: though my kids can use computers, they cannot use them at school. In other parts of society—offices, hospitals, factories—technology has revolutionized the way work is done. The computer has changed the world, redefining what it means to be literate. Schools, however, remain much as they were when I was a boy. More than twenty years after the advent of the personal computer, school is the only place where the technology is still not taken seriously

This oversight persists despite a rapidly-growing body of evidence showing that access by students to computers, on a one-to-one basis, can lead to a dramatic transformation in the nature of their learning. Especially at schools where students each have their own laptops which, because portable, can be carried home from school and used there, too.

Specifically, kids with their own portable computers become *fluent* in the new medium. They do more and better writing, more and better projects, more and better presentations, more collaborative work (at school), and more independent learning (at home). They do fewer mindless tasks, like copying notes from the board (downloading them instead from the school web site) and watch far less TV. Girls no longer have to compete for access with boys, and vault ahead as a result. Children with learning difficulties gain self-esteem from their work because it looks just as good as everyone else's.

The technology-enabled transformation of schools into learning communities has a profound effect on educators, too. Computers force teachers to rethink what they want to achieve. In a seeming paradox, teachers teach less, but students learn more. The technology frees teachers from the need to lecture, allowing them to do more individual guidance with their students. Teachers become learners, students become teachers. Educators collaborate more with their colleagues

1

and ask each other's advice. Teachers with laptop computers think more highly of their work and by extension themselves. They develop a new-found sense of professional pride.

Parents have consistently demonstrated that they are prepared to make extraordinary commitments in order to provide laptops for their children. They want to bridge the ever-widening chasms that have opened up between workplace and school, and between rich and poor. In their enthusiasm, parents often become deeply involved in supporting their local school systems. This, in itself, is a highly desirable outcome.

Computers are of course not a panacea for all the problems that afflict school. But the experience at hundreds of laptop schools has thus far been that the impact of the computers is benign. Absenteeism tends to drop, discipline to improve; students take more responsibility for their work. And, if only because the kids are at school more often, and participating more actively in academic programs, their test scores tend to improve.[1]

◆   ◆   ◆

Unbeknownst to me as I struggled to memorize my times tables, a revolution was underway. It began in 1947, before I was born, with the invention of the transistor. Twelve years later, while I was still at primary school, came the first microchip. That inspired Moore's Law, the principle that the number of transistors on a chip doubles every 18 months even as the cost of the chip halves. More-for-less led to laptop computers, the first of which appeared in the early 1980s. By the turn of the century, laptops had shrunk to become notebooks. Though no bigger or heavier than my old slate tablet, these machines packed infinitely more power.

A watershed in the microelectronic revolution was the launch by the Soviet Union in 1957 of Sputnik, the first man-made satellite. Sputnik not only provided the impetus for the development of the microchip (to lighten US rocket payloads), it also came as a wake-up call for American education. Competing in the space race would require better schooling in math and science. The federal government made money available for innovative approaches—like using technology in the classroom.

---

1.   For details, see for example the extensive work done over many years by the consulting firm Rockman et al <www.rockman.com>

Experiments began very early on, when computers themselves were still in their infancy. Initial attempts concentrated on improving the efficiency of instruction. Then, beginning in the mid 1960s, it was realized that rather than a replacement for the teacher, a better use for the machine would be as an unprecedented new medium for learning, to boost the intellectual opportunity of the student.

First to formulate this idea was Seymour Papert, a professor of mathematics at Massachusetts Institute of Technology. During the 1980s, thousands of heroic grade school teachers attempted to implement Papert's vision. But their efforts were doomed, in large part by the lack of hardware. Many classrooms were equipped with just a single computer. The computer might be a powerful new type of pencil but, as Papert put it scathingly, What good is one pencil between thirty pupils?

The fire that the professor had kindled was not entirely extinguished. It burst back into flame in a most unlikely place, at the opposite end of the planet. In 1990, Methodist Ladies' College in Melbourne, Australia, instigated a policy of compulsory laptop computers for its girls, beginning with the ten-year-olds in fifth-grade classes, with their parents paying for the computers. The reason was simply that David Loader, the College's visionary principal, believed that the technology would empower his students.

Unlike previous attempts to insert computers into the classroom, this was not an experiment. Entrusting the youngsters with a laptop—the most powerful tool known to society—was a gesture, a way of welcoming the kids to the world of serious intellectual pursuits. In that instance, as in almost every instance since, the students rose to the occasion.[2]

The affluent inner suburbs where Methodist Ladies' College is located boast an unusual concentration of private schools. In part for competitive reasons, it became necessary for other schools to implement laptop programs, too. Within a few years, tens of thousands of laptops were in the hands of Australian kids and—equally important—their teachers. The success of such programs drew flocks of visitors from near and far.

In 1995, beguiled by the idea of grade-school kids using its office software, Microsoft flew ten US educators from Seattle to Australia for a fact-finding mission. The Americans were astonished by what they saw happening in antipodean

---

2. Gary Stager, "Laptops in School—A Wonderfully Cautionary Tale", 2000 <stager.org/articles/laptopbookchapter.html>

classrooms. They went home determined to adapt the Australian experience to US conditions.

This led to the formation the following year of an initiative that came to be known as Anytime Anywhere Learning. By 2002, several hundred schools all over the United States, along with others in half a dozen countries around the world, had taken up the challenge of equipping every kid with a computer.

A second, related US initiative that drew heavily on the Australian experience was the Teacher Leadership Project, which began in 1997. Since then this grass-roots project has trained almost 4,000 teachers in the use of technology in the classroom in the state of Washington and elsewhere.

The ripples continue to spread. In Fall 2002, under Papert's guidance, and citing American emulations of the Australian initiative, Maine became the first US state to mandate laptop computers for every student in its seventh-grade classes. It was the largest educational technology project in American history, and one which its instigator, Governor Angus King believed, would "fundamentally transform K-12 education throughout our State and, ultimately, the nation."

With the price of hardware continuing to drop, other states will likely follow Maine's lead. ("As goes Maine, so goes the nation"). But before all kids at America's hundred-thousand-plus schools have their own laptops, and all teachers have been taught to use the technology effectively, there is still a very long way to go.

◆   ◆   ◆

My point of entry to this extraordinary educational odyssey was a 1997 magazine assignment to find out what was happening with computers in Australian schools. It didn't take me long to discover that Methodist Ladies' College in Melbourne was the epicenter of the laptop movement. I visited the school, and was amazed by what I saw there. I subsequently went back many times. The more I looked, the more I became convinced that something truly remarkable was going on there.

With computers, for what is probably the first time in history of the world, kids know more about something important than adults. I vividly recall one morning at MLC coming across three tenth-graders giving instructions on the implementation of a real-world project—a multimedia installation at an inner city facility—to two besuited computer company executives. The suits were hanging on the girls' every word. Truly, this was empowerment in action.

I wondered why Papert's powerful ideas had taken root and flourished so far from their place of origin? And, having flourished, how the fruits had been transplanted back to their home country? My editor in San Francisco countered with a deterministic argument: the nature of digital technology was such, he asserted, that the germination could have happened anywhere.

Not so! I believe that contingency dictates the time and place where momentous events occur. Exceptional individuals acting in response to specific stimuli and constraints are always crucial to outcomes. This book tells the story of some of these educational heroes and heroines. It does not pretend to be comprehensive: if I have left out some developments, it is not because they are unimportant, but because they are not directly related to the story I want to tell.

The book divides roughly into two halves. The first half deals with the efforts of researchers and experimentalists; the second, with those of teachers and implementers. I begin by sketching some background. As Diane Ravitch, doyenne of US education history, writes, "We cannot understand where we are and where we are heading without knowing where we have been."[3]

Part One looks at the earliest attempts to introduce teaching machines and computer terminals into the classroom. It shows how behavioristic strategies, computer-aided instruction, and the primitive nature of the technology led to so-called "computer laboratories".

Alas, despite huge improvements in computers, laboratories remain to this day the dominant response of schools to the challenge of technology. Most US schools now have a computer lab. The problem is that the labs are "down the hall and once a week." Portable computing is all about liberation. It is about taking power away from the director of technology—the person who keeps the key to the school's computer lab—and giving it, via unlimited access, to all staff and students.

Part Two deals with Seymour Papert, Logo, *Mindstorms,* and the rise and fall of programming in US schools. It also shows how educational imperatives stemming directly from Papert's work have played an important role in shaping the development of portable computers, notably the laptop itself.

Part Three tells the story of how Methodist Ladies' College in Melbourne came to be the first school in the world to introduce mandatory laptop computers for its students. It examines the extraordinary metamorphosis that took place at the school following the implementation of the computers, how other Australian schools joined the movement, and how they succeeded in institutionalizing the change.

---

3.   Diane Ravitch, "Left Back: A Century of Failed School Reforms", Simon & Schuster, New York, 2000, p14

Part Four traces the transfer of the one-to-one paradigm from Australia to the US. It details how the model and its derivatives spread through mechanisms like the Anytime Anywhere Learning program, the Teacher Leadership Project in Washington State, and Maine's Lunchboxes to Laptops initiative. It gives examples of schools where learning has been transformed by laptops, and concludes with some thoughts about what still needs to be done.

Laptops, notebooks, portable computers—call them what you will, they are clearly the way of the future. In May 2003, for the first time, US sales of laptop computers overtook those of desktops. "The laptop", says Papert, "is the prime instrument for today's intellectual work." Regarding the future, one thing at least is certain—the price of the technology will continue to drop. For this, if for no other reason, it is hard to imagine a classroom anywhere in the Western world by, say, the year 2020 in which kids do *not* each have their own laptop or notebook computer. The recent introduction of wireless technology makes connecting up individual computers to a network straightforward and relatively inexpensive. Educators who try to oppose the oncoming tide of technology—and the transformation in learning that it can bring—will find themselves on the wrong side of history.

Ubiquitous computing has been successfully implemented in schools all over the world for more than a decade now: it should no longer be thought of as an experiment the outcome of which is uncertain. Ubiquitous computing "is coming," Papert insists, "the only question is not whether to do it, but are we going to let it come upon us unprepared, or are we getting ready for it and adapting ourselves to it right now?" Bette Manchester, who directs professional development for Maine's laptop program, likes to ask teachers to imagine what kind of world their seventh-graders are going to live in when they grow up. Then she asks the teachers to think about their classrooms, and whether they fit that world.

At the same time, it is important not to get carried away. One must remember that culture change does not happen overnight. Innovations typically take a long time to work their way into the mainstream. Printed books were invented in 1452, but it was not until the end of the eighteenth century—some three hundred and fifty years later—that textbooks became extensively used in schools. Let us hope that, this time, the change will not take so long.

It is vital that schools should see ubiquitous computing as more than a way of improving the efficiency of conventional learning. Or, as simply a method of skilling students for the twenty-first century workplace. In particular, educators must not attempt to use computers to try and micro-manage their students, keystroke by keystroke.

Many people make the mistake of thinking that the arrival of computers in the classroom is in itself of prime importance. It is not. As Alan Kay says, "the music is not in the piano." Never mind the laptops—what's important is rather the kind of learning that kids do using the technology. Creativity, autonomy, persistence, risk-taking: such desirable qualities cannot be taught (or tested). But you can put students in an environment which fosters their development. By virtue of its flexible, open-ended nature, the computer helps to create such an environment.

As the evidence I present here shows, the coming of portable computers represents a wonderful opportunity to bring about a fundamental transformation in the nature of school and the process of learning. Making sure that this revitalization happens is our responsibility. Here are some of the things we must do:

- Parents already understand that acquiring fluency in the use of computers is crucial to their children's future prospects. They must demand that schools prepare their kids for tomorrow's world, not yesterday's. Parents must also recognize that, if the one-kid-one-computer paradigm is to become pervasive, they must work together with schools to create alternative revenue streams to fund laptop programs. Failure to do so will ensure that the digital divide—the technology gap between rich and poor, between independent and public schools—will widen still further.

- Teachers are amongst the greatest resistors to change. For many, computers threaten what they do and how they do it. The changing of the generations will help overcome the problem, but not in the short term. In most Western countries including the US, the average age of teachers is rising. Educators must embrace the future, not cling to the past. They must become learners themselves and in so doing, rediscover the joy of learning.

- Principals must show leadership. They must support the innovators among their staff, while making it clear to the laggards that they have to keep up. Principals must also be sure to provide teachers with laptops, not expect them to buy their own.

- School districts must resist the temptation to squander their limited funds on the latest—hence most expensive—hardware. Instead, they must invest more in their most precious resource, their teachers. Administrators must ensure staff get the professional development and in-service training that they need to be comfortable with computers.

- Teachers' ed colleges must take a long hard look at how they prepare teachers for the twenty-first century classroom. They must try hard to identify best practice in technology-rich environments, then vigorously propagate it. If the educational establishment cannot overcome its inertia, then it is headed for the scrapheap.

- Politicians and other elected officials like superintendents must resist the temptation to play on people's fears, asserting that improving test scores is all that matters in education. To maintain, as some do, that what was good enough for our parents is good enough for our children is simply absurd.

- Business leaders must do a better job of communicating to education departments the requirements of the contemporary workplace. Employers should emphasize their need for young people who are flexible enough to act on their own initiative as well as to work collaboratively with others.

- Computer makers must go beyond trying to sell boxes. They must stop regarding education merely as "the market of last resort". It is very much in their long-term interest to cooperate with educators to make sure that school computer systems get up and, once up, stay running.

- Journalists must try harder to understand the nature of the momentous change that is happening. They must stop relying on the outdated opinions of a few curmudgeons, thus constantly reinforcing a negative stereotype about computers in the classroom. Rather, they should go out to schools, talk to teachers, and feature those who are using technology to do innovative things.

- Humanists must disabuse themselves of misguided notions of the computer as a mechanical instrument of oppression. Society as a whole is still not getting the message about technology in schools. Ultimately, the greatest challenge we face is how to provide equity of access for all our kids. Though making such a provision is and will continue to be hard, it must not be used as an excuse for inaction.

What has thus far been implemented only in exceptional schools and classrooms, through the heroic efforts of visionary leaders like the ones described in this book, men and women who simply wouldn't take no for an answer, must become the norm. The leadership and the will to make it happen for every student at every school is still lacking. In many ways, the epic struggle to transform learning via technology has only just begun.

PART I
BROOM CLOSET DAYS

1

GUIDED BY PIGEONS

Beep-beeep! On 4 October, 1957, the Soviet Union launched Sputnik, the world's first man-made satellite. The silvery basketball-sized object whizzed over the US seven times a day, emitting an infernal beeping noise as it went. "Americans were stunned. How could the Russians have beaten us into outer space? Something must be wrong with American education."[1]

"Sputnik became an instant metaphor", wrote historian Diane Ravitch, "for the poor quality of US schools."[2] Critics such as Elmer Hutchisson, the then-director of the American Institute of Physics, warned that American educators had better pull their socks up. It was time, he told a reporter from the *New York Times*, to substitute the '"highly accumulative" scientific knowledge that can be taught by rigorous discipline' (such as that found in Soviet classrooms) for the "namby-pamby kind of learning" practiced by US schools. Failure to do so, the chief physicist was certain, would doom the American way of life "to rapid extinction".[3]

Popular pressure for a response to the Russian space threat forced the federal government to take swift action. In September 1958, Congress passed the National Defense Educational Act, which provided funds to improve teaching, particularly of science and mathematics. Money supplied by Washington and private institutions like the Carnegie and Ford Foundations made it possible during the early 1960s for schools to experiment with novel educational methods.

---

1. B.F. Skinner, "Programmed Instruction Revisited", *Phi Delta Kappan*, October 1986, p105
2. Diane Ravitch, "Left Back: A Century of Failed School Reforms", Simon & Schuster, New York, 2000, p361
3. Harold M. Schmeck, "Nation Is Warned to Stress Science, Faces Doom Unless Youth Learns Its Importance", *New York Times*, October 8, 1957 [page number unknown]

Among them, one was particularly prominent. It was, according to a feature article in the October 1960 edition of *Fortune* magazine, "the most radical innovation in education since John Dewey introduced his 'progressive theories' [read: namby-pamby kind of learning] more than half a century ago..."

"The familiar routine of school—lectures, textbook study, recitation, regular quizzes, and even, to a certain extent, teachers—has been all but eliminated." Were it to live up to its early promise, gushed the article, the new method "could in the next decade or two revolutionize education. Indeed, so fundamental would be its effects that it could conceivably "upset the whole social structure of American youth."[4]

This revolutionary new method was called "programmed instruction". It was delivered via purpose-built devices known as "teaching machines". The method's inventor and principle advocate was Harvard professor Burrhus Frederick—"Fred"—Skinner.

In 1957 B.F. Skinner was probably America's most celebrated psychologist. Judging by a contemporary photograph taken in his lab, Skinner certainly looked the part. A receding hairline accentuates an already higher-than-average forehead, giving the impression of a man with a truly enormous brain (and, no doubt, a truly enormous ego to match).

Skinner is best-known as a behaviorist. Behaviorists are most famous (or infamous) for their experiments on rats. In fact, Skinner's favorite subjects were not rodents, but pigeons. The pigeon, he wrote approvingly, was "a healthy, docile animal with good color vision."[5]

Skinner demonstrated that it was possible to teach pigeons complex and subtle behaviors, the like of which had "probably never previously been reached by members of their species."[6] Such behaviors included modified versions of bowling and ping pong, neither of them particularly obvious milestones on any conceivable pigeon evolutionary path.

When it performed in the desired manner, a hungry bird in a small box would immediately be rewarded with a kernel of corn. (In Skinner-speak, its behavior was "shaped" by "reinforcement".) Though devised in the laboratory, this technique turned out to have practical applications. Some of these were unexpected—like guiding missiles to their targets, for example.

---

4.   George A.W. Boehm, "Can People Be Taught Like Pigeons?", *Fortune*, October 1960, p176

5.   B.F. Skinner, "Teaching Machines", *Scientific American*, 205 (November), 1961, p92

6.   Ibid, p94

"Project Pigeon" began during World War II in response to a problem that bedeviled early rocket-powered weaponry. Namely, that control signals transmitted to the rocket by radio were easy for the enemy to jam. Some sort of self-contained guidance system was clearly called for. Among possible solutions to this problem, the US Navy hit on the idea of using pigeons. It hired Skinner to train them.

Confined in a missile's nose cone, the pigeon was supposed to peck at an image of the target—an enemy ship, say—projected via a lens onto a touch-sensitive screen connected to the missile's guidance servo-mechanisms. To guard against momentary distractions, and to guarantee reliability, three pigeons were used. If the missile was on course, all three pigeons would peck the middle of the screen.

After the war the research was revived, from 1948 to 1951, under the title of Project Orcon (for "organic control"). In simulated rocket tests, the pigeons produced "surprisingly good results". Eventually, the birds were able to track a target image jumping all over the screen, for more than a minute at a time. They were capable of delivering four pecks per second, over 80 percent of them within a quarter inch of the target.[7]

Project Orcon was abandoned, in favor of inertial guidance, because of the limited range of its optical system and the fact that it could only be used during daylight hours. But, as Skinner explained, there was a direct link between pigeon guidance and teaching machines. "The project had forced us to consider the education of large numbers of pigeons....One great lesson of our experimental work seemed clear: it is unthinkable to try to arrange by hand the subtle contingencies of reinforcement that shape behavior. Instrumentation is essential. Why not teach students by machine also?"[8]

Why not, indeed? Skinner had always been a tinkerer, in his youth building Rube Goldberg contraptions. Now he put that skill to good use by designing a series of teaching machines, the first of which he demonstrated at a psychology meeting at the University of Pittsburgh in 1954.

At the time, Skinner was unaware of similar work done by Sydney Pressey, a psychology professor at Ohio State University, back in the mid 1920s. Pressey's machine was designed to test his students' knowledge by presenting them with multiple-choice answers to questions. The student responded by pressing one of

7. Steve Scrupski, "Navy Declassifies Details of Pigeon Guidance Project", *Electronic Design*, November 22, 1999, Volume 47, Number 24
8. B.F. Skinner, "Teaching Machines", *Scientific American*, 205 (November), 1961, p95

four keys. If his choice was correct, the machine moved on to the next item; if incorrect, the student pressed another key. The machine kept track of errors, so that when the student took the test a second time, it would stop only on questions which he had answered incorrectly the first time. Pressey's machine thus functioned as teacher as well as tester. It also featured a reward-dial that could be set for any desired score. Once that score was attained, the machine automatically dispensed a candy.

The professor was gratified to discover that his students learned faster this way than they did from reading textbooks. He wrote excitedly about "the coming 'industrial revolution' in education".[9] But the world was not yet ready for teaching machines. "At that time there was no shortage of teachers and little public pressure to speed up the pace of education ['cultural inertia', scoffed Skinner], and Pressey's ideas were ignored by educators."[10] In 1932, Pressey gave up work on automating education, citing lack of funds.

A quarter century later, Skinner's machines would take a different tack. Students would come to them not to be tested, but to learn. Instead of choosing from prepared answers (multiple-choices notoriously increasing the probability of students remembering the wrong answer) they would write their own replies. Third, and most importantly, Pressey's machine merely gave an evaluation of each response. Whereas, "in my machine", Skinner wrote, "the items were arranged in a special sequence, so that, after completing the material in frame 1, the students were better able to tackle frame 2, and their behavior became steadily more effective as they passed from frame to frame. I began to speak of 'programmed instruction.'"[11]

In 1958, Skinner had a dozen of his machines installed in a self-study room in Sever Hall, Harvard Yard, to teach an undergraduate course (Natural Sciences 114) on, appropriately enough, human behavior. The machines were about the size of a typewriter, though mechanically much simpler. A commercial version, dubbed the Didak, was marketed by Rheem-Califone in 1960. It retailed for $157.50.

The programs consisted of a sequence of up to several thousand small steps, or "frames", printed on fan-folded paper and loaded into the machine. Rolling the paper forward exposed a single frame in a window. Each frame consisted of a sen-

9.   Sidney L. Pressey, "A Third and Fourth Contribution Toward the Coming 'Industrial Revolution' in Education", *School and Society*, vol 36, 1932, p934

10.   Boehm, p177

11.   B.F. Skinner, "Programmed Instruction Revisited", *Phi Delta Kappan*, October 1986, p104

tence with one or more missing words. For example, the first of the 2,300-odd items in Natural Sciences 114 read, "A doctor taps your knee (patellar tendon) with a rubber hammer to test your _____."[12]

The student wrote his or her (Radcliffe girls also took the course) response, in pencil, on a separate roll of paper located in a smaller window to the right of the text. Pulling a knob on a slider located above the windows rolled both frame and response forward, uncovering the correct answer—in this case, "reflexes"—while at the same time covering the response with a transparent shield, to prevent the student from cheating. The students graded their answers as correct or incorrect by inserting a pencil point in one of two holes and making a mark.

Feedback was important, because too many errors—more than 5 to 10 percent—indicated that the program needed improvement. "Effective Skinnerian programming requires instructional sequences so simple that the learner hardly ever makes a mistake."[13] To write such programs meant atomizing the subject matter into tiny pieces. The idea behind making each step as small as possible was that it would maximize the frequency of reinforcement. Students, it turned out, were more malleable than pigeons—no corn for them, not even candy. Reinforcement was merely the faint glow of self-satisfaction that came from knowing they had got the right answer.

Though producing such programs was not easy, the machines seemed to work. Students spent an average of 15 hours on them during a one-semester course, getting through the equivalent of a 200-page textbook. "Although it is less convenient to go to a self-study room than to pick up a textbook in one's own room," Skinner wrote, "most students feel that machine study has compensating advantages. They work for an hour or so with little effort, and they report that they learn more in less time and with less effort than in conventional ways. An important advantage is that the student always knows where he stands without waiting for a test or a final examination."[14]

There was also another, unexpected benefit. While demonstrably labor-saving devices, teaching machines in no way resembled a mass production line. In fact, "the effect on each student is surprisingly like that of a private tutor."[15] Skinner pointed out that there was a constant exchange between program and student

---

12. Ibid
13. Paul Saettler, "The Evolution of American Educational Technology", Libraries Unlimited, Englewood, Colorado, 1990, p296
14. B.F. Skinner, "Teaching Machines", *Scientific American*, 205 (November), 1961, p96
15. Ibid, p97

which kept the latter on his toes. "Like a good tutor, the machine insists that a given point be understood before moving on." And, by using hints and prompts, it helped the student to come up with the right answer. Finally, by rewarding every correct answer (allowing the student to move on to the next step), the machine managed to hold the student's interest.

Thus far in human history the processes of teaching and learning had been little understood. Now, for the first time, here was "a true technology of education."[16] Never one to shy away from making extravagant claims, Skinner asserted that "machines such as those we use at Harvard could be programmed to teach, in whole and in part, all the subjects taught in elementary and high school and many taught in college."[17]

In addition to the breadth of its applicability, there was also the sheer efficiency of the method. Skinner was soon telling audiences that, "with the help of teaching machines and programmed instruction, students could learn twice as much in the same time and with the same effort as in a standard classroom."[18]

There would be benefits for teachers, too. Programmed instruction would liberate them from the drudgery of what Skinner called "white-collar ditch-digging". Freed from the likes of drilling, the dishing out of routine information, and the correction of homework, the teacher could emerge "in his proper role as an indispensable human being."[19] In addition to which, teachers would no longer have to deal with discipline problems, because schools would be redesigned with classrooms broken up into study booths, like the ones in Sever Hall, with a machine in each booth.

Educators were skeptical. They voiced for the first time concerns that would echo down the coming decades, in seemingly endless debates over the introduction of technology into the classroom. Administrators would use teaching machines to replace teachers. The machines would reduce education to a cold, mechanical process that would turn students into robots. Schools would become factories.

Skinner dismissed such fears as "groundless." His supporters asserted, minting another phrase that would long remain current, that any teachers who thought they could be replaced by a machine, deserved to be.

---

16. Ibid, p91
17. Ibid, p97
18. B.F. Skinner, "Programmed Instruction Revisited", *Phi Delta Kappan*, October 1986, p104
19. Quoted in Boehm, p178

Nonetheless, "American schools were generally slow to adopt programmed instruction."[20] The first field trials of the new method took place in Roanoke, a small city nestled in the heart of Virginia's Blue Ridge mountains. In February 1960, a pilot class of 34 eighth graders at one of the city's public schools took a programmed beginners' course in algebra.

"The children worked on the program for fifty minutes a day. There were no lectures and no homework. The teacher was forbidden to talk to the students about algebra. The result was an overwhelming triumph for the Skinner method. In less than one semester, all 34 pupils completed a full year's work."[21] When tested, 50 percent got a ninth-grade score; the rest scored average for the eighth grade or better.

Following this encouraging success, in the fall of 1960, some nine hundred ninth graders in all of Roanoke's secondary schools participated in a large-scale trial that included a control group. This time, however, the results were inconclusive. The study was disrupted by "a number of uncontrolled variables", most notably a teacher who was so hostile to the idea of programmed instruction, he flunked 30 percent of the students in one of the experimental classes.[22] Undeterred, Roanoke decided to extend programmed instruction to subjects including English and foreign languages, as well as other branches of math.

In June 1960, *Control Engineering* magazine blithely predicted that the market for teaching machines would grow to $100 million within ten years.[23] At least twenty US equipment manufacturers were said to be designing teaching machines or thinking of doing so. Meanwhile, alarmed at the prospect of their textbooks being rendered obsolete, educational publishers rushed to produce programmed texts. By the end of 1962, according to one estimate, some 500 programmed courses were available across a range of elementary, secondary, and college subjects.

By then, however, the fad for programmed instruction had already peaked. There were several reasons why enthusiasm flagged. One was that the method failed to live up to the hype. Following Skinner's hubristic lead, manufacturers and publishers made exaggerated advertising claims without bothering to do corroboratory research. More effort typically went into building the machines than

---

20. Saettler, p297
21. Boehm, p259
22. Saettler, p433
23. "The Coming Boom in Teaching Machines", author unknown, *Control Engineering*, June 1960

into writing programs for them. Hardware was sold—sometimes door-to-door—without sufficient software.

The machines were too expensive for most schools to contemplate. (According to one estimate, "with every student taking several programmed courses, a school might have to invest $50 to $100 per student even after machines got into mass production.") Developing good programming proved more expensive to produce than expected, costing anywhere from $2,000 to $6,000 per student hour. The market, so far from improving the quality of programs, as Skinner had anticipated, was soon flooded with substandard material.

Parents fretted that programmed instruction was more appropriate to an animal psychology lab than to a school. ("I don't want my child taught like a pigeon.") Teachers grumbled about their profession being reduced to the level of machine-shop supervisor. For their part, school boards were mostly too conservative to contemplate abandoning conventional education.

Ultimately, however, the biggest problem with programmed instruction was simply that kids hated it. In fact, it drove them nuts—especially the brighter ones. The rigidity of the seemingly endless, tiny-steps, one-word-answer format bored clever students to tears. They soon found ingenious ways of circumventing the programs and even, in some cases, of sabotaging the machines. A well-placed wad of chewing gum could throw a whole terminal out of whack.

Meanwhile, in academe, the tide was turning. Out went behaviorism, in came cognitive science. Whereas behaviorism had emphasized the external (Skinner at his most outrageous liked to deny there was any such thing as "mind"), the cognitive approach focused on the internal, on the construction of knowledge by the learner. Students were no longer to be *told* things; they were to *discover* things for themselves.

"Cognitive science approaches teaching and learning in a different way. It addresses how the human, as an information processor, functions and uses information. Rather than focusing on teaching facts through expository lectures or demonstrations, the emphasis is, instead, on developing higher-order thinking and problem-solving skills."[24]

The foundations of this new, discovery-based approach to education were laid down at a meeting at Woods Hole on Cape Cod in September 1959. Thirty-five educators—all men—gathered to discuss how to spend the money made available by the National Defense Education Act. At the meeting Skinner demonstrated

---

24.   Andrew R. Molnar, *Computers in Education: A Brief History*, THE Journal, Volume 24, Number 11, June 1997

his teaching machines. The discussion which followed the demonstration was "lively, at times stormy."[25] The group's conclusions were reported by its director Jerome Bruner, who in 1960 co-founded the Center for Cognitive Studies at Harvard, in a hugely influential book published that year, *The Process of Education*.

On the outcome of the man-versus-machine debate, Bruner was prescient. "Clearly, the machine is not going to replace the teacher—indeed, it may create a demand for more and better teachers if the more onerous part of part of teaching can be relegated to automatic devices."[26]

By 1964, programmed instruction in schools was in decline. A disgusted Skinner wrote that "It was as if the automobile industry had been shown how to build cars in half the time at half the cost and had said, 'No'."[27] More than twenty years later, he would take a certain grim satisfaction in pointing out that student grades in science and math were, if anything, somewhat worse than they had been before the Woods Hole meeting.

◆   ◆   ◆

Not all programmed instruction was based on behaviorist principles. During the 1950s, while Skinner was teaching guidance pigeons for the US Navy, Norman Crowder was training US Air Force troubleshooters to find malfunctions in electronic equipment. He came up with a concept called "branching". Where Skinner insisted on a rigidly linear sequence of steps, Crowder allowed the response to one step to determine what the next step should be.

Initially, Crowder embodied branching in the form of instructional books called TutorTexts. At the end of a page of text was a question together with multiple choice answers. If the student chose an incorrect answer, he was sent back to a page designed to remedy the cause of his error; if correct, he could proceed to the next step of the program. Since this might be anywhere in the material, TutorTexts were sometimes referred to as "scrambled books."

Like Skinner, Crowder believed that learning his way was akin to having a personal tutor. Branching allowed lessons to be tailored to the knowledge of the

---

25. Jerome Bruner, *The Process of Education*, Harvard University Press, Cambridge, Massachusetts, 1960, pxxi

26. Ibid, p84

27. B.F. Skinner, "Programmed Instruction Revisited", *Phi Delta Kappan*, October 1986, p105

individual student. To emphasize this personal aspect, Crowder peppered his texts with comments. For example, a wrong answer might elicit a rebuke like, "You aren't paying attention"; or, if the student were to chose "I don't know", the friendly tutor would respond cheerily, "That's the spirit! If you don't know, speak up."

An accomplished engineer, Crowder invented a stand-alone desktop machine called an AutoTutor to deliver his texts. It looked a little like a television set, with a screen for displaying the pages, and a row of push-buttons to the right on which to punch in the answer. Manufactured by the Western Design Division of US Industries in Santa Barbara, California, AutoTutor sold for a whopping $5,000. Of course, this was far too expensive for schools to afford. But it was not beyond the budget of other organizations with an interest in education. These included the US Air Force, and IBM.

At the corporation's laboratories at Poughkipsie, NY, a young researcher named Harvey Long bought eight AutoTutors for a teaching machines center he had set up there. Outside his office door at the center, a group of pigeons nested. Given the behaviorist nature of his research this was, Long thought, a nice irony.

Long joined IBM in 1957 as a mathematician. But he also had a degree from teachers college, and one of the first things he did at the corporation was to write a Skinner-style programmed text to teach a brand-new computer language called FORTRAN. Long decided that the tiny-steps style lacked the ability to motivate. Students—mostly IBM engineers—got bored very quickly. The Crowder method seemed better suited to the task. "I could give a pre-test, and on the basis of the results, I could branch to the areas where my analysis showed there was a deficiency."

Using the AutoTutors, Long ran a comparison study between machine-delivered and text-delivered versions of his program. The idea was to demonstrate that machines would provide a degree of control that text could not. There would be, for example, no cheating, no turning of the page to look at the answer and saying "O sure, I should have known that."

Forty years on, Long could not recall whether the machine-delivered instruction produced any significant improvement over the text-delivered version. "But the machine was sort of a fascinating thing that IBM was interested enough in to think about having it as a commercial product." Indeed, the corporation's Electric Typewriter Division had already been working with Skinner on the development of a mechanical device, a patent for which was issued in 1960.

In that year, IBM was still primarily a maker of punched card machines for accounting applications. By then, however, it was clear that computers would be the source of Big Blue's future growth. The corporation had predicted that it would sell 1,000 of its 1401 mainframe computers, introduced in October 1959. In fact, IBM eventually produced 12,000 of the machines.[28] Unexpected new markets for computers were popping up all over the place. Education might well turn out to be one of them.

IBM's own experience pointed to the existence of demand for educational programs from business. The corporation was itself spending over thirty million dollars a year running "one of the costliest universities in the world"—its in-house education programs. Crowder had already demonstrated that there was a military market, selling 18 of his machines to the Kessler Air Force Base at Biloxi, Mississippi. But by far the biggest potential target was the school market, which Long reckoned could be worth as much as $26.5 billion over four years.

In July 1961, he published his findings in a confidential in-house technical report. It was entitled, "Should the Digital Computer be a Teacher?"[29]

Long answered his own question: Yes. His report concluded that automated teaching was more than a passing fancy. To meet the demands of the new market, Long recommended that "IBM should use its own nearly ready-made teaching machine, the present IBM digital computer...".

28. Martin Campbell-Kelly & William Aspray, *Computer: A History of the Information Machine*, Basic Books, New York, 1996, p134
29. Harvey S. Long, "Should the Digital Computer be a Teacher?", *IBM Technical Report* 00.817, July 5, 1961

2

YOUR OWN PRIVATE ARISTOTLE

It was a tense moment. The director of the National Science Foundation had flown out from Washington DC to see for himself how things were progressing on an experimental educational project in which the foundation had invested what was, for it, serious money.

The year was 1966, the location a custom-built classroom at Brentwood School, an elementary school in East Palo Alto. This was a run-down, primarily black neighborhood just off the wrong side of Highway 101, the main artery of what would shortly become known as Silicon Valley.

On opposing sides of the classroom were five library-like booths, in each booth an extraordinary set of hardware. The terminals of the IBM 1500 System—a machine built by Big Blue, as Harvey Long had recommended, specifically for the education market—were way ahead of their time.

To the right of the booth was a cathode ray tube console and keyboard equipped with a light pen that enabled the student, in those pre-mouse days, to choose an item on the screen by pointing at it with the pen. To the left was a second, somewhat wider screen that displayed, under computer control, film and colored slides. There was also a set of headphones, through which the computer could "speak" to the student.

Now here was this little African-American girl leaning back, feet dangling, spinning slowly to and fro on her office-style chair, apparently oblivious to the arithmetic lesson taking place on the screen in front of her. And to the presence of the NSF director, hovering impatiently behind her.

The director frowned. What was the girl doing? It looked as though she and her classmates were just wasting their time. What he didn't notice was that the first-grader had her headphones on. She was listening to a question. Pretty soon the little girl spun round to the keyboard and typed in the answer. Seeing this, the director felt relieved. As did his host, the project leader, Patrick Suppes.

Nominally a professor of philosophy at Stanford University, Suppes was already then, and would remain over the course of a long career that spanned five decades, one of the gallant pioneers in the field of educational technology.

◆   ◆   ◆

Pat Suppes is a man of great charm, formidable intellect, and tremendous determination. In his late seventies he still cut a dashing figure. Tall and rangy with a weatherbeaten complexion, Suppes wore his curly hair long and swept back like the frontiersman Wild Bill Hickok. He favored Donegal tweed suits from Kevin and Howlin of Dublin, a style not often seen under the Spanish Gothic arches of the Stanford hacienda. A sartorial tip of the hat (as if the christian name were not giveaway enough) to the fact that, on his mother's side, Suppes is Irish Catholic.

Born in Tulsa, Oklahoma, in 1922, the scion of wealthy independent oil men of German Huguenot descent, Suppes was himself the recipient of an unusual high school education. One that, he recalled, "was more influential on my development than is often the case."[1] Sponsored by the Progressive Education Association, this was an experiment in accelerated learning. The students were chosen on the basis of examinations taken in the sixth grade and given the best teachers available. At Tulsa Central High School they were encouraged to speak out about a wide range of current issues, and anything else that interested them. "As is often the case, this led to some unusual lines of effort. I can remember very well being chagrined at fourteen if I were not able to name the senators from every state in the union."

"They encouraged us to think for ourselves, that was part of the progressive attitude—to have critical attitudes, to be willing to challenge the teacher, they broke the mold of a lot of standard classroom behavior in the twenties and thirties," Suppes noted, adding that "we're much more conformist in schools now." The classes were the most competitive he was ever in, Suppes remembered, and that included graduate school. Intellectual life at the University of Oklahoma he found pedestrian by comparison.

---

1.   Patrick Suppes, "Intellectual Autobiography", 1978, www.stanford.edu/~psuppes/autobio1.html, p1

Suppes switched from Oklahoma to the University of Chicago, from which he graduated with a degree in meteorology. In 1943, Suppes was called up into the Army, which sent him to the South Pacific. He whiled away two years on Solomon Islands, occupying himself with "swimming, poker, Aristotle and a couple of correspondence courses in mathematics and French."[2]

After his discharge, Suppes entered Columbia University as a graduate student in philosophy. Thanks to the philosophy department's easy-going policy, he spent a good deal of time taking non-philosophical courses. "I thus developed early the habits of absorbing a wide variety of information and feeling at home in the problem of learning a subject in which I had not had much prior training or guidance." Suppes received his PhD in 1950 and took off for Stanford, "full of energy and brimming with ideas".[3] He has been there ever since.

Suppes' interest in education began in 1956, when his eldest child, Patricia, entered elementary school. Feeling that his daughter was not being intellectually challenged, and frustrated at the lack of any geometry in the curriculum—"it's kind of natural to have intuitive geometry for kids"—he and a colleague took turns teaching classes, ultimately co-authoring two primary-grade geometry textbooks. "This practical interest in the mathematics curriculum in the schools almost inevitably led to trying to understand better how children learn mathematical concepts."[4]

Suppes saw that using conventional techniques to do detailed quantitative research on learning would be extremely complicated. The task cried out for automation. So, in the fall of 1962, he and his slightly younger colleague Richard Atkinson (later President of the University of California) submitted a proposal to the Carnegie Corporation for the construction of an automated computer-based psychology laboratory for the study of the learning of mathematics and other school subjects. The proposal was funded—"we got a million dollars, which was a lot of money in 1962"—and by late the following year, the computer (a Digital Equipment Corporation PDP-1 shared with Stanford's newly-established artificial intelligence laboratory) was in place and their lab—dubbed the Institute for Mathematical Studies in the Social Sciences—was up and running.

"As we got into it, we realized that this was really a way to provide 'computer-assisted instruction'", also known as computer-aided instruction, or CAI. In other words, rather than being merely a tool for analyzing how kids learned, the

---

2.   Ibid, p2
3.   Ibid, p3
4.   Ibid, p14

computer could itself be used to dispense the learning. Suppes concentrated on elementary mathematics, Atkinson on basic reading.

At first, the students—two groups of six first-graders—were brought in to the laboratory for twenty-minute sessions five days a week. This proved logistically difficult. The researchers quickly realized that, if they really wanted to study the long-term impact of computers on learning, then they had better get the equipment out of the lab and into actual school classrooms.

Easier said than done. There were school principals to convince, at a time when computers were still almost impossibly exotic objects. "The big thing at first was people just not knowing what you were talking about," Suppes recalled. "'What do you mean, computers in the classroom?' It didn't make sense." A common fear in those days was that computers would cause a regimentation of the education process, leading to a loss of individuality. In this context, Orwell's dystopian novel *Nineteen Eighty-Four* was often cited.[5]

"Suppes started out when everybody said that nothing could really be done for education, things were too expensive and difficult," said Andrew Molnar, the then-director of the US Office of Computer Activities, a branch of the National Science Foundation. "And he demonstrated that, using the computer, in terms of rote memory or transmitting concepts, it was viable, it was doable in schools, and that there were improvements in the student performance. And at that time that was very significant because people were writing off computers as merely mathematical tools for digital logic."

Of course, it would not be practical to put the computer itself in the classroom. Though relatively small—it was one of the first all-transistor machines, hence did not require its own air conditioner—the DEC PDP-1 was still a mainframe computer, a huge set of cabinets packed with power-hungry circuits. However, it was possible to instal "dumb" terminals remotely connected to the host computer via a phone line.

That meant fighting the phone company, because in those days sending digital information down phone lines was illegal. But Suppes was bold and a smooth operator, and somehow he always managed to get things done. "I tend to be venturesome with my ideas," he allowed, "y'know—let's just go out there and try it with some of these kids."

The biggest problem for schools was, where to put the terminals? In the baby-boom years of the early sixties, schools were already overcrowded, and the broom

---

5.   Apple Computer played on this fear in its famous Superbowl commercial, which aired in January 1984, for the introduction of the Macintosh.

closet was often the only available space. Such isolation also had its advantages, since the terminals they used in those early days were typically "teletypewriters" linked to a mainframe computer via phone line.

The Teletype Model 33 ASR ("automatic send-receive") was a monstrous machine that hummed, clattered, and emitted fumes of oil. It incorporated a simplified typewriter keyboard and tickertape punch embedded in its own base and (wheel-less) stand. The Model 33 was capable of printing ten—upper-case only—characters per second. That's about one page every three minutes in today's terms, except that Teletypes printed on a continuous roll of paper, not pages. But clunky though it was, early computer users saw the Teletype as a magical machine, because it enabled them to communicate directly with the central computer. "Teletypewriters are the Volkswagens of computer terminals," wrote one besotted user, "rugged and dependable; inexpensive, ugly and noisy."

In 1964, Suppes arranged for a Teletype terminal to be installed in a closet at Walter Hays Elementary School on the Mountain View edge of Palo Alto, about ten miles down the road from Stanford. By the following year, the school had been equipped with eight Teletypes, each with its own phone line, one for each classroom. The students took turns at the machines in a fixed order, one session a day, while to minimize disruption, the researchers looked on through one-way observation mirrors. What the kids did, mostly, was drill-and-practice exercises.

Sessions were limited to ten minutes, which was about the extent of a kid's attention span. Drills began with the instruction, "Please type in your name". This was fun: "it is our experience that every child greatly enjoys learning how to type his own name."[6] The computer would then look up the pupil's file, and determine a set of exercises based on the previous day's performance.

Exercises typically consisted of twenty questions devoted to a single concept, such as identifying the lowest common multiple of two numbers. Students had ten seconds to answer each question. If they answered wrongly, the computer would provide them with the correct answer. At the end of the drill, the computer printed out the student's score, plus the combined average for this and earlier drills in the same series. The exercise concluded with a cheery farewell—"Good bye, O fearless drill tester."[7]

Such hard-nosed drills were of course very similar to the programs produced for teaching machines. Suppes protested that he did not believe in Skinnerian

6.   Patrick Suppes, "The Uses of Computers in Education", Scientific American, 215 [September], 1966, p217

7.   Ibid, p216

behaviorist reductionism. What he advocated was "a kind of methodological behaviorism," which he also called "neobehaviorism." This was "anti-reductionist in spirit, and wholly compatible with mentalistic concepts."[8] For the layman, however, it was hard to tell the difference.

Like Skinner, Suppes was excited by the machine's potential to act as a personal tutor, tailoring instruction to the individual student's style of learning. The computer could, he thought, give every kid the kind of personalized education under which he himself had thrived. "The computer makes the individualization of instruction easier because it can be programmed to follow each student's history of learning successes and failures and to use his past performance as a basis for selecting the new problems and new concepts to which he should be exposed next."[9]

As a result of such individualized instruction, "students will be less subject to regimentation and moving in lock step". At Stanford, in a tutorial program in fourth-grade mathematics, the overlap between the brightest student and the slowest student was not more than 25 percent of the curriculum.[10] The computer thus had the potential, Suppes claimed, to effect a radical improvement of learning.

Suppes identified three levels of interaction between computer and student. Of these, drill and practice programs were the most basic, being "merely supplements to a regular curriculum taught by a teacher."

The next level would be the tutorial system, where the aim was "to take over from the classroom teacher the main responsibility for instruction." The idea was exemplified by teaching first-graders concepts like "top" and "bottom", having them point with the light pen to boxes on the computer screen. Instruction could accommodate the needs of bright and deprived children using Crowder-style branches to more or less challenging material.

Under the tutorial system, the teacher would be relegated to functioning like a nurse in a kind of educational intensive care unit, waiting at a "proctor station" to respond to the individual needs of students who were having difficulty mastering a concept. To this end, programs at Stanford included an instruction named Teacher Call.

---

8.   'Intellectual Autobiography", p16

9.   "The Uses of Computers in Education", p208

10.   Patrick Suppes, "The Teacher and Computer-assisted Instruction", reprinted in "The Computer in the School: Tutor, Tool, Tutee", ed Robert Taylor, *Teachers College Press*, New York, 1980, p234, (article originally appeared in NEA Journal, February 1967)

The third and most sophisticated level of computer-student interaction would be "dialog systems"—having the computer respond to questions asked by the student, doing away with the teacher altogether. But implementing this would require two technological breakthroughs. The computer would have to be able to understand the question. Older students could type their questions in. For elementary school kids, however, the computer would have to recognize the children's spoken words. More than 35 years later, while speech recognition has made great strides, natural language processing remains a largely unsolved problem.

Back then, however, the obstacles seemed eminently superable. In a much-quoted article in the September 1966 issue of *Scientific American*, Suppes made a confident prediction. "In a few more years millions of school children will have access to what Philip of Macedon's son Alexander enjoyed as a royal prerogative: the personal services of a tutor as well-informed and responsive as Aristotle."[11]

Nor was Suppes the only one making such extravagant claims. Lawrence Stolurow, director of the Computer-Aided Instruction Laboratory at Harvard, asserted that CAI was "comparable to Gutenberg's invention of the printing press in terms of the potential effect it will have upon education."[12] As late as 1978 Al Bork, founder and director of the Educational Technology Center at UC Irvine and a prime exponent of dialog-system-style CAI, predicted that "by the year 2000 the *major* way of learning at all levels, and in almost all subject areas will be through the interactive use of computers."[13]

By 1967, almost three thousand children in seven California schools, and in rural schools as distant as Mississippi and Kentucky, were receiving Stanford's computerized instruction, in reading, spelling, and elementary Russian (!), as well as arithmetic. Suppes claimed that "the first school system in the world to have the opportunity of every elementary-school child's doing daily work at a computer terminal was in McComb, Mississippi" (pop: 13,000), the birthplace of Bo Diddley.

(Getting funding for such far-flung locations had been an uphill battle. "Government officials were initially resistant", wrote the NSF's Molnar, "because they did not believe that the project would be cost-effective. Suppes argued that it would, since the Stanford computer in California would run three additional

---

11.   "The Uses of Computers in Education", p207
12.   Charles E. Silberman, "Crisis in the Classroom: The Remaking of American Education", Random House, New York, 1970, p187
13.   Alfred Bork, "Interactive Learning", reprinted in "The Computer in the School: Tutor, Tool, Tutee", ed Robert Taylor, *Teachers College Press*, New York, 1980, p53

hours a day due to the time-zone differences. That led someone to wonder if the computer were in Hawaii, whether the computer would be even more effective, since then it could run six hours a day. Suppes countered with the suggestion that, if they really wanted to be cost-effective, he would move the computer to the other side of the international dateline and have it run for 48 hours a day. The project was funded as proposed.")[14]

Student math scores were increasingly nicely.[15] Suppes was always very focused on outcomes. Colleagues remember him saying repeatedly, We want to be sure that it makes a measurable difference. "Suppes was able to go into very poorly-run educational environments and produce results immediately."[16]

By 1967 the program at Stanford involved almost 200 people, including staff, research associates, and graduate students. Such a large-scale activity could not continue on campus indefinitely. That year, Suppes and Atkinson started up a company, Computer Curriculum Corporation (CCC) based in nearby Sunnyvale, to develop and market CAI drill-and-practice elementary school courses in "basic skills"—mathematics, reading, and language arts. To help get the firm off the ground, Suppes chipped in $50,000 of his own money.[17]

This was a daring venture, especially in an era when it was far less common for academics to become involved in commerce than it is now. "We were ahead of our times and were quite lucky to survive the first five or six years," Suppes recalled. "We were breaking the ice, and it was thick ice to break."

In its first year, CCC made a profit thanks largely to a contract with the disadvantaged-student program in the Chicago public school district.

But after that it was hard going, with the company losing money every year until 1973. At one point in that year, Suppes as the CEO of CCC underwent what is reckoned to be a rite of passage for the true entrepreneur—paying employees' salaries out of his own pocket. For the most part, however, Suppes enjoyed steering the company's development. "I find that the kind of carefully thought-out and tough decisions required to keep a small business going suits my temperament well."[18]

---

14. Andrew Molnar, "Computers in Education: A Historical Perspective of the Unfinished Task", THE Journal, Vol 18, No 4, November 1990, pp80–83

15. Ibid, p249

16. Andrew Molnar, interviewed by William Aspray, Charles Babbage Institute, University of Minnesota, Minneapolis, 25 September 1991

17. Lorna Fernandez, "Firm helps teach kids a thing or two", *San Jose Business Journal*, 18 July 1997, p2

18. "Intellectual Autobiography", p22

CCC did not just sell courses, it provided schools with a complete package including mainframe computer and terminals. But the hardware was rudimentary compared with the fancy dual-screen terminals of the IBM 1500. It had proved impossible to bring the cost of these down sufficiently. "We lost so much money on this system in IBM," Harvey Long recalled ruefully, "we only built 27 of them." It would be another 30 years before classroom computing could match the multimedia capabilities offered by the 1500 System in 1966.

The utopian dream of the computer as your own private Aristotle soon faded. By 1970, just three and a half years after the *Scientific American* article, Suppes was writing that having a tutor of the quality of Socrates or Aristotle was, "as a general approach to mass education...clearly prohibitive economically."[19] According to one contemporary estimate, the cost of CAI worked out to nearly ten times the cost of conventional instruction. Critics disparaged the computer as "a thousand-dollar flash card."

But, starting with the Johnson Administration in the mid 1960s, federal funding was made available for remedial education, to give an extra boost to under-performing poor and minority students at inner-city schools. By then, the post-Sputnik enthusiasm for academic improvement had evaporated, to be replaced by "urban crisis" as the leading topic in education.

In 1977, for example, the Compton Unified School District, in Los Angeles County, California, drew on the Emergency School Aid Act of 1972 to order 544 terminals from CCC to be installed in twelve of its schools at an annual cost of over $1.1 million. This would cover equipment rental, curriculum lease and system support, a type of turnkey package would later be termed an "integrated learning system". CCC's largest contract to date would, Suppes said, "give over 19,500 individual lessons in mathematics and reading every school day. The program selects, presents and grades questions automatically and provides diagnostic reports to the students' teachers."[20]

By that point, CCC had installed systems in schools in sixteen states. In addition to his other skills, Suppes also developed a talent for marketing, pioneering a concept known as "performance contracting". CCC would set up a contract with, say, the State of Texas, guaranteeing that CAI would improve students' performance by a certain amount. If it did not, then the state need not pay. "He was very much a risk taker," said Long.

---

19.   Patrick Suppes, *New York Times Annual Education Review*, 12 January 1970, quoted in "Crisis in the Classroom: The Remaking of American Education", p188

20.   "Installation Begins for Largest School Computer Order", *People's Computer Company*, (date unknown)1977

"Early in the game Suppes, in some of the better controlled experiments at that time, found that some of the control groups were doing as well as the CAI groups, which was astonishing," Molnar recalled. "What he found was teachers who said, 'We aren't gonna let those computers beat us, kids—we're gonna work like heck day and night, and we're gonna do as much as we can to beat them.' And they did as well, and that became a component of the sales pitch—that is, the idea was that, yes, teachers and students could do well, but they had to include special pressure, and in those cases where you didn't have the teachers and you didn't have that motivation, the technology did do it well."[21]

Throughout the 1980s, CCC reported double-digit growth. In 1990, Suppes won the nation's highest honor for researchers, the National Medal of Science. That year, he sold the firm to Simon & Schuster, which itself was subsequently taken over by Viacom. "I was 68 years old and the company was doing well," he said. "It was just a good time to step back."[22]

Suppes got a good price for his company, and he was generous with the proceeds. He gave a donation to Stanford that was reportedly the biggest individual gift to the university that year. (Suppes refused to specify the amount, but it was rumored to be more than ten million dollars.) The following year, on the eve of his official retirement, the indefatigable Suppes initiated a new education program, this time for gifted youth, a distance learning initiative that would be entirely computer based.

To him, this style was nothing new. For twenty years, from 1972 to 1992, Suppes had taught Stanford's standard introduction to logic course by computer only. In 1974, he introduced a second course, in axiomatic set theory. Thanks to these courses, which ran every term, three terms a year, year after year, Suppes could proudly claim that he had carried the largest teaching load of any professor at the university.

In 1997, CCC celebrated its thirtieth anniversary. The firm claimed to have assisted more than ten million students learn at more than 10,000 schools. By the end of the decade, however, after yet another takeover the company, no longer known as CCC, seemed in disarray.

While CCC and one or two other firms had enjoyed modest commercial success thanks to federal funding of disadvantaged schools, in the wider world "it was clear by the mid-70s that CAI had not succeeded."[23] There were a number of

---

21. Molnar, 1991. The phenomenon of subjects trying harder because they are in the control group is known to psychologists as the Hawthorne Effect.
22. "Firm helps teach kids a thing or two", p2

reasons for this failure. One was that, as with programmed instruction, "CAI had been oversold and had not delivered on its promises."[24] Once again, it proved difficult to extend the scope of drills beyond relatively simple parts of the curriculum like arithmetic. And whereas performance in mathematics improved significantly, in other areas such as reading, it did not.

Part of CAI's mystique was based upon the idea that teaching could become scientific. But learning—even such an apparently simple subject as elementary mathematics—turned out to be much more complex than anyone had anticipated. Nor, much to the rigorous-minded Suppes' disgust, was the level of scholarship in the field of education particularly high.

There was the predictable antagonism from teachers concerned about being replaced by computers. "They are bewildered, misinformed and—more often than not—disinterested."[25] Educators either did not understand that the system was drill and practice, not teaching content, or they chose not to understand. For the most part, however, teachers were able simply to ignore the phenomenon. The decision to instal computers would be made by the school's administration. A room—designated the computer lab—would be allocated, together with a specialist teacher to run it. This person would dictate who could use the equipment and when.

From an administrative point of view, computer laboratories are convenient for the twin purposes of insurance (they can be locked up safely) and PR (they can be shown off to parents). The kids typically go to the lab for one period a week. There is little or no attempt to integrate what they did there with what went on in the rest of the school. This lab-based model of computer usage continues the dominant one in present-day schools.

As with programmed instruction, it proved difficult to write good software for CAI. "Programmers, hurriedly attempting to demonstrate the new machines and infatuated with the ease with which they can make their words appear on the screen, are producing programs as bad as the home movies of an amateur."[26]

In addition to which, the hardware was primitive. Often the system was so slow that, by the time the student managed to log on, their ten minutes of assigned drill was over. Even when the system was working properly, not all kids

---

23. Paul Saettler, "The Evolution of American Educational Technology", Libraries Unlimited, Englewood, Colorado, 1990, p307

24. Ibid

25. James Martin & Adrian R.D. Norman, "The Computerized Society", Prentice Hall, Englewood Cliffs, NJ, 1970, p19

26. Ibid, p129

were prepared to sit obediently and do exactly as they were told. For some, especially the brighter ones, drill-and-practice was more like "drill and kill." They found other ways of occupying their allotted time at the terminal. A visitor to one of Suppes' experimental school sites was observing a child working with a CAI multiplication program, when he noticed something strange was going on:

"I had seen the child do several multiplications quickly and accurately. Then I saw him give a series of wrong answers to easier problems. It took me awhile to realize that the child had become bored with the program and was having a better time playing a game of his own invention. It redefined the 'correct' answer to the computer's questions as the answer that would generate the most computer activity when the program spewed out explanations of the 'mistake'."[27]

Then there was the kid who ignored the drill entirely, and used his ten minutes to take the Teletypewriter apart and put it back together again. "And who was learning more?" the champions of discovery-led learning demanded.

Suppes would have none of it. "People who don't recognize the need for practice," he said, "are only romantics out of touch with the real word." A real world in which drill and practice were crucial to many walks of life, for example in training pilots and surgeons. Ultimately, Suppes was less concerned about *how* learning was going to take place than that it *should* take place at all.

"My thesis about learning," he explained in 1998 to a visitor to Ventura Hall, the converted mansion at Stanford where Suppes bases his activities, "is that it's enormously robust, but it has to have an opportunity to happen. I'm focused on getting [the students] going, so that those who want to shoot ahead can do so.

"I think we're stuck," he continued, "the curriculum in the US is enormously conservative—the high-school curriculum is not drastically different than what I had, and I'm 76 years old…I'm very interested in radical transformation…what I feel about the computer is that there is a sort of robust effect that's much more important than all these detailed arguments we get into about how something ought to be taught. The robust effect is that, with the computer, you can deeply individualize the learning, so that a student who is slow can go slowly, and a student who is fast can go fast."

---

27. Seymour Papert, "The Children's Machine: Rethinking School in the Age of the Computer", Basic Books, New York, 1993, pp165–6

◆   ◆   ◆

In addition to the intense debate over how the computer should be used in the classroom, there was also something else that emerged from those early days, something new and completely unexpected. That was, the first signs of what Seymour Papert would later describe as "a passionate and enduring love affair" between kids and computers.

At the Brentwood School in East Palo Alto, "the children loved playing with the terminals and their teachers had to 'peel them off the machines' to get them back to their lessons."[28] In New York, Harvey Long was working on his doctoral thesis with an IBM 1500 at the corporation's Systems Research Institute, which was located in central Manhattan, right across the street from the United Nations. The students were transported in from around the city to Long's lab, where there were ten terminals.

"And the kids would not randomly pick out a terminal, they would go to their terminal, they had a personal identification with that terminal, they gave the terminals names." Occasionally, a terminal would be out of order and the researchers would put a sign on it saying that it was not usable that day. "When they came in, it was definitely a letdown for them not to be able to use their terminal. And these were juniors and seniors at high school."

Then there was Bob Lash, whose first—unforgettable—exposure to computers came at age 6 in 1963, as a subject in Suppes' accelerated mathematics experiment at Stanford.

"I was taken to a small room with what I now know was a CRT display and an intercom. I was asked to push some keys in response to some shapes on the screen. Afterwards, they showed me around a large room filled with big cabinets, some with lots of blinking white lights.

"They said it was a 'computer' and its name was the 'PDP-1'. A tall thin man [Suppes?] asked me to hit a key on a console to make a 'deck tape'. I had absolutely no idea what a 'DEC tape' was at the time, but when I hit the key, a small pair of reels BEGAN TO TURN!! It was a moment I would never forget."[29]

Power!

---

28.   "The Computerized Society", p123
29.   Bob Lash, "Memoir of a Homebrew Computer Club Member", www.bambi.net/bob/homebrew.html, 5 July 2001 (last update)

3

THE ELECTRONIC ACADEMY

Pat Suppes was not the only one interested in the educational applications of computers. On campuses around the US during the 1960s, a handful of other pioneers were also exploring the pedagogical possibilities of the new technology. Prime among them was Don Bitzer, an idealistic young graduate student at the University of Illinois at Champaign-Urbana.

Bitzer was an electrical engineer at the Coordinated Science Laboratory, a facility whose principle concern was defense-related research. The laboratory's focus was things like the processing of radar data from airborne reconnaissance. "We were always interested in working on long-range problems that might be related to needs for defense," Bitzer recalled. Unlikely though it may seem, education was one such problem. "It turns out that the largest schools in the world are military schools," he explained, "so solving educational problems fit into our guidelines."

In 1959 the dean of engineering at Illinois convened a committee to look at teaching machines and the prospects for technology in higher education. Its brief was to consider whether the school ought to take some new initiatives. Terrible fights ensued. "Those that knew about computers weren't interested in education, and those that knew about education didn't know anything about computers." The committee concluded that nothing could be done.

The chairman of this committee happened to be the director of Bitzer's lab. He drafted a letter to the dean reporting the committee's negative conclusions, but before sending it, the director called Bitzer into his office. He wanted his young graduate's opinion, because Bitzer was one of the few people in the lab who actually used computers and therefore knew what they could and could not do. Bitzer read the letter, then told his boss to tear it up because, in his view, it was all wrong. "I said, There's something we can do and we can do it immediately."

Bitzer had always been interested in education. It bugged him that public school systems, in particular the large inner-city schools like the ones in nearby Chicago, were failing in their function, turning out students who were likely to be functionally illiterate in society. He was keen to investigate whether it was possible to use computers to help solve this problem.

Described in one near-contemporary account as "a crew-cut, huggy-bear sort of a fellow", Bitzer was by all accounts a brilliant engineer.[1] He was also a great salesman. Bitzer knew that the most important part of making a successful invention was selling it. Which he was well-qualified to do, having put himself through undergraduate school by selling used cars at his father's dealership in Collinsville, the southern Illinois town where Bitzer was born.

Bitzer set to work, quickly cobbling together a primitive CAI system. It consisted of an old Motorola TV (his own) and a little sixteen-key keyboard used in aircraft identification. This makeshift terminal connected to none other than ILLIAC-1, the first-ever computer to be owned by an academic institution. When it was built, in 1952, ILLIAC-1 was the most powerful computer of its time, packing a full four kilobits of RAM. Today, your watch probably has more computing power.

His new system needed a name, and Bitzer wanted it to be a good one. After pondering for several days he came up with the acronym PLATO, which stood for Programmed Logic for Automatic Teaching Operations. Plato was of course the Greek philosopher who founded the Academy. Now, the electronic academy was up and running.

The first two iterations of PLATO were confined to the laboratory, hampered by the need to share precious computer time with the rest of the university. At first, an hour of computer a day was all Bitzer could wangle. Then, in 1963, William Norris, the maverick president of Minneapolis-based Control Data Corporation, let Bitzer's group have a refurbished 1604 computer rent-free. This powerful machine was to be used solely for the development of instructional applications. Thanks to it, PLATO Mark III was able to support up to twenty terminals. Twelve of them were installed at half a dozen locations, including University High School, a school for talented students in the Champaign-Urbana

---

1.   Ted Nelson, "Computer Lib/Dream Machines", Tempus Books, Redmond, Washington, 1974 (revised edition: 1987], p93

area, and Mercy Hospital School of Nursing, where Bitzer's wife Maryanne worked.

PLATO's early terminals were simply portable TV sets plus a device for collecting keyset data and sending it back to the lab. Up until that point—the early 1960s—computer terminals were typically Teletypes, only capable of handling text. From the outset, however, Bitzer wanted a system that could act as a blackboard, capable of delivering diagrams and displaying pictures, what would much later be known as "multimedia". Such features could be achieved using a TV set, but it was clumsy and, with microchip memory still years away, prohibitively expensive.

"By 1963," Bitzer wrote, "it was clear that we needed a drastically different type of display to expand the PLATO project outside the laboratory. The display had to have graphics capability, be low in cost, have inherent memory…and had to be flat and transparent so that selected slide images could be superimposed by rear projection. Such a display did not exist, but the requirements suggested that it be made of gas (for light-generation and memory) and glass (for rear-projection transparency)."[2]

The following year, the ingenious Bitzer and his colleague Gene Slottow came up with the goods. They called their screen a "plasma display panel". To the uninitiated, the prototype did not look like much—an inch-square lump of glass with wires sticking out of it. This first flat-panel display consisted of just four neon-filled cells that would light up on command. "You see this?" Bitzer, ever the salesman, would insist, "This is a computer screen!"

One early believer was Alan Kay, perhaps the computer industry's best-known visionary, whom we shall meet in Chapter 12. Having seen Bitzer's plasma display demo, Kay conceived the Dynabook, an image of the laptop computer.

More importantly for the future of PLATO, Bitzer also used his crude prototype to sell major manufacturers—notably local glass container producer Owens-Illinois—on the idea of producing plasma display panels for his student terminals. The first panels were delivered to the university around 1970. They were beautiful to behold, producing bright orange text and graphics against a black background on a nine-inch, 512 x 512 pixel screen. "The images were so sharp because they were precise and [unlike pictures on a TV screen] never moved," Bitzer recalled, "it was fantastic!" Certainly, it was a huge improvement over a Teletype.

---

2.   Donald L. Bitzer, "Inventing the ac Plasma", *Information Display*, 2/99, p22

In addition to sharp graphics, the terminals could display, under computer control, any of 256 images stored on microfiche cards. To select and back-project an image took only a tenth of second, a much faster response than any other terminal of that period. "A few minutes' intercourse with a PLATO terminal makes anyone an enthusiast for the system," raved a contemporary review, "PLATO is the world's greatest computer display system."

The terminals could do more than just display. There was also a speaker so that the computer could "speak" and play music. An infrared touch screen was a unique feature that enabled students to put their finger on an object and move it around the screen. This feature left an indelible impression on many who saw it, including Adele Goldberg, a researcher who worked with Pat Suppes and later Alan Kay. Some thirty years later, Goldberg could still close her eyes and picture "the first time I touched that screen, and how real it was to pick up something, like a little chicken facing left, to be put in the left bucket, learning left and right. I remember holding the chicken in my finger and feeling compelled to put it back!"

One example of a program that made use of the terminal's graphic capabilities was Speedway, a drill intended to test basic arithmetic skills. It began by asking the student to choose among four races, Daytona, Grand Prix, Sebring, and Indianapolis 500. The student was then presented with a simple line-drawing of a racetrack complete with grandstand, spectators, flags, two race-cars, and a starter. The drill consisted of ten problems, addition, subtraction, multiplication, and division, the cars indicating current speed of answering versus past performance, with the computer doing the timing. Differences in the time taken to answer a given number of problems correctly were also displayed in the form of a bar graph, thus neatly exposing students to different ways of representing data.[3]

Many years later Amy Fahey, one of the children in the Champaign Unit 4 school district who participated in the first version of this experimental drill in 1974 distinctly remembered "the excitement of looking forward to working on the computer and playing a game [sic] called Speedway. "We even had 'touch screens' installed later that year, which as an 11-year-old, I'm sure I thought were the coolest."[4]

Bitzer now had a superb mechanism for the delivery of instructional materials. For an engineer like him, building the hardware had been the primary challenge.

---

3.   Cynthia Solomon, "Computer Environments for Children", The MIT Press, Cambridge, Massachusetts, 1987, pp 44–45
4.   Amy Fahey, http://lrs.ed.uiuc.edu/students/afahey/Activity8.htm#past

What ran on the system was not his business. "Bitzer's philosophy was that any-body could write programs," the NSF's Andy Molnar recalled, "and anybody that wanted to write programs knew what they wanted to teach. That was all you had to worry about educationally, providing them with the resources to teach."

But you also had to make it easy for educators to write programs. In 1965 the university's life sciences department assigned a graduate biologist, Paul Tenczar, to see whether he could use PLATO to teach genetics. He discovered an unsatis-factory state of affairs. Programming the machine was complex, involving a mix-ture of languages, hence very difficult to learn. And, since the system was in continuous use during the day, programming could only be done at night. After six tortuous months, all Tenczar had to show for his efforts was a five-page lesson that asked some simple questions.

One night, as he trudged disconsolately home, Tenczar muttered to himself, "Hell, there's no future here, at this rate it'll never become cost effective. All these people—say 50 researchers at the PLATO lab and perhaps 50 teachers in many departments at the university—are wasting their time!" Tenczar continued to brood about the problem through the night. Finally he decided that something had to be done to speed up the production of courseware.

Next day, Tenczar sat down and designed a new language especially for instructional use. He spent the whole of the following night checking it out on the computer. "By the next morning, I could write a single-page interaction with a student in about five minutes! This was great progress—I could now do in min-utes what had previously taken months." This language, which was said to be "utterly strange to computer people", was dubbed TUTOR. After a few months, practically everyone was using it. Within a year, over 200 hours of lesson material had been created, a twentyfold increase over the previous five years.

PLATO seems to have been popular with undergraduates. Molnar remem-bered visiting the University of Illinois in the late sixties, at a time when student riots were going on. It was 10 o'clock at night, and student demonstrators were out tearing up the campus. Meanwhile, in the computer facility, "there were hun-dreds of students working on the PLATO system, doing their homework, and that was interesting, to say the least."[5]

By the early 1970s, custom software and hardware were in place, together with more powerful mainframe computers to run them. It was now possible to con-

---

5.   Andrew Molnar, interviewed by William Aspray, Charles Babbage Institute, Univer-sity of Minnesota, Minneapolis, 25 September 1991

template scaling up PLATO to a system that could support hundreds, if not thousands, of users simultaneously.

But who would pay for such a system? Among funding agencies there was still considerable skepticism about computers and what they could do. "We gave a demonstration to the Ford Foundation once," Bitzer recalled, "at their place, live, with a remote plasma panel terminal, and I'll never forget one of the heads of that foundation saying, 'Now this isn't really practical, because how many people do you have back there typing in these interactions when you have a question?' He took a long time to grasp the concept that there was <u>nobody</u> back there, that this was all being handled by a computer."

But Bitzer, drawing on his experience as a used-car salesman, proved to be a superb demonstrator. He confronted an extremely skeptical board at the National Science Foundation, taking with him Stan Smith, a chemistry professor from the University of Illinois. Smith would ask the chemists on the board what they wanted to illustrate. Bitzer would type in the code, and the results—chemical symbols and simulations—would pop up on the screen. "The NSF's chemists were astonished," Molnar recalled, "they didn't believe this could be done." That demonstration convinced the board to support a major national trial of the PLATO system.[6]

Funded by several million dollars from the NSF, PLATO Mark IV went into operation in 1972. The system began with 950 plasma display terminals located at 140 sites around the country. It offered about 8,000 hours of instructional material contributed by over 3,000 authors. In 1974, the Educational Testing Service of Princeton was called in to evaluate the system's effectiveness. Not surprisingly, given the enormous range and variety of material, the results of the evaluation were mixed. One thing, however, was crystal clear: the cost of PLATO was too high to support its use in schools.

To his credit, Bitzer was the first to acknowledge this. To be able to compete with human instruction, you had to be able to deliver CAI at a dollar per student-hour. If it cost $10 an hour for a student to sit at a terminal, forget it. Bitzer argued that he could achieve the magic dollar-an-hour figure through economies of scale, with 10,000 terminals, the terminals accounting for a large part of the cost. With less than a thousand, the system could never compete.

In 1974, a PLATO terminal cost $4,000. But while the price of CRT monitors continued to drop, plasma displays stayed expensive—and unreliable. Another huge expense was communications. In the system's early days, it cost

---

6.   Molnar interview, 1991

over $10,000 a year to run just eight terminals.[7] Bitzer begged the phone company to let him have an educational discount on the long-distance lines needed to run the system, but even he was unable to persuade them. To get around using phone lines, the ever-resourceful Bitzer proposed using cable or broadcast bands. But the FCC refused to approve his request.

By 1975, with federal support dwindling, PLATO was in trouble. To the rescue rode Bill Norris, by now chairman of Control Data Corporation, which had long provided the mainframe computers the system used. For years, Norris had believed that technology had the potential to transform education. Now, he predicted that education would ultimately become Control Data's principal source of income. He envisioned installing PLATO terminals in schools, projecting one million installations by 1980. The company poured money—hundreds of millions of dollars according to some sources—into developing a commercial version of the system.[8] Hard sell was the order of the day. "If you want to improve youngsters one grade level in reading," a Control Data executive told *Time* magazine, "our PLATO program with teacher supervision can do it up to four times faster and for 40 percent less expense than teachers alone."[9] But schools were not interested in PLATO.

In addition to the high cost of the system, there were the usual objections from educators worried about the threat to their jobs. This was, after all, a system explicitly designed for *automatic teaching*. Bitzer would never forget one presentation he gave to a meeting of University of Illinois faculty. A professor whose specialty was working with dysfunctional students got up and told the president that Bitzer should be stopped from working in this area. PLATO was obviously going to wipe out his field, which was unfair. Obviously the professor assumed that the system would work. Bitzer assured him that he was wrong, that they would be lucky if PLATO made even a small dent in the problem of student failure.

Bitzer's sidekick Tenczar vividly remembered an experience he had while demonstrating PLATO to a group of around 250 faculty at a major university. "In the middle of my talk, one lady stood up and started to shout hysterically that this would take jobs away from her and other teachers. She had to be led out of the room."

---

7.   Nelson, p95
8.   See, for example, Robert Slater, "Portraits in Silicon", The MIT Press, Cambridge, Massachusetts, 1989, p123, "Norris would spend over $900 million on the project."
9.   "Machine of the Year: The Computer Moves In", *Time*, 3 January 1983, <www.time.com/time/special/moy/1982.html>

Tenczar insisted that there was never any thought of PLATO replacing teachers, merely of augmenting teaching with the unique abilities of the digital computer. "A computer was always patient and never got bent out of shape by the student. Once something was programmed, the computer would present it again and again without fail, fatigue, or forgetfulness. We saw this as a great boon for teachers. It could free up teachers from the mundane repetitive process of much of teaching to address single students for their unique problems.

"In my case, teaching beginning genetics, I specifically got involved with computers to help students understand how genes are passed from parents to offspring. A teacher presents this in front of a class with diagrams on the board of how the genes 'flow' from mom and dad to the children and in specific ratios. Invariably, most of the class looks at you without any understanding of the small amount of probability theory involved. You end up having to take students one-at-a-time through the flow. My thought was that I could program this beginning genetics on a computer and thus free up time to spend on more complex issues.

"Most of us realized that you could use the computer to simulate the real world and thus present teaching situations impossible in any other way. ... I wrote a simulation of a fruit fly laboratory. The student would 'mate' flies and see a sampling of the offspring. Like in the real experiment, the student would have to count up the offspring and prepare a written report of what heredity principles are involved with a statistical analysis supporting the conclusions. This could all be done in one or two class periods. Interestingly enough, at this time (late '60s) the real fruit fly experiment was being dropped at the University of Illinois and elsewhere, due to the cost and time involved (two to three months). I remember having to keep the lab open until midnight so that the students could collect virgin females needed for the real experiments."

At least one other useful lesson was also derived from PLATO—the importance of collaboration among students. At an NSF-sponsored conference, during a report on early experiences teaching arithmetic on PLATO, Adele Goldberg noticed that, out of three classes, all had done well, but one had done much better than the other two. Why was that? she quizzed Bob Davis, who was in charge of the elementary mathematics project at University High School, which taught talented students in the Champaign-Urbana area.

"And so we really talked through this situation—you have a classroom with closets at the back of the room, and the idea was that there were two PLATO terminals per classroom, one in each closet, and the students would rotate to go back for their 10 or 15 minutes, doing their exercises, which wasn't all that much different from what we were doing at Stanford. But one of the classrooms only had one closet, so they put the two machines in there, and guess what? That was the classroom that did better!

"So I said to him, It's obvious—working alone, there's nothing there that gives me, as a child, any help. So if I get stuck, I'm twiddling, I'm doing nothing for all that time. But if I'm in a room with someone else—What are we supposed to be doing here? And boom, I'm off and running. Or, I look and see what the other kid's doing and, O that's pretty neat, and it's motivating. And they never saw how important the environment was in affecting how well the kids would do."

When Goldberg and Alan Kay of the Xerox PARC Learning Research Group set up their experiments in schools in 1972, they made sure that all the equipment was in one place "so that the kids could motivate each other, and look over the shoulder and see what the other was doing. We always did everything in groups rather than in isolation."

Control Data continued to use PLATO for in-house training and for social goals such as rehabilitation programs in prisons. In the mid 1980s, the computer market shifted from large machines to personal systems, forcing the company to radically downsize.

Having sold the name PLATO to Control Data, Bitzer and his team regrouped and formed a company called University Communications. This firm developed a PLATO-like integrated learning system called NovaNet. By 1999, NovaNet was offering 10,000 hours of curriculum to students in more than 800 schools, community colleges, and other learning environments. In that year, through a series of mergers and acquisitions, a company called NSC Learn was formed as a subsidiary of the Pearson group. It brought together under one roof the battered remnants of the two pioneering CAI outfits, Bitzer's NovaNet/PLATO and Suppes' Computer Curriculum Corporation.

4

EINSTEIN'S ASSISTANT

Dartmouth College was not the obvious setting for a revolution. For one thing this smallest of Ivy League schools is, even today, quite remote. The picturesque little campus, its historic buildings arrayed around three sides of a spacious green, is located way up north in Hanover, New Hampshire, about four hours' drive from Boston. Long before you arrive there, dark woods close in around you. Dartmouth is no place for claustrophobics.

The college was founded in 1769, right at the end of the colonial period. Its motto is *vox clamantis in deserto*, "a voice crying in the wilderness", Dartmouth's original purpose having been to convert Native Americans to Christianity. By the 1950s, the college had long since turned into a liberal arts school that attracted "hearty types", sports-loving young men—the college was not open to women—who would on graduation join big-city banks, brokerages, and legal practices. Its faculty was clogged with dead wood, old geezers on the verge of retirement. Then one day in early 1954, in swept John Kemeny. Nothing at Dartmouth would ever be the same again.

Kemeny was then just 27 years old. A star mathematician, the dapper, mustached, round-faced young professor had been lured to Dartmouth with the promise of carte blanche, to do whatever it took to drag the college's math department into the second half of the twentieth century. Kemeny was a visionary who was always keen to try out new things. At Dartmouth, he would implement a revolution in the way computers were used in education, one whose full potential has still not been realized.

John Kemeny was a prodigy, a latterday addition to that extraordinary group of Hungarians who between them had been responsible for some of the greatest scientific discoveries of the modern era.[1] Born in Budapest in 1926, Kemeny fled

---

1. The group includes Leo Szilard, Eugene Wigner, Dennis Gabor, John von Neumann, and Edward Teller. See Vaclav Smil, "Genius Loci: The twentieth century was made in Budapest", *Nature*, vol 409, 4 January 2001, p21

with his family to the US in 1940, Jewish refugees from the Nazis. On entering New York City's George Washington High School, he spoke virtually no English. Three years later, Kemeny graduated first in his class. He was accepted by Princeton, at that time the school with the best math department in the world.

Kemeny first heard about computers from the horse's mouth. During World War II, he worked at the computation center at Los Alamos. Run by Richard Feynman, this was a sweat shop which kept mechanical bookkeeping machines cranking round the clock solving equations necessary for the design of the atomic bomb. There in 1946, Kemeny attended a prophetic lecture in which the great Hungarian-born mathematician John von Neumann outlined the basis for the electronic computers of the future. He identified for the first time what would later come to be known as "programs". Though Kemeny felt sure that von Neumann's dream of computers would one day be realized, "I wondered whether I would live long enough to use one of those magnificent beasts."[2]

After the War, Kemeny returned to Princeton. While writing his dissertation he served as Albert Einstein's research assistant at the Institute of Advanced Studies. In later years, when asked why the great man needed a mathematician, "Einstein didn't need any help with his physics," the soft-spoken Kemeny would reply with a shy smile, "but he wasn't very good at math."[3] At the institute Einstein and Kemeny sometimes encountered von Neumann, and the conversation would turn to computers. "Here was the brilliant mathematician playing around with the nuts and bolts of a computing machine and raising profound philosophic questions about the relation between humans and machines."[4]

At Dartmouth Kemeny immediately set about recruiting talent to rebuild the school's math department. One of his first hires was a bespectacled, crew-cut statistician from Illinois named Tom Kurtz. Kemeny did more than just hire the best faculty he could find. He went out scouting for the brightest students, too. Steve Garland recalled participating as a high school student in a National Science Foundation summer institute for training math teachers. "There were four people who came from universities there," he recalled, "and John Kemeny was one of them.'" Garland signed up for Dartmouth.

---

2.   John G. Kemeny, "Man and the Computer", Charles Scribner's Sons, New York, 1972, p7. See also, "Man Viewed as a Machine", in which Kemeny summarizes a series of lectures von Neumann gave at Princeton, *Scientific American*, April 1955

3.   Nardi Reeder Campion, "True Basic: A Sketch of John Kemeny", Dartmouth Alumni Magazine, 11 May, 1999

4.   Author and date unknown, http://www.columbia.edu/~jrh29/kemeny.html

At first there was no computer at the college. Faculty who needed access had to commute 135 miles each way by train to Cambridge to use the computer at the Massachusetts Institute of Technology. Then, in 1959, Kemeny and Kurtz drove down to Boston with their wives and returned with a baby computer loaded in the back of their station wagon. The Librascope General Precision LGP-30 looked like an oversized office desk. At $30,000 it was also one of the cheapest computers ever offered. By today's standards the machine was tiny and very slow. But puny though it was, the LGP-30 was big enough to spark a remarkable discovery.

To make the computer easier for undergraduates to use in math courses, it was first necessary to write some software. For this, Kurtz turned to Garland and another of the other bright kids Kemeny had recruited. "For the first time our students acquired hands-on experience with the computers," Kemeny wrote, "and we were absolutely amazed at [their] ingenuity and creativity."[5]

"Our undergraduates were able to make this little computer jump through hoops," Kurtz agreed. Having made this discovery, the logical next step was to try and extend the experience. Kurtz said to Kemeny, "I think we ought to allow all Dartmouth students to learn how to use the computer." This was an outrageous suggestion, one which—as Kemeny well knew—was not physically possible given the limitations of Dartmouth's tiny computer, which could only be used by one student at a time. But Kurtz was aware of a recent breakthrough that would make it practicable to open up computer access to hundreds, and eventually to thousands, of students.

To earn extra money, Kurtz had been working as a research associate at the brand-new Computation Center at MIT. (IBM had donated a computer that the institute shared with the company's local scientific office and a consortium of New England colleges including Dartmouth, each getting eight hours a day on the precious machine.) Once every two weeks Kurtz visited the institute, travelling down by train. There he would meet John McCarthy, himself a former Kemeny hire at Dartmouth, and one of the leading figures in computer science at that period. McCarthy was working on an experimental new technology known as "time-sharing" which, for the first time, would allow more than one user to work on a computer simultaneously. One day in late 1962, McCarthy said to Kurtz, "You guys ought to do time-sharing." As soon as he got back to Dartmouth, Kurtz passed on McCarthy's suggestion to Kemeny.

---

5.   Kemeny, p9

Time-sharing would bring about a fundamental change in the relationship between man and machine. "For the first two decades of the existence of high-speed computers," Kemeny wrote in his seminal 1972 book, *Man and the Computer*, "machines were so scarce and so expensive that man approached the computer the way an ancient Greek approached an oracle. A man submitted his request to the machine and then waited patiently until it was convenient for the machine to work out the problem. There was a certain degree of mysticism in the relationship, even to the extent that only specially selected acolytes were allowed to have direct communication with the computer. While computers solved many problems that were previously beyond man's power, true communication between the two was impossible."[6]

The original mode of using computers was known as "batch processing". The human user punched his program into a stack of special cards and submitted the stack—passed it through a hole in the glass wall that protected the "great pagan temple"—to an acolyte-operator. The operator collected hundreds of such jobs then fed them to the machine in a batch. The computer processed the problems one at a time. When a given batch session was completed, the results were printed out and distributed by the priests to the human users. "This was considered an extremely efficient use of the computers…but it was a rather inhuman use of the human beings. The typical user had to wait twenty-four hours to receive the solution."

Or rather, the initial step on the road to the solution. A first-pass printout from a batch processing session would typically include messages like "illegal instruction on card 27." Thus would begin the long process of finding errors, known as debugging. Often the first few days were needed just to correct the key-punching errors. Any error required tearing up the card and starting over, since there was no way of plugging up the little holes. For anyone with less than excellent typing skills, that could mean punching several cards for every one that was correct. Then you had to figure out how to fix the logical errors. And maybe, after about a week or so, you might get a result.

Kemeny had discovered the deficiencies of batch processing while working as a consultant to the RAND Corporation in the summer of 1956. There, he watched bemused as the corporation's highly-paid experts would stand in line for hours just to get a five-second debugging shot on the computer. Highly desirable though computers might be, not everyone was prepared to put up with such inconveniences. The ideal, Kemeny saw, would be for each user "to have a com-

---

6.   Kemeny, p21

puter of his own, which he can use privately at his own convenience, correcting his ten to twenty errors in one session and not quitting until he has obtained his results." But in 1962, the ideal was still prohibitively expensive.

What McCarthy had realized at MIT was that the huge differential between the time computers took to process—a matter of microseconds—and the time humans took to react—a matter of seconds—could be exploited to allow multiple users to interact with the computer simultaneously. "In a time-sharing system a hundred individuals all use the same computer at the same time and enjoy the illusion that the computer's sole purpose is to help them." The age of interactive computing was at hand.

Kemeny was a born optimist. When Kurtz told him about the potential of time-sharing to extend the use of computers to all students at Dartmouth, he immediately replied, "Let's do it." So Dartmouth, this little school in the middle of nowhere, became—along with mighty MIT and R&D powerhouse Bolt Beranek and Newman—one of the pioneers of time-sharing. Kemeny and Kurtz assembled a team consisting of two faculty members working part-time, plus a dozen undergraduate research assistants. "We said, OK, here's the disk drive, here's the communications thing that interfaces with students, here's the main computer, and there's wires going like this," Kurtz recalled. "So that's what we put together, and by God it worked."

The hardware arrived in February 1964; the prototype time-sharing system was operational by that Fall. Outside referees had warned the National Science Foundation that they would be foolish to fund such a difficult project. But despite the difficulties, the Dartmouth team succeeded. The secret of their success, Kemeny would later insist, was that instead of hiring professionals they had tapped the strength of students. "Undergraduates will work endless hours," he said, "are open to new ideas, creative, and willing to take on impossible tasks."

Time-sharing changed everything, for everyone. Without time-sharing there would, for example, have been no way for Suppes at Stanford and Bitzer at Illinois to extend access to their computers out of the lab and into the classroom.

But the time-sharing system represented only one half of Dartmouth's revolutionary innovations. In the midst of planning time-sharing, Kemeny made a suggestion to his colleague: "Tom, if we design this great new system, why don't we also create a really nice language?"[7] Kemeny had witnessed the introduction in 1957 of FORTRAN—FORmula TRANslator—the first "high-level" language,

---

7.   John G. Kemeny & Thomas E. Kurtz, "Back to BASIC", True BASIC In, Hanover, NH, 2000, p7

which enabled scientific programs to be coded in English words and algebraic notation. This had extended computer access far beyond those few specialists who could program in low-level "machine" or "assembly" language, both of which required an intimate knowledge of the specifics of the individual hardware.

Reasoning that they would be able to use their knowledge in the outside world, Kurtz argued that Dartmouth students should learn a standard language such as FORTRAN. For once, Kemeny disagreed. FORTRAN was a highly formal language intended for experts. It required great attention to detail, and could take as long as two months to learn. He wanted a general-purpose language that would be immediately accessible to the average college student. Starting around September 1963, Kemeny and Kurtz sat down and designed a new language. To christen it, they chose an acronym that summed up their design philosophy: BASIC, for Beginners All-purpose Symbolic Instruction Code. The initial word was particularly significant: "No matter how powerful the language became, we never forgot the needs of beginners."[8]

The first BASIC program ran at 4AM—Kemeny was famously a night person—on 1 May 1964. The initial version of BASIC consisted of just fourteen commands—mostly simple English words like LET, FOR, NEXT, and RUN—enough for elementary programming. Users would need very little training before writing their first computer programs.

"Dartmouth freshmen listen to two one-hour lectures and then read a short manual," Kemeny wrote some years later. "Before the end of the first week of the course, the typical student is able to write at least one usable program. For the rest of the term his learning experience consists entirely of sitting at a terminal and typing in and 'debugging' his own programs. Each student, during a ten-week term, must write four test programs entirely on his own and work on them until they are errorless."[9]

A test program might involve approximating pi, by computing the perimeter of an inscribed triangle, then doing the same for an inscribed hexagon (using only trigonometry), and so on. The program would be about six lines long.

The time-sharing system went into operation at Dartmouth in June of 1964. Access was via eleven Teletypes in the college computer center. Just seven months after the equipment arrived, hundreds of students were learning on the system. "Students started turning in homework assignments printed out on the yellow

---

8.   Ibid, p1
9.   Kemeny, p30

paper the Teletypes used," Kurtz recalled, "and faculty went, What's going on here?"

Each quarter a few more terminals would pop up somewhere on campus. "People'd say, 'Gee we've got to have one of those down here so we don't have to walk to the computer center'." By 1970, there were 150 Teletypes located in twenty-five buildings around campus. Kemeny estimated that ninety percent of Dartmouth's 3,000 undergraduates knew how to use a computer. A survey showed that the average undergraduate spent slightly over an hour a week on a terminal. Most frequent users were sophomores not yet swept up in dating.[10]

From the outset, Kurtz insisted that access to computing should be open to all, at any time of day and free of charge, just like the university library, for whatever purpose students wanted to use it. Computing was a fixed cost, he told Dartmouth trustees—it cost the same whether it was used or not—so why not let the students use it? When alumni demanded to know why the school was giving away computing for free, Kemeny would ask them whether they would charge students for taking a book out of the library? (And he would jokingly add that sometimes he felt like paying students to take books out.)

Meanwhile at other schools, if students wanted to use the computer, they had to fill in an application and submit it for approval. This made it difficult for the average undergraduate even at a school like MIT, which was famous for its computers, to get their hands on a machine. At Dartmouth, by contrast, everybody was on. "And that changed everything," Andy Molnar said, "because at the time the computer was an expensive toy, and all people used it for was simple things like calculations."

With characteristic modesty, Kemeny and Kurtz did not seek publicity for their achievements. In early 1969, however, a staff reporter from the big city, Victor McElheny of *The Boston Globe*, visited Hanover. McElheny wrote a glowing account of the goings-on up in the woods. Under the headline "They're addicted to a friendly computer", his article begins by dismissing the contemporary fear that computers would turn people into robots. "For the past four years, Dartmouth College has been experiencing a computer revolution which shows that electronic calculating machines make people more individualistic, not less."[11]

The article goes on to cite "friendly" examples of computer use. For instance, a program called Climat-1, which introduces itself with a chatty "Hi. I am called

---

10.   Ibid, pp32,33
11.   Victor K. McElheny, "They're addicted to a friendly computer", Boston Sunday Globe, 16 February 1969

Miss Teletype. What would you like me to call you?" The program was intended to teach basic ideas in geography, thus freeing up time "for new lectures on the problems of urban ghettos in America".

Climat-1 was computer-aided instruction much like that being dispensed around the same time by CCC and PLATO. But there was more to computing at Dartmouth than CAI. The *Globe* article quotes Myron Tribus, dean of engineering at the college and a long-time supporter of Kemeny and Kurtz: "The Dartmouth time-sharing system is not really an elaborate teaching machine. Rather, it is a 'being-taught' machine, one that acts like a pupil with any user."

Kemeny was fascinated with this reversal of roles between man and machine. By 1970 he had come to see computer-aided instruction as "a false start." In a chapter in his book entitled *Computers and Education*, Kemeny begins by rehearsing the advantages of CAI as a substitute teacher.[12] The computer enabled students to proceed at their own speed, had infinite patience, allowed students to make their mistakes in private, could drill hundreds of students simultaneously, and never made a mistake.

But Kemeny goes on to confess that he had "two major prejudices against CAI." The first was that "the computer is a very expensive substitute for a book". Rather than have the computer take over entirely from conventional methods of instruction, he asserted that "it is much more sensible to let students read a page, or better a chapter, of a book on their own and then go to the computer terminal to be drilled or tested."

Kemeny's second objection to CAI was that "it is a very poor substitute for a teacher." Kemeny was loath to see the computer usurp this function. He loved teaching and was himself a brilliant teacher. Indeed, in 1970, when Kemeny was invited to become president of Dartmouth College, he agreed on one condition: that he be allowed to continue to teach.

"There are very few CAI applications," wrote Kemeny, "in which a computer can give the same quality of education that a human teacher can provide....In writing a CAI program the instructor must anticipate every possible response to a long series of questions. The more freedom provided for the student, the harder it is to anticipate the responses. Therefore there is an almost irresistible temptation to straight-jacket the student." CAI, he concluded, was most effective for rote learning and mechanical drill. But even in such humble applications CAI could produce much frustration, he noted, since most schoolchildren are poor spellers, and even poorer typists.

---

12.   Kemeny, pp72–80

At Dartmouth, Kemeny reckoned, CAI accounted for less than one percent of total computer usage. The computer was used mostly as a powerful tool. "The opportunity to put a modern computer at the fingertips of all the students," he wrote (using for the first time what would two decades later become a catch phrase), "has made the Dartmouth mathematics and science courses both more palatable and meaningful. Students do not spend endless hours doing mathematical calculations....Instead, it is their job to grasp the principles taught in mathematics and science classes; all the messy arithmetic is left to the computer."

In the social sciences, the potential of the computer for information retrieval had made a vast difference. It was now possible for sociology students at Dartmouth to access vast data bases such as the latest United States census, extract the desired information, and carry out a variety of statistical analyses upon it. Kemeny pointed out that such applications supplemented classroom activity. They posed no threat to the job of the teacher.

But the most important educational impact of the Dartmouth time-sharing system was one not foreseen by its designers. Writing programs turned out to be an extraordinarily effective way of developing thinking skills. In the process of programming the computer, Kemeny wrote, "the student is the teacher and the computer is the student. The student learns an enormous amount by being forced to teach the computer how to solve a given problem.

"Much of the teaching mathematics and science consists in the development of algorithms, or recipes, for the solution of problems. In traditional education, the student is supposed to absorb an algorithm by working out three examples of it. Quite typically the student gets so involved in the complexities of the arithmetic or algebra involved that he completely loses track of the algorithm itself. When he programs a computer to work out the examples, the exact opposite occurs. The student must concentrate on the basic principles; he must understand the algorithm thoroughly in order to explain it to the computer. On the other hand, he does not have to do any of the arithmetic or the algebra. At Dartmouth we have seen hundreds of examples of spectacular success of learning through teaching the computer."

The introduction of computers also produced another unintended educational outcome, one that would be observed and wondered at in many other schools down the years. This stemmed from the fact that with computers, unlike with other areas of intellectual activity, students and teachers started from the same baseline.

According to Art Luehrman, who taught physics at Dartmouth from 1965 to 1977, "students and faculty were learning together and finding mutually interest-

ing projects to do. So you got very interesting, cross-generational collaboration....When an English professor got interested in something, it was because he
had a student who was interested in that, and who would do a lot of the grunt
work to get some programs up. And the interaction would take off from
there—the teacher would say, O that's nice, now can we do this? And they would
be mutually teaching each other."

It was Luehrman who, at a conference in Boston in 1972, coined the phrase
"computer literacy.' "I was blasting away at a computer priesthood who wanted
to keep the congregation illiterate," he recalled.

Dartmouth graduates were willy-nilly computer-literate, with an understanding of what computers were and how they could be used. This often gave them a
head start in their working life. The vast majority of the school's graduates were
not mathematicians, but humanities and social science students. But they could
write simple programs and understand computer-ese. A lot of them went on to
get good jobs by virtue of what was then a rare set of skills. "They didn't think
anything of it," Kurtz said, "until they got to their job in a big New York bank
and discovered that they were worth their weight in gold."

In the late 1970s, while other universities were having difficulty in attracting
students, Dartmouth accepted one in eight. A survey of applicants found that the
most frequently cited reason for wishing to attend was the college's reputation for
instructional computing.[13]

The influence of BASIC and the time-sharing system extended well beyond
Dartmouth. Soon after its introduction at the college, the system began supplying computer instruction via phone lines and Teletype terminals to around 50
colleges and secondary schools in northern New England. These included local
public schools like Hanover High, and exclusive private schools like Mount Hermon, just on the Massachusetts side of the New Hampshire state line. Kurtz
believed that Mount Hermon was the first secondary school in the world to
require computer instruction of all of its students.

At the same time General Electric, which supplied the computers used at the
college, hired some Dartmouth students in their summer vacation to help the
company build a commercial version of the time-sharing system. This was the
start of what would become the world's largest commercial time-sharing service.
And whenever GE sold computer time, the company bundled BASIC as part of
the package.

---

13.   Andrew Molnar, "The Next Great Crisis in American Education: Computer Liter-
      acy", THE Journal, Vol 5, No 4, July/August 1978, pp35–38

Among the many thousands of high-school students who gained their first experience of computing in this way was Bill Gates. Using the proceeds of a mothers club rummage sale Lakeside, the exclusive Seattle private school which Gates attended, bought a Teletype machine and some computer time from a GE time-sharing bureau. Mastering the operation of this machine became a contest between the students (the teachers were too intimidated). Computer time was expensive, and after a very short time the donation from the mothers club was exhausted. Obtaining free computer time became top priority for Gates and his friends.[14]

BASIC was the first language they encountered because that was what the GE computer system used. Gates & co would spend hours reading the BASIC manuals, teaching themselves the code, and making extensions to it. "The teachers thought we were quite unusual. And pretty quickly there were four of us who got more addicted, more involved and understood it better than the others." They included Gates and Paul Allen. In January 1975, the pair were walking through Harvard Square when they spotted a copy of *Popular Electronics* magazine with a picture of the Altair 8800, the world's first microcomputer, on the cover.[15] Gates and Allen immediately fired off a letter to MITS, the company which made the Altair, offering to write a version of BASIC for the new computer. Later that year, they founded Microsoft to license their version of BASIC to other computer makers.

Like the good academics they were, Kemeny and Kurtz had put BASIC in the public domain so that anyone who wanted to could use it, free of charge. The easy-to-learn language became a key component in the explosive growth of the personal computer industry. In the industry's early days, it would have been unthinkable to market a machine that did not come with (its own version of) BASIC. Millions of schoolchildren learned to program in the language. Even today, though the emphasis in computer instruction has long since shifted away

---

14. David Allison, transcript of an interview with Bill Gates, Smithsonian Institution, 1993
     http://americanhistory.si.edu/csr/comphist/gates.htm#tc2
15. This is Gates version of the story. An alternate version goes "Gates's friend Paul Allen ran through Harvard Square with the article and waved it in front of Gates's face, saying, "Look, it's going to happen! I told you this was going to happen! And we're going to miss it!" quoted in Paul Freiberger & Michael Swain, "Fire in the Valley: The Making of the Personal Computer", [2nd ed] McGraw-Hill, New York, 2000, p178. The title of article was "World's First Minicomputer Kit to Rival Commercial Models".

from programming, with advanced placement courses relegating it to the status of a specialist subject in the US, many kids all over the world still learn to program computers using BASIC or its descendants.

Kemeny served as president of Dartmouth from 1970 to 1981. During this time he ushered in profound changes in the college—the introduction of female students, the renewal of Native American education, the active recruitment of minority students. In 1979 recognition of his leadership ability, President Carter selected Kemeny to chair the commission of inquiry into the accident at the Three Mile Island nuclear plant. In 1982 he returned to full-time teaching.

John Kemeny died unexpectedly in December 1992, at the age of 66. In an interview the year before his death, he voiced his frustration at the slow progress of computers in education.[16] More than a decade later, most of his criticisms still ring true. Asked to list what were the problems of getting computers into the curriculum, Kemeny responded that there were essentially three. The first was hardware, but this was less difficult than formerly, being mostly a question of money. Second was the lack of good educational software. But third, and by far the most difficult problem, was how to change faculty attitudes.

"Some take to computing naturally," Kemeny said, "but that is a minority. A very typical attitude is, 'I've taught this course extremely well for 25 years, and I see no reason at all why I should change it.' Some of my best friends fit that description....You have to convince them that what was good enough 25 years ago is no longer good enough with the availability of computers.

"Underlying their arrogance may be fear...they hate to admit that they don't know how to use a computer, they fear that they would make some terrible mistake with this frightening gadget right in front of their students. [To get around this problem] takes some training and some help."

Kemeny lamented that "the potential that we saw 25 years ago at Dartmouth has still not been realized at most institutions. I'm looking forward to the day when no-one teaches a math course for which computers are obviously appropriate without using a computer. The sad fact today in math and most other disciplines is that the vast majority of courses which should use computers do not."

---

16.   Ken King, "The Computer and the Campus", video interview with John Kemeny, Educom, 1991, www.dartmouth.edu/~kemeny/

5

THE DUTCHMAN, THE DRAGON, & THE OREGON TRAIL

Lud Braun's epiphany took place one afternoon in 1970 at the Graduate Center of the Polytechnic Institute of Brooklyn, where Braun taught electrical engineering. There, as he looked on in astonishment, the real world ceased to exist for two high-school kids, a boy and a girl aged around 16. Their eyes lit up as they tried to save a stream full of fish from being poisoned by pollution. Or rather some virtual fish, for this was a trial run of POLUT, a computer simulation designed for use in high school biology class.

The program simulated a body of water into which pollutants were dumped. The students had control over five parameters. They could select the kind of water (pond, slow-moving stream, fast-moving stream), the kind of pollution dumped into it (industrial waste, sewage), the extent to which pollutants were processed before dumping (no treatment, primary treatment, secondary treatment), their rate of injection, and the temperature of the water (warm or cold, according to the season).

The computer monitored the concentration of pollutants and dissolved oxygen in the water. It printed out a report on a Teletypewriter in the form of a crude graph made up of Xs and Os. The machine would alert students when fish began to die, which happened when the oxygen dropped below five parts per million. The teachers that Braun was working with thought POLUT was hot stuff. But he wanted to see for himself how students would react to his simulation. So Braun asked one of the teachers to lend him two kids for a couple of hours for a trial run at the center, which was located in Farmingdale, Long Island.

"I sat them down at the computer and explained what the program was about," Braun said, "then I went to the back of the room and just watched." What happened was that the students' imagination quickly took over, transporting them to the riverbank. Despite the constant clackety-clack of the Teletype-writer—a very noisy device—Braun was convinced that "those kids heard water rippling over the stones in the brook." They were in short, he reckoned, entranced. And whenever the computer reported that fish were starting to die, the students reacted "with great sadness, and they went back to the drawing board determined to do something to keep to keep the fish alive."

This demonstration had a profound effect on Braun. Henceforth, he vowed, he would go "on an evangelical journey to let the world know what I had discovered about kids and computers." From 1968 to about 1985, Braun travelled all over the US. "Anytime anybody invited me to come speak about computers in education anywhere I did it, all they had to do was pay my transportation and I came. Nobody ever paid me, or if they did they paid me a hundred bucks. Most of the time I waived the fee, I was so excited about what computers would do for kids."

Braun—aided by his students who, he said admiringly, were "some of the best programmers in the world"—would be responsible for developing some of the most innovative and widely-used software programs in the early years of educational computing.

The son of German immigrants to the US, Ludwig Braun entered educational computing through the back door. In 1963, one of his students told him, scathingly, that no-one over 30 years old knew anything about computers. Braun, who was then 37, rose to the challenge. He said to himself, "Nuts to you, I'm gonna learn. So I started learning FORTRAN, and punching cards, and all that awful kind of stuff."

Two years later Braun joined in a post-Sputnik initiative called the Man-Made World.[1] The purpose of this project was to give college-bound kids taking non-science subjects an understanding of important engineering concepts and devices, such as feedback and computers. His colleagues wanted to teach kids how a computer worked using FORTRAN and assembly language. Braun argued that such difficult technology was not appropriate for the target audience. He had heard about what Kemeny and Kurtz were doing. He went to Dartmouth College several times to see for himself what was going on up there.

Braun caught the BASIC bug. To him BASIC was a people-oriented language and he embraced it wholeheartedly. "Now we could thumb our noses at the computer center and its FORTRAN punched-card system" Here was a wonderful opportunity to do something, he told his colleagues. They were unconvinced.

---

1.   Officially known as the Engineering Concepts Curriculum Project

They did not take into account what Braun called his Germanic persistence. "I'm a thick-headed Dutchman," he laughed, "and when they get their minds set, German people tend to press forward, no matter what."[2]

Unlike most of the other pioneers of educational computing, Braun was not an elitist working at an elite institution. He was a veteran, a product of the GI Bill, which had paid for his entire education. "If it hadn't been for the GI Bill," he allowed, "I would probably have been a laborer."

Braun kept making loud noises until finally the people who ran the project gave him some money to try out time-sharing terminals in a few high schools. In those early days, very little software was available for schools and what there was not very good. Nonetheless, the results were encouraging. "It really worked," Braun recalled, "the teachers and students were enthusiastic, even without lots of software."

Building on this initial success would take serious money. The indefatigable Braun journeyed to Washington to tell the National Science Foundation how he thought computers should be applied to the education of kids. By a happy coincidence, the NSF had just opened its Office of Computer Activities and the forward-thinking Andy Molnar was a program director. "For two decades Andy had the vision and the courage to fight the federal bureaucracy from within for funding for educational technology," a grateful Braun recalled. Molnar liked what Braun had to say, and the NSF ended up backing him to the tune of three million dollars.

Thus began what became known as the Huntington Project, named for the suburban Long Island town of Huntington, the birthplace of Walt Whitman. Huntington was chosen because there were ten schools in the immediate vicinity. This made it easy for Braun to gather teachers together at the nearby Farmingdale graduate center for training sessions and progress reports.

In the summer of 1967, he assembled around eighty high-school teachers across a wide range of subject areas. These included biology, chemistry, earth sciences, history, language arts, mathematics, physics, and social sciences. The teachers learned BASIC and discussed ways in which it might be applied to support them in the classroom. The idea was that the kids would do more than just programming. "We went through some mighty contortions in the early days, trying to identify what was useful and what wasn't," Braun said.

---

2.   American readers will not need to be reminded that "Dutchman" means German (Dutch = Deutsch).

"In the first year of our project, we tried doing some programmed instruction on the computer, and some simulations. And everybody agreed that the simulations were much more valuable, they had much more staying power than anything else we tried. Students were bored by the programmed instruction and stimulated by the simulations; teachers felt that their students learned much more from the simulations, going back repeatedly to explore further."

Braun pressed hard for what he considered a more intelligent use of the computer than drill and practice, which he dismissed as mere programmed page-turning. "One of my guiding principles has been that I see the computer as an intellect amplifier for every kid," he said, "I think it enhances their intellectual prowess dramatically."

(Years later, succumbing to the unfortunate tendency to make extravagant predictions that is so characteristic of educational computer pioneers, Braun would write that he was "convinced that children who grow up with a computer available to them will be part of a race of intellectual giants.")

Braun was particularly alert to the power of simulation because he used it extensively in his own research. He had worked with doctors at the respiratory disease unit of the downstate medical center in Brooklyn, developing a computer model to help them improve patient diagnosis and devise better tests. "I was able to show physicians things about the respiratory system that they had never understood before," Braun said. This prompted him to think about ways in which simulation could be used to help high-school kids understand the world around them.

The first phase of the project was such a success that the NSF funded a second round, known as Huntington Two. The project used the same schools and equipment, but focused efforts on biology and social studies because they had very large student populations nationwide. Mathematics was excluded because other groups were working in that area.

"The Huntington simulations opened a lot of people's eyes that you could do real interesting things in science and social science and kind of be outside the math classroom," said Dan Klassen, a software developer who worked on the project, "that was the big breakthrough."

Simulation would be the mode of choice because almost no-one else was doing it, certainly not at the high-school level. "I really liked the simulations," recalled Sue Talley, then a high-school teacher of English. "There was something about their open-ended nature that said to me, This is gonna be a really good way for kids to learn."

The program development phase of Huntington Two lasted four years, from 1970 to '74. It produced twenty-two simulations, POLUT being one of the first. Others included LIMITS, a simplified model of world dynamics that encompassed future changes in population, food supply, non-renewable resources, industrial production, and pollution. Students could alter the program's assumptions and let the computer project results up to 125 years hence. In many ways, LIMITS prefigures Sim City, the hugely popular simulation game launched fifteen years later, in 1989. (Sim City has sold millions of copies. Today, along with its derivatives, it is widely used in schools and colleges.)

With its emphasis on simulation, the Huntington Project was a radical departure. "It was head and shoulders better than anything the NSF had done to bring computer stuff to teachers," said Bob Albrecht, who used the software in workshops for teachers on the West Coast.

In addition to the simulations themselves, Braun and his team worked hard to develop support documentation to make the programs as attractive as possible to teachers. The documentation included a student manual and a brief teacher's manual. The latter outlined a statement of objectives, student level, suggestions for the preparation of students, and post-program questions and activities.

The Huntington Two simulations went on to become perhaps the most widely used computer-related materials in high schools until the coming of the personal computer. The publisher, Digital Equipment Corporation, sold over 50,000 student manuals and more than 100,000 manuals in total. Braun estimated that by 1980, some hundreds of thousands of students had used the programs.[3]

◆   ◆   ◆

What was a computer manufacturer like DEC doing publishing educational materials? The answer is, promoting sales of the corporation's PDP-8, a new and dramatically different type of computer. At the time, people could not believe how small the PDP-8 was. Before it, serious computers—"big iron" the industry called them—came in multiple cabinets that lived in a glassed-off, air-conditioned room. The PDP-8 by contrast was a stand-alone unit which occupied just eight cubic feet and weighed a mere 250 pounds. Though it took four hefty men to lift the machine, it was nonetheless portable and could be installed more or less

---

3.   Ludwig Braun, "An Odyssey Into Educational Computing," unpublished paper, c 1980

anywhere. The PDP-8's logic modules were mounted in two symmetrical towers enclosed in smoked plastic which rose above its control panel. "It looked like a giant stereo receiver with flashing lights instead of an FM dial, and a row of switches in front."[4] The minimum configuration came with 4K of memory.

The PDP-8 first shipped in 1965, the era of mini skirts and mini cars. One of DEC's English salesmen came up with a catchy name for the new machine: he called it a "minicomputer". The name quickly caught on. The PDP-8 is sometimes described as the Model-T Ford of the computer industry because it was the first machine to be mass-produced and was easy to maintain. Initially priced at $18,000—including Teletype terminal—it was cheap enough for almost any institution to afford. Small colleges and large public school systems were some of DEC's best customers for the system. By 1973, the PDP-8 had become the best-selling computer in the world, a ranking it would retain until the coming of the Apple II.

Five of the schools in Huntington Two used terminals hooked up to remote time-sharing systems, the other half had a minicomputer installed in one of their classrooms. Though both types of system were educationally effective, there was a dramatic difference in the students' response to them. "The kids in the PDP-8 schools really fell in love with their computers," Braun recalled. It was right there in the classroom, and it was *their* box.

The computers were typically placed in rooms with large windows so that everyone could see them as they passed by. Perhaps because they could see, touch, and operate machines directly, "the kids formed emotional attachments with the stand-alone computers." They gave their minicomputers names, even wrote poems to them. In one school, the captain of the football team was so enamored of the PDP-8, he took it under his protection, making it clear that if anyone horsed around with his computer, they would have to answer to him.

Though the technology was primitive—programs had to be fed into the machines on paper tape—teachers preferred the stand-alone computers because they were much more reliable than the remote ones. Administrators preferred to own the machine rather than renting it, because it meant they didn't have to ask for funds for computing each year. They also liked the fact that there was no need to pay for communications, the cost of which on time-sharing systems was often as much as the computer time.

The Huntington Project was thus successful both in demonstrating the value of a new type of educational software (simulations) and in establishing a new way

---

4.   Steven Levy, "Hackers", Dell Books, New York, 1984, p173

to deliver that software (stand-alones). However, as Braun ruefully concluded, the project was "unable to achieve the impact we had hoped for because funding was not available to produce the number of units we felt were required." As new and more powerful computers became available, there was no money to upgrade the programs. But though few now remember the Huntington Project, it did inspire at least one significant successor. This originated in, of all places, Minnesota.

◆   ◆   ◆

Minnesotans, being sensible people, have an ordinance known as the "joint powers law." This enables state government agencies to band together to perform a particular function. In 1973, recognizing the need to coordinate educational computing activities across the entire state, and seeking to avoid wasteful duplication, the government invoked the joint powers law to form the Minnesota Educational Computing Corporation, or MECC. The new joint agency was run by a board consisting of representatives from the University of Minnesota, the state university system, the community college system, the department of education, which was responsible for the 400-odd K-12 school districts in the state, and the state's department of administration.

MECC's first major achievement was to set up a state-wide time-sharing system. The idea was that any student anywhere in Minnesota would have equal access to computing resources no matter whether they lived in a big city, up on the Canadian border, or in a rural backwater. Teletype terminals were installed in appropriate locations and hooked up via telephone lines to a Control Data mainframe computer in Minneapolis. By the early 1970s, the state had more than 200 schools and 50,000 kids with access to the network.[5]

With this unique, state-wide network in place, the next question was, what would run on it? The cooperative spirit in Minnesota dictated that the software schools needed should be developed at the grass-roots level. So when a young history teacher named Don Rawitsch joined MECC in 1974 and inquired whether any additional programs were required, the answer was: Yes—all the time!

It so happened that a couple of years earlier, while finishing teacher training at nearby Carleton College, Rawitsch had spent several months doing teaching practice at schools in Minneapolis. There he shared an apartment with a couple

---

5.   Bob Albrecht, quoted in Stewart Brand, "Spacewar", *Rolling Stone*, 7 December 1972

of trainee math teachers who knew a little bit about computer programming. On the weekends they used to bring home a Teletype terminal and an acoustic coupler using which they would dial into the time-sharing system that the Minneapolis school system ran.[6]

"They were doing things for their math classes," Rawitsch recalled, "and finally it just dawned on me that there must be something I could do in my teaching of history." (A brave idea: in the Huntington Project, history had been one of only two subjects in which it proved impossible to find anything useful for the computer to do.) The three trainees put together a crude game based on their recollections of the nature of westward migration in the United States in the 1840s. Since this was a topic that was almost always covered in history, Rawitsch was able to use the game in his classes. Then, when he had finished his practice teaching, he forgot all about it. Fortunately, Rawitsch had the foresight to keep a print-out of the code. This crude game formed the basis for *The Oregon Trail*, which would become one of the software publishing industry's largest-selling—and longest-lasting—programs.

When Rawitsch found out about the desperate shortage of educational software, he pulled out the listing and reentered the code into the MECC computer. During the ensuing year, he took it upon himself to go to the library to do further research on the actual historical facts of the migrant trails. As it happened, there were more materials on the Oregon Trail than on any of the others. Materials included diaries of emigrants who had made the epic overland journey. It took an average of six months to travel the 2,000 miles from the Missouri River to Oregon. The diaries contained entries recording the kinds of things the migrants experienced and the frequency with which they experienced them. Based on this data, Rawitsch modified the programming of the simulation, "so that the probability of things happening would be more accurate, the prices that you paid for things along the way were more reflective of the pricings of the time, and so forth."

For the program Rawitsch also wrote a teacher's manual, which was very much influenced by the Huntington materials. It helped that Dan Klassen, one of Lud Braun's team of developers, who had come out to join MECC as an executive, was on hand to offer advice.

---

6.   An acoustic coupler was a device that used the handset of an ordinary phone to connect the terminal to the phone line. On the slanted face of the Teletype, there was a cradle into which you put the handset.

Since the original *Oregon Trail* ran via a Teletype, it had no graphics whatsoever. All the prompts for the students to do something were simply printed out as text messages. The program proceeded in a series of turns, each turn representing two weeks on the trail. Each period started with you having to make some decisions about how fast you would drive your wagon, and whether you wanted to buy some extra supplies. You also had the opportunity to go hunting, to replenish your food supply without spending precious cash.

To simulate hunting animals for food, Rawitsch and his co-developers came up with an original idea. When you were ready to hunt, you hit the return key on the Teletype, and the computer would ask you to type in a word like BANG. The system had the ability to time your response. So you would type in the word, then hit return again. The computer would know whether you'd spelt the word correctly, and how long it had taken. If you had misspelt the word, of course you wouldn't get any more food; if you'd spelt it right, there was a formula that give you more or less food, depending on how fast a typist you were.

One of the intriguing things about *The Oregon Trail* was that there were so many possible combinations of events and decisions, it never played the same way twice. You made your decisions then the mathematical model in the computer would determine, based on those decisions, at what rate your supplies were used up for those two weeks. The model also kept a measure of the health of the people in the wagon, so it knew if you were eating poorly.

Since there was only one terminal, the students had to operate in groups. This encouraged collaboration. "In those days I had the opportunity to work with classes of [junior high school] students and to observe groups of them using the program," Rawitsch recalled. "And it was always very interesting to me that they tended to invent some social processes without really knowing that they were doing that. For example, they generally came up with a system of specialization, so that somebody would become the leader, and the person who was the best typist would always be the one who would take care of the shooting, and someone else might be following the map, and somebody else might be helping to track the supplies."

Another useful byproduct was a lesson in decision-making. "When a small group of students first started playing, as each decision came up, everyone would be shouting at once and trying to make themselves heard as to what should be done. And pretty soon they figured out maybe they could invent democracy and start taking votes on these things, and it would go more smoothly."

The Oregon Trail was a big hit with teachers, too. Most social studies teachers had thus far not had much involvement with computers, compared to their colleagues in other fields. Here at last was an application that was easy to master and that related directly to what they were teaching.

By 1980, people had begun to realize that educational software had business potential. Initially formed as a state-owned corporation, MECC during the '80s weaned itself off public funding and operated more or less as a regular business. In 1991, the state of Minnesota sold the corporation to private investors. Though MECC produced a range of other programs, including popular titles like *Number Munchers*, *The Oregon Trail* was by far its best-selling product. Now published by Broderbund, the software is still going strong, something that few if any other twenty-five-year-old programs can claim. The current edition—the fifth—features color graphics and 3D.

Rawitsch earns no royalties from sales of his creation. "Back then, no-one knew that software would become a business," he said, "but it's given me many years of notoriety, which has been just fine." Looking back Rawitsch saw the early period of educational computing as a kind of golden age. "There was a tremendous amount of creative energy released back in the old days," he said. "Not only was the technology exciting, but in developing products, you could bring to bear everything that you valued in curriculum as well."

◆   ◆   ◆

Few pioneers had more creative energy—or more notoriety—than Lud Braun's good friend, brother in spirit, and fellow computer evangelist Bob Albrecht. "Bob has probably impacted more children and young people in the United States than anybody," Braun thought.

Albrecht began his impacting early. In 1962 he was a buttoned-down young applications analyst working for the computer company Control Data in Denver. His next door neighbor, a math teacher at a local school, George Washington High, invited Albrecht to give a talk to his kids. A couple of days after the talk, a redheaded kid named Bob Kahn called to say that he and some of his friends would like to learn more about computers. Albrecht told him, "OK you assemble a group of students, and I'll run a course for them, free". Every Wednesday evening 7 to 10PM that summer he taught around 35 sixteen-year-olds at the Control Data office, where a small computer was available. Most stuck it out. "The summer course was merely an appetizer for many of the students. They clamored for more training."

Soon Albrecht had the kids teaching their peers. Albrecht persuaded his employers to lend him a computer for a week. Kahn and three other whizzes put the machine through its paces for math classes at the school, among other things showing how it could be programmed to do homework exercises. As a result of these demonstrations, sixty students signed up for computer classes. "We had so much fun," Albrecht recalled, "we...extended the program to eight other schools"[7]

Albrecht persuaded the National Science Foundation to fund him to teach teachers about computers, evenings and weekends at the University of Colorado's Denver Center. As instructors, once again he used his star students from high school, a role reversal that some teachers found—and continue to find—disturbing.

Pretty soon Albrecht was traveling all round the country running workshops for teachers at educational conferences like National Council of Teachers of Mathematics meetings. "I'd go a couple of days early and take a bunch of kids and teach them how to program," Albrecht recalled, "and then they'd put on a show at the conference."

In 1964 Control Data transferred him to Minneapolis. There Albrecht taught at the University of Minnesota's Laboratory High School. Thus far, he had been mostly teaching FORTRAN. Then the school managed to get access to the Dartmouth time-sharing system, and Albrecht discovered BASIC. It was love at first sight. "I said, that's it!"

Albrecht quit his job to crusade for BASIC. When the national math teachers council debated whether to support FORTRAN or BASIC, Albrecht tirelessly championed the interactive language. He even went so far as to hand out business cards and buttons for what he called the Society to Help Abolish FORTRAN Teaching, otherwise known as SHAFT.

In January 1966, Albrecht began work on his first book. Over the next three decades, he would write or co-author more than 30 how-to books, most about programming in BASIC. The most successful of these was *My Computer Likes Me When I Speak BASIC*. Published by DEC, it would sell over a quarter of a million copies. That made Albrecht probably the greatest popularizer of the easy-to-learn language.

The previous month Minnesota had endured 23 days of below-zero weather. Too much for Albrecht, who piled everything he owned into his Volkswagen bug convertible and set out for San Francisco. It was a propitious choice: the city had a long-established liberal tradition, and was fast becoming a mecca for all things counter-cultural. From then on, the Bay Area would be his base.

---

7.   Bob Albrecht, "A Modern-Day Medicine Show", Datamation, July 1963, pp31–33

There, together with Stewart Brand, Albrecht co-founded the Portola Institute, a nonprofit foundation that published the *Whole Earth Catalog*. As a result of the institute's educational activities, Albrecht was invited by a teacher named LeRoy Finkel to demonstrate computers at a progressive peninsula school called Woodside High. The two hit it off, forming a partnership that would last until Finkel's untimely death in 1993. Albrecht was the outsider, ranting and raving about alternate ways of using computers, Finkel played the straight man. An educator with his feet firmly grounded in reality, he provided the solid information that teachers and administrators needed to select the right equipment for their schools.

Finkel, Albrecht, and Kahn traveled all over California. "Collectively we taught on seven campuses of the University of California," Albrecht recalled, "running extension courses called Computers in the Classroom I and II, and Games Computers Play I and II. We'd go to Hewlett Packard and DEC to collect the computers they loaned to us, drive in my red VW bus to, let's say, UC San Diego, teach all weekend, pack up the computers, and drive home."

Albrecht estimated that perhaps as many as a thousand teachers attended these workshops, and those teachers went out and spread the good word to others. "We taught them how to program in BASIC," Albrecht said. "We also introduced the teachers to games—with names like Hurkle, Snark, and Bagels—because in those days all the games were written in BASIC."

Games would also play a big part in Albrecht's best-known venture, the People's Computer Company, which he set up in 1972. At a time when computers were often seen in the popular mind as sinister instruments of control, this was an attempt to turn ordinary people on to the joys of computing.

The People's Computer Company was a non-profit corporation that existed both as a monthly newspaper and, in physical form, as "a center of subversion, where computer time was wasted on mere fun." The newspaper was put together entirely by volunteers. Its content, though often whimsical in tone, was largely education-oriented, offering practical advice for people who wanted to learn about computers. It circulated nationally, ultimately attracting some 8,000 paying subscribers, many of them teachers.

The center was located in a storefront in Menlo Park, "the most comfortable, cruising-the-strip postwar suburb imaginable", according to the critic Greil Marcus, whose home town it was. An eminently suitable place to set up a center of subversion.

The storefront housed a PDP-8 and three Teletypes that DEC gave Albrecht in exchange for writing a couple of BASIC primers. The PCC was intended to be the first of what Albrecht hoped would become many neighborhood computer centers, "where people can walk in like they do to a bowling alley or a penny arcade and find out how to have fun with computers—just walk in the door and pay $2 to mess around with whatever is going on." Pretty soon, "the place was full of long-haired, populist computer freaks, many of them of high-school age."[8]

One such habitue was Bob Lash, who we last met as a 6-year-old in Pat Suppes' lab. "The People's Computer Center was a really cool place for computer hobbyists at that time," Lash wrote, "the best public access for 'real people'!"[9] Many would go on to found, or work for, Silicon Valley personal computer companies, most notably Apple.

Albrecht was beginning to make a name for himself. Ted Nelson hailed him as "the caliph of counterculture computerdom". As author of the hackers' bible, *Computer Lib*, this was a title to which Nelson had some claim himself.

In 1973, the magazine *Saturday Review of Education* published a two-page spread entitled "Computer Confrontation", which pitted the "romantic" views of Albrecht against those of "the self-proclaimed White Knight of the Behaviorists", Pat Suppes.[10] Albrecht's page is dominated by a mugshot in which his determined face is framed by a moustache-less, Amish-style beard. Not a bad look for an evangelist.

Albrecht began his side of the debate by asserting that "Kids who continually interact with a computer in a situation where all the control is on the computer's side, where all they do is respond and the computer says you're right or wrong, are likely to become susceptible to computer control. Drill and practice programs where the computer is in full control are all right as part of the learning environment—if you also teach kids how to control the computers.

"When kids first come to the People's Computer Company, they usually play games. Sometimes for two or three weeks. But some point almost every child asks, 'How does the computer play these games?" How can I write a game?' 'How can I make the computer do this?'

"After a kid has learned some mathematics—by drill and practice maybe—then we can teach him a simple program to teach some other kids. Then he knows how it was done to him. Then all the mystery is dispelled. And maybe his program will be better for kids than the program written by a behavioral scientist sitting in an ivory tower somewhere." By Suppes, that is, who was working

8.   Steven Levy, "Hackers", Dell Books, New York, 1984, p173
9.   Bob Lash, "Memoir of a Homebrew Computer Club Member", www.bambi.net/bob/homebrew.html, 5 July 2001 (last update)
10.   "Compute Confrontation", Saturday Review of Education, May 1973, pp48–49

at Stanford, just a few minutes' drive from the People's Computer Company. "I wish that Suppes could have seen some of the things that I saw happening with kids," Albrecht recalled, "that happened spontaneously just because they had access that wasn't tightly controlled."

Unlike Suppes and the Computer Curriculum Corporation, Albrecht's involvement with the People's Computer Company did not last long. Albrecht confessed that his tendency was to get something started, then move on to other things. The mainstream education community did its best to ignore his populist initiatives. Many people found Albrecht a little...unconventional. He was fond of a drink and devoted to Greek dancing, a passion which dated back to his early days in San Francisco. Having learned to dance himself, Albrecht was characteristically keen to teach others. Many a pot-luck dinner at the Center would end with him leading an exuberant Zorba-style knees-up. There was also the matter of Albrecht's somewhat eccentric identification with dragons, notably his alter-ego and sometime co-author, "George Firedrake".

◆   ◆   ◆

Albrecht was not the only one to witness extraordinary things happening spontaneously when kids were let loose on terminals. Working on the other side of the country was a researcher with a highly unusual provenance whose work with young children and computers and its remarkable consequences we will examine in Part Two.

PART II
POWERFUL IDEAS

6

OUT OF (SOUTH) AFRICA

Christmas Eve, 1953: though the immigration office in Cape Town, South Africa's principal port, was nominally still open for business, the yuletide booze had long since begun to flow. When a dark-eyed young man wandered in and pulled out a bottle of hooch, he was welcomed like a long-lost friend and invited to join the fun. Amidst this great merriment, after a while, the stranger happened to mention that he was in urgent need of a passport. His timing was perfect: eager to get on with the party, the officials issued their newfound acquaintance his travel documents on the spot.

That came as a huge relief for the young man. As an anti-apartheid activist and sometime member of the local Young Communists League—a banned political organization—he had been afraid that the authorities would not let him leave the country, to take up a postgraduate scholarship at Cambridge University in England. So much so that, to apply for his passport, rather than try his luck at home in Johannesburg, he had travelled hundreds of miles down to Cape Town, where he was not known. Now, with his papers in order, the young man fled South Africa. It would be twenty-five years before he returned.

An unconventional end to an unconventional beginning for Seymour Papert, certainly the most radical and arguably the most influential of all the pioneers of educational computing.

Papert is a richly complex human being. A full beard and dishevelled mop of curly hair frame a benign, slightly mischievous-looking face. Geniuses tend to talk down to lesser mortals. Papert, by contrast, is a generous spirit. He has "a splendid gift for making you believe that he regards your intellect seriously."[1] Women have been known to fall in love—sometimes at first sight—with this rumpled, gentle, soulful man.

---

1. Pamela McCorduck, "Machines Who Think'" W.H. Freeman and Company, San Francisco, 1979, p131

Papert has tremendous charm and indeed charisma. An adoring audience of thirty parents might fall under the spell cast by Papert's soft, cultured, mellifluous voice, in which it is still possible to detect the characteristic, shifted vowels of a South African accent. But Papert is equally capable of falling apart in public, in front of two thousand people, losing the place in his speech, scattering sheets of paper all over the stage. Over the years more than a few audiences never even got to hear Papert, on account of his having failed to show up. Organization was never his strong suit.

Papert is, to be sure, your classic absent-minded professor. His friend and colleague Nicholas Negroponte recalled one time when Papert boarded a plane bound for Europe before remembering that he had left his wife waiting for him on the corner of New York's 57th Street and Park Avenue. Papert has been observed ambling down the Infinite Corridor at MIT, where he works, bumping into a pillar and politely saying Excuse me, Mr Magoo-style, before continuing on his way. On one occasion in Texas, Papert ended up not getting to where he was supposed to be because he forgot where he had put the key to his rental car. It finally turned up, in the lock of the car's trunk.

At the same time, however, Papert is also the possessor of a laser-sharp mind, one which is capable of piercing insights. "Seymour's really brilliant at getting to the essence of something," said his former collaborator Cynthia Solomon, "and helping you to see what that essence is."

Mitchell Marcus experienced this intense clarity of vision as a graduate student at the first meeting of his PhD thesis committee at MIT circa 1975. Papert "proceeded, with a scalpel to slice away all the parts of my program that were fluff," recalled Marcus, who is now a professor at the University of Pennsylvania. "He separated the parts I hadn't really thought through from the parts that it was clear to him I understood. It was really Papert who ended up focusing on what I was trying to do. Later he read the first two chapters of my thesis and said, 'This is really very interesting,' and then didn't show up for the thesis defense."[2]

Your appointment with Papert might be at two in the afternoon, and he might not show up until five or six o'clock. But you always knew that when he did finally give you his attention, it would be well worth waiting for.

For all his lapses and failures to deliver, Papert was nonetheless capable of attracting and inspiring some of the most creative young talent at MIT, and winning the lasting devotion of many. And to his great credit, he has remained for

---

2.   Jeremy Bernstein, "Three Degrees Above Zero", Cambridge University Press, Cambridge, 1984, p64

almost forty years in the vanguard of the struggle to transform education via technology.

◆   ◆   ◆

Seymour Aubrey Papert was born in Pretoria on 1 March 1928, the scion of a Jewish family who emigrated to South Africa in the late nineteenth century. Like many of their coreligionists, the Paperts left the pogroms and poverty of their native Lithuania lured by the news that diamonds and gold had been discovered in the Transvaal.

Papert's father Jack was a scientist, an entomologist who mapped the migration patterns of the tsetse fly. This little pest was responsible for transmitting sleeping sickness, a terrible scourge that caused widespread death and destruction (not least among gold miners). Jack Papert's method was to head off to some remote part of Swaziland, a region on Africa's southeast coast, and set up camp for several months. There he would trap the flies, then mark and release them. Later, when marked flies were caught, he would record the location. On these trips he took with him his wife and their infant son.

For the first seven years of his life, young Seymour grew up as a nomad, without acquiring the racial prejudice normal to South African whites. A curious child free to roam as he pleased, he made new discoveries every day. "It was my first taste of life, where everything was visible and understandable and self-contained," he recalled.[3] This school-less idyll came to an abrupt end one day when a black mamba, Africa's deadliest snake, was discovered dangling from the rafters of his hut. The snake was about to drop down and bite the lad when his father picked up a shovel and killed it. After this incident—not the first of its kind—his mother, Betty, put her foot down. Other children were on the way; high time to move to a house in the big city.

Johannesburg is South Africa's largest city and the center of its gold-mining industry. Located a mile above sea-level Johannesburg is blessed with a delightful climate, the best in the world some say. The sun shines every day of the year, the rain coming predictably, in half-hour bursts on summer evenings. But despite the perpetual good weather, the political atmosphere in the 1930s and '40s was already dark and highly charged. Although apartheid was not officially introduced until 1948, South Africa had been since its earliest days, in Papert's words," a powerfully segregated society."

---

3.   Tom Weber, "Signing on to Revolution", *Bangor Daily News*, 3 February 1997, pA2

In the backyard of every middle-class suburban Jo'burg home lived Africans, referred to by the whites as "natives". Black servants did the cooking, nursed the babies, made the beds, cleaned the floors, washed the clothes, polished the shoes, mowed the lawns, and trimmed the hedges. "They ate on enamel plates and drank out of chipped cups with no handles, which were known as the boy's cup or girl's cup and kept separate from the rest of our china. They spoke broken English or Afrikaans, wore old clothes, had no money and no last names."[4]

Growing up amid such extremes of inequality, Papert developed from an early age a strong and deeply-felt social conscience, one that would subsequently inform his educational philosophy. Under the tutelage of Father Trevor Huddleston, a turbulent Anglican priest who was known for doing what were then regarded as outrageous things (like raising his hat in friendly greeting to an uneducated black cleaning woman sweeping a veranda)[5], he became an activist.

To raise money for literacy programs, Papert and a friend put on various activities at his school, including a cake sale and a play. The issue of black literacy ended up getting him thrown out of high school. To teach the black servants of their community how to read and write, Papert and a group of his teenage pals attempted to organize after-hours night classes. They asked for permission to use their classroom from the school principal, who turned them down flat. Undaunted, Papert and his friends called a meeting of parents, certain that they would support the proposal. "But it turned out that the parents were even more against it than the school," Papert recalled. "One parent said that the servants might have diseases, so they couldn't be allowed to sit on the same benches that the kids sat in."

"We argued that these were the same people that cooked our food and cared for our kids, but we couldn't budge them."[6] The parents' arguments horrified Papert. How could these grown-ups be so irrational? How could they possibly think about blacks the way they did? These were questions that would continue to torment him. As a result, Papert became passionately interested in logic, and how thinking happened. If you could figure out how people's minds worked, then perhaps you could stop them having such illogical thoughts. How to bring

---

4. Rian Malan, "My Traitor's Heart", Vintage Books, New York, 1990, p43
5. The woman in question being the mother of Desmond Tutu. "I had never seen anyone do this to a black woman, let alone an uneducated woman like my mother," Archbishop Tutu remembered. "It was a great influence on me." He named his son Trevor in honor of Huddleston.
6. Weber

about such a radical transformation in society became, and would remain, his main intellectual interest.

Eventually, Papert would conclude that it was the kind of learning which people do when they are young that plays a dominant role in determining how they think in later life. This conclusion would ultimately lead him to computers "as instruments of change that might alter, and possibly improve, the way people learn and think."[7]

In late adolescence Papert had constant run-ins with adults he knew to be otherwise fundamentally decent good people, but who somehow supported a brutal discriminatory social order. Like many others of his generation, the experience pushed him in the direction of politics, and the desire to change the world. The idealistic young radical became a Marxist, briefly joining the Young Communists League, and making connections with various Trotskyist and other left-wing, non-Soviet-oriented, groups.

In 1945, aged 17, Papert entered the local University of Witwatersrand (known locally as Wits) where he met and befriended others who thought along similar lines. Many would also go on to leave South Africa and make international names for themselves, most notably his contemporary, the renowned microbiologist Sydney Brenner.

In his first year at Wits, attempting to demonstrate that logic could be formalized, Papert built a little logic machine. It was in effect a primitive computer, though at the time he didn't know the word "computer" and was unaware of similar efforts elsewhere. Made out of pushbuttons, switches, and lights, the machine could perform deductions based on the input of premises (eg, Socrates is a man, and all men are mortal).

As an undergraduate, Papert studied philosophy, but he soon found this arid and took up mathematics instead. Having earned his doctorate, Papert escaped to England, as we have seen, in somewhat dramatic circumstances. Cambridge University, however, was not to his liking. "It was amusing for the first couple of months, playing Middle Ages while dressed in academic gowns," he recalled with a grin. But Papert felt uncomfortable in the snobbish, class-ridden social atmosphere of the place. He was, at this time, a very political being: "What was important in the world", it seemed to him, "was to be politically involved." The young South African preferred London, where he moved in left-wing circles, leaving a lasting impression on some of those he met. "Seymour was the most intellectual,

---

7. Seymour Papert, "Mindstorms: Children, Computers, and Powerful Ideas", Basic Books, New York 1980, p209

the most critical and open-minded, and the least pretentious person that I encountered in the workers' movement in London," the veteran socialist James Young recalled.[8]

Having fulfilled his requirements at Cambridge, Papert got permission to finish the thesis for his second doctorate in Paris, at the Henri Poincare Institute, the mathematics wing of the Sorbonne. This was much more to Papert's liking. In the 1950s Paris was a hotbed of mathematical revolution, with the maverick Bourbaki group laying down an entirely new foundation for mathematics. He became involved with a splinter group of Trotskyite anarchists called Socialisme ou Barbarie—"Socialism or Barbarity"—contributing regular articles to the magazine of the same name.

"As a young radical, I was drawn to this atmosphere of change and its possibilities," Papert said. "For the first time I envisaged not going back home to South Africa. It was an agonizing time for me, yet going back seemed futile. I certainly would have been imprisoned."[9] At this point, the South African government having revoked his passport, Papert was effectively stateless. Then, in 1959, Jean Piaget intervened in his life.

◆   ◆   ◆

The great student of children's thinking, "the giant of the nursery" as he has been called, was teaching a course at the Sorbonne. For an investigation into how children develop ideas about number, Piaget needed a mathematician. One of his scouts fingered Papert as a possible candidate, and a lunch was arranged. From the outset, the chemistry was good: Piaget asked Papert what he thought of Bertrand Russell. Not much, came the precocious reply, a good logician but a bad epistemologist. The great man was delighted with this answer, further lunches were organized, until at last the question was popped: Would Papert like to come and spend a year with Piaget in his center at the University of Geneva?

At first, Papert dismissed the idea: he was still attempting to decide whether to stay in Paris and be a mathematician, or go back to South Africa and be a revolutionary. But Piaget wouldn't take no for an answer. A letter arrived saying, Here's your appointment to a position and your salary will be this much. Papert's initial reaction was, What a cheek! But indignation quickly gave way to curiosity: he

8.   <http://www.redsw.fsnet.co.uk/RSW02/CLRJames.htm>
9.   Weber

went to Geneva for a look, liked what he saw, signed on for one year and stayed for four.

Though often described as a child psychologist, Piaget (1896–1980) never thought of himself as such. "His real interest was epistemology—the theory of knowledge—which, like physics before Newton, was considered a branch of philosophy until Piaget came along and made it a science in its own right."[10]

Piaget believed that studying how knowledge develops in children would elucidate the nature of knowledge in general. He was thus the first to take children's thinking seriously. "Piaget is best-known for demonstrating that, so far from being empty vessels to be filled with knowledge (as traditional pedagogical theory has it), children are actually active builders of knowledge—little scientists who are constantly creating and testing their own theories of the world."[11] In John Dewey's phrase, the child learns through doing, without being taught. Piaget's theory was that children's cognitive development proceeds through four, genetically-determined stages that always occur in the same sequence, moving from concrete experience to abstract thinking. His ideas provided the intellectual foundations for the educational reformers of the 1960s and '70s.

Living in a Swiss Alpine village and working with Piaget, Papert focused his attention "on children, on the nature of thinking, and on how children become thinkers." But in addition to studying cognitive development, there were also other emerging approaches to intelligence. Particularly promising among them was the attempt to build mechanical models of the mind, a field that was originally called "cybernetics" but that would subsequently come to be known as "artificial intelligence" or AI. One of the pioneers of this new field was Warren McCulloch, a neurophysiologist at the Massachusetts Institute of Technology. In 1943, together with a mathematician named Walter Pitts, McCulloch published a paper which proposed ways in which neurons—nerve cells—could be connected up in a network to form computer-like machines.

Piaget was sympathetic to developments in AI, and Papert worked on mathematical models of what would later be known as "neural nets". For this work, he needed access to a computer, but there was none in Geneva. An opportunity arose to schedule a little time on the Automatic Computing Engine—ACE—a huge batch-processing monster of a machine located at the National Physical Laboratory in Teddington, England. "Everything about this machine was iso-

---

10. Seymour Papert, "The Century's Greatest Minds", Time, 29 March 1999, p105
11. Ibid

lated and idiosyncratic."[12] With its well-spaced racks of tubes, it looked more like a library than a computer.

Papert began commuting to Teddington, a small town southwest of London, averaging a couple of days a week at the laboratory. At a conference there in 1961, he met McCulloch. The latter had decided that he was too old to make any further new contributions to science. His role was now was to identify talented young people who could carry on the torch. McCulloch immediately invited Papert to come to MIT. Papert, who was then 33, jumped at the offer.

Geneva had been an exciting formative experience, but the ageing Piaget did not want to have to deal with computers. Papert was ready to move on. In particular, he wanted to go somewhere where there were computers. Nowhere had more computers—or a more highly-developed computer culture—than MIT. And nobody was more involved with those computers than Marvin Minsky, a young colleague of McCulloch's, who was also at the conference. He gave a paper that was virtually identical to Papert's, although the two had never even heard of each other before. This amazing coincidence initiated what would be a very fruitful and longlasting collaboration.

Though the attraction of MIT was enormously strong, it took Papert a couple of years to get to the transatlantic Cambridge. The US government was loath to grant a visa to a person without a passport, a man moreover who had been involved in left-wing political activities back home. A particular sticking point was that Papert could not obtain a police report from his country of origin, since from the South African government's point of view he was out of the country illegally. But McCulloch would not give up, he kept hammering away until in 1963 the immigration people gave in. Papert eventually obtained a British passport and became a professor of applied mathematics at MIT.

No sooner had he arrived, in fact on just his second day at the institute, than Papert had an epiphany. He was supposed to be meeting Minsky, was hanging around the latter's corner office on the eighth floor of Technology Square, home of MIT's computer science laboratory, wondering when Minsky would show up, unaware that—characteristically—he had got the day wrong. There was a terminal in the office. Papert started fooling around on the computer.

"I realized that, Hey, I can write a program on this!" he recalled. "It was a pretty bad program, but it solved a problem. And that really staggered me because I had really grappled with that problem, but I couldn't solve it, didn't know how to go about it, it was too big a chore."

---

12.   Seymour Papert, "The Connected Family", Longstreet Press, Marietta, 1996, p57

"What struck me most forcibly was that certain problems that had been abstract and hard to grasp became concrete and transparent, and certain projects that had seemed interesting but too complex to undertake became manageable. At the same time I had my first experience of the holding power that keeps people working all night with their computers."[13]

◆   ◆   ◆

Papert had arrived at MIT at a propitious time. The early 1960s was the hey-day of hackers at the institute. Hackers, wrote Steven Levy in his enjoyable exposition of the phenomenon, were "adventurers, visionaries, risk-takers, artists...and the ones who most clearly saw why the computer was a revolutionary tool." They had developed an idealistic philosophy "of sharing, openness, decentralization, and getting your hands on machines at any cost—to improve the machines, and to improve the world."[14]

The computer that Papert was fooling around on was the hackers' favorite machine. The PDP-1, "a downright heavenly toy", had been donated by DEC to MIT in 1961. In the next few weeks, in all-night sessions on the PDP-1, he joined in the hacking with his new colleagues, experiencing "a volcanic explosion of creativity" that resulted from this sudden unlimited access to the best machine in the world.

"It was pure play. We were finding out what could be done with a computer, and anything interesting could be worthwhile. Nobody yet knew enough to decree that some things were more serious than others. We were like infants discovering the world."[15]

This policy of hands-on discovery in a playful atmosphere was actively promoted by Minsky. For what was the world's first laboratory in artificial intelligence he needed all the programming skills he could muster. The aim of this new lab was simply, How to build machines that think? In other words, how to replicate the brain, which the provocative Minsky delighted in referring to as "a meat machine." He invited Papert to be the AI Laboratory's co-director.

---

13. Seymour Papert, "The Children's Machine: Rethinking School in the Age of the Computer", Basic Books, New York, 1993, p13
14. Steven Levy, "Hackers: Heroes of the Computer Revolution", Dell, New York, 1984, p7
15. "The Children's Machine," p33

It would seem natural that a researcher who had worked for years with children, and who was then translated to a place where there were undergraduates—many of them still in their teens—who played with computers, would make an immediate connection between children and machines. In fact, it took Papert a couple of years to put the two together in his mind. The conjunction happened while he was walking on a mountain in Cyprus in 1965, where Papert had gone for a holiday with his first wife, a Greek Cypriot, and their baby daughter.

"Here on this remote Mediterranean island I was feeling my absence from a life in which computers were a constant presence. This in turn stirred up thoughts about how much I had learned since coming to MIT...how concepts related to computers were changing my thinking in many different areas." Then, "like a thunderbolt"—not a bad metaphor under the more-or-less Olympian circumstances—the "obvious" idea hit him.

"What computers had offered me was exactly what they should offer children! They should serve children as instruments to work with and to think with, as the means to carry out projects, the source of concepts to think new ideas....I became obsessed with the question, Could access to computers allow children something like the kind of intellectual boost I felt I had gained from access to computers at MIT?"

It was a thought that would change his life.

"In search of good examples of what children might actually do with computers, my mind raced through my own activities, making lists of ways in which I thought I had benefitted from computers and asking myself whether something similar could be made available for children. For a while I simply passed over the first entry on my list: artificial intelligence, the principal interest that had brought me to MIT. 'Obviously not for children.'

"Then I remembered a conversation with Piaget a few years before in which we had engaged in playful speculation about what would happen if children could play at building little artificial minds....If psychologists could benefit from making concrete models of the mind, why shouldn't children, whose need was much greater, also benefit?...Neither of us thought of it as very real...but now suddenly, on a mountain in Cyprus, the idea changed for me from a philosophical speculation to a real project."

The change derived from the fact that, as a result of his work in the AI Lab, Papert now had a very concrete idea of what it meant to "do" artificial intelligence. AI researchers worked by selecting a piece of human mental activity, playing chess, say, "then they write a computer program that will do something similar; and finally they discuss…whether the computer program 'really' does what the human does." Papert had done a lot of this kind of thing, and had been greatly stimulated by it. It seemed plausible to him that "doing elementary AI could give children, too, a new context for thinking about thinking."

Chess was obviously too complex, so Papert cast around for a simpler example to work with. He settled on the matchstick game known as nim, in which two players take turns in removing one, two, or three matches, the loser being the one who takes the last match. The idea was that children should carefully observe the game being played, then try to come up with rules to put in a program to make the computer behave similarly. Matches would be represented by rows of Xs printed out on a Teletype. But what language would they program in?

"It seemed intuitively obvious that nothing good would come of trying to have third-or even fifth-graders make game-playing programs from scratch in any of the then-current programming languages such as FORTRAN…". These were designed for adults. The only sensible approach was thus "to take a first shot at making a programming language that had a better chance of matching the needs and capabilities of younger people than the existing ones."

Getting from the mountain in Cyprus to a place where young people could actually do something like the scenario he had envisaged would take Papert two years, but get there he would.

7

ENTER THE TURTLE

"But where is their math?" the woman screamed as she ran out of the classroom, hands clutching her head, agitated to the point of tearing her hair out. For months, this math coordinator from one of the neighboring towns had been begging to see what was going on at the Muzzey Junior High School in Lexington, Massachusetts. But when eventually allowed to visit in the Spring of 1969, the coordinator was confronted by a dozen seventh-graders doing something called "random sentence generators". The Teletype was printing out gibberish like "INSANE RETARD MAKES BECAUSE SWEET SNOOPY SCREAMS".[1] And the teachers of the class, Seymour Papert and Cynthia Solomon, seemed to think that this was pure poetry.

Papert and Solomon felt that they had good reason to be pleased. They had seen how profound learning could result from such an apparently meaningless activity as generating random sentences. One of the kids, a girl named Jenny, had initially wondered why she had been chosen for this experimental computer class. After all, she was not "a brain". Then, "one day Jenny came in very excited. She had made a discovery. 'Now I know why we have nouns and verbs,' she said."

Years of grammar lessons had left Jenny cold. She simply could not grasp what grammar was for. "But now, as she tried to get the computer to generate poetry, something remarkable happened. She found herself classifying words into categories, not because she had been told to, but because she needed to. In order to 'teach' her computer to make strings of words that would look like English, she had to teach it to choose words of an appropriate class."[2]

"That was a revelation," Papert said, "it was exciting not just because she was doing something that kids hadn't been able to do before, but because it gave

---

1. See Seymour Papert, "Mindstorms: Children, Computers, and Powerful Ideas", Basic Books, New York 1980, p49

2. Ibid

meaning to a whole range of experience that hadn't been meaningful before. Muzzey was the first time I saw that."

The language in which Jenny had been programming the computer was called Logo. The name came, appropriately enough, from the Greek "logos" meaning "word". It was chosen by Wallace Feurzeig, a mathematician at Bolt Beranek and Newman. BBN was a high-powered research and development consultancy—"the third university in Cambridge" some called it—that by the early 1960s had made computer technology its focus. Along with MIT and Dartmouth College, BBN was a hotbed of work on time sharing systems.

Feurzeig arrived at BBN in 1962, one of many young talents recruited by the great visionary of interactive computing, J.C.R. Licklider. (The latter had himself seen, at first hand, the potential of educational computing, if only for conventional drill-and-practice. "[W]ith only a small computer, a [Teletype], and a few nights of programming," Licklider said in a lecture given to celebrate MIT's centennial in 1961, "some of us have already created 'motivational traps' for our children, and we are sure that a computer teaching machine can be made more attractive than television. The youngsters love real-time interaction with a thing like the computer...[they] will sit there and punch the keys for hours learning spelling and language vocabulary.")[3]

Inspired by Licklider, at BBN, Feurzeig was interested in the possibilities of using interactive computing for education. But computer-aided instruction, the then-dominant way of applying education to technology, was anathema to him: CAI was insulting, Feurzeig said, "the notion that a kid was a vessel into which one poured knowledge." He wanted to build a system in which the student had equal rights with the computer.[4]

In 1965 Feurzeig founded an educational technology group at BBN. He recruited Dan Bobrow, one of Marvin Minsky's graduate students from the AI Lab at MIT, and Cynthia Solomon, Minsky's former secretary, who was learning to be a programmer. Bobrow introduced Feurzeig to Papert, whom he hired as a consultant on the basis of his experience with Piaget.

"Seymour and Wally and I started talking about how we could teach better at the youngest grades," Bobrow recalled, "and the whole process of programming itself we thought was very illuminating from the point of view of getting kids, if

---

3. "Computers and the World of the Future," Martin Greenberger (ed), MIT Press, Cambridge, 1962, p208

4. Angelos Agalianos, "A Cultural Studies Analysis of Logo in Education", [unpublished doctoral thesis], Institute of Education, Policy Studies, and Mathematical Sciences, London, 1997, p127

they could program, to be able to think about the process of getting a process to happen....What we were trying to avoid was the notion that you're either right or wrong. And so this whole notion that there could be some incremental way of getting from wrong to right was something than we all strongly believed in."

"Many children are held back in their learning because they have a model of learning in which you have either 'got it' or 'got it wrong'", Papert wrote. "But when you learn to program a computer, you almost never get it right the first time. Learning to be a master programmer is learning to become highly skilled at isolating and correcting 'bugs', the parts that keep the program from working."[5] Debugging was not just a technique—it was a powerful idea.

At first the group employed Telcomp, an existing BASIC-like language, in experiments to teach problem solving in math at some local schools. The results were encouraging: "I saw that kids were really engaged in doing mathematics," Feurzeig recalled, "it was a very different kind of experience from the usual way of presentation...they really liked the notion of building simple programs and running them...it turned the classroom into a beehive of activity, and we said, This is a very real thing, we obviously need to do more."

It was also obvious that a new language was needed. Not a hand-me-down from engineering, an algebraic language that presupposed you knew algebra, but one that was specifically designed for use by kids. The group discussed how to build such a language. "And Seymour said, 'Children's purpose is to learn by playing,'" Solomon recalled, "and he said, 'What do they play with? They don't use numbers, they use words and sentences.'" So the metaphor for the language they were designing became to imitate the way children learn to talk.

Soon it became clear to Bobrow that what they were proposing was to re-invent LISP, a programming language developed by John McCarthy for use in artificial intelligence. Instead of numbers Lisp processed information in the form of lists of symbols. Beginning with simple functions, it was possible to build up complex programs, a style well-suited to exploratory research. Papert agreed that it was all right to adopt LISP as the basis for the new language, but if kids were to be able to use it, then it must have a radically simplified syntax.

And so the new language was born, as a dialect of LISP, and christened Logo. "The notion was that computers were not just for doing science or math or technical things; they could be used for language, for music, for all kinds of things," Feurzeig said, "we were interested not only in mathematics but other areas, too."

---

5.   Papert, Mindstorms, p23

Logo's original goals were not modest. "We hoped that this would be transformational," Feurzeig said, "that this was going to really revolutionize education. It was a very, very different view about what computers and programming and kids were all about from what people were doing with other technologies like CAI or with BASIC...the hope was that Logo would really get kids to think in a more fundamental way about thinking in all kinds of contexts, to become strategic thinkers, to become more involved in designing and building of knowledge."[6]

Papert went even further. "From the beginning," he said, "I was thinking of a radical transformation of society." In addition to revolution, there was also derring-do. "Logo was fueled", Papert wrote, "by a Robin Hood vision of stealing programming from the technologically privileged (what I would in those early days in the 1960s have called the military-industrial complex) and giving it to children."[7]

Because it was designed for use with young children, Logo would acquire the reputation of being a toy language, suitable for simple tasks only. In fact, however, as would later be amply demonstrated, Logo could handle problems of considerable complexity. "Just as in English you can start off with baby talk," Papert said, "but the same language is also the vehicle for the expression of poets and philosophers." The language had, in a phrase coined to describe it early on, "a low threshold and no ceiling."

A pilot version of Logo was trialled in the summer of 1967, around the time when Pat Suppes was starting up Computer Curriculum Corporation. The guinea pigs were fifth and sixth graders at a school at Hanscom Air Force Base just outside Cambridge. (Since the Office of Naval Research was providing funding for the trial, it was deemed politic to recruit children of military personnel.) The goal was to test whether kids were capable of programming in Logo, and of understanding key concepts such as debugging. They were. On the basis of the experience, the language was revised, in particular, to give more precise feedback in the form of clearer error messages.

Muzzey Junior High, a small school in the upper middle class Boston suburb of Lexington, was chosen as the test bed for Logo's first major trial, because Feurzeig lived in Lexington and had a good relationship with the local superintendent of schools. Twelve kids of average academic ability were selected for the experiment. For the academic year beginning Fall 1968 Papert and Solomon

---

6.   Agalianos, p133
7.   Seymour Papert, The Children's Machine: Rethinking School in the Age of the
      Computer, Basic Books, New York, 1993, p180

taught them two days a week each, using a couple of Teletypes connected to the PDP-1 at BBN.

That first year they flew by the seat of their pants, never knowing what they were going to do next. Solomon started the students off playing primitive (graphics-less) computer games, then told them that they could not play any more unless they wrote the games themselves. That led to the kids to programming the nim game, which worked wonderfully well. Then they moved on to sentence generators and computer poetry. There were also math generators, which produced sentences like "A plus three equals what?" The kids loved writing what were, in effect, their own CAI programs. ("We have at last discovered the true role of CAI in education", Papert and Solomon would later write triumphantly.)[8]

In Spring 1969, at a meeting in Boston of the Association for Computing Machinery, the industry's premier society, a demonstration was arranged. Teachers and superintendents from all over Massachusetts were invited. The kids were well-prepared, the demo went smoothly, but the reaction was unexpectedly negative. Solomon recalled that some attendees got upset at how knowledgeable the children were, "because at that time people didn't think that kids could learn to program." Teachers would ask the kids difficult questions, then be annoyed that they knew the answers.

◆   ◆   ◆

By the end of the school year, Papert was both happy and frustrated. Happy, because the experiment at Muzzey had showed that twelve-year-old seventh-graders could handle Logo and do significant things with it. "There was no doubt that some of the students did get an intellectual boost," he wrote. "I felt confirmed and was beginning to dream ambitiously of really making a difference in how children learn." Frustrated, because "seventh-graders are scarcely children…and I felt that if contact with computers were destined to have an important effect it would be at a much younger age." But this was not simply a matter of developing appropriate pedagogical techniques. Teaching elementary school children to program would require a radically different idea.[9]

It came to Papert one day as he was doodling on the computer, wondering how on earth a child could capture in computational form something physical

---

8.   Seymour Papert & Cynthia Solomon, Twenty Things to Do with a Computer, MIT AI Laboratory, Logo Memo No. 3, June 1971

9.   Papert, The Children's Machine, p173

like drawing or walking. The answer was, via "an object to think with", a robot that the kids could actually see.

Building a robot was not an unusual idea in the context of the AI Lab, where robotics was one of the major activities. Hackers loved building robots almost as much as they loved programming computers. Robotics provided the perfect medium for testing ideas about the nature of intelligence. Minsky's dictum was, build a machine, see if it works; if it doesn't, then your idea probably isn't a very good one. In the late 1960s, he and Papert collaborated on a project to combine a mechanical hand, a television camera, and a computer into a robot that could build with children's building-blocks. The project, Minsky liked to think, "gave us glimpses of what happens inside certain parts of children's minds when they learn to 'play' with simple toys."[10]

The first Logo robot was a big clunky thing that looked like a cannister-type vacuum cleaner on wheels. Painted yellow, it had a headlight in front and a cable trailing from its rear end that connected it to a computer terminal. The robot's hard metal carapace made it look a bit like a turtle. Paul Wexelblat, the engineer at BBN who built it, named the turtle Irving.

Irving had a distinguished pedigree. In 1948 Grey Walter, a British neuro-physiologist, built a pair of cybernetic tortoises that, despite the simplicity of their circuits, could behave in remarkably lifelike ways. (In British English, the word "turtle" is used to refer to the larger, sea-going members of the family.) Based on inputs from the two sensors each carried, Elmer and Elsie would scurry towards a light until it got too bright, then turn away. When their batteries ran low, the creatures would retreat to their hutches to recharge. Papert had known Walter and seen his pet tortoises when he was in England. The differences was that, whereas Walter's mechanical tortoises had been autonomous, Papert's turtles were programmable.

By typing in simple commands on the computer, you could order them to go forward and back a certain number of steps, and to turn left and right a certain angle. You could also tell the turtle to lower the pen it carried in its belly to make "turtle tracks", a trace of its journey on large pieces of butcher paper taped to the floor. The idea of programming was introduced through the children "teaching" the turtle new words.

Thus, a program to make the turtle draw a square would begin with a title ("TO SQUARE") followed by two instructions ("FORWARD 100", "RIGHT 90") repeated four times, and finish with a conclusion ("END").

---

10.   Marvin Minsky,"The Society of Mind", Simon & Schuster, New York, 1985

It sounds trivial to the uninitiated. But in fact it was—and is—really powerful. With just two commands, FORWARD and RIGHT, it was possible to draw almost anything. Getting the turtle to do something as simple as write their initials was so compelling that kids would beg to be allowed to stay after school to finish it. For some kids, it was just having control over the turtle. One of the powerful aspects of Logo was the ability to give the program a name (in the above example, SQUARE), and then to re-use that name in the creation of something more complex.

"What was most remarkable was that by giving Logo the handful of new commands needed to control the turtle" [eg, PEN DOWN], Papert wrote, "the spirit of what could be done with it changed dramatically. Whereas the day before I was worrying about how to descend a year from the seventh grade, now there was an area of 'baby AI' that seemed plausibly accessible to children well below school age."[11]

The mechanical beast brought the body into math. The turtle was chosen as a metaphor because it was easy for kids to identify with it. They solved problems by putting themselves in the robot's place, for example, turning their bodies, then trying to guess how many degrees they had turned. Then going back and creating programs based on their own actions.

From the outset, kids loved the turtle. On initial exposure, at Bridge Elementary School in Lexington in September 1969, a group of twelve fifth graders jumped on its back and demanded rides. Then, when the students discovered that the beast could be programmed to move and to draw, they became even more excited. The kids would spend hours and hours working with the turtle, making it draw pictures. Starting with simple geometric shapes like squares and circles, they progressed to stick figures, then to quite realistic line drawings of, among other things, birds and spiders.[12]

Early that December, the group decided on a collective project. The turtle would be programmed to write 'Happy Christmas' on a huge paper banner to be strung across the corridor outside the classroom. The words were divided up so that each group would write programs for two or three letters. But the snowstorms of a Boston winter and other disruptions delayed the work and, by the time the last week of school arrived, the banner was not finished.

A particularly sticky problem was the letter "P". As a general rule, Papert and Solomon left it up to the kids to work out how to do things. But with the holi-

---

11.   Ibid, p176
12.   See Papert & Solomon, Twenty Things to Do with a Computer, pp7,8

days almost upon them, time was running out. One evening, on her terminal at home, Solomon dashed off a program to draw the letter. Next day, she gave the program to one of the kids, a ten-year-old boy named Peter, to debug. But Peter couldn't get the turtle to draw the letter properly. He turned to his teachers for guidance.

Solomon and Papert couldn't figure out where the bug was. Seeing the two of them on their knees examining the turtle and scratching their heads came as a revelation to the boy. At first he thought that the adults were just teasing, that they actually did know how to fix the problem. Finally Peter realized that they honestly were stumped, and he was astonished. "It was a breathtaking experience for me," Solomon recalled, "because it made me realize how kids feel tricked in school," when teachers say Let's do this together, when all the time they know the answer. "Discovery cannot be a setup," Papert wrote, "invention cannot be scheduled."[13]

Towards the end of 1969, it became difficult for Feurzeig to get funding to continue the Logo project at BBN. The National Science Foundation was reluctant to underwrite research at the firm, because it was not a university. A dollar spent at BBN didn't go as far as one spent at MIT, because MIT graduate students cost less than BBN employees. With Minsky's support, Papert set up a new organization at MIT. He called it the Logo Lab.

◆   ◆   ◆

The late sixties were a time of great turmoil on university campuses across the United States. In November 1969 an anti-war student protest march climaxed outside 545 Technology Square. The AI Lab, of which the Logo Lab was an offshoot, was targeted because it was known to be funded by the Department of Defense. The CIA had offices in the same building. (The graffiti in the building's elevator read, "Intelligence: Artificial, Ninth Floor; Central, Third Floor".)

In this period of student uprising and general social unrest, the educational pendulum began to swing back towards a revival of progressivism. Having lost currency in the 1950s as a result of the post-Sputnik conservative backlash, the ideas of John Dewey and William Kilpatrick—child-centered schooling, project-

---

13.   Cynthia Solomon, Computer Environments for Children: A Reflection on Theories of Learning and Education, MIT Press, Cambridge, MA, 1986, pp159,160. See also Papert's version in Mindstorms, pp114,115

based learning, and so on—came roaring back into fashion. Chief product of this new progressivism was "a substantial body of educational protest literature."[14]

The forerunner of the new movement was *Summerhill: A Radical Approach to Child Rearing* by A.S. Neill[15] . This was the story of an ultraprogressive school in England as told by its founder. "My view is that a child is innately wise and realistic," wrote Neill, echoing Rousseau. "If left to himself without adult suggestion of any kind, he will develop as far as he is capable of developing."[16] Published in the US in 1960, by the end of the decade *Summerhill* was selling more than 200,00 copies a year. It would go on to rack up more than four million sales, a truly astonishing figure.[17] "A housemate of mine happened to leave [a copy of *Summerhill*] lying around one day," recalled Brian Harvey, a politically active AI Lab hacker who would go on to write a series of Logo textbooks, "and I just picked it up and read it, and went Wow, this is fascinating!"

After *Summerhill* came a deluge of books that delivered radical critiques of US public schools. They included John Holt's *How Children Fail* (1964), Jonathan Kozol's *Death at an Early Age* (1967), Herbert Kohl's *36 Children* (1967), and Everett Reimer's *School is Dead* (1971). This "literature of rage", to use Tracy Kidder's phrase, reached a crescendo in 1970—the year Papert established the Logo Lab—with the publication of Ivan Illich's *Deschooling Society*, which called for the total disestablishment of school.

"The indictment of the school was overwhelming", wrote historian of education Diane Ravitch. "In the eyes of the critics, the school destroyed the souls of children, whether black or white, middle-class or poor. It coerced unwilling youths to sit through hours of stultifying classes, breaking their spirits before turning them out as either rebellious misfits or conforming cogs in the great industrial machine. It neglected the needs of individuals while slighting the history and culture of diverse minorities. It clung to a boring irrelevant curriculum and to methods that obliterated whatever curiosity children brought with them.

---

14. Diane Ravitch, "The Troubled Crusade: American Education 1945–1980, Basic Books, New York,1983, p235

15. A.S. Neill, "Summerhill: A Radical Approach to Child Rearing", St Martin's Press, New York, 1960
     Neill was born in 1883, in Forfar, Scotland, which by coincidence also happens to be where the present writer was born. Neill's father was the "dominie" of a local two-room primary school much like the one I attended.

16. Neill, Summerhill, revised edition (1992), p9

17. Sales figure quoted on the cover of the revised and expanded edition, 1992, published under the title "Summerhill School: A New View of Childhood"

It drove away creative teachers and gave tenure to petty martinets. For those who agreed with the critics, there was no alternative other than to change the schools or abandon them."[18]

Out of this consensus that change was required sprang several movements. Hundreds of private "free schools" based loosely on the Summerhill model sprang up. Some public schools established "alternative schools" within themselves. Home schoolers simply opted out of the system altogether. Then there was the "open education" movement, which aimed to reform public schools along the supposed lines of a British model.

In 1970 yet another book, Charles Silberman's best-selling *Crisis in the Classroom*, propelled open education into a full-scale phenomenon that promised to solve all of education's problems.[19] In the ideal open classroom, the teacher became a "facilitator" of children's discoveries rather than the font of all knowledge. For the next few years enthusiasm for open education raged. By the middle of the decade, however, disillusion had set in. The pendulum was swinging away from progressivism. Demands that schools go "back to basics" were beginning to be heard across the country.

But while the mood for change prevailed, the federal government became a major promoter of innovative practices. "By the early 1970s, about 10 percent of all federal funds for public schools was allocated specifically to promote educational innovations; in 1974, this amounted to about $350 million annually, spent through a wide variety of programs."[20] Some of that money, shepherded through the peer reviews of the National Science Foundation by Andy Molnar, would wind up funding the Logo Lab at MIT.

◆   ◆   ◆

Papert gave the first public talk about Logo on 11 April 1970. Entitled "Teaching Children Thinking", it was held in Room 26-100 at MIT, a lecture theater with a seating capacity of 560. "We sent out a massive mailing," Solomon recalled, "and the room was full." A discussion panel of computer educators was on hand, including Pat Suppes who—unexpectedly—turned out to be an old acquaintance of Papert.

---

18. Ravitch, p237
19. Charles Silberman, "Crisis in the Classroom: The Remaking of American Education", Random House, New York, 1970
20. Ravitch, p257

(The two first met in 1959 in Africa, at a conference in Ghana, where Suppes was running a US Aid project in new math. For years they carried on a running argument about the role of computers in education. Also, about the philosophy of science, Suppes summing up his position by saying that he would rather be precisely wrong than vaguely right. Papert saw this as emblematic of the fundamental problem of teaching.)[21]

In his keynote address, Papert began by attacking the "intellectual timidity" of the behaviorist approach to educational computing. "The phrase 'technology and education' usually means inventing new gadgets to teach the same old stuff in a thinly-disguised version of the same old way. Moreover, if the gadgets are computers, the same old teaching becomes incredibly more expensive and biased towards its dullest parts, namely the kind of rote learning in which measurable results can be obtained by treating the children like pigeons in a Skinner box."

Papert said he had "a grander vision" to present, "an educational system in which technology is used not in the form of machines for processing children but as something the child himself will learn to manipulate, to extend, to apply to projects, thereby gaining a greater and more articulate mastery of the world, a sense of the power of applied knowledge and a self-confidently realistic image of himself as an intellectual agent. Stated more simply, I believe, with Dewey, Montessori, and Piaget that children learn by doing and by thinking about what they do. And so the fundamental ingredients of educational innovation must be better things to do and better ways to think about oneself doing those things.

"I claim that computation is by far the richest known source of these ingredients."[22]

This sort of stuff went down well with an MIT audience consisting mostly of ardent technophiles. The Logo Lab was soon attracting some of the institute's brightest young students. They included Hal Abelson, a mathematician, who was responsible for translating the turtle from the floor to the computer screen. There, it became a blinking triangular cursor that rotated to point in any direction, "an oriented blob" that like the robot could be used to draw shapes and pictures, only much quicker and more precisely. These images came to be known as "turtle graphics". Abelson and Andy di Sessa, a physicist who joined the Logo Lab in 1972, would go on to write a book called *Turtle Geometry*[23], which demonstrated that Logo was not just for kids.

---

21.   Papert, "The Children's Machine", p167
22.   Seymour Papert, "Teaching Children Thinking", reprinted in The Computer in the School: Tutor, Tool, Tutee, Robert Taylor [ed], Teachers College Press, New York, p161

A visitor to the lab in summer 1970 was Victor McElheny, staff reporter for the *Boston Globe*, whom we last met interviewing John Kemeny at Dartmouth College the previous year. Once again, McElheny began his article—headlined "Giving Power to the People"—by dismissing contemporary fears about technology. Papert's experiments with kids and turtle graphics, he wrote, represented "thinking exactly opposite to the cliche about computers turning people into robots." On the evidence of this and other work at MIT, it was "very clear", McElheny asserted, "that some of the leaders in developing computers do not agree that these ever-faster, ever-more powerful electronic machines must inevitably end up as tools for enslaving people to all-powerful organizations."[24]

Based on their work in local schools and at the institute, Papert and Solomon began issuing, under the imprimatur of the AI Lab, a series of memos, informal working papers which also served as recruiting tools. In the third of these, entitled *Twenty Things to Do with a Computer*, published in June 1971, the authors concluded with an extraordinary assertion:

"Some school administrators and town politicians still consider the cost of using computers at all as too high....At the moment a good estimate of what computation ought to cost is $30 per student per year, for one hour per student of terminal time....The price could be halved within a year if several hundred schools a year would commit themselves to installing identical systems. *Only inertia and prejudice, not economics or the lack of good educational ideas, stand in the way of providing every child in the world with the kind of experience of which we have tried to give you some glimpses.* [emphasis in the original] If every child were to be given access to a computer, computers would be cheap enough for every child to be given access to a computer."[25]

Papert was the first to predict that computers would become a significant part of every child's life. Soon, he would begin to talk of the computer as a pencil. That is, as a tool that should be as freely available as pencils and used for as broad a range of activities. What use is one pencil between thirty pupils? he would demand of critics who argued that there was already a computer in every classroom.

---

23.   Turtle Geometry: The Computer as a Medium for Exploring Mathematics. MIT Press, Cambridge, 1981
      "They begin with the simplest of turtle dances and end up in the General Theory of Relativity. Along the way they show how to generate some nifty graphics." Bob Brill <http://users.migate.net/~bobbrill/Erun.htm>
24.   Victor McElheny, "Giving Power to the People", Boston Globe, 26 July 1976, p4-A
25.   Papert & Solomon, Twenty Things to Do with a Computer, p40

But in the early 1970s, the idea of one-kid-one-computer struck most people as completely crazy, the ravings of an academic idealist with his head stuck in the clouds. It would be twenty years before Papert's vision of ubiquitous computers came to pass in an actual school, at the other end of the world.

8

FRIDAYS WE DRAW ON THE TABLE

545 Tech Square, the building whose top floor housed the Al Lab, was not literally an ivory tower. At nine stories, the rectangular office block wasn't particularly tall, even by the standards of low-rise Cambridge. Its concrete walls were light gray, not yellowish white. Metaphorically, however, in the sense of being aloof from worldly concerns, Tech Square was the ivoriest of towers.

The building perches on the northeast edge of campus in a decrepit industrial district, just across from a starch factory. Railroad tracks separate Tech Square—officially known as Building NE43—from the rest of MIT. The institute rented floors 5, 8, and 9 for computer related projects. In the early days, the word was that the value of the computers on those three floors was more than that of the real estate.

"Each office floor had maybe 60 offices, singles and doubles, wrapped around the elevator core. Almost all the offices had windows: none opened. The air conditioning wasn't enough for the load of people and machines in the building on really hot summer days, and failed every year, forcing us to shut down the computers before they roasted themselves. Fluorescent lights, linoleum floors, hard walls, doors that locked; they were nice offices."[1]

Up on the ninth floor there was a "playroom", a big common space where in the early 1970s everyone used to sit around for an hour and a half at lunchtime and argue. The intellectual atmosphere at the AI Lab was extremely intense. Both students and faculty were extraordinary—very smart, very motivated, and very sure of themselves. "If you lacked any of those three things you were in trouble. But it was a wonderful place for people who had them."[2]

---

1. Tom Van Vleck, Multic, Tech Square, <www.multicians.org/tech-square.html>, posted 28 March 1993

One person who undoubtedly had them was Danny Hillis, who would go on to become, among other things, the world's leading designer of parallel super-computers. For Hillis, the AI Lab was "like Mecca—all the great stuff I was excited about was happening there." Initially however he was intimidated by the lab's reputation, feeling that a teenage undergraduate like himself could not just show up and expect to be part of the action. So Hillis set about looking for a way to ingratiate himself.

He found what he was after in a copy of the AI Lab's funding proposals to the National Science Foundation. Like most grant proposals, these largely dealt with problems that had already been solved. But there was one problem that was iden-tified as unsolved: how to have children that don't know how to read and write use a computer. "OK, that's my in," Hillis said to himself, "they don't know how to do that—I'll invent a way to do that."

The determined young man thought about the problem for awhile until he had figured out a scheme. Then Hillis took off for Tech Square and knocked on Seymour Papert's door. Papert liked the young man's plan, and allocated him some money to implement it. "And so I built something that actually worked." Known as the slot machine, it had cards with pictures of actions—of the turtle going forward, turning, tooting its horn, etc—which the kids would arrange in rows on the front of the machine. It had lights next to each card, which would light up as the turtle performed the action shown on the card. "So it was a very concrete way of programming, and kids as young as four years old would come in and get the turtle to do things."

By an odd coincidence, Hillis's upbringing resembled Papert's. His father was an epidemiologist who travelled extensively for his research. Hillis grew up in central Africa, in countries like Rwanda, Burundi, Zaire, and Kenya. "We were typically out in the middle of the jungle, so I was taught at home," he said. Papert took the young undergraduate under his wing: "he was friendly to me and open to a student he didn't know anything about, and I felt quite unintimidated by him." Among other things, Papert taught Hillis how to juggle and to make a soufflé.

Juggling was Papert's favorite metaphor for thinking about programming—a complex skill made up of simple acts (throw a ball, catch it). It was a way of using the concrete as a bridge to the abstract. Papert was evidently proud of his skill as a juggler. He would show it off to anyone, anywhere—including, on one notable

---

2.   Mitchell Marcus, quoted in Jeremy Bernstein, "Three Degrees Above Zero", Cam-
      bridge University Press, Cambridge, 1984, pp56–57

occasion, the waiting lounge at Boston's Logan Airport. There, to the astonishment of his fellow travellers, the professor put on an impromptu display of juggling glass ashtrays.[3]

Papert had always considered learning as a hobby. Seeking insights into the nature of learning, he would deliberately go out of his way to acquire new skills. These included reading Chinese characters, flying airplanes (while still in Switzerland), memorizing the names of flowers, mastering the cooking of tricky delicacies—eg, soufflés and croissants—and, most famously, for weeks on end wearing glasses that reversed left and right.

Hillis found this spirit of playfulness and willingness to learn new things inspiring. "It was very exciting to me to be around an adult who was always willing to approach something even if he didn't know anything about it, and to do something that he wasn't good at yet." It is perhaps uncommon for professors to give their students the impression that they are less than omniscient.

Hillis demonstrated the playful spirit of Tech Square in a famous "hack" (MIT slang for practical joke). He put the building's elevators under control of the lab's computers. This involved picking the lock on the elevator room and tapping into the wiring. Since there was no way to hide the illicit connections, Hillis put them in a box that said "Warning: Do not remove without authorization" and stuck it in the elevator. For years, it was possible to dispatch elevators to different floors by sending signals from anyplace that was connected to the ARPAnet. This infuriated the building's owners, but they never did find out where Hillis's connections were hidden.

After his initial triumph with the slot machine, Hillis also built hardware for other members of the Logo Lab, including Jeanne Bamberger, who was working on musical applications of Logo. She wanted the kids to be able to visualize rhythm patterns via pieces of paper tape which they marked as they tapped out the rhythm. Hillis built her a big orange box containing paper tapes, complete with pushbuttons and a crank-handle. On the outside he stuck a big label saying 'Time Machine'. Hillis recalled that, as he carried this box into the bowels of Tech Square, he got weird looks from people.

Hillis was delighted to have met and hit it off with Papert. Now he was keen to meet the lab's other co-director, Marvin Minsky. But despite the fact that everyone was always talking about him, Minsky never seemed to be there. Hillis asked around until finally someone told him that Minsky only came in at nights. You could find him working down in the building's basement where he was

---

3.   McCorduck, pp299–300

building a Logo computer. Though intimidated by the idea of encountering the famously acerbic Minsky, Hillis went down there one night. Sure enough the director was toiling away, building this big wire-wrap board based on a circuit diagram. The undergrad peeked over the great man's shoulder at the diagram and noticed...a mistake!

Summoning up all his courage, the precocious young man cleared his throat and pointed out the error. "And [Minsky] was like, O well, why don't you fix it? So I corrected it on the diagram, and he said, Fix it on the machine, too." So Hillis did that, then noticed another improvement that could be made. This went on for some time, and "after a while, Marvin just sort of assumed that I worked for him. So that's how I got to know Marvin—I would go in every night, and pretty soon I did work for him."

The computer Hillis helped Minsky build was the General Turtle 2500. This machine, like its better-known contemporary, the Alto at Xerox PARC, was a sort of proto personal computer. General Turtle was a start-up formed by Papert and Minsky in 1973, with Papert's engineer brother Alan as president. "It was a mistake," Papert admitted many years later, "but there wasn't any reasonably-priced computer that a school of that time could have gone out and bought."

Like other early education-use machines, the GT 2500 had two screens, one for text, on which to do programming and editing, the other for displaying graphics. To begin with, other than a simplified version of Logo, the machine had no software. "In those days, there wasn't really a software industry," Hillis explained, "at least not for small computers." The hardware was considered the difficult part; the software was just something that the hackers could program afterwards. So, fuelled by a diet of french fries and vinegar, Hillis wrote the software for the GT 2500. For the first program, Hillis wanted to demonstrate something fun. So besides Right and Forward, he threw in two new Logo commands, Spin and Grow.

Spin caused succeeding inputs to rotate at a specified rate; Grow caused lines to continue in the specified direction. Together they could produce some spectacular displays. "The first thing I did was make it draw a picture of a ferris wheel. And everyone was amazed when they walked in and there was the ferris wheel rolling around with the cars on it. So that was a great moment when it came up and [the ferris wheel] started working."

Spin and Grow were very much a product of the attitude at the AI Lab—if you wanted the computer to do something, you could wire something into it, or change the operating system. But Hillis's participation in the activities of the

Logo Lab were not restricted to building and programming computers. He was also called upon to work as a volunteer teacher at a Boston elementary school.

◆   ◆   ◆

In its early years, the Logo Lab was not much interested in schools. This was partly because the lab had a faction of younger members who, infected with the prevailing literature of rage against conventional education, saw schools as obsolete. This faction included Hillis, Minsky's daughter Margaret, and Brian Silverman, who all lived communally in a huge loft in Boston's Chinatown.

"A lot of us in the early days were real educational revolutionaries," Logo Lab young turk and sometime SDS activist Brian Harvey recalled, "we wanted essentially to do away with the whole institution of school."

The revolutionaries took their lead from Papert himself, whose views on reactionary institutions had been forged in the anti-apartheid struggle. Then, he had been against apartheid as a system that kept races from mingling. Now, he was against school as a system that kept children from learning.

Seen from the exalted heights of Tech Square, there seemed plenty of things wrong with school. Brian Silverman explained this perception. "From a fairly normal high school I went to MIT, and the first thing I learned was that everything they had told me about the process of science was made up.

"Among the things they didn't tell me at school the first one—which was really obvious—is that scientists are really passionate about what they do. And that was really stunning, because I had come out the other end of science education thinking that it was all pretty dry. And yet, suddenly, here were these people who stayed up all night, and who were crazy.

"The other thing that really shook my view about high-school science was that, in high-school science, you're supposed to get the expected answer. But in real science, what gets real working scientists the most excited is when something unexpected happens."

Much as they would have liked to, however, the revolutionaries could not afford to ignore school entirely. Papert and his merry band of young engineers and computer scientists needed actual kids on whom to try out their ideas. As a result, it was necessary to bring into the group people who could understand their language but who were also connected to schools.

The first of these human interfaces was Paul Goldenberg, who joined the lab in 1971 after hearing Papert's first Logo talk at MIT the previous year. A mathematics teacher from a local school who had worked extensively with computers,

Goldenberg was able "to translate between the needs of teaching and the systems programmers who were building [new versions of Logo]."

In those early days, Goldenberg remembered, there was "constant debate" within the Logo Lab. On the one hand, there was "Seymour's vision of transformed education which he believed would be unattainable if any concessions were made towards the structures of current schools." Opposed to this was another view, which was, "if you wanted to transform education, you had to be somehow part of it." Evolution, in other words, not revolution.

Goldenberg and one or two older members of the group argued in favor of this latter view, seeing Logo as something that could achieve educational transformation from within. They believed that if kids were going to get any benefit from Logo, most of it was going to come in schools. Once there, the computer could act as a Trojan Horse: just sneak the machine into the classroom, and it would subtly subvert the education process.

◆   ◆   ◆

By the mid 1970s, the word was beginning to filter out: something intriguing was going on at Tech Square. A stream of visitors started coming through the Logo Lab. Some of them left puzzled by lab's elitist culture. Dan Watt, a teacher who replaced Goldenberg as the lab's principle interface with the real world in 1976, recalled the elitist attitude that prevailed among its members. "If you understand what we're talking about, you're with us; if you don't, we don't have time to bother with you."

There were other types of confrontation. Some of the hackers more or less lived in the lab, and personal hygiene was not always high on their list of priorities. It was acceptable not to wash for weeks. Straitlaced teachers would come in for workshops and find students crashed out on bean bags. Culture shock.

But some visitors were captivated by the radically different vision of learning emerging from MIT. One such was Scott Brownell, an Australian educational researcher who swung by the Logo Lab in 1974, on his way home to Tasmania from a scholarship in England.

Brownell recalled that the lab was "having groups of students in, often disadvantaged students, using Logo and the turtles. And the thing that was most impressive for me was that I'd always thought of computer programming as being a fairly exotic sort of a pursuit, designed for academics and highly intelligent people and so on, because the closest I'd got to programming was learning Algol [a computer language] at university as part of a degree. So to me programming was something that really clever people did, not something that kids did. Their idea was that you could use Logo-type technology to do everything from teaching elementary mathematics or geometry to physics and in fact English. And it had never occurred to me that something like Logo could be used to enhance the ordinary opportunity of young children."

According to another visitor, the laboratory itself was a spartan environment with, "a surprising lack of amenities." Mostly there was "a lot of not especially appetizing hunks of machinery...sitting around on the bare tile floors, and wires dangling from the ceiling in what seems haphazard fashion. The whole place looks unfinished...."[4] The machinery included the floor turtle, which in its second generation had shrunk to become a much smaller machine, covered by a transparent plastic dome. Other toys lying around included Logo-controlled spiders, worms, music boxes, train sets, and vans. Few of them ever worked for longer than was necessary to demonstrate "proof of concept." At MIT, creativity always took precedence over reliability.

The robots were built in two tiny rooms in the basement of Tech Square, which as we have seen also served as the headquarters of General Turtle. The firm offered a "starter system", which sold for $3,705. Basic equipment included a turtle with touch sensors, music box, plotter, and a simplified input device known as a "button box" which replaced the Teletype keyboard. Among the company's first customers was the education department of Tasmania, which bought a turtle on Brownell's enthusiastic recommendation. This, as we shall see, would lead to dramatic developments Down Under.

◆   ◆   ◆

In early experiments with Logo at MIT, teachers like Goldenberg would bring in kids from their schools to the "children's learning environment" at the lab. Research and development continued under the determinist assumption that once the right technology was created it would win success on its own merit. Other than the odd visitor and counterparts at a few other academic institutes—notably the University of Edinburgh—the rest of the world showed little interest.

In 1977, the National Science Foundation, which was funding most of the research at the lab, finally lost patience. Logo would either prove its worth as an

---

4.   Pamela McCorduck, "Machines Who Think'" W.H. Freeman and Company, San Francisco, 1979, p296

educational tool in actual school classrooms, or there would be no more cash. Time to descend from the ivory tower.

The late seventies witnessed several projects intended to demonstrate Logo in US schools. The first of these was held in a public elementary school in Brookline, an inner suburb of Boston. An elderly redbrick building on a main street, the Lincoln School catered to the children of upper-middle-class parents, many of them Jewish.

Brookline, according to Dan Watt, who had been a classroom teacher at the Lincoln School for seven years prior to his involvement with the Logo Lab, was "a place where people pay well for their schools and expect a lot of them. They have good teachers, good curriculum, they always have the best of everything they can identify." The Logo project was "just one of many innovations that were going on all the time—they expected people to be doing things, doing research." The school allocated the project a large basement room, a cool place for heat-generating computers. In this space four large machines were installed, rented $15,000 General Turtle 3500s (a commercial version of the machine that Minsky and Hillis had built).

The focus of the Brookline study was 16 sixth-grade students, chosen to represent a range of academic abilities from very low to very high. But the school insisted that during the year the experience should also be open to all fifty of its sixth graders. That meant having to recruit MIT undergraduates like Danny Hillis to do the additional teaching.

On the twenty-year-old volunteer teacher's first day in the Lincoln School computer room, the kids wanted to know what they could and could not do. What are the rules? they demanded. At first, Hillis was dumbfounded; then, spying a table on which there were some crayons, inspiration suddenly came to him. He told the kids, "OK, the first rule is that…on Fridays we draw on the table!"

The fact that the kids seemed conditioned to perform certain classroom rituals came as a surprise to Hillis. "It was kind of like, Give us our worksheets, what do we have to know for the test?" For him and all the other volunteers from MIT, working in an actual school was "a shocking experience of how you could take something great and just assimilate it into the normal patterns of class and it wouldn't be great anymore." One of the most frustrating things for Hillis was that "when Logo got in the class, I think we all assumed that it would just completely change the style that learning happened in. And the answer was, it did, but only if you had a great teacher."

With a doctor's degree in engineering from Cornell, Dan Watt was exceptionally well-qualified for an elementary school teacher. An anti-war activist and lover of traditional folk music, Watt had become excited about applying his scientific knowledge to the education of younger kids. Like many of his progressive contemporaries in the early 1970s, he adopted open education as his philosophy. Watt had been on the left of the progressive movement in schools. Now, at the Logo Lab, he found himself on the right in terms of how he wanted to get things working in the classroom. At the same time, he really liked the lab's idealistic young revolutionaries, Hillis in particular.

At Lincoln Elementary, the students came in groups of four, one to each computer, a ratio which at that time was reckoned to be ideal. (Later, it would be realized that it was better to have kids collaborate in pairs or groups.) Over the course of the year, each student got between 20 and 40 hours of hands-on experience with the computers. "The emphasis of the research was to observe and document what...[the] students actually learned, rather than assess whether they had achieved a set of preplanned objectives."[5]

The main vehicle used to observe their learning was something called a "dribble file". Whatever the students typed in was saved in this file. After each class, the teacher went through the files, painstakingly tracing exactly what the kids had done, and where they had got stuck. This took hours, but it gave the teachers a level of insight that they could never have gained by simply observing goings-on in a regular classroom.

For Watt, analyzing the dribble files was "a wonderful experience—I've never had anything like it before or since in terms of being able to get inside kids' heads." It was also, he conceded, totally unrealistic to expect regular teachers with a class of 25 kids to spend what little free time they had poring over dribbles.

Though the dribble files Watt discovered that an African-American girl called Tammy was developing a very unusual relationship with the computer. Whereas the other kids all focused on writing programs, producing pictures made up of geometrical shapes of varying complexity, Tammy used Logo as a writing tool. And this was remarkable, because she was a student with severe learning disabilities, who had never really written anything before.

From the outset, Tammy formed a intensely personal connection with one of the computers, calling it Peter, and refusing to let any of the other kids use it. This personalization of the hardware, as we have seen in earlier chapters, was by no means uncommon. But Tammy became more involved with her computer than most. She discovered how to clear text from the screen by using the return key, and how to erase the last character input by using the delete key. Writing by

---

5.   Daniel Watt, "Logo in the Schools", Byte, August 1982, p130,132

hand had discouraged her, because Tammy was a perfectionist who found her own handwriting ugly. She would throw the paper away after making a single mistake. Now, Tammy found she could print out clean copies of her efforts, which she would proudly distribute to her friends, family, and teachers.

A special program was created for Tammy's use, to enable her to type directly into the computer without her input having to be part of a program. From then on, Tammy devoted most of her time at the computer to writing stories which, as the year went by, became more and more complex. Two years after the project had ended, despite the subsequent lack of access to the computer, she was still writing, mostly poetry, a volume of which on graduation she presented to the school library.[6]

The researchers were delighted with Tammy's transformation. They would perhaps have been less so if they had realized what it portended. With the coming of the microcomputer, programming would rapidly be displaced as the dominant application of the computer in the classroom by word processing, an activity with which most teachers felt much more comfortable.

For the time being, however, as the year drew to an end at the Lincoln school, there was reason to be optimistic. All students, regardless of ability, had been successful in the Logo classes. Unfortunately, the researchers had no way to measure this success. Standardized sixth-grade math tests could not assess the students' ability to use turtle geometry. Special tests devised by project staff proved inconclusive. "The research reports had no strict before-and-after evaluative character and thus failed to produce demonstrable quantitative test results ('hard' evidence) about Logo, something which was at odds with the 'hard', quantitative approaches to educational research at the time."[7]

A second Brookline project was organized to address the concerns of those who wondered whether Logo really made a difference. Also, in a victory for the Logo Lab's moderate faction, to develop a curriculum to support further classroom use of the language. (Papert had always been vehemently opposed to curriculum development, arguing that if learning were to be truly Piagetian, then there could be no curriculum.)

In this phase of the project, which ran from 1978 to '79, two computers were circulated among several classrooms, each classroom having exclusive use of the

---

6.   Sherry Turkle, "The Second Self: Computers and the Human Spirit", Simon & Schuster, 1984, p126
     In Turkle's version of the story, she uses the pseudonym Tanya; the girl's real name was Tammy
7.   Agalianos, p297

machine for eight to twelve weeks. During this time, students worked on their own at the computers, individually or in pairs, while the rest of the class went on with its regular work.

One interesting aspect that emerged in this second project was the way that "clandestine knowledge"—how to do certain things on the computers that the kids were not supposed to know—was discovered, without it being taught, and passed from student to student by word of mouth. Within a matter of hours, virtually all the kids knew about it. This phenomenon would be repeatedly observed down the years in computer-rich environments.

Even more interesting was the way in which students emerged as Logo teachers. By virtue of their experience with computers at Lincoln Elementary the previous year, the kids from the sixth grade had become experts. Teachers throughout the school routinely began to ask these students when they needed help.

Perhaps for the first time in the history of the world, kids knew more about something important than their teachers. The MIT researchers, for whom status was derived from hacking ability rather than age, were ecstatic. But in the coming decades, many teachers would be profoundly disturbed by the prospect of their privileged position as the *fons et origo* of all knowledge being usurped in this way.

◆   ◆   ◆

Brookline paved the way for an even more ambitious Logo project. This began in 1979 at the Lamplighter School, a richly-endowed private elementary school in Dallas, Texas. In this project, conditions could hardly have been better. The school had 400 pupils aged between 3 and 9 with a pupil-teacher ratio of 10:1. Children were encouraged, in the best progressive tradition, to follow their own direction. They learned in purpose-built, open-plan classrooms where scheduling was flexible. Even the name of the school—which derived from the old adage that "a child is not a vessel to be filled but a lamp to be lighted"—was perfect.

The project came about as a joint effort between the school, the Logo Lab, and Texas Instruments. TI's chairman, Erik Jonsson was a former mayor of Dallas and a man whose breadth of vision Papert much admired. He was also chairman of the school's board and a major benefactor of Lamplighter. Jonsson arranged for his company, which was headquartered nearby, to donate 50 computers to the school. The idea was that this would provide Lamplighter with enough hardware that access to computers would not be a limitation on what students could learn. These were not $15,000 monsters like those used in the Brookline project, but $1,000 microcomputers.

The age of the microcomputer had dawned in April 1977 with the introduction of the Apple II. Unlike previous microcomputers, the Apple II was not a kit for hobbyists to build in their garages: it came pre-assembled. All you had to do was plug it into an ordinary color TV and off you went. Other companies soon piled into the new market, including Texas Instruments, whose bargain-basement TI-99/4—the computer used in the Lamplighter project—would briefly be the best-selling microcomputer in the country. The school was to provide a test-bed for the machine.

A special version of Logo was written for this project. Though the software had to be pared down to fit into the microcomputer's extremely limited memory, the hardware included a special experimental feature. This was a chip designed by Hillis, that allowed multiple characters—he called them "sprites"—to be superimposed on a background and moved independently.

(Though TI never made a successful product based on this chip, it became the basis for the "family entertainment system" sold by a previously-unknown Japanese game maker called Nintendo, with Super Mario and his friends replacing the turtles. Yet another example of how educational imperatives have driven the development of technology that has had a huge impact in the wider world.)[8]

The intention at Lamplighter was "to simulate a future where computers would be everyday objects in the life of the child."[9] When Dan Watts visited the school in the second year of the project, he was "struck by just how comfortable the children are with computers," preschool kids included.

In a third-grade classroom, Watt came across "several children clustered around two computers. One of them had written a 'secret' animation program that made a number of sprites move continuously in a dynamically unfolding spiral. Three boys were trying to duplicate the procedure on the adjoining computer. Another child was designing a sprite shape for the center of the screen that would look as if it was emitting spiraling sprites. Competition, cooperation, communication, problem solving, programming, geometry, and artistry were all happening at once."[10]

But despite the "unique, exciting, and wonderful things" happening at the Lamplighter School, Watt came away worried. "Except for the school staff, who

---

8.   Perhaps in gratitude, in 1990 Nintendo would donate $3 million to support Papert's work at MIT.
9.   Turkle, p97
10.   Daniel Watt, "Logo in the Schools", *Byte*, August 1982, p130,132

usually are too busy to write, study, and reflect on the situation," he wrote in *Byte* magazine, "one gets the feeling that 'nobody's watching.'"

His concern was understandable. Outside of a handful of experimental implementations at exceptional schools in the US like Lincoln and Lamplighter, plus a few isolated sites in far-away places like Edinburgh and Tasmania, Logo was still virtually unknown.

All that was about to change. In 1980 Papert published his manifesto in the form of a book called *Mindstorms: Children, Computers, and Powerful Ideas.*[11] Soon, everyone would be watching to see what Logo could do.

11. Seymour Papert, "Mindstorms: Children, Computers, and Powerful Ideas", Basic Books, New York, 1980

9

TURTLE FEVER

The first wave of personal computers hit the stores in 1977. Useful software packages—spreadsheets, databases, and, above all, wordprocessors—followed soon after. Sales of microcomputers soared as a result. In 1980, the year Papert published *Mindstorms*, two dozen firms—including Apple, Commodore, Radio Shack, and Texas Instruments—sold 724,000 personal computers. In 1981, the year that IBM joined the fray with its PC, sales doubled. Next year they doubled again, with 100 companies selling some 2.8 million units worth almost $5 billion.

In January 1983, in an unprecedented anthropomorphization, the editors of *Time* named the computer as the magazine's "Man of the Year".[1] "[T]here is an inevitability about the computerization of America," the cover story asserted. "Commercial efficiency requires it. Big Government requires it, modern life requires it, and so it is coming to pass. But the essential element in this sense of inevitability is the way in which the young take to computers…the computer is a screen that responds to them, hooked to a machine that can be programmed to respond the way they want it to. That is power."

Time's reporter had obviously been talking to the folks up at MIT. The article goes on to mention *Mindstorms* and to quote, among others, Papert himself, his then-wife Sherry Turkle, his colleague Marvin Minsky, and his friend and fellow visionary Alan Kay.

According to a poll *Time* commissioned, 68 percent of those surveyed expected that the computer would improve the quality of learning. "Many Americans concerned about the erosion of the schools put faith in the computer as a possible savior of their children's education…."

Microcomputers were starting to pop up in classrooms. *Time* estimated that in 1982 there were more than 100,000 machines in US schools, roughly one for

---

1.   Otto Friedrich, "Machine of the Year: The Computer Moves In", *Time*, 3 January 1983, <www.time.com/time/special/moy/1982.html>

every 400 pupils. Among the states, Minnesota was leading the way with a pupil-to-computer ratio of 50 to 1 and a home-grown collection of educational software programs like *The Oregon Trail.*

By 1983, according to *Popular Computing* magazine, "computer mania" had gripped America's schools.[2] Nor did the publication that year of *A Nation at Risk* by the Reagan-appointed National Commission on Educational Excellence, do anything to calm the frenzy. Quite the reverse, in fact: the report called for a return to "older values" through the introduction of "five new basics": English, math, science, social studies—and computer science.[3]

"Computer literacy", the term coined by Art Luehrman in 1972, had become a prime educational objective. But how to achieve this new form of literacy? From the schools' point of view, the best way was far from clear. Should they invest in an "integrated learning system" like PLATO, which supposedly guaranteed improvements in reading and arithmetic via drill and practice? Or should they go with micros and teach programming in BASIC?

Now it appeared that there was also a third way—Papert's vision, as laid out in *Mindstorms,* of the computer as a vehicle for the implementation of new educational ideas. His book was soon bolstered by the publication of *Turtle Geometry,* which demonstrated (in more conventional terms) Logo's potential as a tool for exploring math. Then Logo Computer Systems Inc., LCSI, a start-up formed across a kitchen table in Montreal one evening in 1981 by Papert, Minsky, Brian Silverman, and other Logo Lab stalwarts, introduced a version of Logo for the Apple II.

This combination of manifesto plus the means to implement it convinced thousands of teachers in schools across the country and around the world. It was the answer that they had been looking for.

◆   ◆   ◆

It is not hard to see why Papert's book proved popular. Though largely concerned with the learning of mathematics, *Mindstorms* is a highly romantic work. "We are at a point in the history of education when radical change is possible," prophesies Papert, the self-confessed "educational utopian," "and the possibility for that change is directly tied to the impact of the computer."[4]

---

2.   Editorial, Popular Computing, August 1983, p83
3.   <www.ed.gov/pubs/NatAtRisk/risk.html>

The book's original title was *Brainstorms*, evoking the no-holds-barred discussions at the AI Lab. By coincidence, a month or two before publication in 1980, a book of that title by the philosopher Daniel Dennett was announced. *Brainstorms* became *Mindstorms*, which Papert said he preferred. The brain was after all merely meat; the mind had long been the focus of his study. Besides, "Mindstorms" was a brand-new word, entirely appropriate for a book with such novel contents.

Mindstorms is easy to read (although not always, given the profundity of the issues it discusses, easy to grasp). The style is refreshingly direct, without jargon and obfuscation, lamentable characteristics that encumber many books written by academics.

As its subtitle promises, *Mindstorms* is concerned with powerful ideas. "Ideas burst from the pages of this book", enthused one reviewer, "like black kittens from a burlap bag."[5] At the same time, *Mindstorms* is also a personal work in which Papert offers up the fruits of his experience, using anecdotes—by now, well-polished—from his life and work with kids in Boston schools.

The book begins with Papert telling the story of how, as a very young child, he fell in love with rotating objects, in particular, the gears of automobiles. These concrete examples later served as a model for him to assimilate the abstract ideas of mathematics. Of course, gears would not aid the learning of every child; but the computer, "the Proteus of machines"—in the guise of a friendly turtle—might.[6] "Education has very little to do with explanation," he would say, "it has to do with engagement, with falling in love with the material."

Papert premises *Mindstorms* on "a massive penetration of powerful computers into people's lives." "That this will happen," he predicts confidently—and, as it turns out, correctly—"there can be no doubt."[7] With ubiquity a given, Papert posits a new kind of learning environment, one in which children can freely interact with the machines.

Computers could be designed so that children learn to communicate with them naturally, like learning French in France (as Papert himself had done). By analogy, to overcome widespread "mathophobia", the natural way to learn math would be in "mathland", via conversations with a math-speaking entity like the computer. The student programs the computer. By teaching the machine to do

---

4.   Seymour Papert, "Mindstorms: Children, Computers, and Powerful Ideas", Basic Books, New York 1980, pp36–37

5.   Bill Higginson, from a review in *Mathematics Teaching*, 1981, pp60–62

6.   "Mindstorms", p viii

7.   Ibid, p23

things, the child learns to speak the language of math, in the process becoming a mathematician.

(Of course, the student programming the computer rather than vice versa was not an entirely new idea. As we have seen, John Kemeny understood its importance in the late sixties with BASIC and the time-sharing system at Dartmouth College. But Kemeny was thinking of undergraduates, not elementary school children. And at Dartmouth, all the problems to be solved via programming were defined by teachers.)

Papert devotes several pages to explaining why BASIC, which by 1980 was already established as the language of choice for teaching programming to high school kids, was no match for Logo in terms of the intellectual benefits it conferred. BASIC was to programming computers as QWERTY was to typewriter keyboards—a historical artifact that arose when the technology (in the case of computers, memory) was limited, but which was now an anachronism that threatened to hold up progress. Entering computer culture via BASIC was, Papert asserted, like reading poetry in pidgin English.

Ultimately, learning to master computers could change the way children learned everything else. But such learning could not occur inside conventional classrooms, which were artificial and inefficient. It should take place outside the classroom. "Schools as we know them today will have no place in the future." The computer, Papert predicted in 1984, would "blow up the school."[8]

Where would children learn, then? Papert suggests a somewhat fanciful alternative model—the "samba schools" he had discovered during a summer spent in Brazil. Samba schools are neighborhood clubs which compete for prizes in the famous carnival held in Rio de Janeiro each year in late February or early March. In preparation, the schools create an original routine, which they rehearse for the rest of the year. "Members of samba schools range in age from children to grandparents and in ability from novice to professional. But they dance together and as they dance everyone is learning and teaching as well as dancing."

"Logo environments are like samba schools in some ways…the resemblance comes from the fact that in them mathematics is a real activity that can be shared by novices and experts. The activity is so varied, so discovery rich, that even in the first day of programming, the student may do something that is new and exciting to the teacher."[9]

---

8. Seymour Papert, "Trying to Predict the Future", *Popular Computing*, October 1984, p38
9. "Mindstorms", pp 178–179

◆   ◆   ◆

This sort of thing was of course music to the ears of neoprogressive enthusiasts like Dan Watt and his wife, Molly, a former math teacher turned teacher trainer. "The ideas [in Mindstorms] weren't radical to me," she said, "I was already in those ideas."[10] Though Papert would acknowledge working in the progressive tradition of Dewey, he was critical of the progressives' failure to dramatically improve learning. Previous experimenters had lacked the tools that would allow them to create new methods of learning. Now, with computers and Logo to give child-centered learning backbone, kids finally had the opportunity for real discovery.

Mindstorms would eventually sell between three and four hundred thousand copies. It was translated officially into seventeen languages, including French, Spanish, Italian, German, Japanese, and Norwegian; and unofficially into several more. The book captured the imagination of visionary teachers all over the US. A grassroots Logo movement sprang up. Many teachers used their own money to buy microcomputers and sneaked them into the classroom without the permission of school authorities.

Much to his surprise, Papert was inundated with hundreds of adulatory letters from teachers who had read his book—some of them many times—and been inspired by it. Fifty-year-old schoolmarms from Alabama would pour out their hearts in multi-page biographical effusions, telling about their yearnings and frustrations, and how he had captured their experience to a tee.

(Papert would subsequently claim that he had not written the book with teachers in mind. But it is hard to imagine who else might have constituted the book's primary readership—certainly not the despised education research community. During that period, Papert seems not to have been thinking in terms of school at all.)

"When the book came out, I discovered that there were an awful lot of teachers out there who had always felt they could do much better than schools were allowing them to do," Papert said. "They didn't know there were others who thought like that and wanted to do exciting things."[11]

---

10. Angelos Agalianos, "A Cultural Studies Analysis of Logo in Education", [unpublished doctoral thesis], Institute of Education, Policy Studies, and Mathematical Sciences, London, 1997, p209

11. Tom Weber, "Signing on to Revolution", *Bangor Daily News*, 3 February 1997, pA2

Some teachers were grateful to Papert for showing them a way of implementing their vision of educational change. Others saw him as a Martin-Luther-King-like figure—a man with a dream, the most eloquent spokesman for their beliefs.[12] He was flooded with invitations to give speeches and seminars, visit schools, and participate in projects.

One such project was a workshop that Papert and his graduate students put on at the Children's Museum in Washington, DC, showcasing Logo and the power of the language for programming. Janet Graeber, a young kindergarten teacher at Stone Ridge Country Day School of the Sacred Heart in Bethesda, Maryland, was excited about Logo and its potential for young children, who are very visual at pre-school age. The MIT group gave her a copy of Logo to use on the Apple II in her classroom.

The computer sat on a rug on the floor in a part of the classroom known as "the block corner", because that was where wooden blocks for building structures were kept. Graeber thought it a kick that the kids wanted the computer on the floor so that it could be at eye-level with them. The movie *Star Wars* had recently been released and the computer became part of their "space ship." The rug made it much easier for the kids to be the turtle, crawling or walking on the floor to give directions.

Twenty years later, Graeber could still vividly remember sitting on the rug, surrounded by eighteen five-year-olds staring at the computer in front of them. "A mixture of voices and clicking noises permeated the space as the children eagerly suggested the next direction for the 'turtle' to go on the computer screen. 'Turn left; go straight; no, go left some more; send him backwards,' they said. In reply, I asked 'How far to turn, how far to walk?' One child jumped up and said, 'Watch me—this is how much to turn.' As she moved her body, we tried to guess how many degrees she turned. A group teachable moment—90 degrees, 180 degrees, numbers that might help the screen 'turtle' create a square or a rectangle. Each student waiting impatiently for her turn to be the 'turtle' driver."[13]

---

12. Agalianos, p302
13. Transforming Learning: An Anthology of Miracles in Technology-Rich Classrooms, ed Jenny Little & Bruce Dixon, Kids Technology Foundation, Melbourne, 2000, p69

◆   ◆   ◆

"The school year 1983/84 was one of incredible growth for Logo in the US. Thousands of teachers across the country started to use it in their class-rooms…primarily in grades 3-6."[14] By mid 1983, LCSI had contracts to develop versions of Logo for 15 different machines. By 1986, the company had sold about 150,000 copies of the Apple II version of the language in the US and Can-ada. A bibliography in that year listed over five hundred publications explicitly about Logo. "Turtle fever" had reached epidemic proportions.

"The whole phenomenon of Logo was kind of an amazing surprise to us," said Andy di Sessa, the co-author of *Turtle Geometry*. "When I started with Logo, I remember telling my brother-in-law what we were doing [letting kids program computers] and he just thought I was completely off-the-wall, just crazy, couldn't imagine what was going on. And in the course of a year or two my brother-in-law became the Logo coordinator for his junior high school…it was an incredible phenomenon."

Also in this period came the first corroboration of Logo's potential from out-side the group at MIT. Starting in 1982, researchers at Queens University in Ontario examined the creative use of microcomputers in Canadian elementary schools. Initially over 400 students at 13 sites were involved; in the second year, the study concentrated on 40 kids and five teachers. "We chose the folks who did interesting things to focus on," said Bill Higginson, one of the project's leaders, "and in those classrooms you got pretty strong glimpses of *Mindstorms*-ish things happening."[15]

Papert subsequently invited Higginson to come to MIT. There the Canadian researcher helped Papert choose the site for Project Headlight, what would be the final attempt in a US school to demonstrate the difference that using Logo could make to learning outcomes. This time, it was not an upper-middle-class citadel like Lincoln or Lamplighter. The James E. Hennigan School was a tough, inner-city Boston public school.

"It's the kind of place that's easy to find parking near," wrote Stewart Brand, who visited Hennigan in early 1986, "a random-feeling, freeway-bruised, non-

---

14.   Agalianos, p272
15.   See Higginson et al, "Computers, Children and Classrooms: A Multisite Evaluation of the Creative Use of Microcomputers by Elementary School Children", Ontario Institute for Studies in Education, Toronto, 1985

neighborhood. The concrete slab walls of the school, built in 1972, are covered with faded graffiti."[16] "It was pretty grim," Higginson recalled, "you really did worry for your safety getting in and out. But there was a bit of a spark, and there were some teachers there who were trying to do some things, which was the reason we chose it."

As a teenager, Papert had tried to teach reading and writing to the black domestic servants of Johannesburg. Now, he deliberately chose to work in a school where eighty percent of the kids were African-American or Hispanic, many of them from single-parent, illiterate homes. "The social conscience part of him wanted to show that [Logo] could be a really powerful device for moving society in a more egalitarian direction," Higginson thought.

By 1985, there were about a million computers in American schools, and about 50 million students, which meant that each student got about an hour's computer time a week. At Hennigan, there were 100 computers for 220 students, meaning each student could get several hours on a machine per day. In addition, there were also twenty-five undergraduate volunteers from MIT on hand at the school to help out.

"The kids were quite fascinated by the undergraduates," Higginson recalled, "they really had not seen folks like this at all....The key thing was just seeing people who were very good at something doing it, and having the kids realize that it's not just the answers at the back of the book and there are some people who are smart and some people who are dumb and the smart ones get it right all the time right away and the dumb ones never get it right no matter what they do, to seeing that Hey, even the smart guys, when they first start something, screw up. And that was powerful—it just shattered every image they had of anybody who was even remotely close to being a teacher."

Though Project Headlight was deemed a success, many shook their heads and wondered whether that success could be reproduced. After all, the teachers at Hennigan had been enthusiastic about the idea of using Logo, it was not imposed on them by fiat. And they had had the support of 25 high-powered smart-ass students from MIT, which was not going to be the case anywhere else.

This was just one of many doubts that were being expressed about Logo. In fact, questions about the practicality of Papert's proposals had been raised from quite early on. For example, in 1984, in a paper presented at the first of three National Logo Conferences held in successive years at MIT, Higginson pointed out that "[v]ery few elementary school teachers have the scientific/mathematical

---

16.   Stewart Brand, "The Media Lab", Viking, New York, 1987, p120

background to appreciate fully the potential of Logo...[n]or, without considerable personal sacrifice, do they have the time to learn about the higher levels of the language."[17]

In Ontario, Higginson had seen what could happen even to teachers with an aptitude for Logo-style learning. "They were doing wonderful stuff, but they were just burning themselves out, making themselves sick, their personal lives were going down the toilet, their colleagues hated them—they'd come in to school at seven o'clock in the morning, do all the necessary stuff with the computers, the kids would come early to work before school, [the teachers]'d stay at recess, they'd eat their lunch from a brown paper bag, they'd go off at 3:30 to do a workshop at some other school, they were never in the staff room, and that was fine with their colleagues, because they didn't like what they were doing at all."

That learning with Logo was hard work had been clear right from the very earliest days. Back in 1968–69 at Muzzey Junior High Cynthia Solomon remembered working 16 and 18 hours a day. But Papert never told people about this side of his vision. "That was something I felt was being kept as a dark secret," Solomon said. "Seymour made it sound like anybody could do it, any kids could do it with some help. But the teachers teaching it, they had to know something."

"Programming was a serious intellectual endeavor," Dan Watt agreed, "it wasn't, as Seymour Papert led a lot of people to believe, something you could just sit kids down at the computer with this wonderful Logo and they would learn it—it needed teachers who understood what they were doing."

Soon it became clear that many teachers did not have a clue as to the significance of what their students were doing. "When the students made something with Logo, the teachers didn't know if it was good or not," said Watts, whose missionary work with his wife Molly—"Mr & Mrs Logo", some called them—included writing best-selling books on Logo and running two-week, samba-school-style summer courses at their peripatetic Logo Institutes.[18]

"Even if it looked good on screen, was it really intellectually sound? So you could have kids who were patient and persistent produce a beautiful-looking picture that was made with a string of instructions that they could never look back and understand. And that would be considered a great success."

---

17. William Higginson, "About that Rose Garden: Remarks on Logo, Learning, Children and Schools", Pre-Proceedings of the 1984 National Logo Conference, MIT, 26–29 June1984

18. For example, Daniel Watt, "Learning With Logo", McGraw-Hill, New York, 1983; Watt, M. and Watt, D. "Teaching with Logo", Addison-Wesley, 1986.

If insiders like Watt and Higginson were concerned, so too were outsiders like Dave Moursund, a professor of computer science at the University of Oregon. "Logo frightens me", Moursund stated in an editorial in the December-January 1983–1984 issue of *The Computing Teacher*.[19] On the one hand, Moursund feared that Logo was being oversold: "Some people are developing unreasonable and unrealizable objectives about what Logo can do for education." And on the other, he was afraid that Logo would not reach its potential.

"Understanding the Logo phenomenon is difficult," Moursund wrote. "It is accompanied by an almost-religious enthusiasm. In talking with many Logo-oriented educators, I am led to believe that Logo not only will make their students computer literate and substantially improve their problem-solving skills, but will make a major contribution to rectifying many of the current ills of education. These claims may prove to be true, but it is important to acknowledge that, to date, such deeply-held beliefs in Logo go largely unsubstantiated. A number of my graduate students have done careful surveys of the Logo literature, searching for solid research to back up the widely-voiced claims. The literature is sparse. It consists mainly of descriptions of teachers using Logo with students, most concluding that the students enjoyed using Logo to draw pictures. One could say the same thing about students provided with a set of paints and a brush."

Moursund conceded that the Brookline project had given "a strong hint" of Logo's potential. But he cautioned that "one must view with suspicion an experiment in which the elementary school teacher [Dan Watt] has a doctorate in engineering. Indeed, few of the so-called experiments have been done making use of 'ordinary' teachers—those with a very modest level of training, experience and interest in the computer field."

"We asked a lot of the teachers," admitted Adele Goldberg, Pat Suppes' former research associate, who had gone on in 1973 to work with Alan Kay in the Learning Research Group at Xerox PARC, "we expected them to learn a lot of stuff, and they're very busy. If you look at what the average teacher has to contend with…there's an enormous amount of administrative overhead and a lot of things that take up their day. The times I spent in school I always left overwhelmed, thinking O my God, I don't know if I could do this. So I would just be in awe of the teachers.…What Seymour and Alan and probably myself didn't really quite see as strongly as we should have was what we were asking of the

19.   David Moursund, "Logo Frightens Me", *The Computing Teacher*, December–January 1983–84, p3

teachers in their context. And we have to be very conscious of that…because without that, the teachers will fight it, simply for their sanity's sake."

It did not help that Papert himself was no ordinary pedagogue; in fact, he loved kids and was brilliant in the classroom. "He's one of the best teachers I've ever seen," Watt admitted, "he would light up whenever there was a child around." "Seymour's fabulous with kids," agreed Solomon, "his whole body language changes when he's with them—I remember someone coming to video him about something, and he looked so stern, so I ran to find a child because I knew he would, y'know—just change."

But personal charisma would only stretch so far. "It's really not that hard making a pilot project that works," Brian Silverman mused. "It's even not that hard growing something to the point where the people who are really at the center of it talk to all the people who are doing things. What's really hard is when it becomes big enough that you only have third-and fourth-hand contact with the ultimate audience.

"When we first started getting Logo out commercially, instead of it being five or ten schools, suddenly it was 5,000 schools, and we didn't really have a good way of talking about the powerful ideas in *Mindstorms*. It was one of those things where everyone was talking about it, everybody wanted to get involved, and it was really the cutting edge and if you were involved in that you were doing something important."

As had happened so often in educational computing, the hype had got out of hand. Logo had acquired the aura of a charismatic religious cult. Fanatical believers were running around telling people that Logo was the be-all answer for computers in education. "In the US…Logo advocacy became synonymous with messianic zeal as many early Logo enthusiasts saw it as a panacea for the ills of an educational system in crisis." People came to expect miracles, and when they didn't get miracles, they got disillusioned.

Along the way, Papert had made many enemies. He had attacked the education research community both directly and indirectly. At first, the community had done its best to ignore him. "Seymour was never viewed as a serious researcher," di Sessa asserted, "he never played that game, never published in standard journals, never did a research study that could pass peer review in a journal, his books are inspirational and only very loosely based on what actually happened." In particular, what was missing was mention of the effort that teachers had to put in to produce the results Papert claimed happened spontaneously. (Papert never mentioned the fact that he himself used a bag of tricks in the classroom.)

But as turtle fever spread, the education research community could no longer afford to ignore Papert. They looked around for an intellectual basis to discredit his vision of using computers. And in 1985, with the publication of the results of a study at the Bank Street College in New York, they found one.

10

BACKLASH ON BANK STREET

By no means all progressive educators were pro-computer; indeed, many were actively antagonistic. A prominent opponent was the physicist Philip Morrison, who had been one of the leading figures in early post-Sputnik classroom initiatives and was still, even in retirement, a major thinker in science education. Morrison argued eloquently against using the machines in schools. At one of the MIT Logo Conferences he gave a talk, saying that there was so much rich experience available in the world, it would be a shame for kids to sit in front of the computer screen when they could be out on a field trip, studying a pond, say, and what lives in it. "Hands-on learning" meant hands on real materials, not hands on the computer.

This was a philosophy that Bank Street College, one of the bastions of progressive education, had heartily endorsed. Established in 1916 in New York's Greenwich Village, the college was deeply imbued with John Dewey's ideas of child-centered pedagogy. But by the late 1970s Bank Street College had become a very staid institution devoted to the preservation of fuddy-duddy modes of education. (It was no longer even in Bank Street, having moved uptown in 1970 to a new base in West 112th Street, on Columbia University's southern flank).

Then the college got a new president, Dick Ruopp, a visionary who saw that technology was going to change education in fundamental ways. Ruopp (pronounced "Roop") hired bright young post-doctoral researchers who had been bitten by the computer bug and who were ambitious to make a name for themselves. They included Roy Pea, whose thesis advisor at Oxford University had been Jerome Bruner, US champion of the cognitive approach to education, and a Canadian, Midian Kurland. In September 1981, Ruopp founded the Center for Children and Technology at the college. The center's first project would be to study how kids learn with computer programming. And what better topic for Pea and Kurland to focus on than Logo, the hot item of the moment, about which Seymour Papert was making such extravagant claims?

The methodology the MIT Logo Lab adopted in its projects had been qualitative, relying on observations, interviews, and documentation. No control groups had been used, nor had behavioral measurements been made. "Papert and his students didn't believe in experimental logic and experimental results," explained the NSF's Andy Molnar, "they refrained from testing, they believed that the drama of what the kids did was convincing enough, and therefore they didn't believe in using any ways to evaluate the outcome. And [Papert] had just outstanding students who did outstanding things with kids that were really very compelling. But there was no way to demonstrate that to the experimentalists, or to the educationalists, who believed that test results were the only way to confirm and validate the importance."

"It was all so individual and anecdotal that we could never really capture any principle out of it," admitted Danny Hillis. To a skeptical outsider, of whom there were many, the MIT crowd seemed interested merely in creating a situation in which kids could mess around, and if one kid did something really neat, then that justified the entire experience for all 25 kids for the last six months. So the question remained: Did Logo affect the kids' thinking, and if so, how? Pea and Kurland set out to find the answer.

At Bank Street College, Pea wrote, "[t]eachers and researchers alike were enthusiastic in beginning the Logo project and were devoted to its success". The setting for the experiment would be the college's own laboratory school, "a very fertile environment for receiving what were perceived to be the many compatible ideas expressed in Papert's progressivist text, *Mindstorms*. In fact we were often cautioned at the outset of our project that no one would believe positive findings demonstrating Logo's influence on children's thinking because the classrooms were so unrepresentatively well-matched to the Logo pedagogy (as compared to most American schools) which stresses discovery-learning and student-planned project work."[1]

The school was highly unrepresentative in another way, too. "It was very computer-saturated for its time (1981–83: each of two classrooms had six computers each for its 25 children). Two teachers from the school participated in Logo training planned and organized by Papert, who was also an early advisor to the project." In one class, the kids were aged between eight and nine; in the other,

---

1.   Roy Pea, "The Aims of Software Criticism: Reply to Professor Papert", Educational Researcher, June–July 1987, p7

between eleven and twelve. "The computer programming activities during the first year were intended by the teachers to be largely child-initiated, so as to encourage the child-centered Piagetian learning 'without curriculum' advocated for Logo."[2]

Fertile environment or no, things soon started to go awry. "To the surprise and consternation of all involved...children and teachers began to have difficulty in making headway with the discovery-oriented vision for Logo in the ongoing classroom activities of children." In the second year, the teachers took a more directive role in guiding their students. Each student had about two 45-minute work periods per week. Logs kept at each computer showed that, on the average, the children spent about 30 hours a year programming in Logo.

To test whether Logo was having any effect on the children's thinking, and whether they could transfer any newly-acquired skills to solve other types of problem, Pea and Kurland devised the following task. The kids were asked to make up a plan to perform six chores for an imaginary classroom—washing the blackboards, watering the plants, etc—in the optimum order. Never mind that chore scheduling was not exactly a topic guaranteed to fire the imagination of a pre-teen Manhattanite, it fit the classical paradigm for psychological research.

Unsurprisingly, relations between Bank Street and the Logo Lab, which had previously been cordial, began to sour. Pea went up to MIT to try and convince Papert that he and his colleagues "were doing something sensible in figuring out whether and how children were learning in Bank Street's Logo classrooms." In April 1983, an "infamous"—Pea's word—symposium was held at the American Educational Research Association in Montreal. Papert was a keynote speaker. A group from Logo Computer Systems Inc. was on hand to represent the true faith, Montreal being the company's home base. Kurland remembered the meeting as the "coming-out party for the first wave of Bank Street research that started to deflate the overly inflated Logo balloon."

Pea announced that, in testing the kids who had been programming in Logo against a control group, he and his colleagues had found no significant difference between them as problem solvers. A clash between the two camps ensued, the debate grew heated, and *ad hominem* remarks were made.

The argument continued in print, in academic journals over the next few years. Pea and Kurland accused Papert of having "naive technoromantic ideas"[3] ;

---

2.   Ibid
3.   Roy Pea & Midian Kurland, "On the Cognitive Effects of Learning Computer Pro-gramming," New Ideas in Psychology, 1984, Vol 2, p138

Papert countered that the Bank Streeters were "technocentric" in their thinking. Computers and Logo were only components: what was really important were people and cultures. "The context for human development is always a culture, never an isolated technology."[4]

"It was such a specious research project", growled Dan Watt who, more than 15 years later, was still bitterly angry at Pea and Kurland. "I think they totally misunderstood the nature of the enterprise." The Bank Street research had had a huge impact, Watt thought, outside the narrow field of educational research. "What happened," he explained, "was that schools had decided to use Logo, for a lot of reasons. Most of them had not really thought it through and seen what [Logo] was doing, and what it would take to implement Logo, and made a commitment to do that. Mostly it was because they wanted their kids to have computer literacy, and Logo seemed like a good vehicle for that, plus it had all this wonderful problem-solving that kids were going to learn.

"It wasn't Pea and Kurland's research that got spread around everywhere, it was some other people that used their research and were widely published in educational trade magazines that lots of people read. And basically it came to be common knowledge that 'Logo wasn't working'. This wasn't just Pea and Kurland's research, there was a lot of reality to it, because people didn't know what to do with [Logo], they didn't know how to make it work, they weren't trained. And even when you had teachers who were trained, and schools that had made a temporary commitment to it to the extent that teachers could be trained, the higher-ups didn't have a long-term commitment to it.

"In fact, as soon as the first easy-to-use wordprocessors came along, people said, O that's what we should be doing with our few computers in the schools, let's have the kids do wordprocessing. And boy, everybody could see the value of that—except for a few curmudgeons—but mainly that was universal, and you didn't have to learn anything specific, other than a few technical things, about how to make it work. The technical benefits were tangible in the product—you could see something that looked like something. When kids took home a Logo product, their parents couldn't make sense of it. But when kids took home a wordprocessed document, their parents said, I'm gonna get one of these for you!"

Wordprocessing quickly replaced programming as *the* thing to do with computers in the classroom. And the source of the most popular wordprocessor in the early days was, ironically enough, Bank Street College.

---

4.   Seymour Papert, "Computer Criticism vs Technocentric Thinking", Educational Researcher, January–February 1987, p23

◆   ◆   ◆

The sponsor of the program was, once again, Dick Ruopp, the college's visionary president. Bank Street had recently purchased a couple of wordprocessors—dedicated machines made by IBM and Wang costing about $9,000 each—for the use of its secretaries. "Dick was just captivated at the thought of What if kids could write with these machines?" Kurland recalled. "Apple IIs were beginning to emerge on the landscape, so Dick just decided that he was going to back the development of a wordprocessor for kids that would run on the Apple. And based on no idea if there was any market for this, or any interest in this—or anything—just by force of personality, he got the project going, got some money committed, got some partners, and the development of the *Bank Street Writer* was underway."[5]

Kurland became one of the program's chief developers. "The early eighties was a wonderful era to be doing software development," he said. "Since nobody knew how wordprocessors were supposed to work, whether for kids or adults, there was no standard. We didn't know, Should there be menus or not, and if there were menus, what kind of menus, and did they go on the top of the screen or the bottom? Y'know, how does text scroll—from the top down, or the bottom up like a typewriter? Just all of these issues to deal with which now seem kind of obvious since everybody's used something like *Microsoft Word* for a number of years. But back then, everything was up for grabs."

The program they developed, *Bank Street Writer*, was way ahead of its time. It was much simpler than the most popular package of the day, *WordStar*, which because of its multitude of control characters was horrendously complicated for kids to learn. It was much more flexible than *AppleWriter*, which could only handle uppercase letters. And it was also fast.

For all the *Writer*'s virtues, however, finding a publisher for it was hard. "None of the educational publishers wanted to touch it, because market research had clearly indicated that there was no market for such a thing. In fact, [leading publisher] Sunburst had just done a survey, they'd asked teachers to rank sixteen different product categories, from math drill-and-practice all the way down to wordprocessors, and wordprocessors finished dead last. So they took a pass on the *Writer*."

---

5.   Dick Ruopp died, of Lou Gehrig's disease, in 1998.

Eventually Broderbund signed up to publish the program for the home market on a gut call by the firm's founder, Doug Carlson, with another company, Scholastic, subsequently agreeing to take the school rights. *Bank Street Writer* appeared in 1981. Much to everyone's surprise, it took off like a rocket, selling close to a million copies. At one point something like 80 percent of the schools in the country had a copy of the program.

Teachers took to wordprocessing with alacrity. Here was a form of computer literacy that, unlike programming, they could understand and use to support mainstream curriculum. Early uses of wordprocessing were often trivial, taking no advantage of the power of the tool: teachers would reward a good essay by allowing the kid to make it look pretty by typing it in and printing it out.

Fortuitously, however, the arrival of wordprocessing happened to coincide with, and be a natural fit for, one of the more enduring educational innovations of recent decades. The "process writing" movement was kicked off in the late 1970s by such educators as Donald Graves of the University of New Hampshire. It consisted in essence of the revolutionary notion that children should be taught to write like real writers. In other words, instead of the conventional classroom practice of one-shot-is-all-you-get style composition, kids should be allowed to refine their work through successive drafts. ("Prose is like hair," instructs Flaubert, a real writer if ever there was one, "it shines through combing.")

"So the whole appeal of the wordprocessor" for teachers, Kurland said, was that, "My Goodness, we can have kids write, then we can go through and mark their writing and comment on it, and have them do a second draft without the onerous imposition of making them copy over, in a tedious way, parts that in fact didn't need changing." Or, he might have added, like medieval scribes, introducing mistakes that were not there in the first draft.

Papert had seen this coming. "For most children rewriting a text is so laborious", he wrote in *Mindstorms,* "that the first draft is the final copy, and the skill of rereading with a critical eye is never acquired. This changes dramatically when children have access to computers capable of manipulating text. The first draft is composed at the keyboard. Corrections are made easily. The current copy is always neat and tidy. I have seen a child [Tammy, whom we met in Chapter Eight] move from total rejection of writing to an intense involvement (accompanied by a rapid improvement of quality) within a few weeks of beginning to write with a computer."

Nor was she an exception. What teachers repeatedly observed with wordprocessing—when there was enough hardware to go round—was that kids wrote more, more often, and better. For Papert, wordprocessing was simply another instance of empowerment by machine. "What is good for professionals is good for children...I believe the computer as writing instrument offers children an opportunity to become more like adults...in their relationship to their intellectual products and to themselves."[6]

◆   ◆   ◆

In 1985, responding to the challenge of the *Bank Street Writer*, LCSI introduced *LogoWriter*, which added wordprocessing to Logo's capabilities. This temporarily reinvigorated the Logo community, extending its bounds beyond math to include subjects like English and social studies. By the late 1980s, however, the vision of the computer as Trojan horse, as vehicle for radical change, was fading fast. In part, this came about, paradoxically, by the proliferation of computers in schools. By 1988, according to one estimate, there were perhaps three million machines in US classrooms.[7]

"When there were few computers in the school," Papert wrote, "the administration was content to leave them in the classrooms of teachers who showed the greatest enthusiasm, and these were generally teachers who were excited about the computer as an instrument of change. But as the numbers grew and computers became something of a status symbol, the administration moved in. From an administrator's point of view, it made more sense to put the computers together in one room—misleadingly named 'computer lab'—under the control of a specialized computer teacher. Now all the children could come together and study computers for an hour a week. By an inexorable logic the next step was to introduce a curriculum for the computer. Thus, little by little the subversive features of the computer were eroded away: Instead of cutting across and so challenging the very idea of subject boundaries, the computer now defined a new subject; instead of changing the emphasis from impersonal curriculum to excited live exploration by students, the computer was now used to reinforce School's ways."[8]

Boston's elementary schools, which had hosted so many of the early Logo experiments, instituted a special computer curriculum. By 1987, to Papert's horror, children attending them were even required to take a test in Logo. "It's like

---

6.   Seymour Papert, "Mindstorms", Basic Books, New York, 1980, pp30–31

7.   Paul Saettler, The Evolution of American Educational Technology, Libraries Unlimited, Englewood, Colorado, 1990, p457

8.   Seymour Papert, "The Children's Machine: Rethinking School in the Age of the Computer", Basic Books, New York, 1993, pp38–38

taking a riding test before you're allowed to ride a bike," he groaned. "And then it turns out that there are too few bicycles—if you pass the riding test you can ride the bike for five minutes a week."[9] At least the Boston schools still had Logo. Elsewhere, drill-and-practice had become the usual computer activity in elementary schools, with programming increasingly being marginalized to advanced placement courses in secondary schools.

"It was clear from most of the computer literature that the computer was viewed as the further extension and embodiment of the traditional goals of education. The primary forces that pushed computers on the schools—the computer industry, the parents, and the educators themselves—all called for a return to basics. As a result, an increasingly conservative form of educational software began to be produced by publishers because they knew compliance with the demands of school boards and state-level adoption agencies would make it more likely that their products would be sold to the state system. Thus, so-called 'wrap-around packages' consisting of drill-and-practice type diskettes and correlated text-books were produced and promoted."[10]

What had gone wrong? Robert Taylor, director of the program in computing in education at Columbia University's Teachers College and editor of a seminal work on computers in schools, couched his answer in theological terms.[11] "When you study the Old Testament or Judaism," Taylor explained, "you see that there's a constant tension between the priestly and the prophetic. Papert is a prophetic figure—he's iconoclastic, comes in, breaks down ideas, and so on. The schools, including universities, are all priestly—their job is to keep things going, in order, with lots of rituals to reassure everybody, so you know where everything is, and you know this is going on in this way. And so anytime you have a prophetic idea enter the educational stream, it's gonna be an uphill battle, because it's blasting away at the priests, and most human beings feel more comfortable with a priestly orientation than a prophetic one. Prophetic is very scary, because the ground can disappear from under your feet while you're standing there listening to this guy."

---

9.   Angelos Agalianos, "A Cultural Studies Analysis of Logo in Education", [unpublished doctoral thesis], Institute of Education, Policy Studies, and Mathematical Sciences, London, 1997, p239

10. Saettler

11. "The Computer in the School: Tutor, Tool, Tutee", ed Robert Taylor, *Teachers College Press*, New York, 1980

◆   ◆   ◆

In 1988, at the eleventh hour, came vindication for Papert and his philosophy. Idit Harel, one of his graduate students who had done experiments at the Hennigan School, produced in her doctoral thesis the first hard—that is to say, academically acceptable—evidence that Logo worked. Harel got a class of fourth graders at the school to use *LogoWriter* to build educational software to help third graders learn about fractions. The topic was chosen deliberately because it was widely recognized that kids had difficulty with fractions.

At the outset Harel determined through interviews and standardized tests that her fourth graders did not understand fractions, nor did they know anything about programming. By the end of the project, each student had developed a relatively complex piece of interactive software, in the process learning a lot about both programming and fractions. In fact, rigorous post-testing showed that Harel's students learned significantly more on all measures than students in control groups who had studied fractions and programming in traditional settings. Other researchers proceeded to replicate her results.

In 1991 Harel's work was published in commercial form. Entitled *Children Designers*, the study won that year's Outstanding Book Award from the American Education Research Association.[12] It was a triumphant rebuttal to Pea and Kurland. By that time, however, it was also too late.

LogoWriter was soon overtaken by the rapid development of flashy new software that took advantage of the graphical user interfaces of the Mac and the *Windows* PC. It took LCSI until 1993 to respond with a multimedia, mouse-and-menu-driven product called *MicroWorlds*. (Papert had first used the word "microworlds" in *Mindstorms*, to describe self-contained worlds like "mathland" which children could explore in depth, like they would a video game, "undisturbed by extraneous questions.")[13] But though Logo diehards continue to swear by *Micro-Worlds*, it has proved difficult for the product of a tiny firm like LCSI to compete in the classroom against the commercial packages of giants like Microsoft.

A more successful legacy of Logo was its incorporation in robotics construction kits launched in 1998 by the Danish toymaker Lego. The Lego-Logo con-

---

12.   Idit Harel, "Children Designers: Interdisciplinary Constructions for Learning and Knowing Mathematics in a Computer-Rich School," Ablex Publishing, Norwood, New Jersey, 1991
13.   Mindstorms, p117

nection dates back to 1984, when company CEO Kjeld Kirk Kristiansen visited Papert's lab at MIT. There he was delighted to discover that one of Papert's students, Mitch Resnick, had built a robot out of Lego bricks wired to an Apple II. The relationship blossomed, with Lego bankrolling the following year a whole group at MIT's newly-established Media Lab, complete with an endowed chair of learning research for Papert. At the Hennigan school, the kids built robots out of Lego and programmed them using Logo. The robots were controlled by motors and input from sensors. In 1987, the MIT group invented a "programmable brick" which put a microcomputer inside a piece of Lego, dispensing with the need for wires.

In homage to Papert, Lego named the kits "Mindstorms". They recapitulate, at the elementary school level, the robotics experiments of the AI Lab. The kits also represent another instance of Papert's 1965 insight that technology should offer children the same things it offered adults. Like the floor turtle, programmable Lego bricks were objects to think with. The difference was that now, the kids could create their own turtles—and all sorts of other artificial creatures—as well as programming them.

The Mindstorms kits were an immediate hit, selling 100,000 in their first year on the market. To Lego's surprise, the bulk of these early sales went not to children, but to young adults. In a development amusingly reminiscent of the early days of computing at MIT, within two weeks and a half weeks of the product's launch, hackers had cracked the system's proprietary code and posted it on the Internet. They then proceeded to write an alternate operating system, plus a bunch of advanced applications to go with it. "They kept coming up with stuff we had never thought of," commented a bemused Danish executive. The new—freely available—software made the kits more attractive. Today, over seventy percent of Mindstorms users are kids. The system is used in more than 15,000 elementary and middle schools.[14]

◆   ◆   ◆

In 1988 Seymour Papert turned 60, an age when most people would be thinking of retirement. In that year, however, he was approached by IBM to go to the Central American republic of Costa Rica as a consultant. The forward-thinking president Oscar Arias, winner the previous year of the Nobel Peace Prize, was

---

14.   See Paul Keegan, "Lego: Intellectual Property Is Not a Toy", Business 2.0, September 2001, <www.business2.com/articles/mag/0,1640,17011,FF.html>

determined to improve the quality of education in his country. Arias wanted elementary school children in rural and slum areas to have access to technology. The original idea had been to buy one computer for every school. Papert advised against this, recommending instead that it would be better to select a smaller number of schools, install lots of computers, and give a core group of teachers an intensive course in how to use them.

An experiment was arranged in which some teachers, most of them women, participated in an intensive three-week Logo workshop arranged by Papert and members of his group. The results brought tears to his eyes. "Here were these women, who had never touched a computer, never even replaced a lightbulb, learning an advanced programming language. They felt empowered, it gave them a chance to learn, and that in turn got transmitted to the children."

Since its inception, the Costa Rican program has reached over one and a half million children, teachers, and adults. The still-growing initiative has put Logo in the hands of more than half of Costa Rica's elementary school children. One indication of its success was that, in 1998 ten years to the day since the educational computing project began, the giant chipmaker Intel chose to locate its first Latin American test and assembly plant in Costa Rica. Another was a fourfold increase in the number of Costa Ricans studying computer science at university.

Papert found it instructive that a tiny developing country with a population [3.8 million] less than that of greater Boston could succeed where the US had failed. "The United States is in some ways the best, but in so many ways it's the worst place for educational innovation," he said, "because people here are really smug and self-satisfied. I mean, they'll bitch a lot about how bad the schools are and how they've got to improve them, but basically their idea of America and everything in it is that, This is the best in the world, and it couldn't be better—except it's broken here and there and let's fix it. So there's a fix-it mentality that is not really conducive to making far-reaching changes."

By contrast, Costa Rica had set up an innovative organization outside the education department. The Omar Dengo Foundation, directed by the redoubtable Clothilde Fonseca, has a fulltime staff of 35 people. It provides a system for the training and support of teachers using technology that few if any developing countries can match.

In addition to Costa Rica, beginning in the late eighties, Papert would also begin working in his adopted home state of Maine. In 1993, he and his third wife moved to an 1815 farmhouse in the picturesque little port town of Blue Hill. There, as we shall see in Part Four, he would continue to be an activist in the cause of what he had begun to call "educational megachange" in various ways—some of them potentially of great significance for the future.

MicroWorlds and Mindstorms, Costa Rica and Maine, these are directly attributable to Papert's influence. But there were also at least two important indirect legacies of his work. As we shall see in the next two chapters, one was what would become perhaps the most used educational software in contemporary schools. The other was the portable hardware that would increasingly be adopted by schools in preference to the desktops in the computer laboratory—the laptop computer.

11

GLaD ALL OVER

Charlie Dietrich is the math teacher we all wish we'd had. After almost forty years at the chalkface, Charlie's joy in imparting a proof of the Pythagorean Theorem, or the Quadratic Formula or—better yet—of the area of a circle, remains undiminished. For him, it's simply exhilarating. "What really matters, and what is obvious to the students", Charlie says, "are my enthusiasm for teaching math, my eagerness for them to see the light as well, and my happiness when they do."

Charlie has high expectations for each and every student that he teaches at Greens Farms Academy. This is an independent college preparatory school housed in a Tudor-style mansion that was once a Vanderbilt family summer home in Westport, Connecticut, some 45 miles northeast of New York City. Expectations vary from student to student, of course, and not all students rise to the challenge. One way or another, though, Charlie seems to be able to get his students to work.

Perhaps it's the humor that Charlie strives to interject into every class he teaches, as often as he can, without reducing the seriousness of what he is trying to teach. Humor is "the horse I ride", he says, "and it enhances everything I do…goodness knows, these kids need to relax and have fun while they study mathematics. I ensure that."

One thing Charlie takes pains never to do is to check up on a student's background in math. He takes kids the way they come, and tries to change them for the better. But when two precocious fourteen-year-olds, Dave Goldenheim and Dan Litchfield, arrived in Charlie's accelerated math course in the summer of 1995, their reputations as outstanding students preceded them. "I was prepared for a fascinating and challenging time", he said. But in his wildest dreams Charlie, who was then 55, could not have imagined what was about to happen.

In mid-July that year, as a last minute challenge on his way to lunch, Charlie assigned the two bright sparks a well-known geometry problem. First posed (and answered) by the Greek mathematician Euclid more than 2,000 years ago, the problem was: Given a line of any length, divide it into any number of equal parts, without using a ruler. Find the solution, he told them, and there would be extra credit. "And by the way fellas," Charlie added encouragingly, "you don't have a prayer of figuring this out."

Blissfully unaware of Euclid's solution, the pair got out their laptops. They fired up a program called *The Geometer's Sketchpad*, which allowed them to draw lines and then manipulate them. Then the pair started, as Dan said, "to mess around." After less than a couple of hours of experimentation, the boys reckoned they'd licked the problem. They went to find Mr Dietrich to show him their solution.

When Charlie saw what his ninth-graders had done, he nearly had a heart attack. "My instincts screamed at me that this construction was unique and original—in fact, a discovery." Mathematicians tend to regard Euclidian geometry as a branch of their subject that has been done to death. Now, for perhaps the first time since antiquity, here was something new. (Their creation was later named the GLaD construction, for <u>G</u>oldenheim, <u>L</u>itchfield, <u>a</u>nd <u>D</u>ietrich.)[1]

And there was more. To verify their approach, the pair had gone back over their previous trials, which was easy to do since *Sketchpad* had saved them all. In one of their early attempts the boys noticed something weird about the numbers the program had generated. It turned out to be nothing less than the Fibonacci sequence, in which each number is the sum of the previous two. This is a pattern that fascinates mathematicians because it crops up repeatedly in nature. The Fibonacci sequence? This was too much for poor Charlie: "I had to lie down," he said.

He soon bounced back up again, getting the pair—who still had no idea why their teacher was freaking out—to write up their results. These were published in the January 1997 edition of *Mathematics Teacher*, a leading scholarly journal.[2] An avalanche of attention followed. It began with a glowing write-up in the *Wall Street Journal* and climaxed in July 1998, with a meeting with US Education Secretary Richard Riley in Washington DC.[3] (Both boys subsequently entered Harvard University.)

---

1.   A "construction" in geometry is a drawing of a figure which satisfies certain conditions, and which is used in solving a problem or proving a theorem.

2.   Dan Litchfield and Dave Goldenheim, with support from Charles Dietrich, "Euclid, Fibonacci, and Sketchpad", Mathematics Teacher, Vol 90, No 1, January 1997 <www.nctm,org/mt/1997/01/vol90-no1-euclid1.htm>

3.   Guatam Naik, "Teen Math Whizzes Go Euclid One Better", Wall Street Journal, 9 December 1996, pB1

"I suspect that most teachers in their entire careers do not see anything approaching the caliber of these students' efforts," wrote Harry Tunis of the National Council of Teachers of Mathematics, the publisher of *Mathematics Teacher*, in his letter of acceptance to Charlie. "You are very fortunate."[4]

Charlie knew it. An emotional man, he would still get tears of joy more than six years after the fact, just thinking about what had happened. "I have been the luckiest math teacher...ever," he said.

◆   ◆   ◆

What had happened at Greens Farms Academy that summer was a perfect illustration of the Logo principle, "low threshold, no ceiling". *The Geometer's Sketchpad* works all the way from fourth grade right up through Stanford Medical School, where they use the software to look at what happens to bones in car crashes. (It's fundamentally a geometric problem: they deform.)

Without computers and *Sketchpad*, it is highly unlikely that Dan and Dave would have discovered the GLaD construction. "We could have done the whole thing with pencil and paper," said Dave, "but it would have been much harder to visualize. We probably would have gotten frustrated and thrown the whole thing in the garbage."[5] It was, after all, said Dan dismissively, "just an extra credit problem."

Charlie had had the good sense to leave his students to discover things for themselves. And to allow them to work as a team. ("Dave and I come at things from completely different places," said Dan, "and then we get really creative together.")[6] All in all, it was a beautiful example of what by the mid 1980s educational theorists, following Piaget, were beginning to call "constructivism" in action.

Papert preferred to use his own, slightly different word: "constructionism". "The word with the v expresses the theory that knowledge is built by the learner, not supplied by the teacher", he explained. "The word with the n expresses the further idea that this happens especially felicitously when the learner is engaged in the construction of something external or at least shareable...a sand castle, a

---

4.   Letter dated 30 October 1996
5.   Quoted in Leslie Chess Feller, "The Eternal Challenge of Euclid's Geometry", *New York Times*, Sunday 7 March 1999, (page number unknown)
6.   Ibid

machine, a computer program, a book." (Or, he might have added, a geometrical construction.)

Constructionism could be seen in opposition to instructionism, the dominant mode of learning in schools. Instruction was not in itself necessarily bad, Papert wrote, it was just not a good way to bring about significant change in education. *"Better learning will not come from finding better ways for the teacher to instruct but from giving the teacher better ways to construct."*[7] [Emphasis in the original]

Although not directly derived from Logo Lab activities, *The Geometer's Sketchpad* did have some roots at MIT. To begin with, there was the name: *Sketchpad* was so called in honor of an program written at MIT in 1963—the same year that Papert arrived at the institute—by an engineering student called Ivan Sutherland for his doctoral thesis. The original Sketchpad was the first program that allowed the creation and manipulation of graphic images directly on a display screen (contemporary displays could only handle text). It was an early indication that computers could be used for something other than data processing. Sketchpad was thus the progenitor of the now-ubiquitous graphical user interface. It made a profound impression on all those who saw it including, as we shall see in the next chapter, Alan Kay.

Then there was the precursor, *The Geometric Supposer.* This was a program written for the Apple II in 1985 by Judah Schwartz and Michal Yerushalmy at MIT's Educational Development Center. It encouraged users to experiment and make their own discoveries, albeit only, as Papert pointed out, within the framework of traditional geometry. (There had been heated debates at the institute about how far one should go in empowering students with computers.)

Finally, there were the genes of *Sketchpad's* author, Nick Jackiw (pronounced "Jackeev"), whose father Roman is a professor of physics at MIT. "*Sketchpad* inherits the Logo tradition through the *Suppose*r," Nick Jackiw thought, "it's really sort of a third turn of this constructive software design philosophy that characterizes all three of those genres of program." Since its introduction in 1991, *Sketchpad* has made a major contribution to the rejuvenation of geometry in schools everywhere. In the process, it has become perhaps the most widely-used piece of purely educational software in the world.

Jackiw is an engaging, highly articulate young man with intense light blue eyes set in a triangular face whose apex is tipped with a blond goatee. Rangy of frame, he dresses in a latterday beatnik style slightly reminiscent of the young Bob

---

7.   Seymour Papert, "Constructionist Learning", Introduction, MIT Media Laboratory, 1990, p3

Dylan. Jackiw began programming at the age of nine, back when the dominant vision of programming was as counter-culture rather than computer science. Magazines like *Creative Computing* and Bob Albrecht's *People's Computer Company* were early influences. By his teenage years, personal computers had arrived, and Jackiw was writing—and selling—games.

But Jackiw was not a maths whiz. "I had no mathematical background prior to my work in *Sketchpad*," he said, "all of my secondary [school] experience was such that I didn't want to take any mathematics at college." Jackiw arrived at Swarthmore in 1984 intending to major in English. But, as fate would have it, a mathematician named Eugene Klotz had been assigned by mistake as his undergraduate advisor.

Before the error could be rectified and they went their separate ways, Klotz and Jackiw chatted about the recently-introduced Apple Macintosh computer, which the freshman had already begun to program. Three years later, in 1987, when Klotz received a National Science Foundation grant to develop visual geometry programs for the Mac, he remembered the young man's prowess. He called Jackiw up and offered him a summer job.

The fact that Jackiw was not a professional mathematician turned out to be an advantage. "*Sketchpad* came about largely out of my attempting to relearn school geometry," Jackiw recalled, "while at the same time building a tool that would help me play with the ideas that I was learning....I think there's some sort of perspective on the subject that I brought as a learner that gets propagated by the program, as opposed to the traditional tone of mathematical materials that kids encounter, which is an expert tone—'I, the textbook, know what I'm talking about, and your job is to memorize it.'

"*Sketchpad* starts with a blank screen—it's up to you to do what you want, it's not about teaching you what it knows. And, to take it back to Piaget, that's very much the model of how knowledge is built, knowledge is not transmitted from an authority to some sort of empty vessel, it's something you build for yourself. And the appropriate role for teachers or tools is to set up conditions in which you'll be motivated, encouraged, and ultimately successful in your encounters with, and attempts to manufacture personal knowledge about extrinsic objects." To use Papert's term, *Sketchpad* is a microworld.

At the heart of *Sketchpad* is a powerful idea, which is simply that geometry should be dynamic. Traditionally, much of the time in geometry class has been taken up with drawing, with fiddling about with compasses, protractors, and rulers, often with unsatisfactory results, especially for those with poor motor skills. It leaves little time for more important matters, like learning how to make and test hypotheses. But with the arrival of the Mac, which came with a built-in program called MacDraw, drawing was suddenly trivial.

Moreover, the Mac made it possible to "drag" on-screen objects with the mouse. This ability to create geometric diagrams quickly—clickety-click-click—then manipulate them dynamically is *Sketchpad's* most celebrated feature. The idea grows out of the technology: create one triangle, and just by dragging the apex you can make it into any triangle. But *Sketchpad* was more than just an extension of the Mac, it was actually, as Jackiw liked to say, "a spreadsheet that worked with graphics." Having created your triangle, you could add up the angles-on screen, then watch as the total always remains 180 no matter how much you experiment with the shape.

When the grant money ran out, there was a strong push from the NSF to commercialize the results of the Swarthmore project. This was, after all, the Reagan era. In the foundation's view, too much academic research on education wound up in a nice binder on the shelf of the researcher who had produced it. "They more or less twisted our arm into looking at commercial publishers," Jackiw recalled. At first, the researchers approached the corporate conglomerates that dominate educational publishing. "And they'd send out marketing people who just didn't speak the language that we spoke at Swarthmore and didn't wear the right clothes."

Enter Key Curriculum Press, a tiny publisher of supplementary math materials based in Emeryville, an industrial district just over the Bay Bridge from San Francisco. Key had just made a splash as innovators in geometry education by virtue of a textbook—one of the first to be put together using the tools of desktop publishing—that espoused the new math-as-experimental-science philosophy as laid out in standards established by the National Council of Teachers of Mathematics in 1989. Key's president Steve Rasmussen flew over to the East Coast, spent two days evaluating *Sketchpad*, then told Jackiw, This is how it ought to be done—we'd love to work with you. "I basically got sold with the software," Jackiw said. He came out to California to field-test *Sketchpad* for a year in California schools, then stayed on as Key's software strategist.

Sketchpad was an instant hit. Since its launch in 1991, the program has remained hugely popular, a rarity in the software industry where titles seldom last long. One reason for this enduring success was that math teachers like Charlie Dietrich took to *Sketchpad* like ducks to water. "It was love at first sight," Charlie recalled, "the visual impact of that technology, the changing of the static to the dynamic simply was magical to me and made the subject of mathematics come ALIVE!"

Meanwhile, developments in the wider world, most notably video games and computer graphics, have combined to produce a renaissance in geometry. Playing computer games like *Doom* has given kids a very good sense of solid geometry. In addition to which, a further attraction is that, as Jackiw points out, "you can now win an Oscar for being a geometer—I mean, the people at [computer animation specialists] Pixar do it all the time, and kids are very aware of this."

When Jackiw visits high school classrooms, his favorite source of math problems for the kids to investigate is computer graphics. "Everyone's seen a morph on TV," he said, "but nobody's thought about the mathematics of a morph. But when kids realize that they can bring their high-school mathematics to that problem and really generate [morphs] themselves, that's a powerful thing for them. So it's nice to have this two-way feedback, where technology is showing us new things about geometry, but where geometry is also something that's driving the technology."

◆   ◆   ◆

Solid geometry mapped naturally onto the computer. Transforming other subjects has not proved so easy. Nor has success in one part of the curriculum been deemed relevant in others. You might suppose that, having seen their students achieve a feat unique in the annals of high school scholarship, the authorities at Greens Farms Academy would have changed their attitude to the use of computers in the classroom. After all, unlike at most schools, there were no financial constraints at Greens Farms. Fairfield County, where the school is located, is one of the wealthiest counties in the United States. "The parents are smart and pushy," Charlie says, "[they] will spend whatever is necessary to give their children the best education possible." They can afford all the computers they want.

At the same time, however, Greens Farms is a pretty conservative place, still emphasizing the basics throughout its curriculum. Computers are for the most part confined to the lab. (Thanks to the arrival of *Sketchpad*, the math department was granted one extra class per week for geometry in the computer room.) Though students use computers as wordprocessors for most subjects—all English and History assignments must be typed—Dan and Dave were the first two students granted permission to use their laptops in class. This was in 1994, when the pair started seventh grade. Seven years later, in 2001, it pained Charlie to have to report that there were still only two kids who used laptops in every class. "Our faculty endorses them, but we will not require them," he says.

The stumbling block is the Academic Committee, which is responsible for what goes on in the school's classrooms. The committee must vote its approval for any changes of a major kind, such as making laptops mandatory. "It seems that each year the computer department and the math department take a proposal to the Academic Committee regarding mandatory use of laptops," Charlie says, "and we get nowhere. The non-math and non-science types just don't see any need for it in any of their History, English, Language, Art, Music, Philosophy, etc courses. I wish I could predict a reversal in their thinking, but it's hard to teach old dogs new tricks."

According to Charlie, "there is always a curiosity involving more computers in the classroom, but not much of a debate. Heads of Departments go to other schools at which much computer usage takes place, but they come back with hundreds of questions, ifs and buts, and then decide as a department to keep with the status quo." Prime among the skeptics is the school's headmaster. He was one of two who had to stifle a laugh when Charlie told them that his students had created an original proof. (The other, much to Charlie's chagrin, was his brother.)

Kids need teachers like Charlie to have faith in them and to recognize their achievements. He remembers that, in the wake of all the publicity that followed publication of Dan and Dave's discovery, came poignant e-mails from two men in their eighties. Each said that they had made the same construction back when they were in high school, but their teachers had ignored them. "When they read about us," Charlie says, "they felt vindicated and quite thrilled for themselves, and for us."

Though much better endowed than your average high school, Greens Farms Academy is by no means atypical in its attitude to technology. "I never cease to be surprised at how inertial the whole school system really is," said Nick Jackiw, "from the parent loop, where anything that's different—'It's not how I learned my multiplication, therefore it's not math'—to the teachers who, for ninety-five percent of their working lives, have complete autonomy in the classroom—they basically do the same thing every year—but don't have any sort of culture of professionalism.

"We don't think of teaching as a set of professional skills that you groom, maintain, and develop in a community, in a profession. And without any sort of model of how things can change, nothing does. How you insert a model into that without seeming like Goths at the gates is really difficult."

But while the rate of change in the classroom may be glacial, in the computer industry, it is torrential. And for as long as anyone can remember, nowhere has the rate of change been faster than in the field of portable machines.

12

CRYSTALLIZED DREAMS

Alan Kay thought he was going to be killed. It was late 1968 and Kay had flown to Boston to behold the work that Seymour Papert, Wally Feurzeig, and Cynthia Solomon were doing with Logo at Bridge Elementary School in Lexington. It turned out to be a meeting of like minds: "I felt for the first time that I had an ally in the world," Papert said. In the car on the way back from the school, Papert drove, Kay sat in the back seat. As the discussion became excited, Papert kept turning around to talk to him. There were, Kay recalled with a shudder, "some very scary traffic incidents".

In addition to a near-death experience, this encounter would produce an even more memorable outcome. It would lead, indirectly, to the laptop computer. Indeed, to the very model that would be used, more than twenty years later, by the first school to fulfil the vision that Papert and Kay shared. That is, of computer-as-pencil, "used as casually and as personally for an even greater diversity of purposes."[1]

Louis Pasteur said that chance favors the prepared mind. Seldom can there have been a mind as well prepared as Kay's for what he observed that day in Boston. Ever since he arrived at the University of Utah in 1966 as a 26-year-old graduate student, Kay had been intent on inventing the future of computing. On virtually his first day in Salt Lake City, he had been handed Ivan Sutherland's Sketchpad thesis outlining the first graphical user interface. In early 1967, Doug Englebart, "a prophet of biblical dimensions", visited Utah and demonstrated his revolutionary mouse-based text-editing system. Kay designed an interactive desktop machine called FLEX, which incorporated many ideas from Sutherland, Englebart, and other pioneers.

The paradigm, it was a-shifting. For Kay, the implications of Moore's Law alone were staggering.[2] The sun no longer circled the earth. "Computing as we

---

1. Seymour Papert, "Mindstorms: Children, Computers, and Powerful Ideas", Basic Books, New York 1980, p210

knew it couldn't survive," he wrote. "Instead of at most a few thousand *institutional* mainframes in the world…there would be millions of *personal* machines and users, mostly out of direct institutional control."[3]

In his doctoral thesis, Kay became the first person to couple the words "personal" and "computer".[4] Though modelled on a time-sharing terminal, FLEX bore an uncanny resemblance to the Apple II, introduced ten years later. (Or at least his drawings of it did, since an actual FLEX machine was never built.) FLEX was not bad for a first attempt, but its over-complicated interface "repelled end users instead of drawing them closer to the hearth". The components had been cobbled together; they refused to gel. "It was like trying to bake a pie from random ingredients in a kitchen: baloney instead of apples, ground-up Cheerios instead of flour."[5]

In July 1968 Kay presented his vision of personal computing to a skeptical (though, he thought, supportive) audience of fellow post-grads at a conference held at the University of Illinois's Allerton House. After his talk, during a tour of the university, came "the big whammy".

"I saw a one-inch-square lump of glass and neon gas in which individual spots would light up on command" to form letters. This was the plasma screen Don Bitzer had designed for PLATO terminals—one of the first flat panel displays. "I spent the rest of the conference calculating just when the silicon of the FLEX machine could be put on the back of the display." According to Moore's Law, the answer seemed to be sometime in the late seventies or early eighties.[6] (A pretty accurate estimate, it turned out: the first laptop computer, as we shall see, was introduced in 1982.)

Later that year came a second whammy: *Understanding Media*, the seminal text by Canadian communications theorist Marshall McLuhan.[7] Like many peo-

---

2.   The notion, formulated in 1965, that electronic circuits become cheaper and more powerful as they become smaller.

3.   Alan Kay, "The Early History of Smalltalk", manuscript version c 1992, p7 (reprinted in "History of Programming Languages", ed. Thomas J. Bergin & Richard G. Gibson, ACM Press, New York, 1996)

4.   Alan Kay, "The Reactive Engine", University of Utah, 1969. The abstract describes "the design and implementation of the 'FLEX machine', a personal, reactive, minicomputer which communicates in text and pictures by means of keyboard, line-drawing CRT, and tablet."

5.   Alan Kay, "User Interface: A Personal View", from "The Art of Human-Computer Interface Design", ed Brenda Laurel, Addison-Wesley, Reading, Massachusetts, 1990, p192

6.   Kay, "Early History of Smalltalk", pp9–10

ple, Kay put his own construction on McLuhan's best known—and least comprehensible—dictum. "[A]nyone who wants to receive a message embedded in a medium", he wrote, "must first have internalized the medium so that it can be 'subtracted' out to leave the message behind. When [McLuhan] said 'the medium is the message' he meant you have to *become* the medium if you use it."

Hitherto, Kay had followed Englebart in envisaging the personal computer as a vehicle. It was like a private car that would let you go wherever you wanted, as opposed to a mainframe, which was like a railroad train that would only stop at certain destinations. Now, with a shock that still reverberated in him more than two decades later, Kay realized: "The computer is a medium!" And if McLuhan was right, a medium that would change the thought patterns of those who internalized it.

A beguiling vision beckoned: "The intensely interactive and involving nature of the personal computer seemed an antiparticle that could annihilate the passive boredom invoked by television. But it also promised to surpass the book to bring about a new kind of renaissance by going beyond static representations to dynamic simulation. What kind of thinker would you become if you grew up with an active simulator connected, not just to one point of view, but to all the points of view of the ages represented so they could be dynamically tried out and compared?"[8]

At a ski lodge meeting held in Park City, Utah, in Spring 1968, Kay had heard a talk by Marvin Minsky. The caustic Minsky let loose "a terrific diatribe against traditional education methods". He spoke "about how we think about complex situations and why schools are really bad places to learn those skills." From Minsky, for the first time, Kay heard—and was intrigued by—the ideas of Piaget and Papert. Now it was time to pay the latter a visit to find out what he was up to with kids and computers at the Lexington school.[9]

Kay was amazed by what he saw there. Twelve-year-old children writing real programs that generated poetry, created arithmetic environments, and translated English into Pig Latin ("igpay atinlay"). He immediately recognized the importance of becoming literate in this new medium. If the computer was a vehicle, you could wait until high school to teach "drivers ed". But if it was a medium, you had to make the computer accessible—like reading and writing—at a much

---

7.   Marshall McLuhan, "Understanding Media; the Extensions of Man", McGraw-Hill, New York, 1964
8.   Kay, User Interface", p193
9.   Kay, "Early History of Smalltalk", p9

earlier age. The next time Kay tried to design a computer, it would be with elementary-school children in mind.

Considering children as young as six years old as the primary users brought the design problems strongly into focus. It was clear, for example, that kids needed as much computing power as adults—or more. "The best that time-sharing has to offer is slow control of crude, wire-frame, green-tinted graphics and square-wave musical tones," Kay wrote later. "Kids, on the other hand, are used to finger paints, water colors, color television, real musical instruments, and records. If 'the medium is the message' then the message of low-bandwidth time-sharing is 'blah'."[10]

Pondering Papert's work on the plane back from Boston, Kay flashed on similarities with the history of printing. The first books printed using movable type—the so-called incunabula—were, in a sense, like mainframe computers—huge, hence immobile, produced in small quantities (in the case of the Gutenburg Bible, just 180 copies), and affordable only by the very rich. It was not until 40 years later that the real impact of the technology began to be felt, when the Venetian printer Aldus Manutius—Aldo Manuzio to his friends—adapted printing to produce small-format, low-cost books that even poor scholars could afford to buy and carry around with them on their travels.

Kay could barely contain his excitement. "I remembered Aldus Manutius put the book into its modern dimensions by making it fit into saddlebags," he wrote. Because children are mobile, the computer would have to be portable—no larger than a notebook. "A clear romantic vision has a marvelous ability to focus thought and will. Now it was easy to know what to do next. I built a cardboard model to see what it would look and feel like [about the size of an A4 page by half an inch thick], and poured in lead pellets to see how light it would have to be (less than two pounds)."[11]

Kay also coined a name for this vision of a handheld, notebook-sized computer for kids that would, one day, capture McLuhan's metaphor in silicon and glass. He called it the "Dynabook".

---

10. Learning Research Group, "Personal Dynamic Media", internal publication, Xerox Palo Alto Research Center, March 1976, p9
11. Kay, "Early History of Smalltalk", p10

◆   ◆   ◆

Alan Curtis Kay knew all about the history of printing because he was himself a prodigious reader. He started reading early, at the age of two and a half. Kay had the advantage of growing up in a household filled with books and, by his own account, had devoured several hundred volumes by the time he got to school. "I wasn't reading Bertrand Russell at age five, but I was interested in different religious systems and I'd read quite a bit about that, and my dad liked ancient Greece, so...."

His dad, Hector, was a physiologist who became one of the best-known names in the field of prosthetic limbs. Hector was born and raised in Melbourne, Australia, then went to Springfield College, Massachusetts, where he met and married Kay's mother, Katherine, a musician. Alan was born in the US, but spent his preschool years in Sydney, where his father ran a kinesiology program. Kay and his mother returned to the US on a war-bride ship, his father rejoining the family a couple of years later.

Elementary school in rural Hadley, Massachusetts, was not at all to the boy wonder's liking. "School systems don't like variant perspectives," Kay said, "they want you to read one book and understand it. So my basic memory in first grade was the teacher saying something and me raising my hand saying, Well, I read a book that says something else in it. And very quickly I got the idea that this was not done, because what they wanted us to do was learn a party line."

Worse was to follow. "In second grade, I was very carefully drawing something when the bell rang—time for recess. And they just wouldn't let me stay in class and finish that drawing, I had to go outside. And I said to them, Why? So that was pretty much it: I had a couple of good teachers in there, but my earliest brushes with school convinced me that they weren't interested in ideas, basically, and they certainly weren't interested in *my* ideas." By third grade, he was more or less educating himself. At ten, the precocious auto-didact was appearing on radio as a National Quiz Kid.

Kay would continue to have run-ins with school authorities throughout his education, getting suspended from Brooklyn Technical High School (for insubordination) and thrown out of Bethany College (for protesting against quotas on Jewish students). He moved out to Denver to join a friend who was living there. To pay for a double major in mathematics and molecular biology at the University of Colorado, Kay enlisted for a two-year stint as a cadet in the US Air Force.

For someone with such a well-developed disregard for authority this was not, to put it mildly, a happy time.

They say that everybody learns something in the army. In the Air Force, Kay learned computer programming and became good at it. On graduating from Colorado, he was accepted as the seventh graduate student in Utah's tiny but up-and-coming department of computer science. For the first time in his life, Kay was in a place where people took him seriously. Much to his own surprise, ideas began to pour out of him.

In 1970, the newly-minted PhD moved to the Stanford AI Lab. There, Kay spent most of his time thinking about a children's computer he called KiddiKomp. In his sketches, the KiddiKomp looks a lot like a Macintosh, introduced fourteen years later. To run on it, he came up with Simulation LOGO—SLOGO for short. This would evolve into Smalltalk, a programming language specifically designed for kids. Kay began consulting for the newly-established Xerox Palo Alto Research Center. By mid 1971, he was working at PARC full-time.[12] There, a Xerox corporate planner asked him what the future of technology was going to be and how the company could defend against it. An exasperated Kay shot back with what would become his signature maxim: "Look," he said, "the best way to predict the future is to invent it."[13]

◆   ◆   ◆

Kay's was a restless intellect, always eager to move on to something new. Like Leonardo da Vinci—a presumptuous comparison perhaps, but one with which Kay himself was not uncomfortable—he found it hard to stay focused long enough to follow through on his ideas. At PARC, Kay finally realized that he needed some backup. He formed a team, called the Learning Research Group, hiring only "those people that got stars in their eyes when they heard about the notebook computer idea." The group's charter may have been vague, but its goal was clear: "When anybody asked me what to do, and I didn't have a strong idea, I would point at the notebook model and say 'Advance that'."[14]

---

12. For a good, book-length account of account of the center's activities, see Michael Hiltzik, "Dealers of Lightning: Xerox PARC and the Dawn of the Computer Age", Harper Collins, New York, 1999
13. Kay, "Early History of Smalltalk", p13
14. Ibid, pp13–14

An excellent musician, Kay used to liken the Dynabook to a sort of musical instrument. It would be something that you strummed, like a guitar perhaps; or, like a flute, "which…responds instantly to its owner's wishes."[15] It struck him that "if you could get the computer off the table and out of the big rooms and into this kind of relationship, you'd have something more like the relationship that musicians have with their instruments."

"During the whole decade of the 1970s," wrote Papert, "Kay's research group at the Xerox Palo Alto Research Center and our group at MIT were the only American workers on computers for children who made a clear decision that significant research could not be based on the primitive computers that were then becoming available in schools, resource centers, and education research laboratories."[16]

The PARC group worked mostly at night. Kay himself performed best from 4 to 8AM. Daytime was spent outside, "playing tennis, bike-riding, drinking beer, eating Chinese food, and constantly talking about the Dynabook and its potential to amplify human reach and bring new ways of thinking to a faltering civilization that desperately needed it." In California in the aftermath of the sixties, with the dehumanizing carnage of Vietnam still in full swing, that kind of goal was quite common, Kay recalled.

Time to crystallize the dream, to build some actual machines to try out on kids. But getting his lab manager at PARC to greenlight this idea proved more difficult than Kay had anticipated. In May 1972, he made his pitch, outlining a personal computer that was way beyond the capabilities of conventional technologies—especially the display, which had to be high-resolution.

"I was very interested in high-quality text and graphical presentations", Kay explained, "because I thought it would be easier to get the Dynabook into schools as a 'Trojan horse' by simply replacing school books rather than to try to explain to teachers and school boards what was really great about personal computing."[17]

He argued that, though still embryonic and expensive, microelectronic components were improving fast and getting cheaper. The manager was unimpressed, shooting down Kay's proposal in flames. The purpose of Xerox's lab was to create the office system of the future, not komputers for kiddies. Kay crawled away to lick his wounds.

---

15. Learning Research Group, "Personal Dynamic Media", internal publication, Xerox Palo Alto Research Center, March 1976, p5
16. Ibid, p14
17. Ibid, p16

He soon recovered. That August, at an Association for Computing Machinery meeting in Boston, Kay presented a paper, *A Personal Computer for Children of All Ages*. It included a hand-drawn illustration that would be widely reproduced. In what appears to be a bucolic setting, a young a boy and girl are happily communicating with each other via tablet-like Dynabooks.[18]

The following month, two of PARC's hardware hotshots sidled up to Kay with an unexpected proposal. "How would you like us to build your little machine for you?" they whispered conspiratorially. The lab manager was going off on a course for a few months, and the pair figured they could "sneak it in" while he was away. "I'd like that a lot," Kay said.[19]

In December, an article by Stewart Brand entitled *Spacewar: Fanatic Life and Symbolic Death Among the Computer Bums* appeared in *Rolling Stone* magazine.[20] Large sections of the piece covered PARC and Kay's work there. "Alan is designing a hand-held stand-alone interactive-graphic computer called the Dynabook," Brand wrote. The description of this fantastic machine and what it would be able to do continues for several paragraphs.

"A Dynabook could link up with other Dynabooks, with library facilities, with the telephone, and it could go and hide where a child hides. Alan is determined to keep the cost below $500 so that school systems could provide Dynabooks free out of their textbook budgets." (A good point, one which is still relevant thirty years on: it demonstrates that here, at least, Kay was actually thinking along practical lines.)

"If Xerox Corporation decides to go with the concept, the Dynabooks could be available in two or three years," the article concluded with breathtaking over-optimism, "but that's up to Product Development, not Alan or the Research Center."

In fact, so far from deciding to "go with the concept," Xerox went berserk. To prevent further breaches, the corporation tightened security at the center and restricted publication. This made it difficult for Kay's group—the "lunatic fringe" as they were known by PARC's other computer scientists—to share ideas and programs with colleagues like Papert.

---

18. Alan Kay, "A Personal Computer for Children of All Ages", Proceedings of the ACM National Conference, Boston, August 1972
19. Kay, "History of Smalltalk", p18; Tekla Perry, Paul Wallich, "Inside the PARC", IEEE Spectrum, October 1985, p65
20. Stewart Brand, "Spacewar: Fanatic Life and Symbolic Death Among the Computer Bums", Rolling Stone, December 1972

Nonetheless, by April 1973, the "little machine", the world's first personal computer, was ready. Dubbed the "interim Dynabook", it was officially known as the Alto. Kay christened the prototype Bilbo. Within minutes of being up and running Bilbo was displaying its first—animated—images, of the Muppet, Cookie Monster, munching a cookie.

The interim Dynabook was a long way from Kay's ideal: it was big—consisting of separate CRT, keyboard, and a rack of hardware that could just about be hidden under a desk—and not very powerful, packing a grand total of just 128 kilobytes of memory. But it was beautiful. And soon, in order to compensate for a relatively small display, the Alto became the first computer to feature overlapping windows.

By summer '73, the Learning Research Group was ready to start experiments with computers and kids. Since none of its members knew anything about working with children, however, it was necessary to find someone who did. Adele Goldberg was a very bright, no-nonsense young woman who had been working with Pat Suppes at Stanford since 1969. She knew Kay via a small Bay Area community which got together once a month to discuss their shared interest in computers in education.

When Kay asked Goldberg to join his group she agreed, because "I felt that Pat Suppes was tied so strongly to his time-shared system that he wasn't willing to entertain small computers where you could get rid of this institutionalization." That is, having to go to a particular place—the school computer lab—where the tools were available, in order to do your learning. "And Alan of course was totally into the Dynabook, and to me that just seemed to be the right way to go, to say It's a tool you carry with you, it's a means to an end, it's not the end itself."

Not everyone found the idea of the Dynabook so intuitively obvious. "In the seventies, we would say to people Everyone's going to want to have a portable computer the size of a notebook," Goldberg recalled, "and people literally thought we were crazy, that we belonged in insane asylums."

One person who thought otherwise was Joan Targ, sister of the chess champion Bobby Fischer. She ran a state-funded program for "mentally gifted minors". At the Jordan Middle School in Palo Alto, Targ had a resource center for doing extra-curricular stuff with students. At first, because access to the Alto machines was restricted, the kids came up Coyote Hill Road to PARC once or twice a week. Later, without the management's knowledge, working on the well-known principle that it is easier to gain forgiveness than permission, Kay and Goldberg smuggled an Alto out of the center one night and set it up at the school center.

Goldberg taught the kids to program in Smalltalk. From past experience, she knew that working in groups was the best way to go, so that the kids could look over each other's shoulders and motivate each other. "Even at this seventh-grade, twelve-year-old level," she recalled, "these kids would very quickly start to build up partnerships—O, he's got good ideas but he doesn't want to sit here programming; I'm more the engineer, I want to program it—and I thought the partnering was the most exciting thing that happened there."

Goldberg began by mimicking Logo turtle graphics, achieving very similar results to Papert's group at MIT. But this seemed rather superficial. Kay felt that since the content of personal computing was interactive tools, the kids should use their newly-acquired computer literacy to create such tools. Goldberg came up with a brilliant idea for teaching programming called Joe the Box. This used a box, an onscreen object like the turtle, that could be commanded to turn, to grow and shrink, to disappear and reappear, and to combine with other boxes to form crude animations.

"What was so wonderful about this idea", Kay wrote, "was the myriad of children's projects that could spring off the humble boxes." Some of the earliest were tools. For example, twelve-year-old Marion Goldeen came up with a painting system which allowed the user to choose from a menu of shapes; another seventh-grader, Susan Hamet, created an illustration program that prefigured MacDraw. "This was when we got really excited."[21]

But though such successes were real, they were not as widespread as Kay and Goldberg had at first thought. It slowly became clear to them that to expect that their triumphs would extend to schools everywhere was unrealistic. After all, the gifted offspring of upper-middle-class Palo Alto families were hardly your average kids. And by no means all even of them had taken to programming as readily as Marion and Susan.

In part, what the researchers were seeing was the "hacker phenomenon"—the fact that five or so percent of people are more or less pre-wired for any given pursuit—they get it right away—whereas the remaining 95 percent find it hard to learn. Another part of the problem was, it took time for Kay to grasp that what was obvious to a computer genius like him was not necessarily obvious to ordinary mortals.

As Goldberg kept reminding him, it was hard to claim success if only some of the children were successful. And if an all-out effort from both children and teachers was required in order to get the successes to happen. "Real pedagogy has

---

21. Kay, "History of Smalltalk", p26

to work in much less idealistic settings and be considerably more robust." An opinion with which Goldberg's old boss, Pat Suppes, would have readily agreed.

◆   ◆   ◆

By late 1975, seven years after his momentous encounter with Papert, Kay felt that the Dynabook idea of a computer for children was slowly fading. The dream obstinately refused to crystallize. Before moving on, he and Goldberg paused to write up the group's results in a 76-page report. It was simultaneously a summation of their efforts to invent the future and a prediction of the shape of computers to come. Entitled *Personal Dynamic Media*, the paper was published internally the following March. [22]

"Imagine having your own self-contained knowledge manipulator in a portable package the size and shape of an ordinary notebook. Suppose it had enough power to outrace your sense of sight and hearing, enough capacity to store for later retrieval thousands of page-equivalents of reference material, poems, letters, recipes, records, drawings, animations, musical scores, waveforms, dynamic simulations, and anything else you would like to remember or change.

"We envision a device as small and portable as possible which could both take in and give out information in quantities approaching that of human sensory systems. Visual output should be, at the least, of higher quality than can be obtained from newsprint. Audio output should adhere to similar high fidelity standards."

The machine would be for everyone—for architects, doctors, animators, composers, homemakers, and executives. ("Those in business can have an active briefcase which can travel with them....") But the Dynabook was envisaged above all as a machine for educators and children.

Teachers could use it "to show complex historical inter-relations in ways not possible with static books" (hypertext links). "Mathematics becomes a living language in which children can cause exciting things to happen" (dynamic geometry). "The production of stylish prose and poetry can be greatly aided by being able to easily edit, file, and 'debug' one's own compositions" (wordprocessing). For kids, the Dynabook could be "an environment in which the natural activities are creative thinking and planning; visualization of effects and their causes...." A Protean machine indeed.

---

22. Learning Research Group, "Personal Dynamic Media", internal publication, Xerox Palo Alto Research Center, March 1976

In 1977 a condensed version of *Personal Dynamic Media* was published in *IEEE Computer*, a magazine read by members of the world's leading organization for computer professionals.[23] Prime among those who sat up and took notice was Tetsuya Mizoguchi, who at the time was in charge of mainframe computer development at Toshiba in Tokyo.

"I read that paper", Mizoguchi said, "and I thought, Ah-ha! this machine can be used for mutual communication between young and old, men and women and computers. You'll be able to read it like a newspaper and listen to audio on it. And I thought that, in the future I really want to develop a Dynabook like [Alan Kay] described." A seed had been planted whose subsequent flourishing, almost a decade later, we shall consider in the next chapter.

Meanwhile Kay put on his thinking cap again. At PARC, professional needs were now pressing. He outlined a new machine that, unlike the Dynabook, could be realized in the near future. It was based on the new microprocessor chips that were starting to become available. In his preliminary sketches, NoteTaker resembles a portable typewriter with a screen that popped up when the lid opened. The same sketches reveal that the machine was designed to sit on its user's lap.[24]

Ideally, NoteTaker would have been light enough for students to carry from class to class and home again at the end of the day. Once again, however, reality lagged behind Kay's imagination. The prototypes were slower, bigger, and, at 45 pounds, much heavier than originally envisioned. Rather than the first laptop—the word had not yet been coined and the machine would in any case have crushed any lap—NoteTaker was actually the first of a short-lived category of portable machines called "luggables". It looked like a suitcase with a bottom that folded down to reveal keyboard and monitor. But NoteTaker worked well, ran on batteries, and fitted under an airline seat, albeit only just.

Xerox didn't want to know. In December 1979 Steve Jobs made his famous raid on PARC. The following May, Kay left the center on sabbatical, never to return. He was hired by the game machine maker Atari to head the West Coast wing of the corporation's research (Cynthia Solomon directed the other wing in Cambridge). Then, in 1984, he joined Apple, the company that had appropriated so many of the innovations made at PARC, as an Apple Fellow. For the next few years, Kay would divide his time between working at a public elementary

---

23.   Alan Kay & Adele Goldberg, "Personal Dynamic Media", IEEE Computer, vol 10, March 1977, pp 31–41
24.   Kay, "History of Smalltalk", p30. Perry & Wallich (IEEE Spectrum, October 1985, p73) credit Goldberg with having originally conceived the NoteTaker. "Poor Adele," [Larry] Tesler said. "The rest of us got involved and kept redefining the project."

school in his new home town, Los Angeles, and overseeing theoretical research at MIT's Media Lab, the new headquarters of his old friend and onetime driver, Seymour Papert.

13

CORPORATE GATLING GUNS

We live in an age, as Alan Kay likes to say, of parallel invention. The modern laptop computer does not descend directly from the Dynabook, which was essentially a dream machine. The idea of a portable computer sprang independently from the mind of John Ellenby, another former Xerox PARC researcher, who conceived it for an altogether different type of user. And it is Ellenby's vision, not Kay's, which holds sway in the contemporary marketplace.

Though little-known, the story of how Ellenby, his partner Glen Edens, and their team at GRiD, the startup they co-founded, developed the world's first laptop computer, then snatched defeat from the jaws of victory, is a classic in the annals of high technology. It begins in 1973 in Edinburgh, where Ellenby, a young Englishman, was simultaneously teaching computer science at the university and consulting for Ferranti, a pioneering computer maker with a history of giving individuals their heads.[1]

At Ferranti, Ellenby worked on a large project to design a family of minicomputers for process control and communications. This experience alerted him to the momentous shift taking place in electronics from discrete components to integrated circuits. And, since display processors were part of his responsibility, he was also aware of the recent emergence from various laboratories of flat panel displays.

Ellenby realized that "at some time in the future it would be possible to make a full computer in a very small footprint that would have a flat panel...and that you could carry around. And that [such a computer] would be very useful to all kinds of people." Then in 1974, as a result of a chance encounter at Edinburgh

---

1.   In February 1951 Ferranti delivered the Mark I, "the world's first commercially available general-purpose computer". <www.computer50.org/mark1/FM1.html>

University with visiting scholar Dan Bobrow (the co-author of Logo, who had gone to PARC after MIT), Ellenby was recruited by Xerox.

For the next five years Ellenby worked at PARC. His job was to turn the Alto from a prototype into a machine that could be efficiently mass produced. In this he was successful, but in trying to get the computer out into the real world he collided with an inflexible and unsympathetic corporate bureaucracy. Frustrated, Ellenby told the company he was leaving. Xerox's lawyers responded by warning that he had better not take any of the people who worked for him. Or go into business making products like those he had worked on at PARC. Otherwise, he would find it very difficult to raise capital. "So I thought, We'll do something new."

In September 1979 Ellenby got together with Edens, an extremely creative engineer who had also, briefly, worked at Xerox. Ellenby was kicking around the notion of doing a portable communications terminal with a modem in it. Edens said, "Well, shoot—let's not do a terminal, let's do a whole portable computer!" Which was a pretty flaky proposition, considering that personal computers had yet to establish themselves as useful devices. So the question, according to Edens, was "I barely know what a personal computer is, why would I want a portable one? But we ignored that."

The concept the pair came up with differed from the Dynabook in several significant respects. "Alan's conception of Dynabook was that it would be a music and media thing," Ellenby recalled, "but I was thinking much more of a general-purpose, communications-oriented machine." Though the main thrust was communications, the idea was to create a device that would also allow business people to take some computing resources with them on the road.

The Dynabook was always something that was not quite practicable, a little bit out of reach. "Which was entirely how Alan thought," Ellenby recalled, "I mean, as soon as you could do something, Alan would start to think about the things you couldn't do." The Dynabook, as we have seen, was designed with children in mind. For Ellenby and Edens, "we pretty much figured that business was going to be the primary user of this technology to start with."

Above all, there was a crucial difference in shape. Kay imagined the Dynabook as a flat, tablet-like machine that kids would carry around under their arms. While on the corporate staff at Xerox, Ellenby had noticed that all the company's executives hefted these big chunky briefcases. The plan was to build a computer that could fit into the bottom half of such a briefcase, leaving enough room in the top for papers, sandwiches, whatever.

"In the latter part of '79," Edens said, "we started working on different physical models—What would this look like, how small could we make it, how heavy would it have to be?" At this early stage, they engaged the services of a talented industrial designer, an Englishman called Bill Moggridge. The first model opened up and laid flat. This was kind of cool, but the more they played with it, the more they realized that this design wasn't going to cut it.

"So we starting doing drawings," Edens said, "we went through every possible combination of how you could combine a keyboard and a display, and where all the parts would be. We must have done a hundred drawings, and the one that we kept coming back to was the clamshell, because that was the most natural to use, it folded up and therefore protected the screen for travel, it gave you the right screen structure." Today, the clamshell design is used in virtually all laptop and notebook computers. It may seem like a no-brainer, but it was actually a brilliant insight, one that took months to figure out.

Moggridge put together a very realistic plastic model. Ellenby and Edens took it around to show investors and potential customers, large companies like Arco and American Airlines, to get a feel for whether they would buy such a machine if it existed. "We got a range of answers from Huh? to Can I have one tomorrow?" Encouraged, they set about writing a business plan.

By mid 1980, the fledgling firm was ready to roll. It had significant funding and a small team of engineers. It also had a name, GRiD, suggested by Ellenby's wife Gillian, to encapsulate the notion of a connected network of machines. Now it was time to build the computer, the target being to have ten functioning prototypes ready in twelve months, and a product on the market within eighteen. At the time they started, however, everything was a problem. Nothing they needed existed—flat panel screens, switching power supplies, modems, small keyboards, memory. So they had to conjure everything up more or less from scratch.

"GRiD made those technologies happen," Ellenby said, "it was really extraordinary that we could make things happen that had never happened before." Edens agreed: "It was really pretty amazing, every day was like a new discovery." Of course, it helped that most of the startup's engineers were too young to know what could not be done. The average age of the team was around 25; Edens himself was barely 30. Several would go on to distinguished careers at other Silicon Valley firms, most notably Jeff Hawkins, the designer of the Palm Pilot.

Having fixed the size of the machine—half a briefcase—"we started to carve up space for everyone," Edens chuckled, "we would just tell every vendor, y'know, this is your cubic inches." Trying to find a suitable keyboard was a nightmare at a time when two inches was considered great for key switches. Eventually they discovered a German maker called Rafi that was willing to shoot for a tiny keyboard with real keys just a quarter of an inch thick.

The modem was merely difficult. At a meeting, executives from the vendor, Racal Vadic, kept telling the GRiD guys they were crazy: a 1200 baud modem was impossible, and even if it were possible, why would anyone ever want to communicate at faster than 300 baud?[2] "But there was an engineer in the corner," Ellenby recalled, "and he looked at me and winked." This engineer had been in touch with his counterparts at GRiD beforehand. He felt that GRiD's specifications could be met, he just lacked the nerve to say so in front of his boss.

Then there was the case. This had to be strong, which meant metal, but light and capable of being injection-molded. That ruled out aluminum, which was light, but not moldable. Instead, they selected magnesium. That seemed ridiculously expensive, until someone pointed out that, since metals are sold by weight and magnesium is much lighter than aluminum, they'd actually end up paying less. The real problem, according to Edens, was that "when you injection-mold stuff, you get all these little flaky bits around it, so you have to come back and sand everything. Well, when you sand magnesium, you create magnesium powder, which is one of the most explosive substances on Earth."

The solution was incredible. "It turns out that there are all these machine shops back East where all the milling and everything is done under water," Edens explained. "We went to some places that were just like big sunken swimming pools—their guys were all walking around and working at the machines in hipwaders with water up to here." Edens reckoned that GRiD was the first company to mass-produce a product from magnesium. The material is still used—albeit in the form of less explosive alloys—in most high-end laptops.

There was also a problem with painting the cases—the black paint they used would chip or wear off. The solution to that one came from a customer, General Motors, whose laboratories in Detroit had developed a wonderfully effective paint for an experimental, all-magnesium Corvette. It was heat-resistant, ductile, and went on easily.

Small disk drives were still several years away, so GRiD adopted a nonvolatile chip technology called "bubble memory". This was made for them by Intel, which in those days was itself still a relatively small firm. Of course it helped that Intel co-founder Bob Noyce was an individual investor in GRiD. "He was incredible," Ellenby recalled, "an absolutely wonderful man."

---

2.   In binary terms, 300 baud equals three hundred bits per second. Current modems can handle many million bits per second.

But the key enabling technology for the portable computer was always going to be the flat panel screen. And in 1980, there were no suitable flat screens available from US manufacturers. To be sure, Owens-Illinois was making a plasma panel—the prototype of which had so excited Alan Kay—for Don Bitzer's PLATO terminal. But by GRiD's standards that was a gigantic, power-hungry thing, with a ton of electronics behind it.

The company's only hope was to take their model over to Japan, and see if they could find anybody there who could make what they needed. "To get the flat panel display," said Edens, "we actually got a five-way race going between a bunch of Japanese companies. We said, Whichever one of you gets there first and meets our specifications, you'll get in the product."

The contestants included Sony with plasma, Toshiba with liquid crystals, and Sharp with a technology called electroluminescence. Looking back almost twenty years later, Edens was struck by how extraordinary the whole thing had been. "I'm not sure how we did it, because a bunch of nutcases from California was asking these companies to make multi-million-dollar investments."

At that time the state-of-the-art, display-wise was a four-line liquid crystal display which could only show characters, 24 of them per line—barely enough for a portable typewriter. GRiD wanted 24 lines by 80 characters, and, just to make life even more difficult, the screen had to be bit-mapped so that it could handle graphics. But it was not just a question of being able to make the displays—whoever won GRiD's business would also have to commit $100 million to building a factory in which to manufacture them.

And yet, remarkably, that is what in early 1981 Sharp agreed to do to do. Their electroluminescent technology produced a beautiful orange-on-black display. EL was much crisper than contemporary monochrome LCDs; people used to talk about its jewel-like quality. "The fact that Sharp decided to make the electroluminescent panels is what really made the laptop business real," Ellenby said.[3]

By August 1981 GRiD had built ten prototypes as planned. The launch date for the product was set for the National Computer Conference the following April. In the meantime, the company's software people wrote the first-ever integrated suite of applications, including wordprocessing, drawing, communications, and database. They also met with Internet pioneer Vint Cerf, who taught GRiD how to do e-mail, in those days still very much in its infancy. To support it, they assembled one of the first nationwide e-mail network services.

---

3. As the only major Japanese electronics firm that did not make its own cathode ray tubes, Sharp has always been the keenest on flat panel displays.

Come the launch and the machine, which weighed 12 pounds, was up there on the podium ready for its first public demonstration in front of an eager crowd. This was not uneventful. On his way to do the demo Edens, who is so short-sighted that he is technically classified as blind, caught his foot on the power cord and yanked the GRiD off the podium. The machine slammed into the concrete tile floor of the hotel. "You could have heard a pin drop," Edens recalled laughing, "so I picked the thing up, put it back on the podium, facing out so that everyone could see it—and it still worked!"

This unexpected ruggedness turned into a sales point. To make sure that machines would not come back under warranty after being dropped or damaged by customers while they were on the road, GRiD's engineers devised an unusual test. They built a box equipped with shock sensors and sent it all over the country to see whether it could survive the tender mercies of parcel shippers and airport luggage handlers. "The joke was that the box got better vacations than the rest of us," Edens laughed.

Initial sales of the GRiD machine were made to individuals. Edens thought that the company's first paying customer was Steve Jobs. The second order came from the writer William F. Buckley Jr ("he just fell in love with the thing"). The initial corporate customers were Chevron and Bank of America, who used their portable computers to give them the edge in financial negotiations. Here, the GRiD machine's ability to handle communications enabled its users to redo calculations on-the-fly, thus run rings around their opposite numbers.

Ellenby remembered one early customer saying that, thanks to the GRiD, "We could just turn inside their decision cycle four times, and that just totally made the difference—we came away with a very profitable deal as a result. You remember those awful pictures of Gatling guns being used against American Indians? she asked. Well that was us, and we were the ones with the Gatling guns."

To such corporate customers, the GRiD machine had a very high value. To be sure, at first they would grumble at the $8,150 price tag, but quite a few subsequently told Ellenby that they would have paid ten times more. Nor did GRiD's clandestine government customers care how much they paid for the machine. The company had accidentally discovered that, because of its all-metal case, the computer did not radiate any telltale electrical signatures. Word of this got out and, soon, spooks started showing up on GRiD's doorstep.

Early adopters of any new technology tend to be insensitive to price. To grow the business, however, GRiD had to cut costs. And, beautiful though they were, electroluminescent displays were simply too expensive. Then Toshiba developed

LCDs that were bigger and more flexible than the character panels. These were nowhere near as beautiful and crisp as EL, but they cost much less. GRiD made the switch to liquid crystal displays in late 1983.

The same year, Tandy introduced the Radio Shack TRS ("Trash")-80 Model 100. With an 8-line display and costing just $800 for an entry-level model, this machine became the first widely used portable. It was especially popular with journalists, who could write stories on location and transmit them via modem to their editors. But the machine was not taken seriously by business users.

(The TRS-80 is also, supposedly, Bill Gates' favorite computer, because it was the last machine for which he wrote the majority of the code.[4] But it was not, as is sometimes thought, the first computer to be referred to as a "laptop". The term was first used in *Byte* magazine in reference to the Epson HX-20 on view at a trade show in November 1981.[5] Confusingly, since both the Trash 80 and the Epson machine are tablet-type machines, they would not today be described as laptops.)

Even with LCDs, the problem for GRiD continued to be profitability. They simply couldn't get the price of the displays down low enough. The company struggled on until December 1987, when it was acquired by Tandy. But GRiD had proved the point that there was a market for laptops, albeit a niche. This was not lost on Toshiba, a big vertically-integrated company that made many of the key components for the portable machines, including the displays and the high-density memory chips. Or on Tetsuya Mizoguchi, the dynamic individual who led the development of personal computers at the corporation.

◆   ◆   ◆

Mizoguchi is very far from being your stereotypical Japanese salaryman. Tall, dark-skinned, with the big-boned frame of a pro wrestler, a shock of graying black hair, and an overbite, Mizoguchi looks like a leader and has about him an aura of power. His manner is similarly atypical—frank and to the point. When we met him in the previous chapter, reading and being deeply impressed by Alan Kay's 1977 vision of the Dynabook, Mizoguchi was in charge of mainframe development at the corporation. But Toshiba was never more than a bit player in big iron; and with the coming of the personal computer, Mizoguchi was one of the first in Japan to focus on the smaller machines.

---

4.   See <www.tcp.com/~lgreenf/bill.htm>
5.   See <www.retrobytes.org/classiccmp/9907/msg01036.html>

Under his direction, in 1985 Toshiba introduced its first laptop. LCDs were not backlit in those days, so the display was relatively hard to read. The following year, the company switched technologies and introduced a model featuring the first plasma display to be used in a laptop. Bright red on black, the more legible screen helped to make this model enormously popular in the US and Europe (the Japanese domestic market for laptops took much longer to take off).

But plasma is a power-hog, which meant that laptops equipped with plasma displays had to remain tethered to the wall-socket. This was unsatisfactory, but had to suffice until the development of better, backlit LCDs. When that low-power technology arrived in 1988, Mizoguchi told his engineers, "Let's develop a battery-powered machine." It took them a year. On 26 June 1989 the company announced a new slim, four-and-a-half pound laptop called...Dynabook. (Never having believed in the concept, Xerox had not troubled to trademark the name.)

The following day, Mizoguchi wrote Alan Kay a letter, saying "We've taken the first step toward making the machine you wrote about in that 1977 paper." They translated the catalog from Japanese into English and enclosed it along with the letter. Mizoguchi knew that Kay had been teaching at the MIT Media Lab, so he sent the materials there. But no answer came. "I waited three weeks," Mizoguchi recalled, "so it must have been mid July. Then I thought—it's the middle of summer, maybe he's gone somewhere?"

Mizoguchi thought some more, then remembered reading somewhere that Kay had been doing research on man-machine interfaces at a primary school in Los Angeles. Perhaps he had an address in LA? Toshiba had a factory in the Los Angeles area, in Irvine, CA. Mizoguchi called and asked them to look in the phone book to see if there was a listing for Alan C. Kay. "So they did that, found his address, and I sent the same letter there. Then I waited three weeks and, again, no answer came."

By this time it was August, and Mizoguchi thought it was odd that Kay hadn't replied, but he really wanted to get hold of him somehow. Then he had another bright idea—every year, around the second week in August, Apple holds its annual MacWorld bash in Boston. "And Kay was an Apple Fellow, so I thought maybe he'd be there and we could ambush him—forget about posting letters! So we sent a couple of section chiefs and a machine over to the US with instructions that, when they met Alan Kay, they were to give it to him along with my letter."

Meanwhile, unbeknownst to Mizoguchi, a freelance Japanese journalist had bought a Dynabook and taken it with him to MacWorld. He went to the Media Lab, where Kay happened to be that day. Kay saw the journalist carrying his machine, asked him what it was, and was told that it was a Dynabook made by

Toshiba. Kay was very surprised and decided, there and then, that he would really like to have one. But the journalist could not be persuaded to part with his, so Kay called the director of the Media Lab, Nicholas Negroponte, and asked him if he knew anyone at Toshiba?

As it happened, there had been a young researcher from Toshiba studying at the Media Lab. But he had gone back to Japan. So Negroponte e-mailed him: "Alan Kay called me last night and asked if I knew anybody at Toshiba through whom I might be able to get a Dynabook. He said it looked like the best of its kind so far." Next day, the section chiefs Mizoguchi had dispatched arrived in Boston and went looking for Kay. They found him and presented him with the Dynabook. Kay was completely bemused: "I only called yesterday, and it's come from Japan already? That's impossible!"

Now that contact had finally been established, Mizoguchi was keen to meet Kay himself. An opportunity arose the following December, when Kay flew in to Tokyo for a conference. Next morning Mizoguchi picked Kay up at his hotel and took him out to the factory where Toshiba made its laptops, 30 miles west of central Tokyo. After a tour of the production line and development department, Mizoguchi assembled his young researchers. Kay talked for twenty minutes on his thoughts and dreams for the computer. "For the youngsters, here was the man who had thought of the Dynabook; it was like God had come to see them," Mizoguchi recalled, laughing. "They were very excited, and determined to try even harder—which was exactly what I had intended!"

After Kay's talk, Mizoguchi got him to sign eight of the laptops. On one he wrote "I'm very happy you made this—Alan Kay." Twenty years on from his original vision, reality had begun to catch up. Indeed, unbeknownst to Kay, the very model that he was signing was about to be used in the world's first laptop class.[6]

◆   ◆   ◆

By 1990, Toshiba was the dominant player in laptop computers. The company had sold more than a million of the machines. Its market share was over forty percent in Japan, over thirty percent in Europe, and twenty percent in the US. But though prices had fallen, laptops were still expensive, costing several thousand dollars each—a long way from Alan Kay's target of $500. And the overwhelming majority of sales went, as Ellenby and Edens had predicted, to busi-

---

6.   Known as the T1000SE. The Dynabook name was only used in Japan.

nessmen and women who needed access to some computing resources and the ability to communicate with head office when they were on the road.

Then word began to filter up from Toshiba's Australian sales office about a school that had adopted laptop computers for all its students. The school, which was located in the city of Melbourne, was called Methodist Ladies' College.

Intrigued, Mizoguchi flew down to Melbourne in Spring 1994 to see for himself what was going on. Much to his surprise, the general manager of Toshiba's information systems division discovered that Methodist Ladies' College was not, as he had thought, a junior college—it was just a girls' school. And the kids using the laptops there were aged from eight to fifteen.

"They let me sit in on various classes," he recalled, "English, math, social studies, science, art—everything. At that time the screens were still monochrome, but for art you have to have color, so there were color monitors in the art room that the kids could connect to. And I went to the library, where they had a server, and the children were using it. During recess, although there were also girls who were playing physical games outside, quite a few were sitting on the floor playing with their computers. And they could use them at home, too, for e-mail and whatever."

Mizoguchi came away deeply impressed by what he had seen. There was nothing like this back in Japan. Nor for that matter, anywhere else in the world. How had this extraordinary situation come to pass? he wondered. Good question.

PART III

MARVELLOUS MELBOURNE

14

VICTORIA SUNRISE

To discover how Seymour Papert's idea of transforming learning through kids each having their own computer was first put into practice at an actual school, it is necessary to journey all the way from MIT almost literally to the opposite end of the Earth. Specifically, to the island of Tasmania, which is about as far south of the equator as Massachusetts is north of it.

Australia's smallest state is more than three times bigger than Massachusetts, but with a population just two thirds that of Boston. Home of Bugs Bunny's nemesis, Taz the Tasmanian Devil, and birthplace of the actor Errol Flynn, Tasmania is best-known for its stunning natural beauty, the desire to sustain which spurred the formation in 1972 of the world's first Green party. During the 1970s "the Apple Isle", as Tasmania is known locally, was also—briefly—a leader in the nascent field of educational computing. Less burdened by bureaucracy, small states can sometimes get the jump on their bigger neighbors.

Geographical isolation makes Australians great travellers. It also makes them eager listeners, especially regarding developments in the UK and US. On a one-year teacher exchange to England Scott Brownell kept his ears open, and (as we saw in Chapter Eight) returned home via MIT. He arrived back in Hobart, the capital of Tasmania, clutching a magnetic-tape copy of Logo. Soon Brownell had Logo up and running on the Tasmanian education department's time-sharing computer system. Then he won a grant from the national government. Brownell used one part of the money to buy a General Turtle robot. Another part went to hire one of his former students, Sandra Wills, to go forth with Logo and teach kids about computers.

Wills started work in early 1976, more than a year before the Brookline Project began in Boston. Every day, she would head off in her little panel van for one of three primary schools. All three were located in housing commission areas, it being a condition of funding that disadvantaged students should be the focus of research. In the back of the van were the turtle, the huge control box that went with it, a $4,000 graphics terminal, plus an acoustic coupler to connect the system to the computer center. On arrival Wills would unload this heavy gear and set it up in the principal's office (typically the only place in the school where there was a phone line). The students would come in, five or six at a time, to play with the turtle. In addition to teaching the kids, Wills also ran workshops for their teachers. At the end of the day, she would pack up the gear, then drive back to the computer center.

The following year saw the launch of the Apple II. An Australian computer scientist called Richard Miller was quick to adapt Logo for the machine. His version of the language came out at least a year ahead of the "official" LCSI Logo. As the Tasmanian computer education program expanded, more robot turtles were needed. But in the interim General Turtle had—predictably—gone bust. Enter a local electronics whiz called Allan Branch, who built his own version of the machine. Known as the Tasman Turtle, this robot was cheaper and more accurate than its predecessor—for example, it could draw a perfect circle. Thanks to some code that Miller wrote, the turtle was soon running under the control of the Apple II. Branch formed a company, Flexible Systems, whose business was making and selling robots. He exported hundreds of them to the US (where the market was mostly home electronics enthusiasts, not schools).

Now, with a second robot, "we were able to program the turtles to bump into each other and back off and dance together," Wills recalled, "it was really good fun." By the time she left the island in 1983, teachers in all 300 of Tasmania's schools had had at least some exposure to Logo.

Meanwhile, over on the Australian mainland, Anne McDougall, a math teacher turned computer programmer, had also discovered Logo. In 1973, Melbourne University hired McDougall to look into the possibility of computerizing some of its courses. Among the hundreds of papers she sifted through, McDougall came across a bound copy of the original memos issued two years earlier by the MIT Logo Lab. They included *Teaching Children Thinking* and *Twenty Things to Do with a Computer*. "These were just *so* different from anything else I was reading," McDougall recalled, "they sounded magic. And I remember thinking as I read them in 1973, I wonder if I will live long enough to see this happen for kids?"

In the course of her research, McDougall had travelled interstate to Tasmania, where she met Wills. The two women kept in touch. During one phone call McDougall happened to mention that she had read the Logo Lab papers. Wills replied that they had Logo running on the PDP-11 at their computer center. On hearing this McDougall was so excited she just about dropped the phone. Wills sent over a copy of the tape, which McDougall implemented on the university's computer. Soon she was using Logo in her teachers ed courses.

◆   ◆   ◆

Mention Australia and most people think of penal colonies, of convicts transported all the way across the world from England to Botany Bay and Van Diemen's Land. And to be sure, both Sydney and Hobart started out as prisons. By contrast Melbourne, Australia's second largest city and capital of the southeastern state of Victoria, was established by free settlers. The city (current population: 3.5 million) takes its name from Lord Melbourne, the British prime minister at the time of its founding in 1835; the state (or colony as it then was), from Victoria, who became Britain's queen two years later. True to its origins, Melbourne has remained a haven for free-thinkers. It prides itself on being a place where ideas are taken seriously, and where authority is challenged. Some go so far as to liken Melbourne and its independent culture to that of Massachusetts. The city even has its own MIT—the Royal *Melbourne* Institute of Technology.

One area in which Melbourne has traditionally been more free-thinking than elsewhere is curriculum development. Particularly in the city's many private schools, there has always been a willingness to ask What do we really want to do? as opposed to accepting whatever the education department tells them to. Such freedom of thought and independence of action would be crucial in establishing the world's first laptop programs in Melbourne's schools.

In 1979 a group of Melbourne-based educators, mostly math teachers, banded together to form a self-help organization called the Computing in Education Group of Victoria, or CEGV. Aware that computer literacy—whatever that meant—was going to be important, they were also frustrated by the state education department's complete failure to take any action on the matter. Interest was keen, educators flocked to join, and within a couple of years the group had over a thousand members. From the outset, one of the organization's goals was to keep its members informed about developments going on elsewhere in the world. They would bring over US luminaries like Don Rawitsch, author of *The Oregon Trail,* to tell them about the simulation software produced by MECC. In 1981, to keynote its third annual conference, the CEGV invited Seymour Papert.

Papert had actually been scheduled to give a paper at a computer conference in Melbourne the previous October. For that occasion Wills and McDougall, as ranking local Logo-philes, were deputized to look after him. Aware that Papert was a notorious no-show, they nervously kept ringing the conference organizers to find out whether he'd arrived. The pair were right to worry—as they later discovered, Papert's mentor Jean Piaget had died and, instead of coming to Melbourne, he had understandably decided to go to Europe for the funeral. Wills eventually got a message from Papert asking her to give his paper for him at the conference.

The following year, feeling confident that, this time, Papert would feel obliged to show up, McDougall and Wills decided to put on something special in his honor. The CEGV conference was due to start on a Monday. For the Sunday, the pair organized a Logo seminar at Melbourne's La Trobe University to which they invited every Logo freak in the country.

Wills met Papert at the airport and, while he was still groggy with jetlag after the long intercontinental flight, brought him to the university. She ushered the professor into the seminar room. There, to his astonishment, Papert found assembled at least 50 Logo devotees, nine or ten Tasman turtles beeping away and performing (perfect) circles, plus a variety of homegrown Logo applications running on Atari and Texas Instruments machines. Then everyone started clapping.

For Papert, it was a deeply emotional moment, one that he later confessed had moved him close to tears. To come all the way to the opposite end of the world and discover that, unbeknownst to him, this hotbed of activity—complete with a new type of turtle—had sprung up based on his ideas; well, it was simultaneously hard to believe—and enormously gratifying.

It was particularly amazing to Papert that Wills and her colleagues were not, like him and his group at MIT, university researchers doing one-off experiments. Rather, they were actual teachers employed by the education department working in real schools.

On the strength of her experience, Papert invited Wills to participate that summer in a ten-day workshop to train teachers in New York City for a computers-in-schools project sponsored by the New York Academy of Sciences. To thank her for coming, Papert generously treated Wills to oysters at the famous Oyster Bar in the Plaza Hotel on Central Park South. "It was just fantastic," Wills recalled, "the best thing to do for someone having their first trip to New York."

There would be even more interesting consequences resulting from Papert's no-show the previous year. One of Ann McDougall's masters-degree students was a computer scientist called Tony Adams. Adams got hold of an advance copy of the proceedings for the 1980 conference at which Papert had been scheduled to present a paper.[1] He showed them to his wife, Pauline, who was at the time studying to be a kindergarten teacher.

"Papert's paper captivated me," Pauline Adams recalled, "his educational philosophy really appealed to me, because what I was learning was very much based on Piaget. Tony and I were talking about it, and he said Right, I'm going to go to that conference and listen to this guy [Papert]. And of course the guy didn't turn up!"

Despite this false start, the Adamses did get involved in Logo. They would play a significant role in popularizing the language via *Learning Logo,* an influential and much-translated series of books for various computers, which they co-authored with McDougall.[2] Pauline Adams got her start in 1981, in her final year of teacher training, when she was asked by her psychology lecturer if she'd be interested in trying out Logo. The subject was a gifted eleven-year-old sixth-grader who needed a bit of extension work.

The kid's name was Charles Nevile and he was a pupil at Glamorgan, a preparatory school located in Toorak, an exclusive inner suburb of Melbourne. "I had an early version of Logo on a disk, and an Apple," Pauline recalled, "and a technical manual because I had no computer background. Each week Charles and I would meet in a room at Glamorgan and we would explore Logo together. And when we came to a problem we didn't understand I'd go home and ask Tony to explain it to me."

Sometimes Pauline would take Charles out to the university where McDougall worked because the latter had better equipment there, including a turtle. Both teacher and student were having great fun exploring with the computer. Then one day, after this had been going on for several weeks, Pauline looked up to find herself confronted by a tall, formidable-looking woman wearing jodhpurs. It was Charles's mother Liddy, and she did not look pleased. Liddy had been out riding with a friend. Now she had a bone to pick with Pauline.

The boy's grandmother claimed to have seen Charles playing with the turtle on television. Liddy was furious that her son had been on TV without her permission. Nor was she impressed by what Pauline had been doing with Charles. "I

---

1. Seymour Papert, "Redefining Childhood: The Computer Presence as an Experiment in Developmental Psychology", Proceedings of the International Federation for Information Processing, Melbourne, 1980,
   <www.papert.org/articles/Redefining Childhood.html>
2. Ann McDougall, Tony Adams & Pauline Adams, "Learning Logo on the Apple II", Prentice Hall of Australia, Sydney, 1982. Others in the series included "Learning Logo on the TRS-80 Color Computer" (1984)

said, You're not wasting my child's time on that," Nevile recalled, "there are a lot of good things, but the computer is not one of them." Though taken aback by this unexpected onslaught, Pauline held her nerve. "I certainly wasn't going to be put off by her, so I explained what I was doing and got Charles to show her."

Nevile's indignation soon wore off, to be replaced with fascination. She was—and is—an extremely bright person who is very quick to pick up on things. Nevile could see how playing with the computer was affecting her son. Now she was keen to know more. She attended lectures and conferences on educational computing. Logo captured her imagination. Within a year, Nevile had a new career playing a central role in the Australian Logo community.

◆   ◆   ◆

Liddy Nevile comes from a wealthy, high-powered family. Like Seymour Papert and Alan Kay, she was the child of a scientist, an eminent neurosurgeon who traveled widely in the course his medical career. "My father was adamant that I should be brought up in the world as opposed to Australia," Nevile recalled. While growing up she met many senior academics her father brought home. Nevile's experience was that, even though she was still a youngster, these top-level people would always take an interest in her.

Though cosmopolitan, hers was an extremely conservative sort of family, in which females were not meant to be intelligent and do things. But there could be no holding such a bright spark back. At university Nevile did a double degree in pure mathematics and law. She taught law, then married and had four children. By the time Nevile encountered Logo, she was in her mid thirties, still a lively young woman and full of energy. Her background in math gave her an unusually deep understanding of the power of the language.

"Liddy's a very forceful personality," said her old school friend, fellow parent, and horse-riding chum Caroline Dowling, "she's an initiator and an inspirer." Though not, as Nevile would herself have been the first to admit, a detail person. The two women formed a symbiotic partnership that lasted several years. Nevile would gallop ahead, throwing off ideas, leaving Dowling "trotting along behind, cleaning up the messes, picking up the bits and putting them into some sort of shape."

Nevile got into hands-on educational computing at Glamorgan, the primary school her children attended, which was flexible enough to accommodate new ideas. "In the early 80s," she recalled, "we had 16 Apples, and every child in the school from kindergarten to grade six used computers twice a week. Some of them hated it, but the point was we had kids from age three up using computers long before anyone else. And I was there every hour of every day that those computers were used, so I had the most amazing exposure to 250 kids and their teachers in all contexts and in all sorts of ways. It was a real luxury experience."

Also a profound one. "I had no prior training," Nevile said, "so I had no preconceptions about what these kids could do, and that was just the biggest bonus. Another thing was, quite by accident, I was working with a bunch of kids who were more than averagely intelligent." It seemed that no matter how hard the children were challenged, they could always go further. "What [Glamorgan] did was to give an opportunity to say, If these kids can do it, then it's an existence proof. I've always worked, not on This is what every kid will do; but on Am I dreaming, or are there kids that can do this? And if there are kids that can do this, then we can ask the question, How do we generalize this?"

One way of generalizing was to write a textbook. Since her friend Dowling was a freelance editor who had done a lot of work for university publishers, she was an obvious choice as a collaborator for Nevile in this venture. *Let's Talk Turtle*, published in 1984, was a practical, well-illustrated introductory course aimed at teaching primary school children Logo. It was also what Papert had adamantly refused to provide—a curriculum for computing in the classroom.[3]

Simultaneously Nevile helped set up an in-service arm of the Computing in Education Group of Victoria. Its mission was to provide computer-based professional development courses for teachers. Tony Adams recalled that "three or four of us put our bank cards on the table, guaranteed $2,000 each, and bought a raft of Apples, some Logo software, and a turtle." Having piled this equipment into the back of Nevile's four-wheel-drive, Dowling remembered, "we'd go out to schools and try to get teachers to have an understanding of [what] you could do with computers and what it might mean, what its broader implications were for education."

But before getting too heavily into in-service work, Nevile and Dowling flew off on a grand tour of educational research establishments overseas. Here too, the instigator and driving force was Nevile. "Liddy thought it would be a frightfully good idea to go and actually meet all these people who were doing things," Dowling recalled. "So we took off for a month and we just sort of rolled up at these places. Liddy would say, Well here we are, we're from Australia, and we do computing…and people were a bit taken aback, but they generally received us very

---

3.   Liddy Nevile & Caroline Dowling, "Let's Talk Turtle", Prentice-Hall of Australia, Sydney, 1984

well...we didn't know very much, but we were full of confidence and enthusiasm, so nobody seemed to mind that we were really starting from nothing."

In the US, the pair visited Stanford, Eugene (Oregon), Minnesota, ultimately arriving at MIT. On that first visit, they did not actually get to see Papert, who was away. (Dowling remembered taking a photograph of Papert's door with his name on it.) But they did meet and befriend other Logo Lab luminaries. During the next few years several of them—including Hal Abelson, Andy di Sessa, Brian Silverman, and Steve Ocko (the originator of Lego-Logo)—would fly down to give talks in Melbourne. Nevile would drag them off the plane, whisk them away to a CEGV meeting somewhere, then prop them up in front of an audience of eager listeners.

Nevile finally met Papert on a subsequent visit to MIT. "I wasn't at all fussed," the bold Australian recalled, "I knocked on his door and said You're Seymour Papert, and I think you probably know stuff that I need to know." The rapport between them was immediate. "She breezed in," Papert said, "and we had some wonderful conversations."

Arriving unannounced with one of her kids at the Media Lab on another occasion, Nevile had an encounter with Papert's collaborator Marvin Minsky that she would never forget. "Marvin wanted to have a Lego robot that would write on the whiteboard for him. He hung this robot thing down on one string, then of course it couldn't move horizontally. So he put it on another long string so that it now had horizontal and vertical movement, and in theory you could teach it to write the alphabet. And Marvin leant across to my ten-year-old and said, You play with Lego, don't you? And within a very short time there was a discussion going on about how you would program this robot to draw squares, which was quite a serious problem.

"There was no sense at all that Marvin had any more answers to that problem than the ten-year-old (though clearly he did). It was just two people, one of whom happened to be bigger than the other, tackling the problem. What happened in the space of a relaxed ten minutes was the greatest demonstration of education you could dream of. It wasn't condescension, Marvin wasn't saying, Come on, little boy, I'll see if you can guess the answer; it was, What do you think about this? The kid was accepted alongside the grownups [as Nevile had herself been accepted as a child by her father's colleagues]. And that was the kind of atmosphere they had created in that place."

In 1987 Nevile took part in an inquiry that looked into the results of spending on educational computing by the Australian federal government. "That was very important for my development," she recalled, "because it allowed me to think about what had been done and what could have been done. And out of that grew the notion of a school of the future and what it would look like."

Nevile subsequently got a job at the Australian Council for Educational Research, an independent non-profit organization. Her brief there was to examine the uses of educational technology. She argued that what was needed was to set up some demonstration projects to show people what could be done. Formally known as the School of the Future, this initiative soon acquired its own, suitably prophetic, banner: Sunrise.

One of the locations she selected to host a school of the future was the Museum of Victoria in central Melbourne. Nevile had what seemed to her good reasons for making this unusual choice. A museum offered collections of cultural artifacts, thus was obviously a more suitable place for kids to learn than a school. Why, she demanded, should kids be constrained by what she termed the "peculiar Victorian world of the classroom? It was an impoverished environment, it was low in adult input, it didn't have any cultural artifacts around it."

Nevile was, it will be noted, no fan of conventional schooling. Her experience with her own children had been that they were learning all the time—except when at school. There, according to their teachers, they went to sleep. The teachers laughed, but Nevile didn't think it was funny: "I got the idea that my kids weren't doing very well in school because school isn't a place for kids to learn." This, as we have seen, was not an unusual idea at the time. Many people, including Papert and his circle, were into de-schooling, opting to take their kids out of the school system and educate them at home.

A space at the museum was made available for the Sunrise school. In a lovely room desktop computers, one for each kid, were set up. Students from a nearby public secondary school would come there two days a week. (A fatal compromise, as it turned out. The kids saw their days at the museum as an addition to ordinary school, and resented the imposition accordingly.)

Nevile and her associates decided to launch the Sunrise school with a bang, by throwing a party. In April 1988 invitations were sent out to various interested persons, including—cheekily—the principals of local schools. "Students and teachers in conventional schools are subject to the culture of their schools", read the information accompanying the invitations, "and generally this does not support autonomous learning by the students or teaching by the teachers. For this reason, a school was not considered to be a suitable site for this project."

The gauntlet had been thrown down. Would anyone dare to pick it up?

15

A PRINCIPAL WITH INTEREST

Melbourne's climate is mild, but famously capricious. The evening of Liddy Nevile's Sunrise school launch party was a shocker; it was raining cats and dogs with the occasional hailstorm thrown in for good measure. To make matters worse, a municipal workers' strike had halted all forms of public transport. Traffic throughout the city's central business district had long since ground to a standstill. The strike had also closed the museum, forcing the location of the party to be switched at the last minute to a nearby church hall. Somehow, amid the chaos the guests all managed eventually to straggle in, many of them dripping wet.

Despite this damp start, the party was a great success. The federal industry minister, a well-known local character, got the ball rolling, cracking jokes that had everyone laughing. The keynote speaker was Bill Higginson, the Canadian researcher who had worked with Papert at MIT. "Bill dropped in some wonderful ideas," Nevile recalled. They infused, she felt, "a strong Seymour presence" to the proceedings.

After the speeches, one of Nevile's staff took her aside and told her that an old man had come in off the street—what should they do? Sure enough, wandering around among the guests was a scruffy-looking, unshaven individual dressed in a bedraggled suit. Nevile guessed that he was a street person, no doubt completely harmless. Probably just wanted somewhere to shelter from the rain and maybe a bite to eat. And since they had heaps of sandwiches, no problem, she told her assistant, just leave him alone.

Some time later, the bedraggled figure approached Nevile. She realized that he wasn't quite as old or as unkempt as she had originally thought. But he was sporting about ten days' growth of beard, at a time when designer stubble was not yet in fashion. The fellow seemed terribly excited about the Sunrise initiative. He asked her lots of questions. An enthusiastic crank, Nevile thought, a crazy man off the street. She dismissed him from her mind.

Later that evening, Nevile was astonished to get a phone call from her friend Caroline Dowling, who happened also to be a board member of Methodist Ladies' College, a local private school. Downing said "Look, I've just had the most bizarre fax from our principal, David Loader. He says we need to set aside $10,000 for research *immediately.*" The money was a consultancy fee for Nevile's employers, the Australian Council for Educational Research, to help MLC set up a Sunrise class of its own.

The identity of the mysterious street person was now revealed. Like the other guests, Loader had been caught in the rain without a coat and got soaked. The explanation for his whiskers was that the principal was growing a beard for the school play.

Loader had been a bit insulted by the invitation to the Sunrise party, which asserted that conventional schools were not suitable places to do experiments on the future of learning. How could a museum of dead artifacts be a better place to learn than a school? At least, in a school, most of the exhibits were still alive.

But the invitation also struck a chord. Loader had never forgotten reading the American education reformer John Holt: "Almost every child, on the first day he sets foot in a school building," Holt wrote in *The Underachieving School*, "is smarter, more curious, less afraid of what he doesn't know, better at finding and figuring things out, more confident, resourceful, persistent, and independent, than he will ever again be in his schooling."[1] For Loader, Holt's criticism of school had always been a challenge. MLC's principal maintained a rare degree of empathy for the children in his care.

Now, interest aroused, Loader checked his diary and found that he already had appointments for the evening of the Sunrise party. The School of the Future would take precedence; the appointments were changed.[2] At the party, Loader was intrigued by what he heard. "I thought, This lady's got something—individual computers for kids might help us achieve what we want to do." Characteristically, he was keen to get cracking right away.

Thus began what is arguably the most important adventure in the history of educational computing. Its instigator and, for the crucial early years, protagonist

---

1.   John Holt, "The Underachieving School", Penguin Books Australia, Sydney, 1971, p23

2.   David Loader, "Reflections of a Learning Community: Views on the Introduction of Laptops at MLC", ed Irene Grasso & Margaret Fallshaw, Methodist Ladies College, Kew, 1993, pp9 & 21

was a maverick in a most unlikely setting—the visionary, risk-taking principal of a conservative private school for girls.

◆　　◆　　◆

Encountered at a gathering of his peers—the headmasters and mistresses of independent schools—David Loader looked out of place. They were either prim-looking ladies dressed in frilly high-necked blouses and blue stockings or solemn-looking men in dark blazers and striped (old-school) ties. Loader wore a slightly-dishevelled tan-colored suit, with the buttons of his shirt collar unfastened. On his wrist was a watch with a web on its face and a spider at the end of its second hand, a touch of whimsy which was also a statement. It said: I am not like you.

David Loader is a slightly-built, thoughtful-looking man of average height, with wavy brown hair, and blue-grey eyes. His signature expression is a huge cheeky grin, which is sometimes accompanied by a matching wink. When doing caricatures of their principal, the kids at MLC would always start by drawing the great toothy grin, then fill in the rest of him around it. His staff could ask Loader to come to middle school assembly dressed as the Mad Professor, give him a white coat and tell him what to say, and he'd just walk in and do it, clowning around to the delight of the girls. On one occasion, he had even ridden a Harley-Davidson into (and around) a school hall where a staff social function was in progress.

But beneath this light-hearted, theatrical exterior, Loader was essentially a shy soul, a loner whose personality compounded sensitivity and naivete with stubborn determination and—as his opponents at tennis, poker, and lawn bowls would tell you—a fierce competitiveness.

Loader's manner is informal, friendly, and inviting; his voice soft, slightly nasal, and warm. Longtime associates assert that while Loader is confident, they have never known him to be arrogant. Teachers—especially senior ones—tend to spend too much of their time in sage mode: they make better talkers than listeners. Loader by contrast will often do his opposite number the courtesy of inquiring, What do you think? At the conclusion of a PTA meeting, he would ask the parents, quite sincerely, if the gathering had been useful for them. And they would go home happy, feeling that they had been involved in a dialog.

Loader's defining characteristic is undoubtedly his openness to innovation. Ideas excited him. He was the sort of person who would say Let's do it, let's run with it, let's not be held back by what-if. Members of the school council would sometimes feel that they almost literally had to grab their principal by the back of his pants, to stop him dashing off in pursuit of some seemingly crazy new idea. To those who accused him of being a dreamer, Loader would in later years respond with a favorite quote from Paulo Coelho: "It is the possibility of having a dream come true that makes life interesting".

Blessed with apparently boundless energy, Loader was by temperament restless. Every few years he would head off overseas on study leave, looking for the next educational thrust. At such times his staff would eye each other anxiously, wondering what David would bring back this time. Returning on one occasion after attending a Quaker retreat in Pendle Hill, Pennsylvania, Loader introduced a non-traditional seating arrangement—concentric squares—at a staff meeting at his school. In such a scheme, because there is no "front" for speakers to face, you cannot always see who is speaking. Loader himself made a point of sitting in the back row, gleefully relishing the discomfort this unconventional format caused some of the teachers.

In addition to backing his own intuition, Loader was also a great supporter of initiative in the teachers under his leadership. A good judge of character, he would always encourage those who worked for him to take risks, not something that many school principals are prepared to do. At MLC, anyone who wanted to try something new and different would be given the opportunity. For this, Loader was adored by his staff—or at least, by its more adventurous members.

"My image is always of David out there in front, racing along with the clouds scattering behind him," laughed Ruth Baker, a teacher who worked with Loader throughout his 18 years as principal of Methodist Ladies' College. "And we're all running behind, sort of picking up the pieces and glueing them together to make actual things happen. And part of David's success, I guess, in whatever was achieved was that he did have a lot of people who got caught up in his ideas and were able to support him enthusiastically. So he had a real fan club of people at MLC who were prepared to give it a go."

◆   ◆   ◆

David Norman Loader was born in Brisbane, Queensland, on 26 January 1941. His father came originally from Victoria, having been transferred to Queensland by the bank he worked for. Loader senior left school early, working his way up to become a branch manager, ultimately heading the bank's internal audit. Two of David's uncles were similarly employed, albeit in different banks. When David was aged five, the bank transferred his father again, this time to Sydney. The family moved down to a new and sparsely populated suburb where the little boy had few playmates. The first school he attended was 25 minutes away by bus. No other local kids went there. Though his was a loving family, Loader grew up a lonely child who lived chiefly in his own imagination.

School made him withdraw even further. "My memory of my classroom", Loader recalled, "was of a place where I didn't quite belong, either socially or academically. Socially it was an artificial environment where we sat in rows facing the front and where we were strongly discouraged from relating to our peers. It was a place where I had no personal authority, my assignment was to do as I was told. This was the teacher's room and not mine. It was a place where I had no personal voice, there were right answers and wrong answers and the teacher's answers were the right ones."[3] "I had been silenced by my education," Loader reflected, "it had taken away my authentic voice, it had taken away my self-confidence and my self-esteem." Not that there had been much of either to begin with.

He was rescued from solitude by religion. Joining the Anglican church gave him entree to a whole other world, one that was full of meaning for the adolescent. He threw himself into teaching Sunday school and youth fellowship activities. At the end of his years at North Sydney Technical High School, Loader won a teaching scholarship to university. Not seeing the need for tertiary education, his father encouraged David to follow in his footsteps at the bank. To please him, the younger Loader even sat the bank's entrance test. He did well in the exam, but chose to continue his studies.

Sydney University was for the most part not much better than school. Loader remained filled with inner doubts about himself. He majored in mathematics, which had been his best subject at school, but his academic record was dismal. Once again, religion was his salvation. Loader joined the Evangelical Union, a university club with several hundred members, participating in it so enthusiastically that he was ultimately elected club president. At one stage he even considered becoming a minister, before finally deciding that teaching was his vocation.

Through his involvement with the Evangelical Union, Loader discovered an unexpected talent for managing people. Also through the EU he met his future wife, Ros, the daughter of an Anglican bishop, who was training to be a social worker. They were married in 1964, the same year Loader began teaching at Cabramatta High School, a public school in a tough West Sydney suburb. For him it was a time of great excitement. "I threw myself into the teaching, set up student clubs, volunteered for too much. As well I worked with young people

---

3.   David Loader, "The Inner Principal", Falmer Press, London, 1997, p116

outside the school in sailing camps and church. There was the fervor of a missionary who was out to change the world."[4] For the first time in his life, Loader had begun to assert himself.

In 1967, impressed by the young man's zeal, a Canadian visitor invited him to come over and work in boys' camps in Alberta. Loader applied to the New South Wales Education Department for a year's leave of absence. When this was refused, displaying a very Australian attitude towards authority, he decided go anyway.

The Canadian experience was in many ways a turning point in his life. For one thing, it meant leaving the security of tenure in the public school system. This was something that, coming from a background of strongly Labor politics, Loader would probably never have otherwise contemplated. The young couple deliberately chose Edmonton because it was the opposite of everything they knew. They exchanged the sun and sea of Sydney for the cold and mountains of the West Canadian prairie. Living in a country where they had no past was, for both of them, a liberating experience.

At this time, the late sixties, the progressive revival was in full swing. In the Canadian senior high schools where he taught, Loader had a revelation. He participated in an experiment where he had to teach two different ways, one didactically; the other where the students had to discover things for themselves. The experience transformed Loader into a lifelong advocate of the ideals of John Dewey. Students should have a voice (as he had not) and take responsibility for their own learning. Teachers should relinquish their dominion over the classroom, giving it back to its rightful owners, the young people.

On returning to Australia, Loader got a job in Sydney at a private boys school, which was run along military lines. The experience was an eye-opener for someone who had no prior knowledge of the private school system, indeed who hardly knew anyone that had been to a private school. Like many schools built on the British model, this one had a compulsory cadet corps.

With the Vietnam War (in which some 8,000 Australians fought alongside Americans) still raging, Loader objected to the notion of mandatory military service. He suggested to the headmaster that the school should offer an alternative. To his surprise, the head agreed and made Loader himself responsible for the creation of a program of social service. It was Loader's first experience of instigating

---

4.   David Loader, in "This I Believe", ed John Marsden, Random House, Sydney, 1996, p212

substantial change in an institution. During this period, he completed his master of education degree. His dissertation was entitled "The Principal as Leader."

Loader did not have to wait long for a chance to put his ideas on leadership into practice. By his thirtieth birthday, he was head of a beautifully-appointed girls' school in the New South Wales country town of Orange. When Loader arrived, the school was on its last legs. Within a few years he had reversed the decline. "It was a time when lots of change was being suggested," Loader recalled, "and with a small school and a hand-picked young staff that you worked with and were influenced by, you were able to do things that you couldn't do in other situations."

Like most small country towns, Orange was a conservative sort of place. To many locals, the mildly-left-leaning Loaders seemed like communists. But the children loved what was happening at their school. "We were into exploration, invention, experimentation, all of those things," Loader said, "and it went down really well with the kids, because they were bored by the alternative. So they went home happy, they told other people, and our enrolments went up."

For six years everything went wonderfully well. Loader managed the difficult transition of the school from single-sex to coed. That meant having to compete with another school in town, an old-fashioned boys' college which was making heavy weather of going coed. Parents started switching their children to Loader's school. Eventually, with the rival institution on the verge of closing down, Loader was asked by church authorities if he would take it over. In a decision he would come to regret, Loader agreed.

The merger meant taking aboard some of the more conservative elements in the community, several of whom joined the school council. Tension grew, as the reactionary parents and council members pushed for a return to basics. To a progressive educator like Loader, this was anathema.

Under intense pressure his health began to suffer. Loader ended up suffering a brain hemorrhage. It was a devastating experience: at one stage his doctor told him that he would never work again. For someone as passionate about his job as Loader was, that would have been a fate worse than death. In the event, he was off work for six months. It took a long time because he had to learn how to walk again. Loader did eventually resume his duties, but the damage had been done. He began applying for jobs at other schools. One of them was Methodist Ladies' College in Melbourne.

The biggest single-sex school in Australia presented a daunting prospect for a country-school principal. Loader's first reaction on seeing MLC at the time of his interview was, appropriately enough under the circumstances, scriptural: he was

David and it was Goliath. Nonetheless, he was determined not to make any con-cessions to conservatism. To send a clear signal that he was an innovator, Loader made a point of wearing a bright red tie at his interview .

He needn't have worried—the selection committee was soon convinced that Loader was the outstanding candidate for the job. The school was stagnating: if it were to survive, change had to be embraced. At 38, David Loader was still very young (and not a Methodist). No matter: in mid 1978 the committee announced that it had appointed him MLC's fifth principal.

16

ABOUT A SCHOOL

When Methodist Ladies' College first opened its doors to students in 1882, Melbourne was a boom town, a shiny new metropolis that could compare—favorably—with that other nineteenth-century urban upstart, San Francisco. Like San Francisco, Melbourne rose to prominence on the back of a gold rush. Gold was discovered in country Victoria in 1851, just two years after similar finds in California.

"The inflow of gold-rush migrants in just two years exceeded the grand total of convicts in the eighty years of transportation....Twice as many migrants came to Australia in the 1850s as went to the United States in the three decades from 1800 to 1830. Golden Victoria was the main goal for these migrants, and its population jumped in ten years from 76,000 to the astonishing total of 540,000."[1]

"The gold-rush generation [was] conspicuously fertile, and during the 1870s and 1880s their offspring were seeking jobs and a place to settle. The mining towns had little to offer, and the focus of economic grown and social energy turned to the metropolis."[2] In much less than a lifetime, a bayside city of remarkable grandeur sprang up, "teeming with wealth and humanity".

Melbourne dazzled new arrivals like the Reverend E.H. Sugden. "The city is enormous and as big in extent as Paris," Sugden wrote in 1886, "It is a world's wonder." The previous year his compatriot, the English journalist George Augustus Sala, coined a phrase to describe the phenomenon. He called it "Marvellous Melbourne."[3]

---

1. Geoffrey Blainey, "A Shorter History of Australia", Mandarin, Melbourne, 1995, p72
2. Janet McCalman, "Journeyings: The Biography of a Middle-Class Generation, 1920–1990", Melbourne University Press, 1993, p38
3. Graeme Davison, "The Rise and Fall of Marvellous Melbourne", Melbourne University Press, 1978, p11

The newcomers brought their religion with them. "Methodism travelled well....It was perfect for the pioneers. It preached the disciplines of self-care and hard work which made the difference between success and failure....[T]he Methodists were often the first to erect a place of worship in the new settlements and towns...."[4]

With so many itinerant Methodist ministers preaching in Victoria, there was a need for a school for their daughters (a school for their sons, Wesley College, had been established in Melbourne some fifteen years earlier). While wishing to provide the best education possible for the girls, the founders of Methodist Ladies' College encapsulated their ultimate purpose in the school's motto: *Deo Domuique*, "For God and Home". At MLC, there would be none of the frivolous pursuits that other schools for young ladies catered for: dancing lessons, for example, were specifically excluded from the college curriculum.

The school was built in the gothic revival style, on a large paddock, in what was then the outer eastern suburb of Kew. The original, three-story edifice is dominated by an elaborately-ornamented tower at the tip of whose spire sits the school's symbol, an eight-pointed star. To see MLC, even today, is to be instantly reminded of Ronald Searle's famous (fictitious) creation, St Trinian's.

Melbourne's Methodists built in humble stuccoed brick, in contrast to the better-endowed Anglicans, Presbyterians, and Catholics, who, as one sharp-eyed observer noted, favored real stone for their schools.[5] "From its earliest years [MLC] has been large relative to other schools...the aim has always been to keep fees as low as efficiency would permit and to admit girls from as wide a socio-economic range as possible."[6] With an enrolment that would top two thousand, the College could not afford to be exclusive.

Though a private school, MLC was never as snobbish as some of its rivals. Unlike them, the College was willing to accept girls whose fathers were "in trade". That is, they were not professional people such as doctors and lawyers, but builders, shopkeepers, and the like. The school prided itself on the fact that many of its parents would scrimp or do without in order to foot the bill for their daughters' schooling.

In its first ninety-seven years, Methodist Ladies' College had just four principals, all of them Methodist ministers. The third, Harold Wood, who presided over the College from 1939 to 1966 was, according to the official school history,

4.   McCalman, pp31–33
5.   Janet McCalman
6.   Ailsa G. Thomson Zainu'ddin, "They Dreamt of a School: A Centenary History of Methodist Ladies' College Kew 1882–1982, Hyland House, Melbourne, 1982, pxix

a man of "great personal charm."[7] Stories about Dr Wood—as he liked to be known—are legion. Former colleagues remembered him as a tremendously dynamic figure, with a prodigious memory for the names and faces of former pupils. After preaching out in the country somewhere, Dr Wood "would meet a woman at the [church] door, and ask her how her how her daughter was, who had left the school 15 years before—and this is the mother he would recognize."

Dr Wood was a strict authoritarian. He believed that every section of the school's affairs should be under the direct control of the principal, who invariably knew what was best. Staff meetings were held as seldom as possible. At such meetings, if a member of staff ever expressed any conclusions contrary to Dr Wood's wishes, he would simply say, "Thank you, but I would point out to you that the final decision is mine."[8]

In some of his students, Dr Wood inspired fear as well as awe. The poet Lynne Strahan, a pupil at the school in the 1950s, recalled MLC as having been run by "a male principal of threatening physical substance who had the face of a cross determined baby...he blew along the corridor in academic cloak and ministerial suit, while girls who weren't quick enough to make a getaway edged into the walls grinning stupidly or smiling unctuously." This frightening figure would materialize suddenly in classes, "like an escapee from a picture in the Last Judgment."[9]

Ruth Baker was another old collegian who looked back on her days at MLC with an unsentimental eye. The daughter of a Methodist minister, Baker recalled being sickened when, in her final year at the school, she was one of several seniors assigned by Dr Wood to take down the names of girls who happened to be talking to boys on the train to and from school, and report them to him. It was, she thought, "an appalling thing to ask a sixteen-year-old girl to do."

Baker was also turned off by the school's arbitrary attitudes to uniform. "The headmistress decided that the girls should wear gray petticoats under their gray skirts. So we had to go home and dye our petticoats gray, and I thought that was an intrusion and an unreasonable thing. And she used to stand at the bottom of the stairs—I mean, this is 1956, we're not back in 1910—and she'd look up our skirts as we walked up the stairs to see if we had our gray petticoats on.

"Then Dr Wood decided that he didn't like the look of the girls wearing gray jumpers with the school's green-check summer dresses. He thought we should all

---

7.   Ibid, pxx
8.   Ibid, p351
9.   Lynne Strahan, "The Half-Open Door", ed Patricia Grimshaw & Lynne Strahan, Hale & Iremonger, Sydney, 1982, pp100 & 104

wear green cardigans. And I was incensed because my mother was a widow by this stage, and we were pretty poor—always had been poor, obviously, being a parson's family—I just thought it was appalling that we had to buy this extra, unnecessary garment just to please Dr Wood's particular, personal taste."

Baker voiced her complaints in a letter to the school magazine. For this act of outspokenness, she was summoned by one of the senior teachers and severely reprimanded. Twenty-some years later, circumstances compelled her to apply for a position as an English teacher at MLC. Dr Wood had retired by this time, to be replaced by Ron Woodgate. He, like his predecessor, had been a missionary in Tonga, but was a milder, less forceful man. Coming back to the school was a shock for Baker, because so little had changed in the interim. "Even the people were the same," she recalled. "I couldn't believe it, the first four people I met had all been my teachers."

MLC was at this time at a fairly low ebb, according to Lawrie Turner, who was then chairman of the school council, the College's governing body. From a peak of over 2,000, enrolments were down to around 1,700. "The school was kept largely alive," Turner felt, "by a group of five or six female teachers who were old girls of the school, and who were committed to it…. But it couldn't continue like that—it needed a principal who was going to take it on."

In the late seventies, society's values were changing rapidly. "Students were beginning to assert their position," Turner said, "staff were beginning to demand more recognition, parents were no longer giving unqualified support to the school. There was a time when a principal could have sent for parents and said, Look, your girl's kicking over the traces, and they would have immediately come down on the side of the school. But this was a period when parents were no longer coming down on the side of the school, [they were saying] If my girl wants to sleep with her boyfriend up in the school dormitory, so what?"

In the last years of the decade MLC soldiered on, a very formal, old-fashioned, hierarchical school. The teachers would be having their tea in the staff room at morning recess, Mr Woodgate would walk in, and they'd all leap to their feet. The principal was always addressed as "Mr Woodgate", a legacy of Dr Wood, who believed that "it savored of cheap familiarity for a minister to allow himself to be addressed by his first name."[10]

Ruth Baker would never forget the first staff meeting that David Loader attended. In strode this handsome young man with a huge grin on his face. His first words were, "Call me David."

---

10.   Zainu'ddin, p288

◆   ◆   ◆

"They were stunned by David's youth," Ros Loader recalled, "he felt very young after the last two incumbents." But the shock soon wore off, to be replaced by a feeling of liberation. "They were ready for change, so it was a very welcoming environment," Ros said. "It felt like a group of women that had been kept in chains, who had never been given titles or leadership or responsibility, so there was a lot of energy to be released."

The first changes were largely symbolic. There was, for example, the matter of the chair in which the principal traditionally sat on the stage at morning assembly. It had a big back, and side arms, and it was elevated above the lesser chairs on which the other members of staff sat. It was, in short, not so much a chair as a throne. "David came home from assembly that first day," Ros recalled, "and he said, I'm not going to sit there."

Then there was the business of the gowns that the teachers wore. Writing about their first days at MLC, the kids would invariably comment on how their teachers seemed like witches in their black cloaks, all sort of medieval-looking. Baker and two of her friends sensed that change was in the air. "We looked at each other one day, and we said Let's stop wearing our gowns and see what happens. And all three of us stopped wearing our gowns, we started going to class without them, and other teachers saw us, and they started leaving their gowns behind, and gradually it spread.

"Some people can't just do things like that, they have to get a ruling from the principal. So somebody asked David what his ruling was, and he said Well, it is the custom. But the message was, I'm not going to discipline people if they don't wear them. So it just spread and spread until, in the end, gowns disappeared and they're only brought out now on formal occasions like speech nights. And it was just one of those little things. If we'd done that previously, I reckon within 48 hours we'd have got a memo to say that we'd been observed not wearing our gowns and would we please wear them. But we were able to do it, and it wasn't just David, people like the chief of staff didn't feel that they needed to come and discipline us. And that had to do with the whole way that David changed people's attitudes."

Pretty soon staff were aware that Loader was asking questions about everything, beginning with the organization of the school. One of his first large-scale initiatives was to create a new structure, dividing up the College into four smaller entities—junior school, junior secondary school, middle school, and senior school. This was a measure designed to reduce the hierarchical nature of the College, to decentralize control and devolve autonomy. At his induction service (in which Dr Wood participated) Loader had made explicit his notion of leadership: "Some principals still see themselves as being at the apex of a pyramid of authority", he said, "I see myself as being at the center of a network of relationships."[11]

In his first years as principal, Loader kept challenging the perceptions of his staff. "He shook everything up in a relatively short period of time," Baker recalled, "David told us that we'd just got to look at what we were doing much more critically." To start examining the issues Loader set up a series of committees. These examined how teachers managed their classrooms, how they taught, what they taught, how they wrote reports, all the way down to details like whether the school motto was still appropriate.

Loader brought in speakers from the outside, the gadflies of the educational institutions of the time, to put up different ways of seeing things. He laid on in-service sessions to enable teachers to update their old skills or learn new ones. (Later, when it came to computers, he would again employ both strategies to good effect.) One way or another, Loader made sure everyone at the College participated in the re-thinking process.

"We saw him as liberating," Baker said, "giving people the opportunity to become involved in discussions, to be in a position where they were part of a decision-making process in a way that hadn't happened before. Before that you were just told: You're an English teacher—go to your classroom and teach your English, this is what you teach, here's a commercial textbook and some novels for the kids to read. So there was no curriculum statement, there was nothing."

Loader demonstrated a knack for picking strong leaders to manage the changes, whether hiring them in from outside or promoting them up from within. It helped that MLC was a big organization with a staff of several hundred teachers. In that big a pool, he only had to find five or ten people to fire with an idea, they would then persuade their colleagues, and so it would ripple out. It also helped to be operating in an institution that was well-established, had prestige, academic credibility, money, and a governing council that was well-disposed toward change.

All of those factors combined to give Loader a solid base from which to operate. It was, Baker thought, "a very supportive environment...he was a male in a school dominated by female teachers who were just emerging at a time when feminism was really taking off. We were being given the opportunity to shape

---

11. Ibid, p396

things, to make decisions, to do things that made a difference on a big scale. So we were willing to go along with him, we were prepared to give him a go."

(The feminist push was one reason why the computer initiative at MLC would ultimately be so successful. Computers were—are—an area in which a strong gender imbalance prevails. Technology tends to be perceived as a boy thing. The idea that girls needed special treatment to redress that imbalance made it easier to get the computer message across.)

By 1985, six years after becoming principal, Loader had turned the school around. Enrolments were up, as the community perceived that the College was an exciting modern place to send its daughters. At the same time, facilities were improving. MLC had celebrated its centenary in 1982 by splurging three and a half million Australian dollars on a new teaching block.

Loader was not the sort to rest on his laurels. Caroline Dowling, who had joined the school council as a parent representative, recalled a big discussion at council meetings. "David wanted something special," she said, something that was going to differentiate MLC from other schools in what was—and remains—a highly competitive market. "For some reason he got it into his head that it should be languages," Dowling recalled. She was horrified: "I thought that this was crazy, because there were other schools at that time that were doing languages, and this wasn't a new thing."

At one council meeting where Loader announced that he was going to make this push for languages, Dowling suggested an alternative. On a piece of paper she wrote, "You've got the wrong end of the stick: if you do want to do something that'll make the school stand out, you've got to get into computing." She folded up the note and passed it to him. Dowling recalled that when Loader read her note, "he looked a bit surprised, then later he asked me, Did I know anyone? And I said Yes, you need to talk to Liddy Nevile."

Shortly after this exchange, Loader got the opportunity to meet Nevile, at the launch party for the Sunrise school. Prior to this encounter, Loader had not been thinking about computers; to use his word, he "stumbled" upon them. Then, having stumbled, he picked himself up and went to see for himself what Nevile was doing at the Sunrise school in the museum.

"What I found", Loader wrote, "were some interesting, highly-motivated people, a constructivist philosophy, and a technology-rich environment. Each student had a computer, not one machine between twenty or thirty students, or even between two or three students, each student had access to a machine. While it was the learning, not the computer, that was the focus of this class, the computer's presence provided the opportunity for the new formulation of the classroom, the means by which a new form of learning could be achieved and the trial of some different roles for teachers."[12]

MLC would pick up the gauntlet that Nevile had thrown down. Loader would show the world that the sun could also rise in an existing school.

◆   ◆   ◆

The Sunrise school was not Loader's first exposure to educational computing. Before Sunrise, however, like many progressives, he had been concerned that the technology might swamp the educational process. It would be a disaster, he felt, if the computer were to dictate, CAI-style, to the teacher and children what they were to do. If that was how computers were going to be, he wanted none of them.

Loader had had a long-running dialog on the subject of computers with Cliff Hooker, one of his oldest and closest friends from Sydney University days. A research physicist turned philosophy professor with an interest in cognitive science, Hooker had been deeply affected by *Mindstorms* and the powerful ideas Logo embodied. He persuaded the kindergarten where his kids went to buy some microcomputers, and implemented Logo on them. Hooker went to the school at nights to help organize their program. "I trained a big team of parent volunteers," Hooker said, "not just in using Logo, but in the philosophy behind Logo, because I didn't want them getting in the road of the kids, telling the kids how to do things. And I was talking to David off and on all that time, whenever we met, about what was going on and what its educational value was."

Hooker recalled that when he told Loader about Logo, his friend got quite excited. But not excited enough to actually do anything. "Cliff said I should read *Mindstorms*," Loader recalled. He did and was very impressed. "So when I met Liddy, who was talking about Papert, she was talking about someone I did know, but in a theoretical sense rather than a practical sense. And at that time I had no sense of the significance of the turtle."

Computers did not click with Loader until he saw the potential inherent in the idea of each kid having a computer. This was entirely consistent with his philosophy of empowering students, of saying that school should be a place where young people have authority. "And for him the empowering is not merely intellectual," Hooker said, "it's emotional, it's intended to give kids what he needed as a young person but didn't get." For David Loader, the technology would always be a means, never an end.

---

12.   David Loader, "The Inner Principal", Falmer Press, London, 1997, p89

17

THE FIFTH OPTION

At 55, with retirement just around the corner, Merle Atherton was an unlikely choice as form teacher for the first Sunrise class at Methodist Ladies' College. A petite, matronly woman with a friendly, open manner, Atherton taught geography and history, as well as coordinating seventh grade at the school. Although a very experienced teacher, she was a low-profile person who seemed quite conservative. But David Loader had excellent reasons for picking Atherton in preference to a younger, more with-it teacher. He knew that her track record and the fact that other teachers trusted her would give the school's computer initiative instant credibility. And he was aware that Atherton's conventional appearance masked an adventurous spirit.

So far from being set in her ways, Atherton was in fact a sprightly enthusiast with a lifelong love of learning. Spending the last few years of her career doing exactly the same as she had done the previous few years would have bored Atherton to tears. And, she felt sure, would have made her a pretty boring teacher.

It was Merle's daughter, Kim, who first got her mother interested in computing. "She said, You'd love computers, Mum, your mind works the right way, you really ought to go and do a course." So Merle did, during the school holidays, in a little church hall, for five days, when she was around 50 years old. "They advertised in the local paper," she recalled, "it said Beginners to Experts—I didn't even know where the computer turned on."

Atherton was soon mad on machines. She went on to complete a graduate diploma in computer education at a local university. One of the electives in this course was Logo. "I did [Logo], and it fascinated me." So much so that Atherton wrote to the principal to ask Can we do Logo? And though his answer (for the moment) was No, Loader gave her full credit for asking.

At MLC, Atherton did everything possible to pursue her new passion. Any time a computer-related in-service course came up, she would apply, and Loader would always allow her the time off to do it. She bought ready-made software for her geography classes that students could use, two at a time. But this was unsatis-factory, because the girls had no real control over these programs. They were little more than games really, just curriculum enhancers.

Loader wrote up his visit to the Sunrise school in the museum in *The Link*, MLC's in-house newsletter. After reading what he had written, Atherton went to the principal to ask his permission to go and see this school. Unbeknownst to her, Ruth Baker had independently done the same thing, as had Alan Mapp, a math teacher. In November 1988, the three got together for a discussion with Loader and Liddy Nevile. Out of this meeting came a proposal by the three teachers, vol-unteering to run a Sunrise class at MLC. This would be a pilot program involving one seventh-grade class.

The program's emphasis, ran the proposal, would be "on the creation of an environment in which an integrated approach to learning would be encouraged. Students would be free to explore ideas, to make connections and to use technol-ogy in an active process in accordance with the concepts developed by Seymour Papert and his associates at the MIT Media Laboratory."[1] The emphasis would be on student-initiated learning activities which fostered independent learning. Teachers and students would be partners in the enterprise.

When they heard about this initiative, some MLC staff members expressed reservations. Loader remembered meetings at which the correctness of what the school was proposing to do was questioned. What if children didn't complete the syllabus? What if parents withdrew their children? What about students who didn't get this opportunity? Overall, however, the staff were supportive and the principal decided to proceed with the trial.

Out of the eight seventh-grade classes MLC ran that year, a class of 30 twelve-year-old girls was chosen, more or less at random. The unsuspecting parents were informed of the choice at a meeting during the first week of term in February (when the Australian school year begins). Atherton was delegated to explain the concept of the Sunrise class. "I put it to them that what we were trying to do was give the girls a little bit of responsibility for their learning." At the same time, she reassured parents that the curriculum would not be abandoned, that computing would be integrated with the regular subjects, like English and History (and Bible Studies).

Not surprisingly, the parents had a lot of concerns. This was, after all, a very new idea in what for all Loader's innovations was still a very traditional school.

---

1.   Merle Atherton, Ruth Baker & Alan Mapp, "The Sunrise Class: An Action Research Project in Year 7", 1989, unpublished paper, November 1988

Atherton did her best to address their concerns honestly. It helped that she was a teacher of vast experience. Most parents seemed positive, but as they later confessed to her, many went away feeling nervous about the experiment.

They needn't have worried: it quickly became apparent that the girls were happy with the new style of learning, and putting it to good use. At this stage, the students did not have the computers in their own classroom. Rather, they had access to a computer room, where they were free to come and go as they pleased. When the girls wanted to work on the computers, they would just write their names on the board, then they could leave the classroom. "They were given a large degree of trust," Atherton recalled. "At the same time, there was a curriculum that they had to get through—it wasn't like one of those schools where if you don't want to do maths or science, you could go and sit in a tree."

Because the initiative had been thrown together so quickly, there had been no time for elaborate preparation. "The first teachers in the Sunrise class needed to acquire knowledge of *LogoWriter* in particular very quickly—over the Christmas vacation," wrote Ruth Baker. "This meant that their experience and understanding were only marginally ahead of the students and, fairly rapidly, some students' knowledge overtook that of the teachers. This was particularly significant in developing their relationship as partners in this new learning experience."[2]

In addition to *LogoWriter*, the girls were also challenged to design build a moving robot creature using Lego-Logo. This was a relatively unstructured experience where they worked in groups. "The ingenuity and originality of their creations was startling", Baker reported.[3] (She remembered attending a conference at which some academic gave a talk on this very difficult and challenging task he'd set his university students, to design and make a moving creature, and what a complex exercise that was. "And I thought Well, we gave it to our year sevens, and we didn't think anything about it being complex, and they jolly well did it!")

LogoWriter allowed the students to write programs that blended graphics and narrative. "It was absolutely brilliant," Atherton recalled. "In history we did a journey down the Nile, and the children could actually draw their own graphics, they drew a map of the Nile, and they put in the Pyramids and the Sphinx." The program took you to the Pyramids, then the page would change to one on which there was a big pyramid, together with some writing about it.

---

2.   Ruth Baker, "Personal Computing for Enhanced Learning," Information Technology & Education Conference, Sydney, March 1994

3.   Ruth Baker, "Sunrise and Beyond: An Overview of Changes in the Junior Secondary School of Methodist Ladies College since 1988", unpublished paper, July 1993

Then came a problem. "One child came to me and said, When I go back from the big pyramid page, I'm back at the start of the map, but I want to be back at the Pyramids page. So I just said to the class, we've got a problem, who can solve it? And two girls responded, one said I'd do it this way; the other said, Yes that's a good idea, but I wouldn't do it that way, I'd do it this way. And they were both things that I hadn't thought of, two totally separate solutions of the problem, and they would share that with the class." Such sharing of ideas went on throughout the year.

The class had several students with learning difficulties. One of the best things to come out of the Sunrise class experience, in Atherton's view, was that these girls took to the computers so well that they became resources for the others. "It was marvellous to see children who came in saying I can't do this, or I'm not very good at that; all the failures they'd had just faded away into the background. The other girls would come to them and say Have you got this working, because I can't?" Such blossomings would be a characteristic feature wherever computer-rich learning environments were adopted.

There was also a gifted student in the Sunrise class, a girl called Louisa who was always willing to assist others. "She would wander round and if somebody said I need help, she would see where the child was stuck and say Look, you could do it this way. Louisa would write this program and ask, Did you understand what I was doing? And if the other girl said Yes, then she'd delete what she'd done and say, Well now you try it. She wouldn't give the girl the answer, she'd show her a possible way."

During the year Liddy Nevile would occasionally drop by MLC to discuss developments and inject new ideas. She had originally been reluctant to work with "twee little girls in green uniforms" because she felt that they would be too obedient. "But what happened", Nevile said, "was they didn't do what they were told, for the simple reason that they weren't told what to do, and they came up with things that their teachers had never thought of telling them."

After classes had finished, Nevile and Loader would often talk late into the evening, over a bottle or two of red wine around the kitchen table at the principal's residence above the school. Ros Loader felt that it was reassuring for David to have a sparring partner, someone with whom "to toss the ball back and forth, and see where it went, without at that point having an end in mind."

The Sunrise class of 1989 could not be classified, the principal confessed, as an audacious experiment. Nevertheless, it was a significant departure from existing practice at MLC. And an indispensable first step towards what would be a much more radical development. After eight months, it was clear that the trial had been a success. The question was now what to do the following year to build on this success? There were four options.

The first option was also the cheapest: to acknowledge that it would be impossible to give each of the College's 2,000 students (not to mention several hundred staff) a computer and leave it at that. This was clearly unsatisfactory. After what they had seen in the Sunrise class, to attempt to ignore computers would have been to bury their heads in the sand.

The second option was for the school to provide a (desktop) computer for every student. This would be prohibitively expensive, involving not only the purchase of hardware, but also the re-wiring of the College. How it could be funded was unclear. An additional drawback was that the computers would only be available during school hours.

The third option was the home solution: computers were important, but since the school could not afford to provide them for every student, parents would be encouraged to buy one for their daughters to use at home. This, in effect, would be passing the buck.

The fourth option addressed the access problem: both school and parents should buy computers so that students could have access at school and home. But this of course was the most expensive—and unrealistic—option of all.

It was at this point, while mulling the problem, that David Loader was persuaded to go to a personal computer show. And there, to his considerable excitement, he discovered that there was also a fifth option.

◆   ◆   ◆

In fact, by 1989, MLC already had several hundred computers. Most were located in the College's business school. Historically, this had been where eleventh- and twelfth-grade girls of modest academic accomplishment went to learn secretarial skills, notably typing. To this end, there was a classroom equipped with manual typewriters. One of David Loader's first acts at MLC had been to support the business school's acquisition of a very expensive wordprocessor. It cost something like twenty thousand Australian dollars.

When Joan Taylor took over as head of business studies at the College in 1982, most training was still done on manual typewriters. But by then it was clear that personal-computer-based wordprocessors were rapidly becoming standard office equipment. In that environment, it was easy to get funding for computers to train the business school girls. For perhaps three years during the mid 1980s the school purchased a hundred thousand dollars' worth of computers annually; first Apple IIe's, switching later to IBMs in ever larger numbers. To house the machines, in addition to the old typewriter room in the business school, two computer laboratories were established in the new Centenary Building.

During this period, Loader and Taylor talked a lot about computing at MLC. Taylor was happy because her primary interest was the business school girls. But Loader was looking at the bigger picture, concerned that the school was focusing on such a small number of students. "We've got 2,000 girls and only about 50 are getting some exposure to computers", he lamented. "It's just this tiny group who are getting this opportunity—we're not making any headway with the vast majority of students in the College."

Since the school couldn't afford to provide desktops for everybody, there had to be some other way. "But we certainly didn't have any idea of what that other way would be," Taylor said. "It was just, there's a huge problem here, and we don't know how to resolve it."

In 1983, MLC hired its first computer studies teacher, an eager young man named David Dimsey. The year he started, the school purchased two Apple IIEs. A mathematics teacher, Dimsey had early on caught the Logo bug and its underlying philosophy of learning. Now, along with the Apples, he introduced programming in Logo to his computer studies classes.

As the number of machines grew, technical problems started occurring. The business studies teachers were mostly women like Taylor, middle-aged mothers with lots of teaching experience but no prior exposure to computers. "It was a nightmare for us to be managing those computer labs," Taylor recalled, "we literally didn't know how to turn the machines on, didn't know anything about them at all. And in those early days, the software was so hard to manage—there was just a blank screen with a little prompt down at the bottom."

Their local Apple vendor was helpful, but when there was a problem you had to call the company. "We located the computer room next to the staff room, where there was a phone," Taylor recalled. "We used to have somebody on the phone and somebody in the computer room, and we'd yell out, one to the other, Try this! Try that! And if anything broke down, we as teachers had to try and solve it, with no skills whatsoever. Since the computers were also semi-networked, that added another degree of complexity."

As they blundered on in those early years, and as more and more computers arrived, another headache was finding places to put them. "The spaces that exist in schools don't lend themselves to desktop computers," Dimsey explained. "A standard classroom is built to accommodate 25 students with a desk and a chair each and a bit of space to put a book. But if you want to put computers on those desks, you need 50 percent more space." At MLC, as at most schools, every room was tied up much of the time. For computer studies teachers like Dimsey, the struggle for space was never-ending. "Where are the biggest classrooms?" he would ask. "Who do I have to fight to get hold of one of those rooms?"

Dimsey did his utmost to help the business studies teachers and, later, the Sunrise class. He was always available, always supportive, always willing to help anybody who was using computers. But there were simply too many things to do, and Dimsey was ultimately overwhelmed. Taylor went to Loader and told him that they needed a technical support person.

In 1987 Julian Burden, a second-year dropout from engineering school, was appointed as MLC's first technical whiz kid. "The chemistry between Julian and David was very strong," Taylor said, "it was like father and son…he had a direct line to David, and David relied on Julian for advice, because he was the tech-head." Burden quickly realized that MLC's biggest problem was access. "The business school students in years 11 and 12 were doing more and more of their work on the computers," he recalled. "They were having to come in extra hours, and we were opening up occasionally on the weekend for them to do their homework, because it had to be done on a computer, and not everybody had one at home."

Then, in mid 1989, one of the students brought in an early-model Toshiba laptop. Burden was impressed. "I'd seen laptops before, but they were big, heavy, and very expensive, whereas this was sort of like a cut-down version that was a lot simpler, a lot lighter, and a lot less expensive." He felt that here was a possible solution to the access problem for the business studies students. Perhaps the school could be persuaded to buy some laptops and rent them out to students on an as-needed basis?

As fate would have it, around that time a personal computer show was being held at Melbourne's Exhibition Building. At Burden's suggestion, he and Loader and the school's finance director went to the show to check out the hardware. At the Toshiba stand, Loader saw his first laptop. Prior to that moment he had not been aware that such a thing existed. Now he struck up a discussion with Robert Ward, a company representative who happened to be enthusiastic about laptops in education. At first Ward did not realize who he was talking to; it was only after about forty minutes that Loader revealed that he was the principal of MLC. Ward had tried to convince visitors from other schools about the potential for laptops, but without success. "David was the first person who ever took it seriously," he recalled.

When Loader got back to MLC, Taylor was working in her office at the business school. "David came in, and he was like a little boy with a new toy. He said, I've seen these things called laptops, and I think they're the solution to our problem." Portable computers meant that the kids could use them both at school and at home. And they were cheap enough that every student could afford to have one.

Taylor thought that one-kid-one-computer was a stupid idea. "We didn't know anything about laptops," she recalled, "and the notion of every girl buying her own machine, and being able to sell that idea to the school community, was crazy." She was however forced to concede that "David was an inspirational leader, he had done other things that were crazy, and he had been able to pull them off. And there had been enough of these to believe that he could do this one too, even though it was more crazy than other things that he'd tried before."

Loader invited Ward to MLC to repeat his spiel to staff. The principal got together a group of teachers who he thought would be supportive. They were not: his carefully selected staff rejected the idea of compulsory laptops out of hand. Doubting Thomases warned of kids flushing disks down the toilets, of computers being dropped or left on trains, of students being robbed. "Many, many things were brought up to try and stop the implementation from happening," Ward recalled, "and it was mainly the staff that were trying to do this…[but] David basically didn't care," "this was his vision, and he was going to carry it forward regardless—he wasn't going to let anybody stop him."

"This is a good idea," Loader told Ward, "we will have more meetings and I will invite different staff to the next one." The second time, some of the staff liked the idea. It was agreed that these staff would introduce laptops into their classes at the school the following year. It was also decided that the laptops would be paid for by parents.[4]

"David's great insight," Dimsey concluded, "was that portable computers would give kids ownership of the machines, and therefore ownership of what they did on them. And before any of us really know what was happening, Boom!, they were in place. And from there, the whole focus of computing changed in the school, it shifted from computers on desks and computer classes, to this whole new model of learning."

---

4.   David Loader, "The Inner Principal", Falmer Press, London, 1997, p91

18

A BIG ASK

One of the less-studied aspects of the 1974 Arab oil embargo is the effect it had on individual destinies. The recession the embargo triggered caused more than a few young college graduates to reconsider their future. Given the parlous state of the economy at home, why not try your luck overseas?

One such was Steve Costa, the teacher who led the world's first laptop classes at MLC. A self-deprecating Midwesterner, Costa grew up in Little Canada, a suburb of St Paul, Minnesota, right across the street from his Sicilian-born grandfather's market garden. Costa was one of those happy kids who always enjoyed school; it was where all his social and sporting activities took place. For him, school work was never hard—not compared to growing vegetables for granddad, anyway—and Costa always thought that teaching would be fun. A man of compact stature, Costa liked to joke that he chose to teach primary school because there, at least, he could be sure of being taller than most of his students.

In St Paul, Costa went to Concordia College, the first of his family to make it as far as university. But when he graduated in 1974, job opportunities for teachers in the US were at an all-time low. In Australia, by contrast, school authorities were crying out for teachers. A desperate government education department took the unprecedented step of dispatching recruiters to the US and Canada. There, they signed up hundreds of adventurous young teachers like Costa and chartered Qantas jets to transport them Down Under. When their contracts were up, most of these exotics went back home. A few, like Costa, married local girls and stayed on.

Having served out his time in education department schools, Costa moved on to work at a prestigious private boys' school in Melbourne. In 1981 the school acquired a couple of Apple IIs. Costa and a colleague were the only ones game enough to investigate what the machines could do. Intrigued, Costa went on to take (via correspondence course) a graduate diploma in computer studies. He discovered Papert, read *Mindstorms*, played with Logo. Pretty soon Costa was using computers in his sixth-grade classes.

"When we first started it was almost all drill-and-practice stuff," he recalled. "Then when Logo was put on, you could actually control the machine, and I think that was when the revelation hit, that these things could actually become a learning tool instead of a teaching tool." Costa had always thought that a teacher could teach better than any machine. Now, he saw that the computer could actually let the kids learn in an open-ended, unstructured way. The ideal had always been to allow for individual differences in your teaching. But how could you teach a class of 32 individuals? It couldn't be done. The computer promised to give teachers that option, of allowing kids to pursue things without you having to actually stand there and give them directions. And Costa noticed that his kids seemed to like doing, instead of being done to.

At the end of the year, Costa and his colleague put on a presentation of their computer work for junior school parents. They were expecting that maybe ten people and a dog might show up, especially since the presentation took place on a weeknight, and the weather that day was exceptionally hot. In fact about 200 parents came, not just from sixth grade, but from all year levels. Such huge interest led to the purchase of more machines, and to Costa becoming the school's computer guru because, as he said with characteristic modesty, "I knew how to turn the machines on." Finding that he enjoyed being the school's go-to guy for technology prompted Costa to learn more.

As computer use blossomed, Logo was employed at his school a great deal. In 1988, Australia's bicentennial year, Costa applied for a position as deputy head of the junior school at MLC. During his interview with David Loader, Costa talked about how he done all this work with computing, set up a network, and run in-service courses for staff as well as workshops for parents and children on weekends. In short order, he got the job.

The following year, at a staff meeting the newly-appointed Costa attended, the principal let it be known that he was considering the introduction of student-owned laptops. True to his radical nature, Loader wanted to impose the program on the whole school, from the eight-year-olds in fourth grade to the eighteen-year-olds in twelfth grade. Cautious voices counseled that one of next year's four seventh-grade Sunrise classes might be a more prudent way to begin. "With hindsight, that was a fairly safe option," Costa said, "because in any group of 300, you're bound to get ten percent that are game for a go at anything: You say Swing from the chandeliers? What the heck…"

From his own teaching experience in primary school, Costa knew how well younger kids cottoned on to computers, and how expert they could become. He piped up with another proposal. "I said to David, There's no reason to start only in year seven, let's start in year five, too. And then you've got two points of entry to the school, which might bolster the eventual acceptance of laptops. And if you can prove you can do it younger, then the reticence of the older brigade will have less power because, I mean—My year nines can't do it, but my year fives can? That's a very good argument."

The junior school set-up, Costa insisted, was almost made for laptops. There was far less movement from one classroom to another, and far fewer teachers, too. From both educational and classroom management standpoints, in fifth grade the program would be much easier to implement. Loader saw his point. He told Costa, "All right, you have the background—if you want to do it, go ahead."

The junior school had other things to commend it. For one thing, it was cut off from the rest of the MLC campus by a private residence and its large adjoining garden, a historical hold-out against the school's expansion program. The junior school had its own building, with its own entrances. No-one from the big school paid much attention to what went on there. If something went wrong with the little kids and their laptops, it would not be a complete disaster.

At the year-five level there were just three classes. When Costa told the other two fifth-grade teachers about the initiative, both said they wanted to be involved, too. If computers were such a great tool for learning, then all the kids deserved to have them, not just a select group. There would be no haves and have-nots. The program would be compulsory.

With the teachers on-side, Loader now had to sell the idea to two other interest groups: the school council, and the year-five parents. As it turned out, the latter would take a lot more convincing than the former.

◆   ◆   ◆

Of the sixteen members who sat on the school council, MLC's board of governors, the most important was Brian Hamley. Since becoming College treasurer in 1976, Hamley had never been afraid to ruffle a few feathers. Early on he had also realized that the school could no longer continue to depend on the loyalty of old collegians as its teachers: in the modern world women required equal pay. To meet the salary increases, Hamley insisted on raising fees substantially. At the time his fellow board members said he was mad, but later they admitted that his timely action had saved the school.

Hamley was chief economist for the National Australia Bank, one of the country's largest financial institutions, which is headquartered in Melbourne. In his research department at the bank, Hamley employed lots of bright young analysts. In the 1970s, they started using computers to produce their forecasts. By 1989, the time of MLC's Sunrise class initiative, all his staff had personal computers on their desks.

Looking towards the future, Hamley was convinced that "well before the year 2000, most young people leaving school would have to be computer literate, otherwise their chances of making their way would be very limited." He thus had no problem with the laptop program—other than to warn, correctly as it turned out, that the program would have an insatiable appetite for recurrent as well as capital investment.

The treasurer had recruited another economist for MLC's board. But whereas Hamley was a conservative from the old school of prudent financial management, Michael Porter was a brash free-market radical. At the time he joined the board in 1986 Porter had just returned to Australia from Stanford's Hoover Institution, where he had been a professor. A leading advocate of privatization, Porter was attempting to start a private university to ginger up the cozy world of Australian academe. When he and Loader first met the latter, fascinated with any educational innovations, asked him how this new university was going to operate. "I said Well every student's going to have their own laptop," Porter recalled. He explained to Loader that economies of scale would make the hardware (relatively) cheap.

At Stanford, Porter had long since been accustomed to computers being part of the furniture. In the early 1970s he had worked at the International Monetary Fund. There, Porter had seen the power that computer-driven access to data could confer. "We had a team in Korea, and we could just dial long-distance using acoustic couplers and download a database from the US. Three minutes later, we'd get these sophisticated graphs of how we saw the Korean economy. So I was really avid for access, it gave us the capacity to totally dominate the finance departments in these countries that were doing a bad job."

In addition to the two economists, the other strong supporter of computers was Caroline Dowling, one of several parent representatives on the school board. As we have seen, she had suggested to Loader that computers should be MLC's differentiator in the marketplace. Also on the council were four representatives of the school's owners, the Uniting Church. The "cloud of clergy", as Porter derisively referred to them, did not have strong views about computers. Finally, there was Lawrie Turner, the powerful Methodist minister who chaired the council.

Extraordinary though it seems, the decision to go ahead with what was probably the most revolutionary program in MLC's history never came up for a vote at council, was never even debated. "David would have regarded it as a management issue," Turner explained. You did not take book lists to council for approval. Same with computers: even though they were a very expensive item, implementing them was ultimately a management decision.

Loader would later joke that compared to the laptop program, it had been much harder to get approval for alcohol to be served at MLC for parent functions. The difference was that booze was an issue of policy, not management, one which went against the Methodist tradition. While Turner was chair, MLC stayed dry.

Of course, the school's governing body was consulted about the laptop program. "David wouldn't have done it if he hadn't had the blessing of the board," Hamley insisted. But Loader had already won council approval for the school's Sunrise class initiative, and some of his enthusiasm for that had rubbed off on them. Loader had by this time been at the school for a decade; the principal had long since established his credibility. He had delivered before, and the board had every confidence that he would deliver again. Nonetheless, the laptops represented a huge risk for Loader. Had the program not worked out, it might well have ended his career.

◆   ◆   ◆

At year seven, the Sunrise program was to expand to three classes, with one class using student-owned laptops and the other two accessing the existing computer lab. Parents were invited to volunteer if they wanted their daughters to be in the laptop class. The Junior School opted for a more radical approach.

In late September 1989, parents of fourth-grade students at MLC received a letter informing them that there was to be a dramatic change in the style of education offered to their daughters. From the beginning of the new school year in 1990, in addition to pens, paper, and books, all grade five students would be required to have their own personal laptop computers.

When this requirement was announced, with very little accompanying information, a group of grade-four parents banded together to vigorously oppose it. Leading the charge against laptops was Chris Jenkins, a tall, imposing woman with piercing blue eyes who happened to be the science coordinator in the middle school at MLC. "I didn't think that the idea was well fleshed-out," Jenkins explained, "it lacked quite a lot of substance." Did David Loader know where he was going with this? Several years later, she remained convinced that he did not.

Jenkins's biggest objection to laptops was not substance, but finance. "My husband and I were struggling to pay two sets of school fees—MLC doesn't offer its staff a discount—and we were confronted with an additional expense which wasn't by any means inconsiderable to us at that stage of our lives," Jenkins said. "So financially it was going to be a burden to us."

And indeed, to many other MLC parents. As we have seen, the school did its best to keep fees low to accommodate as wide a range of the community as possible. Even so, most of the kids at MLC would have had one parent working mainly to pay their school fees. Requiring parents to come up with the extra funds for a laptop computer was a big ask.

The school did not intend to provide the machines. "The capital outlay for 82 laptop computers at an approximate cost of A$1500 each was not within the capacity of MLC.[1] The only option was to approach the parents, explain what we thought was the desirable course of action, and how that they would support us by finding ways of providing their daughters with the laptop that we had selected, the Toshiba T1000SE."[2] (This was the same model that Alan Kay signed on his visit to Toshiba's Tokyo factory at around this time, December 1989.)[3]

Ways of sugaring the pill were worked out. Parents would have the choice of purchasing the laptop through the school at a reduced price, or of hiring one of the machines bought by the school. The hiring charge was set at A$525 a year, high enough to encourage parents to purchase, but low enough to offer a genuine alternative for parents unable to afford the full price. In addition, "[a] major effort was made to find ways of providing staff with the opportunity to purchase a laptop." The school could not afford to buy them machines, but sought to subsidize staff purchases.

Another major issue was insurance. Parents would ring up to find out about the cost of insuring a laptop computer against theft or damage for a ten-year-old

---

1. In January 1990, one Australian dollar was worth approximately US$1.30.
2. Pam Dettman, "A Laptop Revolution", case study in "The Entrepreneurial School", Ashton Scholastic, Sydney, 1991, p63
3. The "super-compact" lightweight T1000SE made its debut in November 1989. The T1000SE was 12.4 inches wide, 10.6 inches long, and 1.78 inches high. "Weighing a mere 5.9 pounds [it] is the company's smallest and lightest battery-operated computer. Its notebook-sized portability allows it to fit neatly into a briefcase, providing a new degree of freedom for professionals on the go." [Source: Toshiba newsletter No.329, December 1989]

child who would take the machine to and from school on public transport. And the insurance company, with no prior figures to base an estimate on, would come back quoting a huge premium.

In the first year, unable to find an acceptable insurer, the school offered a policy of its own. As it turned out, "[p]arents' main concerns—the computer would be left on the train or dropped—were largely unfounded. In the first year not one claim was made for a lost or stolen computer (a condition of the policy was that the laptop had to be carried in the student's school bag)."[4]

There were some hiccups in the early days, though. On one occasion, an eleven-year-old burst into inconsolable tears because her computer wasn't working. It was ten minutes before she had recovered sufficiently to tell her teacher that the machine had been working perfectly the previous evening, when she used it...in the bath. (After two hours in front of a heater, the laptop miraculously came back to life.)

A series of meetings was organized at MLC to deal with parental misgivings. At the first meeting, parents went along to hear details of the proposed project. They were concerned, Jenkins recalled, but open-minded.

"We had to show and tell as much as we could," Costa said, "give the parents concrete examples of what had been done." There were at this time a few computers in the junior school, but they were in a sorry state, old and constantly breaking down. "And then to try to extrapolate from that to, if we can do this with the limited facilities we now have, how much greater will be the learning and confidence if children have their own machine, which they can use not just from 9 to 3:30, but take home and share with their family."

Costa's vision of learning when the kids wanted to, not when they had to, went down well. The idea of acquiring superior computer skills was attractive at a time when, as now, a common fear was that not to have such skills would put children at risk of being left behind. The laptop program also addressed another fear, specific to girls' schools, voiced by Judy McKenzie, the College's vice-principal. "Girls tend to be scared of technology," she said. Early exposure plus the ability to take computers home, where girls could work at their own pace, might help overcome gender-based technophobia.

Naturally, the parents also had lots of apprehensions. They were worried about the effect of laptops on handwriting skills (might not the girls forget how

---

4.   Roger Dedman [MLC Director of Finance], "Learning with Laptops: Who Pays?", Reflections of a Learning Community, ed Irene Grasso & Margaret Fallshaw, MLC, Melbourne, 1993, p57

to write?); about the risk of repetitive strain injury (whatever that might be); about the danger that their daughters would become alienated (because they would only be focusing on their computers, and not socializing with each other); and of course, about the disruptive effect on families that would result from children having superior computer skills to their parents.

"We listened to all the worries that parents had," Costa said, "and tried to address them." But since no-one had ever attempted anything like this program before, there was no precedent to guide them. All they could do was keep listening. To legitimate-sounding suggestions, they would respond *That's reasonable—we can accommodate that.*

Ultimately, the matter was referred to the Parents' Association. There, at the end of a volatile meeting, the laptops won by one vote. The program would proceed. As a result of the decision, two or three students were withdrawn; in addition, three parents remained uncertain. They were brought in for further discussions, one-on-one sessions that sometimes lasted hours. A compromise was offered. If these parents were not prepared to buy laptops, then the school would provide their daughters with a desktop. However, size constraints meant that there would only be room for one desktop in each class. Realizing that it would be unacceptable for their kids to be the odd ones out, and recognizing the overwhelming support from the other parents, the three finally gave in.

"By the end of 1989, every parent had declared their intention to either rent or purchase a Toshiba laptop. The split between the two options was approximately fifty-fifty."[5]

---

5.   Dettman, p63

19

LAPTOP GIRLS

The world's first laptop classes commenced "in a blaze of glory" on Monday 12 February 1990. Reporters from print and electronic media descended on Methodist Ladies' College in droves, eager to interview the principal, teachers, and students about this startling new development in education.

The following day, articles appeared prominently in all the local papers. *The Sun*, a tabloid, ran a photograph across four columns. It shows a grinning David Loader, looking like a latter-day Pied Piper of Hamelin, leading an excited-looking mob of laptop-clutching ten-year-old girls. "We think they are old enough" the caption has him saying.

"Wendy Shang, 10, skipped to school yesterday with a $1000 'notebook' under her arm, and an air of simple-hearted naivety about its implications", begins the piece in *The Age*, Melbourne's daily broadsheet. The article goes on to quote Loader: "This is no longer the future, this is the present. It is going to transform the classroom." As it turned out, he was right.

And so it began, in the fifth grade of the junior school at MLC, with three teachers, 82 students, and MS-DOS-based, no-hard-drive, no-mouse, monochrome laptops. The teachers, Steve Costa, Jenny Cash, and Andrew Strooper were all talented, enthusiastic, and had above average computer skills (in Costa's case, well above). But in those days, the average was not terribly high.

Before classes started, the teachers unboxed the computers, labelled them with the girls' names, and placed them in special lockers in each classroom. "We made sure every computer worked and had the right software," Costa said. "It was a big task, but we left nothing to chance."

Then, on the first morning of school, they presented the computers to the students. The girls were thrilled of course, but their excitement was tempered by a sense of the importance of the occasion and the gravity of the responsibility being placed upon them. The teachers began by introducing the computers. They explained proper handling and maintenance, taking the time to make sure that the girls felt confident about using their machines.

"We did not allow the computers to go home for the first two weeks," Costa said. "We wanted to be certain the girls knew how to use their laptops, so that they could take them home and have things work, and not look confused in front of parents who were concerned about their kids using high-tech stuff." A good impression was vital. The delay meant that, in addition to developing basic skills, the girls were also able to show off to their parents some of their first efforts on the computer.

The students began with the basics. An initial task was learning how to input the time and date on their laptops. Pretty trivial stuff you might think, but it had an important outcome. One girl discovered that she could trick the computer: she put in *the wrong date*...and the machine accepted it! At that time kids (and probably most adults) believed that computers were infallible, too smart to be fooled. Now it turned out—much to the girls' amusement—that the computer wasn't the know-all they had thought it was. The kids started to understand that they could have control over their machines. And, perhaps, over their learning as well.

The teachers were proud of how well the girls cared for their machines. But they were taken aback when, a few weeks later, stickers of ponies and butterflies and fairies started to appear on the cases. They needn't have worried: the stickers (and, sometimes, the pet names the girls gave their machines) simply meant that the students were comfortable with their computers. They had accepted them as part of their world.

♦   ♦   ♦

From the outset, the laptop classes were different. "It was just a totally different style," Costa said, "much more collaborative, much more open. So far from turning into robots, as some of the parents had feared, the kids actually became more social. Sharing and helping one another were an integral part of the process. "We were amazed watching how the kids would stop doing what they were engrossed in, put it down, and happily go help someone else." This was a big change: in the past, individual effort was all that counted. Kids were actively discouraged from looking at each others' work (because that would have been copying).

The laptops had a dramatic effect on how classrooms were used. The conventional classroom furniture—rows of desks, tables, and chairs—no longer mattered. Battery-powered laptops freed the girls to move around as they pleased. Students found that when they needed to collaborate, the hallway was a good spot for three or four of them to sit together. Some girls still preferred to sit at their desks. Others found that for thinking and working, it was easier to stretch out on the floor. "There was no value in telling them to sit at the desks," Costa commented, "they were still learning on the floor, or wherever. We tried not to create another condition to constrict them, we let them have a bit of freedom as long as they were engaged—because engagement is what we're after."

Lesson times became longer as the laptop teachers discovered that they were integrating their lessons more often, melding studies of society and the environment into writing, or maths, or science. "We just blocked our time in larger sections and were less mindful of dividing up our timetable into neat little separate subject periods," Costa recalled. This successful innovation was noted and discussed by other teachers. Everyone started to see the advantage of spending more time in larger blocks on a topic. There was less need for continual reviews eating up lesson time. Though setting-up and packing-up times remained the same, they were done less often.

But the biggest change to classroom practice was that the teachers no longer spent much time standing at the board in front of the class doing "chalk-and-talk". Lessons would kick off with short, sharp show-and-tell sessions. These used a data projector, a gizmo that projects onto a large screen whatever is displayed on the computer to which it is connected. This tool, which the laptop teachers pioneered as their new whiteboard, quickly became indispensable.

Now there was time for more individual guidance. "We moved around the room more, and sat down with the kids more, and talked and listened to them more," Costa said. "To make something work, we had to learn what they knew, or what they could do. We also had to know what they did wrong, to help them fix the problem they were struggling with. Though we didn't have *all* the answers—and told the kids this—we worked very hard to have more answers than not. But we needed to have a better than average degree of teacher credibility. The kids needed to have confidence in us, they had to know their teachers knew how to do this stuff, too."

The teachers worked together. "We shared our knowledge, or lack thereof," Costa said. "We spent hours after school figuring out how to meld the curriculum into this computer program. And that created this very strong group identity, as well as a support group. It made us feel, We don't know all the answers, but if we sink, we sink together. But we won't sink that far, because one of us will pull the others out of the mud."

They struggled on, without a model to guide them, making it up as they went along. Often they would repair to Loader's office for tea and sympathy. The teachers told the principal what they wanted to do, and he responded by asking them what they needed. These meetings were like group-therapy sessions. They played an important role in building camaraderie, plus giving the teachers the reassurance of knowing that Loader was behind them a hundred percent.

"David was very keen," Costa recalled, "to the point where you never had to worry you could outdo his crazy ideas. If you wanted to try something that you thought was crazy, it would be accepted readily because he'd probably thought of something that was ten times more crazy."

◆　　　◆　　　◆

Looking back on those early days, what Costa remembered most vividly was how readily the girls accepted the challenges that confronted them. There was a genuine eagerness to learn. In the past, the kids had had a minimum number of things to do, and they usually did just the minimum. Now, with the laptops, they were doing much more than was expected of them. The teachers often had to stop them and say That's it, we don't want any more, the project's big enough, we're moving on to something else. But the kids would always beg to be allowed to add a few more pages, or a few more slides.

The line between work-time and play-time became blurred. At recess, instead of dashing out to play as usual, the girls would often tell their teachers that they wanted to stay in because they still had a bit more to do. At the start of the laptop program, parents mentioned how the girls would even bring their computers to sleep-overs at each others' houses, spending time working on projects and *Logo Writer* programs.

It helped that the students were very keen. Everything was new to them and even the simplest things that the computer could do were exciting. Since educational software was still pretty crude, the girls were able to create their own. In English, for example, they made up a spelling game which used their own lists of words. The program could tell you if you had spelled a word right or wrong. It gave you your score and, depending on whether your answer was correct, showed a happy or sad face—together with an appropriate noise.

They also programmed games in math. One, called Angle Maker, allowed you to guess the degree of a randomly-drawn angle. (This was later changed to guessing whether the angle was acute, right, or obtuse.) You could also ask the computer to show you what an angle of a certain degree looked like.

They did projects, including one that that showed the solar system as little worlds circling around the screen. Additional screens would tell you your age on Mars or your weight on Venus. All were programmed by the students.

Such games and projects took time to make, but they were fun and, most importantly, generated a lot of self-confidence and self-esteem. The work the girls produced looked almost as good as that of adults. As a result, they developed quite a high opinion of themselves.

Whatever they were working on, the girls always added some interesting touches of their own—whether it was music, sound effects, voice recordings or—as in the solar system project—little aliens waving at you from a corner of the screen. Each project was a combination of modelling and help from the teacher, interaction between students, and choices made by individuals about what they wanted their version to look like.

"If a new concept was vital to the topic," Costa said, "we would demo it, then the kids could modify it and make it better. Generally, the majority were content to use the demo. Some would take it a bit further, but a few would drive you crazy asking for more. Then we really had to go check our manuals and reference books, and consult each other to work it out and see if it could be done!"

Kids and teachers discovered that they could swap roles, with the teachers sometimes doing the learning. This was partly because the students, unlike their perpetually overworked teachers, had the energy and the time—especially because they could work on their laptops at home—to become expert in the minutiae of the machines.

"The kids soon learned heaps about changing screen settings, mouse pointers, adding sounds and music. And their animation stuff beat what staff could do." The girls were also great when it came to working on graphics or drawing pictures. They would use backgrounds to hide their pictures, then hit a key to make the hidden picture magically appear.

"We were learning together, and the staff and students knew this instinctively. We were all proud of one another's' efforts and we were happy to learn and share with each other, and to be supportive when things went awry."

Naturally, things did sometimes go awry: the girls had their down days, too. They learned the hard way that something not saved could not be retrieved. Or that a battery dying in the middle of a burst of inspirational work was a bad thing. Or that the best ideas sometimes don't work. Or that trying to do something could be hard, and they might not be able to do it the first, second, or even the third go.

"The girls had a great commitment because they learned how to make the computer do what they wanted it to," Costa said. "They knew that it wasn't easy, that it was a challenge. But everybody had the same challenge, so we could work at it as a group. It created an environment where it was OK to show each other how to do something. It was OK to say, I don't know how."

In the laptop classes, risk-taking—always championed in educational theory but seldom seen in classroom practice—became an everyday reality. "You actually couldn't get away from [risk-taking] if you wanted to do it the way we were doing it," Costa said. "There was a whole environment of Don't give up, have a go. Everybody would be scratching their heads. But whereas in the past, the five or six smartest kids knew everything, never had a problem, now you had everybody in the classroom from the smartest to least smart struggling over some concept.

"In the past, kids were never encouraged to make mistakes—if you made a mistake it was, OK I'll show you the right answer, don't make that mistake again. Now, it was Did you figure something out from that mistake? OK, use that and try the next thing." The next project might be hard, but having succeeded in the past made the students more willing to take risks. They began to develop a closer connection to their learning. Often they set themselves challenges. The girls wanted to have things happen in a certain way, or look a certain way, and they would stick at it until they had achieved their goal. This change in attitude helped to lift the standard of work. The beauty of it was that the students were the ones who raised the bar.

◆   ◆   ◆

The teachers worked at integrating the computer into the curriculum. A good example was when the kids built, from scratch, a database of endangered species. Next, they created stories that linked the information gained from their research to pictures of the animal. (These had to be drawn using the computer because in those days you could not scan in pictures.) The girls also made up and input their own animal sounds. Then, using pens and pencils, they wrote postcards (cardboard squares) that were supposedly sent from the endangered species they had studied. The postcards ended up dangling from wires across the room.

The teachers attempted to make sure that the computers were not used indiscriminately, only where they would make a difference. "Every time we had lessons we had to see whether the computer would make them better or just be busy work," Costa said. "We made a deal between staff not to do things just because they were possible: it was not enough for the computer just to be like an exercise book, it had to have words and pictures and sound and animation, and it also had to be linked to a subject theme or math concept."

Though the program also embraced wordprocessors, databases, and spreadsheets, *Logo Writer* was the core software. "After studying the works of Seymour Papert we were convinced our students could create learning environments or microworlds where they could explore concepts that were of interest to them," Costa wrote.[1] "The philosophy behind Papert and others who promoted the use of programming—that the kid is in charge of the machine instead of the opposite—is very deep."

At the same time, the MLC teachers recognized that constructionist philosophy had to be mixed with a stiff dash of pragmatism. "Some of the things Papert reports in *Mindstorms* I find impossible," Costa said. "Like all these incredible programs for drawing flowers will just happen if you just give the kids a computer and let them sit there. You've got to have a lot more teacher input than was originally purported in *Mindstorms*."

The trick was to go beyond the rhetoric to find the common-sense pearls of wisdom that grew out of using a constructionist approach. "And you latch onto those and bend them the way you want. I mean, all teachers are great magpies: they're eclectic, they take what works and they ignore what doesn't."

One thing that worked very well was disseminating little bits and pieces of information to individual students who would then, in their enthusiasm, tell the others. For example, a student showed Costa one of her first efforts written on the computer, a story entitled 'A Convict Servant Girl'. She felt that it would have looked much better if she had used a different, "old-fashioned" font. But it was too late: the work was due the next day.

Costa told her "We can change it now", and showed her how. He also demonstrated quickly how to change the size and style of the font. Then he undid the changes and told her she was free to format her story any way she liked before printing it out and handing it in. Next day, when Costa collected the stories from the class, he was astonished to find that ninety percent of them were printed in special fonts, with a variety of sizes and styles. He never actually had to teach a lesson on how to change text.

As this case illustrates, it was often the kids who started the teachers thinking which new bit of skill it was necessary to impart. "When they started to ask, Is

---

1.   Transforming Learning: An Anthology of Miracles in Technology-Rich Classrooms, ed Jenny Little & Bruce Dixon, Kids Technology Foundation, Melbourne, 2000, p69

this possible? Can you do this? Can the computer do this easier? Then we knew that if we could create this skill somehow, we had an eager audience that was ready to learn. And if you could give that skill or bit of knowledge to the right kid at the right time, it would be magic. They would benefit, and the others would also learn in a speedy way—it could spread like wildfire, even though the teacher hadn't told them how to do it." In effect, it was another means for the kids to be in control of their learning, discovering stuff in a roundabout way, from their friends, behind the shed in the playground or wherever."

The laptop teachers found that they could take advantage of the instant knowledge transmission phenomenon to boost the self-esteem of under-achieving kids. Knowing that they were going to start a certain project the following week, and aware that a little bit of programming would be needed to make the project look good, the teacher would single out a particular kid and tell her how to do that bit. This was simple to do, as the teachers moved around the classroom from kid to kid.

"You could easily sit down and say to Mary, Watch this, see how it works, Isn't that cool? Can you do that? Show me. Then, when next week rolled around, you could say to the students Now this is what you can do. And they'd ask But how do we do that? And you'd tell them Well, I can't remember, but I think Mary has the answer, go ask her. And then Mary became the guru for this minor but, in her eyes, major bit of knowledge."

In those early days, when the kids knew very little, the knowledge could be something as simple as copying a file name or moving some text around. Even making a new folder or directory in which to put each project was cool. "And you could feed it to the kids and make them feel better about themselves. Parents always liked it when their kids came home with an I-succeeded story instead of an I-blew-it story."

The constant presence of the laptops in the classroom caused a peculiar thing to happen: the machines effectively disappeared. "The kids were working at their activities using the computer as a tool," Costa said. "They were actually doing something, they were thinking, they were working, they were creating something, and the actual machine itself was secondary to their project."

Outsiders coming into the classroom would focus on the computers, watching open-mouthed as the ten-year-olds blithely scripted multimedia productions, complete with multiple screens, animation, and sound and voice recording. But if the visitors asked them what they were doing, the girls would tell them that they were writing a story with some illustrations. The computer just happened to be the most convenient means to that end.

For their part, the kids were never fazed by the questions that visiting educators would ask. They would happily explain the intricacies of their work with all the aplomb of experts. Which, of course, they were.

◆　　◆　　◆

Costa's hunch that a laptop program would work well in the junior school turned out to be spot-on. Primary schools tend to be much smaller than secondary schools, which means that teachers typically have better rapport with parents. "There's a reason to come to us, to drop off or collect your child, to say hello," Costa explained, "and through those casual meetings you come to know one another. On top of that, because one child has the same teacher for most of their lessons, the parent deals with that person, the child comes home and tells what Mr or Ms So-and-So did that day.

"So there's an understanding of what's happening, an information flow. Also, learning at primary school is concrete. A lot of our product goes home. You see our stories there, our writing, our art. That's why printing out was important, you could print out some Logo work and it would be taken home and stuck on the fridge door, which gave parents an absolute reassurance that things were happening. And because the kids were bringing their computers home, there was an added degree of reassurance—Show me how you did that...O I see, I believe you."

But show-and-tell could also be frustrating for the kids, because parents were seldom able to appreciate how much effort had gone into their programs. In one instance in Costa's class, a girl called Anne did a project based on *Sadako and the Thousand Paper Cranes*. In this classic story by Eleanor Coerr, Sadako is a twelve-year-old Japanese girl who gets leukemia as a result of the atomic bombing of Hiroshima. As an offering to pray for her recovery, her classmates help Sadako make a thousand origami cranes. But she dies, and a memorial statue to her is erected in the city's Peace Park.

One of the brighter kids in the class, Anne determined that she would make a project that told the whole story. She programmed her presentation in *LogoWriter*. It unfolded with little animated figures walking through the Peace Park, people rowing a boat, and a statue of Sadako. Integrated with the pictures was text explaining what had happened to Sadako, concluding with why we should always choose peace over war. The story was accompanied by background music that Anne herself had composed. The music was tinny, the animation low-res and clunky, but the overall effect was extremely touching.

On the first Laptop Open Night at MLC, parents walked through the junior school classrooms admiring the printouts and projects the girls had created. Costa would never forget what happened when Anne's parents came by. "They looked at her machine, said That's good, and just kept walking past. And the kid ran and grabbed these adults and dragged them back to her computer insisting, No, no, you have to watch it from the beginning, it was really hard, I put a lot of work into it—Come back and look at it properly!"

Costa had never seen a student behave like this before. "Kids are often proud of their work," he said, "but rarely so proud that they'll almost make a fool of themselves in public, with their friends around them. And you would see much more of that sort of attitude, where the kids were willing and almost too eager to make you look at their stuff."

Outsiders like Anne's parents could only see the product, not the processes that had gone into its production. But in the laptop program, the emphasis shifted and process became more important. Before, students could create products without much thought, just by cutting and pasting stuff from magazines and newspapers. Now, it was a case of working something through various steps to get to the end.

The students had to create each part of their projects themselves. After doing the research, they typed in text—no downloading from the Internet in those early days. Painstakingly they drew pictures using *LogoWriter* commands to control X and Y coordinates on the screen (axis plotting—math integration here). They keyed in music one note at a time—with durations linked to each note—then played it back, editing by ear for speed and tone. (The most-often-heard tune was the old piano-lesson chestnut, *Fleur de Lys*.) Finally, the girls could sit back and demonstrate the end product on-screen. But they could also go to the underlying code and show you how and why it worked.

"By going through activities that pushed them to their limits, testing their abilities, getting to a point where they felt proud of what they had done because they had had to actually do it themselves," Costa was convinced, "they started to learn what the whole point of education was."

◆　　　◆　　　◆

As the year went by, all the effort the school had put into winning the support of the parents began to pay off. "The parents became part of the program," Costa said, "they were supportive, they were very proud of what their kids were doing. And they were not slow to bask in the reflected glory—at dinner parties they enjoyed showing off the special skills that their daughters were developing. They were also very tolerant when things went wrong, when the battery went dead, or the machine didn't work, or the kids lost their floppies, they were very forgiving, they never came to us and said, You made us buy these damn machines and now look, the thing's eaten my kid's homework."

Not everybody was delighted all the time, though. Prominent among the program's critics was Chris Jenkins. A self-described "science person", Jenkins had been using computers since her university days, and she had two siblings who worked in the computer industry. She was therefore better qualified than most parents to assess what was going on.

"*LogoWriter* ad nauseam did not achieve as much as it could have," Jenkins said. "I mean, I was using computers in science classes, and I could see that they could be useful, but you had to use software that supported the curriculum. And I believe that very often in the early days with the things I saw my daughter or her friends doing, or that were touted at computer evenings and so on, it was the curriculum serving the software."

To be sure, some of the tasks the kids were given were trivial. For example, one of the first things they were asked to do was draw a map of their classroom. It took them three weeks to do something with a computer that could have been done with pen and paper in twenty minutes.

But for all her criticisms, the laptop program stimulated the educator in Jenkins to think, "Well OK, if I find that unacceptable, what ought it to be doing?...And I guess the strength of having a laptop program introduced in a school is to get teachers to think about teaching...to [change] the style of teaching to accommodate different learning styles...that's really what is at the heart of this fundamental change, it's accommodating different kids, and not treating them as if they were all the same."

Soon after, Jenkins left MLC to become deputy principal of another private school in Melbourne. There, to David Loader's great satisfaction, she would help set up a laptop program.

◆   ◆   ◆

At the end of 1990, the laptop kids sat standardized tests. "As we were an independent school they didn't have to sit the tests," Costa said, "but we felt that our kids had worked their butts off doing math, reading, and writing, and it would help vindicate the program if we could show that they were learning lots of basic skills as well as untold amounts of computer skills."

The teachers' intuition proved correct—the girls did wonderfully well, scoring way above average in both math and English. "Kids learn better when they are happy, keen, and eager to come to school," Costa concluded. "They also do well when parents see that they are engaged outside of school at home with their work."

For the junior school teachers, the laptop program changed everything. "Personally, I think it would be very hard to teach without a computer now," Costa said. "I have seen my students become more competent and confident people. They know they have developed skills, they know they can do things on their computer that adults can do, they know they can share their ideas with others, and receive praise and acknowledgement for their skills.

"The students learn to work collaboratively. They learn that they can work together but still make their own projects. They can gather information from anywhere in the world and learn first-hand what is happening elsewhere. They can communicate with friends and parents nearby, or people around the world, be they other kids, or experts. I have seen independent learning become a reality. I have seen how different learning styles can be accommodated in a relatively easy way. The computer allows for a project to be completed in many ways, and each way can be right and good."

"From the introduction of laptops," David Loader wrote, "monumental consequences flowed. A school, its culture, curriculum, and teaching-learning paradigm began to be transformed."[2] This was not the result of the waving of a magic wand, of the simple handing-out of machines and sitting back to let things happen. It took a huge commitment from a group of highly dedicated teachers. As Costa put it, "We just worked our tails off, night and day."

"People see our end products," Costa continued, "and they go, Wow, isn't it amazing that these kids can do this stuff? But there's hard work behind that Wow—it doesn't just happen, it's the hours and hours that teachers have used in their own time to see what the potentials are, and go try it themselves, to come back and demonstrate to the kids, or to throw in little hints: I bet you can try to do this, if you do that. And when they catch on, you go away and let them do it. That's how things happen. But it takes time, so you have to have faith.

"Teachers often give up on computing tasks, whether it's *LogoWriter* or databases or spreadsheets, because they don't get immediate results. And they see this sort of slow learning curve; then, after a few days, they panic because they're not up to page 87, and they haven't done much work. So they have to stop this 'com-

---

2.   David Loader, "The Inner Principal", Falmer Press, London, 1997, p91

puter stuff' and get back to the 'real' work. But if they'd just had faith, and given it enough time before the marriage of the learning how to use the computer and the understanding of what they're doing combines with the actual spelling-reading-writing-whatever, then they'd be amazed that the quality of the work is so high. And it happens fairly quickly."

◆   ◆   ◆

The fact that all the year-five parents had committed to MLC's laptop program turned out to be a very big plus. It meant that the program was much less difficult to sell the following year. This time, there was not the same difficulty convincing parents. Following all the publicity, parents would've had to have been pretty naive not to be aware that they were sending their daughters to a school with an ongoing laptop program.

"If there had been only the one laptop class at year seven, chances are that the program would have fizzled out," Costa reflected later. It was the push from the junior school that did the trick. The original three classes had to continue—in order to win the parents' acceptance, the school had had to guarantee that support for the laptop program would not be allowed to fall off. The original 82 laptop girls gave the program critical mass. And once you have critical mass, there can be no turning back.

For 1991 at MLC "[i]t was decided to extend the Sunrise program to all year seven classes (ten of them) and to offer parents the opportunity to provide a laptop computer for their daughter's use. Surprisingly, almost 80 percent of the parents accepted this offer so that eight of the year-seven classes in 1991 used laptop computers."[3] That year, there would be fifteen laptop classes at the College—the three original year-five classes, which became year six, three new year-five classes, the year-seven laptop class, which was now in year eight, and the eight year-seven classes. In total, more than 400 laptop girls.

---

3.   Ruth Baker, "Sunrise and Beyond: An Overview of Changes in the Junior Secondary School of Methodist Ladies College since 1988", unpublished paper, July 1993

20

MIT MEETS MLC

In July 1990, when the laptop program at MLC was just a few months old, the two poles of the Logo world came briefly together. The venue for the convergence, formally known as the Fifth World Conference on Computing in Education, was not Melbourne, but Sydney's Darling Harbor.

Sandra Wills, who as a graduate student had introduced Logo to Tasmanian schools almost fifteen years earlier, chaired the conference. As "bookend" speakers to keynote the opening and closing sessions, she invited to Australia the old comrades, Alan Kay and Seymour Papert. Local Logo stalwarts Anne McDowell and Caroline Dowling edited the conference proceedings.

Hearing that, as she put it, "half of MIT" was headed Down Under, Liddy Nevile seized the opportunity to recruit her American friends. Brian Silverman, Steve Ocko, and Mitch Resnick from Papert's group at the Media Lab were all prevailed upon to take part in a two-day Lego-Logo workshop Nevile organized that ran in the lead-up to the conference. David Loader, three other MLC staff, and eight of the school's students participated in the workshop. Three of the laptop parents spoke at the conference.

In his closing address, entitled *Perestroika and Epistemological Politics*, Papert spoke stirringly of "the battle for the future of education", and "the revolutionary confrontation that awaits us". He compared bureaucracy-ridden school systems to the then-crumbling Soviet economy, pointing out that both suffered from the same problem—rampant centralism. But as the recent fall of the Berlin Wall and the impending end of apartheid in his native South Africa showed, change could happen rapidly.

Computer teachers should abandon their marginal roles and stride to center stage, there to assume their true vocation, as leaders. Once ubiquitous, the computer would effectively disappear: every teacher would be a computer teacher. "At some point," Papert concluded, dusting off his favorite metaphor, "it will be as

221

ridiculous to have a world conference on computers and education as to have a world conference on pencils and education."[1]

But the conference would be principally remembered not so much for what was said, as for the personal encounters that took place there. Two new actors joined the drama, both of whom would play crucial roles in the startling expansion of laptop learning that was soon to occur in schools in Australia and, subsequently, the US and elsewhere.

The first was Gary Stager, self-styled "educational terrorist". A 27-year-old punk—his word—from New Jersey, Stager was tagging along with Brian Silverman when he bumped into David Loader.

Stager had been fascinated by the presence of the MLC kids at the Lego-Logo workshop. "I'd never been to a conference where kids were allowed to just mess around," he recalled. Stager had had great fun working with them. When he discovered that many of the kids at their school had their own laptops, Stager was intrigued. "At that time, I didn't know any adults who had a laptop—including me," he said. "I mean, I knew they existed; but I'd never really used one, and I thought they were really cool."

Stager told Loader that he'd love to visit the school some time. Forty-five minutes later Loader returned and said, "Right, we've put the money together, When can you come?"

Three weeks later, Stager was back in Australia, working at MLC. That first visit lasted only a week, but the following year he spent three and a half months at MLC. For him, it was the most exciting time in his life. Since then Stager has returned to Australia many times to work. No-one has had more experience of laptop schools than him.

Loader was interested in Stager because the young American represented the solution to a tricky problem. Namely, how to ensure that teachers were properly trained for the laptop program at MLC?

For some years, the College had been using its business school computers to run a range of community education classes in after-school hours. "It was a very buoyant time for computer training generally," community education head Joan Taylor remembered, "people everywhere were clamoring for it." Any classes they organized, local people would enrol. Loader decided that MLC staff could take any of these courses they wanted, no questions asked. Slotting in the staff was

---

1.   Seymour Paper, "Perestroika and Epistemological Politics",
      <el.www.media.mit.edu/groups/el/Papers/memos/memo4/4.PerEpist.html>

simple, and didn't cost anything. It was an easy, cost-effective way to upgrade the computer skills of a large number of teachers.

Such classes worked well for standard subjects like wordprocessing and spread-sheeting. An exotic topic like teaching with *LogoWriter* was a different matter. Thus far, MLC's Sunrise classes had mostly been taken by Logo enthusiasts like Merle Atherton and Steve Costa. As the program rippled up through other grades, however, a progressively larger group of teachers had to be enlisted.

There were some resources available in-house. Each team would include at least one teacher with previous experience in the Sunrise program. Self-teaching materials were provided for *LogoWriter*, but staff lacked confidence in working with these. Inevitably, frustrations arose. At MLC, as someone who had spent most of his adult life trying to make Logo happen, Stager was the right person in the right place at the right time.

◆   ◆   ◆

Gary Stager is a born enthusiast. He fell in love with computers as a seventh-grader at junior high school in his home town of Wayne, New Jersey. Programming, via a Teletype terminal on a time-shared mainframe, became Stager's all-consuming passion. It made him feel powerful, a novel experience for the hitherto deeply insecure kid. Soon he was president of the computer club, running after-school courses in BASIC for other kids.

Stager hated school, was terrible at math. He majored in music, wanted to be a jazz musician, won a scholarship to Berklee College of Music in Boston as a trumpet player. During his freshman year at Berklee, Wynton Marsalis burst on the scene. Stager was enough of a realist to realize that, at that point, being a trumpet player was a bad idea. He returned to New Jersey, started taking education courses at Rutgers, eventually earning a preschool-through-sixth-grade teaching credential. At the end of his freshman year, Stager was hired to run a summer camp computer program out of a converted horse-trailer. Aged 18 and a half, he had found his vocation.

In 1983 Stager got his first job, with the Network for Action in Microcomputer Education, a grass-roots organization created to support computer use in schools. He quickly became NAME's unofficial director of professional development. That year Stager saw Logo for the first time, presented at a conference at Rutgers by Dan Watt. It blew him away. "I became a Logo person," he said, "because it made me feel the way jazz made me feel." A couple of years later Stager attended his first Logo conference at MIT, where he presented a paper.

Afterwards, the organizers took him out to dinner, treated him as part of the Logo community. Stager was thrilled. It seemed like the first time anyone had taken him seriously.

Stager signed up for the Logo Institutes that Watt and his wife Molly ran. These were courses run in rural settings in which anywhere from twenty to sixty people would participate. Two weeks of total immersion would climax in a celebration where the participants showed what they had done and alumni from previous years returned to join in the fun. Despite the fact that at the time he did not have a degree, Stager was billed in the promotional brochure for subsequent institutes as "scholar-in-residence", another much-needed boost to his self-esteem. From Molly Watt, Stager learned how to work with teachers and run professional development courses. This was invaluable preparation for his work in Australia.

◆   ◆   ◆

At MLC, Stager put on demo lessons, showing what was possible with *LogoWriter*. He worked with teachers, helping them solve problems, and writing material for them. For his part, David Loader was determined that teachers would not, as at many other schools, be expected to train unpaid in their own time. He made sure that they were released to attend Stager's in-service workshops during school hours.

Loader allowed the young American complete access to the school. "I could walk into any class of any subject," Stager said, "and comment on the educational issues that I thought were important." Initially his comments had to do with technology, but Stager's brief soon broadened. "I could make recommendations to David on anything," Stager recalled. "Not only that, but I could walk in on him in the middle of a meeting and say, This is great, you must come and see it!" Loader responded remarkably well to these intrusions. Nowhere else would Stager be allowed such liberties. At other schools, he was just Logo Boy, a hired hand.

Knowing that he had the principal's ear made Stager cocky. He spoke loudly, in a broad New Jersey accent, and fast—faster when he was excited or exasperated, which was often. What he said was frequently funny, in a sardonic wise-guy sort of way. Stager was outrageous, sometimes seeming to go out of his way to provoke people, to jolt them out of their complacency. "Gary was very good for David's group because basically the teachers at MLC are conservative middle-class people," said Liddy Nevile, herself by no means averse to being provocative, "and he's this absolute *brat* from New Jersey."

Perhaps *enfant terrible* is better. Stager's brightly colored shirts, canvas basket-ball sneakers, and the Swatch watch he wore all served to emphasize his status as an outsider. In his pocket Stager always carried a yo-yo, which when approached he would ostentatiously pull out and play with. But what people mostly recalled when they thought of Stager was his eating habits. In particular, his refusal to consume anything but Coke, potato chips, and other forms of junk food.

On one occasion, when Stager was billeted with one of the teachers from MLC, his matronly host cooked her guest what she thought was a top-notch Aus-tralian meal of roast chicken. What happened at dinner time was hysterical. "Gary went out to the kitchen, found some noodles and boiled them up, got a tin and emptied this...stuff into the saucepan, mixed it, then came back to our din-ing table and ate his *muck* while we ate the roast."

◆   ◆   ◆

Stager's brash behavior could have unexpected consequences. On one occa-sion, Loader had just hired a new librarian. He used the occasion to muse in the principal's newsletter about how this would help usher in "the era of the paperless school". Stager thought that the paperless school was a stupid idea. He barged in on a meeting in the principal's office between Loader and Joan Taylor and yelled "Stop being such a jerk!" at Loader.

Taylor was impressed by Stager's nerve. She began thinking of productive ways to channel it. This led her to employ him for computer camps that ran in school vacations at the business school. "I can see Gary in a classroom, for a holi-day program with kids and their parents, and it was just alive," Taylor recalled, "everybody was excited."

The four-day camps were invaluable because they provided an opportunity for new students to get up to speed with computers before joining regular classes. A second benefit was that staff members served as class counsellors, which gave them a chance to mentor less-experienced teachers in Logo and robotics.

In his second year at MLC, Stager became frustrated. Progress seemed to have stalled. "The teachers have all memorized the rhetoric [of constructionism]," he told Loader, "but none of them actually know what it means; none of them have had experience of actually making something and solving problems of their own creation." His solution was to replicate what Dan and Molly Watt had done with their Logo Institutes, to take groups of twenty or more staff away from the school on residential retreats. Loader immediately gave Stager's idea his blessing.

Lasting two or three days, these excursions allowed teachers the luxury "to just mess about, free to explore the possibilities of *LogoWriter* programming for themselves, and collaborate and fall in love with learning." (And, sometimes, with each other.) Staff with a wide range of computer abilities would attend. Some were quite familiar with laptops; others had never used them before. The advanced users could assist (and inspire) the beginners.

One of Stager's techniques was to upend a bucket of Lego on the floor, divide teachers into groups of two or three, then go round with a hatful of bits of paper on which were written tasks—eg, "Build a vending machine". There were no instructions, the point was you had to learn by doing, rather than by being taught. Sessions would often go on late into the night.

The most famous of these "pyjama parties" was held at the Melbourne Hilton. The staff—some of whom had never stayed in a hotel before—thought it was wonderful. They were able to luxuriate in the spa between sessions, and to finish a long day with a swim followed by a movie in bed.

At one pyjama party, an extraordinary thing happened. It had begun beforehand, when one of the school's junior secondary school French teachers discovered that *LogoWriter* was available in French (a fortuitous byproduct of the publisher, LCSI, being based in Montreal). Recognizing that here was an opportunity to improve her students' fluency in the language, she approached a math teacher and asked him to teach her how to use Logo. He told her he was too busy, but offered to allow the kids in his seventh grade classes to do their maths work in French.

About a month later, on a visit to his class, she saw something that caused her to run hyperventilating to the principal's office, where Stager happened to be chatting with Loader when she burst in. "She said to us, I have been teaching middle school French for 25 years, but this is first time I have ever heard kids actually speaking French to each other!"

Shortly afterwards, the French teacher came along to the pyjama party, all enthusiastic about learning how to do Logo, to build on what she had seen. The math teacher was also there, grading papers. Stager noticed him sneaking over every so often to speak to her. Curious to know what was going on, he eavesdropped on their conversation. The math teacher was asking how to write his comments on kids' math homework projects in French.

At the same time, infected by the French teacher's excitement, a bunch of her colleagues who had taken French classes at College came up with the idea of offering a seventh-grade French Logo class. They put the proposal to David Loader, who as usual was supportive. The result was that, the following year, a group of seventh-grade girls at MLC used only the French version of *LogoWrtiter*. By 1997, this had developed into an immersion class with tuition in most subjects in French and using only French-language computer software.

"And it all came out of the experience of a teacher falling in love with herself as a learner," Stager said, "and the power of the computer to do things that were unimaginable before." Such collaborations on the applications and use of computers across the curriculum convinced him that "a renaissance in learning" was taking place at the school.

One prime indicator of this change was the conversation in the staff room. At most schools, when teachers repair to the staff room at recess or lunchtime, they swap diet tips and recipes, or discuss what they watched on TV last night. At MLC, the teachers began talking to each other about important things. "Small groups of people started meeting in their own time because they wanted to argue about how kids learned, and whether technology could play a part in that. And they became very animated about what they believed about learning and how it happens."

◆   ◆   ◆

In July 1993, during a school vacation, Methodist Ladies' College hosted an International Logo Conference. The gathering, which Stager chaired, was originally his idea. He had bullied everyone else into going along with him. The conference was intended as a celebration of what MLC was doing, as well as a professional development booster for staff at the College. At the same time, the idea was also to spread the word about the laptop program. A sizable number of half-price registrations were offered to first-and second-year teachers from other schools, all of which were taken up. Altogether about 250 people attended the four-day bash. "It was wonderful," Joan Taylor recalled, "one of those conferences that you talk about forever."

In addition to the local presenters, there were seven international guests handpicked by Stager and flown over from the United States. Several of them—Paul Goldenberg, Brian Harvey, Dan Watt, and Idit Harel—were former members of Papert's group at MIT. Harel gave a memorable talk, showing videos of kids developing their thinking skills doing fractions in the Project Headlight experiment at the Hennigan school in Boston.

But though attendees listened politely to the visitors' rhetoric, what they had really come to hear about—and what really blew them away—were the examples from real classrooms in workshops run by Steve Costa and his colleagues in the junior school at MLC. The MIT folks couldn't provide multiple instances of ten-, eleven-, and twelve-year-olds working with computers right across the curriculum. Costa and his team had been teaching laptop classes at MLC for three and a half years. During this time they had accumulated an unrivalled wealth of experience. "Steve showed example upon example of the most astonishing work done by children," recalled Jeff Richardson, one of the conference planners.

"We didn't just shoot at making mathematical graphics," Costa said, "we were doing stories with *LogoWriter*, we were doing projects and social studies and science with animations and text and graphics. People could see the potential for integration for these applications, so you didn't have to be the computer teacher, or the math teacher—you could be the English teacher, or the history teacher, or the geography teacher and take advantage of these tools. So I think that was possibly the biggest eye-opener, and it made people think, there are other applications I hadn't considered, and maybe they've done some of the groundwork for us to get rid of some of the hard slog of how you actually make it work on a daily basis."

For the overseas visitors, many of the phenomena Costa described were familiar from their own experience working in US schools. But during their time at MLC, they also encountered things they had not seen before. One that particularly impressed Goldenberg was how computers had changed children's attitudes toward copying. "We saw kids downloading information from the school library onto their computers, then somehow realizing that in the process they had not done any work. So their work was the embellishment of this thing that they had gotten so easily for free.

"Kids without a computer would in effect do the same thing—go to the encyclopedia and copy down a whole bunch of stuff—and by the time they had finished that, they really had done a whole lot of work. It was pure plagiarism, but they felt they had worked hard, copying it all, hand-tracing the pictures. So there was this interesting thing about the computer making the copying part so easy, that the kids could get on to do some other piece of work. And the folks down there [at MLC] commented on this.

"They also commented about the kids copying from each other. Somebody would have a Logo project, and give it to another kid, relatively freely, figuring that it was their thing, they were proud of it. And the other kids would be happy to have it, but would be building on it, and they knew where their work began." Before then, it had never crossed Goldenberg's mind that computers could influence the sense of where the actual work was.

Many attendees at the conference were decision-makers from other schools. They had come to find out for themselves what was going on at MLC. What they saw convinced some that laptops could no longer be ignored. But to get laptop programs going at their schools, they would need support. Prime among those providing that support would be Bruce Dixon, the other new actor who entered the drama at the World Conference on Computing in Education.

21

THIS IS GOING TO WORK

Thus far in our story we have been concerned mostly with professors and researchers, with principals and teachers. Now, an entirely different type of character enters, in the shape of an educator-turned-entrepreneur named Bruce Dixon. Unlike most entrepreneurs, Dixon's primary goal was not to turn a profit, but to use his business nous to help bring about substantive changes in classroom practice.

David Loader deserves the credit for initiating the world's first laptop classes. But it was Bruce Dixon who figured out the model for one-to-one computing, and the support system needed to sustain it. He also put together ways of propagating that model to other schools, first in Australia, then in the US, and finally all around the world.

Dixon was the glue between the pieces, the organizer who brought all the players together, the workaholic promoter who had the tenacity to keep things happening. It was Dixon who wheedled long-term (three-year) warranties out of the laptop manufacturers, who coaxed unwilling insurance companies into writing policies that parents could afford, and who developed maintenance procedures that ensured repairs were sufficiently rapid that students would never be without their machines for long.

"Make no mistake, without Bruce Dixon, none of this would exist," Gary Stager asserted. "Bruce put together the kind of nasty business stuff that made all of this possible, while all the time trying to keep education at the forefront of the discussion." In addition, to ensure that the good word about one-to-one computing spread throughout the community, Dixon created information conduits in the form of annual conferences for educators.

By nature humble man, Dixon enters the drama in characteristic fashion, working behind the scenes, as the distributor of *LogoWriter* in Australia for Logo Computer Systems Inc. He had brought out Brian Silverman, *LogoWriter*'s developer, for the World Conference on Computing in Education in Sydney in 1990.

Silverman, in turn, brought along Stager. He introduced the latter to Dixon on the LCSI stand at the conference.

"Gary was this bloody weird guy," Dixon recalled, "walking around ranting with a Coke and a pair of sneakers on." Then David Loader chanced to come by the stand. "He and I got talking and Bang! we just hit it off. I said, Well, why wouldn't we bring this guy [Stager] out to work at MLC? And David went, Yeah, that's a really good idea. And I said, Tell you what, the two of us'll underwrite it."

Bringing Stager out to MLC was just the first in a long line of initiatives that Dixon and his company, Computelec, would underwrite in his determination to use technology to transform learning. "Anytime any money was needed for anything Bruce wrote a check," Stager recalled. Including the International Logo Conference: "I was the chairman, but I didn't know the overhead costs—the conference lost a bunch of money, and Bruce just ate it."

◆　　　◆　　　◆

Bruce Dixon was born in 1950 in the little country town of Mildura—"front door to the outback"—in far northwest Victoria. Dixon is what his fellow-countrymen call a "dinkum [genuine] Aussie". He is a tall man with a powerful physique that derives from ocean swimming and ruddy, square-cut, weather-beaten features that could easily belong to a farmer. His accent is broad, his conversation peppered with colorful Australian slang. They demonstrate that, though his mission takes him all over the world, Dixon has not strayed far from his roots.

In Australian slang a *larrikin* means, roughly, a mischievous person. The word is sometimes used—with approbation—to describe Dixon. It captures the aura of *joie de vivre* he radiates wherever he goes. "Bruce used to come to see us at the business school at MLC," Joan Taylor remembered, "he'd walk in the door, and everybody in my office would light up, people who scarcely knew him, but they just knew that this fellow was great fun. He wasn't the sort of person who gave the impression that he was working hard at cultivating people, it was just that he enjoyed the whole thing so much that he was taking us all along with him."

But the bluff exterior disguises a deeply serious individual. Dixon cares passionately about kids and learning, feels intensely frustrated at progressive education's past failures, and is determined that in the future, if he has anything to do with it, things will be different. He is a big-hearted man who is always positive, always enthusiastic, always encouraging, always first to give credit where it is due, always on the lookout for some new way to bring about substantive—a favorite

Dixon word—change. At the same time, Dixon is as much pragmatist as idealist, very much aware of what will fly, and what will not.

Education was not his original vocation. At the state schools Dixon went to he was never more than an average student. Aged 17 he moved to Melbourne to attend pharmacy college. Pharmacy not being to his liking, he took a position with NCR as a trainee computer programmer. From there Dixon went on to become a systems analyst. The company earmarked him as a rising star. It was the late 1960s and the Vietnam War was raging. In 1970 Dixon marched in support of a moratorium on the fighting. Afterwards he stuck an anti-war badge in his lapel. His boss told him that since NCR was an American company, it was inappropriate to wear that sort of thing. Dixon said "Well I'm sorry, it's my personal belief. And he replied, If you wear that badge, you won't work here. And I said, That makes my decision very easy. So that was the end of my high-flying career in computing."

Dixon next worked at a variety of jobs, spent time travelling overseas. Eventually, aged 27, he decided it was high time to get a career. Teaching was what he most wanted to do. At teacher training college, Dixon became interested in alternative schooling. He devoured the "literature of rage" that had burst forth from the US in the late 1960s. Among the polemics his favorite was *Teaching as a Subversive Activity*. In this book authors Neil Postman and Charles Weingartner assert that the teacher's job is to help kids develop the critical skills they need to survive in a world of rapid change.

When Dixon left college in 1979 he went looking for schools that were doing something different. At one school, he chanced to visit a seminar for gifted kids. The teacher was just finishing her lesson as he came in, and she was waxing lyrical about "Apples". Afterwards Dixon went up to her: "That sounds fantastic," he said, "but what can you do with a piece of fruit? She looked at me and said, I'm talking about computers. I said, you've got to be joking." When he left NCR Dixon thought that he would never again have anything to do with computers. Soon, however, he had bought himself an Apple II with 8K of memory. He started using computers the day he started teaching.

As a teacher Dixon always identified with kids who were not succeeding. In his first class was a boy called Scott who, everybody told him, "was dumb as dishwater, never going to get anywhere." But Scott clicked with the computer. "And once you see that this kid can succeed on one thing, you start asking, Well, why is it that he's not succeeding on other things? Has it got something to do with the learning environment, teaching styles, and those sorts of things? And, of course, it does." Though Scott was the most extreme case, there were also other kids like him for whom, Dixon realized, the computer could provide a very different sort of learning experience.

He noticed other interesting things, too. "Often, when kids would work collaboratively round the computer—because we only had one in the class—you'd find that they could do together things that we'd allowed them to do, that with pen and paper we might not have allowed. So this whole idea of giving them different learning experiences that identified skills that we couldn't otherwise see was part of my growing awareness...I started to see what technology could do."

Dixon remembered in particular one piece of software, called *Lemonade Stand*, written by the Minnesota Educational Computing Corporation. It was a simple simulation of kids selling lemonade from competing stands. Variables included the cost of the lemons, the amount spent on advertising, and the price of the lemonade. Dixon sometimes ran the program with two classes, making up five teams of lemonade stands, other times as one-on-one competitions between peers at lunchtime or after school, with a board set up next to the computer to keep track of the score.

"I watched all the computing—as in mathematical computing—going on, the working out by kids who you wouldn't think would be motivated to do this sort of stuff. It was a simple tool, but they all wanted to see who could sell the most lemonade....It fascinated me, the simulation aspects of creating this little microworld that these kids could explore. And that did influence me a fair bit because I saw the power of that sort of learning environment, rather than dumb drill-and-test stuff."

In the early 1980s Australian schools, like their counterparts in the US and elsewhere, were at the stage of having a single computer at the back of the classroom. Kids were being told that if they used a wordprocessor that was going to change how they wrote. "And it was absolutely the most structured, stale, artificial, intrusive environment you could possibly have," Dixon recalled.

"We used to spend a lot of time working out how we could rotate the kids through, so that they each got their fifteen minutes to do inspired creative writing. The kids'd go there, and it'd take them about five minutes to work out how to get started, with their bloody five-and-a-quarter-inch floppy disk, then they'd spend another five minutes trying to figure out how to use the wordprocessor, then off they'd go with five minutes left in which they were supposed to do some creative writing—it was just absurd. So that frustrated me enormously."

Dixon threw himself into activities at the Computer Education Group of Victoria, among other things running Logo training courses and co-editing (with Caroline Dowling) the group's journal. He recalled a debate at a CEGV conference in about 1984. "We were arguing about whether kids should learn keyboarding skills, and guess what? They didn't have any access to keyboards! We had an average of about one keyboard for every 40 kids. The stupidity of that debate was just beyond belief."

After his initial experience as a teacher, Dixon moved on to become principal of a small elementary school near Melbourne. By this time he had two computers of his own, plus two that the school bought. "There was a period where I had say 15 or 16 kids in the class and four or five computers. I realized that when you had a ratio of one between two or three kids, all of a sudden different things started to happen—kids were starting to turn out really substantive work, kids who didn't normally write were doing really good writing. I started to think, Hang on, what if these kids had one of these to themselves, what could happen here?" And I realized that the whole issue was access."

In addition to limited hardware, a second frustration was the lack of decent educational software. Dixon decided to try and do something to solve this problem. In 1985 he quit teaching and joined a company run by Scott Brownell, who ten years earlier had been responsible for bringing Logo from MIT to Tasmania. Dixon went to the UK looking for suitable software to distribute to Australian schools. On his return, Liddy Nevile introduced him to Michael Quinn, the president of LSCI. Quinn and Dixon hit it off, and *LogoWriter* became one of the products his company distributed. While Dixon was not convinced that Logo was the panacea for everything that its devotees claimed, he was a passionate believer in its underlying let-the-kids-go philosophy of learning.

But despite his best efforts, the access problem remained intractable. Dixon became disheartened. It seemed that the technology-rich approach to which he was committed could never become a reality. He remembered all too well what had happened to the last major attempt at reforming classroom practice, the Open Education movement of the early 1970s. Good ideas had been misinterpreted or badly executed, teachers not trained to adapt to the new environment. The movement failed dismally, the walls between classrooms went back up, and the reactionaries said Told you so.

"So at that point, which was the late eighties, I'm thinking it's hopeless, it'll never work, we'll never solve the problem if we rely on governments and outside sourcing to fund computers in schools." Dixon realized that for his dream to be successful, it had to be embraced in the mainstream. Then out of the blue, at the conference in Sydney, Dixon came across David Loader, who'd had this wonderful idea about introducing laptops. When he got back to Melbourne, Dixon made a beeline for Loader's school.

It was a revelation.

"What I saw with David at MLC was everything I believed in philosophically and educationally being attempted in a very mainstream school. And I thought, Hello, this is going to work, because he's got the confidence and the trust of all these people and he's going to deliver the sorts of results that they'll all want to see once we get down the track. I realized that here was an opportunity to work with someone who was really on the same wavelength, and I think David thought the same thing. I understood the technology, he had the school, and we had a chance to make it happen."

Fortunately the chemistry between Dixon and Loader in those early days was good. "The relationship between Bruce and David had sparkle," Joan Taylor said, "they were two larrikins who enjoyed each other's company a great deal, socialized, played cards, tennis, did all sorts of things together. And that relationship to my mind was tremendously important."

Dixon's company, Computelec, was not just a software distributor, it was also a computer reseller. MLC's original laptop supplier had done a poor job. Computelec won the contract to deliver laptops to the College for 1991, the year of the laptop program's expansion from four to fifteen classes.

◆   ◆   ◆

In 1991 Computelec was a tiny company with only five or six employees. In its first couple of years of supplying laptops to MLC, the firm lost a fortune, "far more than anyone would ever imagine." But Dixon was convinced they were doing something worthwhile. "We invested an enormous amount of money in the original [MLC] program to get it over the line, subsidizing it with systems integration and other forms of mainstream, non-school-related computer business." Eventually Computelec would do well out of selling laptops to schools, but the learning curve was steep.

Dixon himself became intimately involved with MLC, working with the school's staff three or four days a week for a couple of years. Dixon would be there at seven in the morning, sitting in on faculty meetings. He would still be there late in the evening, listening to what was said at parent meetings. All through the trials and tribulations of the early days, Dixon was always on hand, scrutinizing everything that happened, participating in the dialog.

Dixon's great strength was that, having himself been a teacher, he recognized that the school environment was very different from the business one. In addition to the technology, he understood what the teachers required, and what was happening from a learning point of view.

One of the basic requirements was reliability. Computelec made sure that the machines kept working. "We did everything," Dixon recalled, "if there was a problem we'd replace the machine or we'd have someone there to fix it." He developed a system for replacing parts in machines that had broken down and for replacing ones that had been stolen.

It was also Dixon who solved the insurance problem, which on several occasions had threatened to close the laptop program down. In the first year of the program, MLC had had to insure the machines itself. Insurance was a boring, unglamorous issue that no-one wanted to get involved with. Now, Dixon devoted a huge amount of effort to cajoling the companies into developing appropriate products for schools. He fought bloody last-minute battles with balky insurers to get them to provide affordable policies.

Other suppliers could not compete with what Computelec did, because they lacked Dixon's total commitment to the cause. "If you go to your average dealer and tell them you want them to spend a few hundred hours at five or six schools to see if you can get a laptop program started," he explained, "they'll look at you as if you had two heads."

To flourish and bear fruit, the seminal initiative needed constant nurturing. Few were aware of the thousands of hours that Dixon put in husbanding the development of the one-to-one computer movement from a seed to a crop. But all the effort would ultimately pay off. Beginning in 1993, other schools began implementing their own laptop programs. In 1997, in recognition of his efforts, Dixon received an award from the Smithsonian Institute in Washington DC. It was presented to him by none other than Seymour Papert.

"At the end of the day," said Adam Smith, a teacher who joined MLC's laptop program in 1991 (and who as we shall see would himself play a crucial role in its propagation), "lots of people out there sell computers, but Bruce gets excited when he sees something like this, and that's what differentiates him from everyone else. I don't think he'd be happy selling computers for the sake of it, he would only be happy if he felt that he was benefitting the kids. It sounds very altruistic, but that's where he's coming from."

As we shall see in Part Four, Dixon was also instrumental, through his company's connection with Microsoft, in bringing developments in Australia to the attention of American educators. And in promoting the spread to US schools of laptop programs modelled on the Australian experience.

22

FROM A SEED TO A CROP

For the teachers in the early days of the laptop program at MLC, it was a wild ride. "We were the bull-bar on the four-wheel-drive of progress," one of them said, "bouncing along out there, with the mud and the insects and everything hitting us in the face." It was scary, but it was also exhilarating. The teachers knew they were blazing a trail. People like Gary Stager kept egging them on, telling them Nobody else is doing this—you guys are way out in front.

From the outset David Loader made no secret of what was going on at his school. Opening up, warts and all, to anyone who wanted to see gave the program a credibility it would not otherwise have had. For both teachers and students, it reinforced the notion that they were engaged in something special. Sharing ideas also accorded with Methodist tradition. "From those to whom much has been given," old Dr Wood used to say, "much is required."

Loader was also well aware of the need to create critical mass. "If we were only one school, and no other school followed us," he said, "then we would have been left high and dry, lonely and vulnerable. So it was very important that we get out and sell the basis on which we had made our decision."

Visitors were always welcome at MLC, and they came in droves. "It was incredible," laptop class teacher Adam Smith recalled, "there were people coming to your classroom just about every second day." Some days as many as 50 or 60 visitors would come. By 1991, the second year of the laptop program, so many people were knocking on the door asking to be shown around that, in order to let the girls have some peace, the school was forced to impose a by-appointment-only rule.

Eventually, MLC set aside one day every semester for an organized tour, guided by a senior member of staff, complete with a catered lunch. In 1993, for visitors who left wanting to know more, the school published a collection of papers. Entitled *Reflections of a Learning Community*, it was written mostly by David Loader and members of his staff.[1]

"Those early years were so tough," Loader recalled, "a lot of people came to see us, but they really came to criticize, they didn't come to learn. They kept saying This is all for show, it's not for real. And there was a sense in many people's minds that what we were doing was image-building and playing. But in fact it was the opposite, it really was an educational focus."

Cynics scoffed that the laptop initiative was merely an extension of the "typing pool", MLC's secretarial training school. Another classic comment was that the laptops were just a publicity stunt, a gimmick to attract enrolments. Though Loader was not enthusiastic about the idea, it quickly became apparent that the laptops could indeed be used as a marketing tool for MLC. The early years of the laptop program coincided with the recession that followed the Gulf War. No longer able to afford the fees, many parents were pulling their kids out of private schools. Schools were forced to sack staff. Competition for students intensified.

Rivalry between private schools in Melbourne's middle-class heartland had always been vigorous. Large numbers of these schools are concentrated in a relatively small area. In the immediate vicinity of MLC alone are half a dozen other independent colleges, three of them like MLC girls-only schools. The inner suburbs' obsession with private education dated back to the late nineteenth century. Authorities deemed primary education the responsibility of the state; secondary education the preserve of the private sector, which in those days meant mostly religious denominations. Private schools would monopolize secondary education in the city up until the 1950s, when construction of state high schools began.[2]

In this highly competitive environment, laptops were soon perceived as giving MLC a comparative advantage. At the beginning of each school year, the local papers would carry pictures of pretty little girls with laptops tucked under their arms. Seventh-grade laptop classes at MLC filled up eighteen months before they were due to start. ("Embryos were on the waiting list", quipped Gary Stager.) The school was effectively full.

The overwhelming majority of parents had little or no idea about Logo or constructionist philosophy or the enhancement of learning in the broader sense that computers could bring. What they saw mostly was the opportunity for their kids to learn computing, a skill that would stand them in good stead in the job

1. Reflections of a Learning Community: Views on the Introduction of Laptops at MLC, ed Irene Grasso & Margaret Fallshaw, MLC, Melbourne, March 1993 <http://library.mlckew.edu.au/computing/reflections.htm>
2. In Australia, independent (= fee-paying) schools enrol about 30 percent of all students, with state government (= public) schools accounting for the remaining 70 percent.

markets of the future. At a time when unemployment was climbing, that was enough to get parents sucking in their breath and reaching for their check-books.

◆　　　◆　　　◆

Of the initial wave of schools to implement laptop programs, each was in some way unusual. This of course was not unexpected: why should an ordinary school attempt anything so radical as a laptop program? The good is ever the enemy of the better. One pioneer was a new school, another a new principal at an old school, the third a school that was on the verge of going under, the fourth a public high school whose principal was committed to providing equality of educational opportunity (and who unusually had the autonomy to deliver on that commitment.)

The first outsider to take what was going on at MLC seriously and to realize its implications was oddly enough not from Melbourne. Cec [pronounced "Sess"] Munns was the principal of John Paul College, an ecumenical private school in the conservative northeastern Australian state of Queensland (the Deep North, as it is sometimes called).

A veritable steamroller of a man, Munns had fought his way up from humble origins—his father was a fettler, a railroad maintenance worker; his mother, a railroad station mistress— to become the founding principal of his own school. Munns, according to the official history of John Paul College, "tends to attract either adulatory praise or severe criticism. He is not a neutral man. He generates strong emotions in his supporters and in his critics."

His leadership style was very different from that of David Loader. Munns could be "overpowering and autocratic...[having] supreme faith in his own vision and unbounded confidence in his own judgment."[3] Towards his staff, Munns was "a hard task master [demanding] total commitment and dedication to the College." Bruce Dixon referred to him, fondly, as "the Lee Kwan Yew of education."

John Paul College is located on a hillside in Logan, a satellite town on the southern outskirts of Brisbane, the state capital of Queensland. Logan is one of the most disadvantaged parts of the country socio-economically, an area where youth unemployment runs at over thirty percent. It was a new town peopled by

---

3.　Noel Quirke, "The Wind Beneath Their Wings: A History of John Paul College 1982–1992", The Jacaranda Press, Milton, Queensland, 1992, pp118 & 119

families who do not have, as Munns put it delicately, "a tremendous amount of excess finance". On average, they were far less well-off than MLC parents.

John Paul is a school that likes to control everything, one which prides itself on attention to detail. A visitor could hardly fail to notice how well-kept were its grounds—every blade of grass cut to the exact same height and not a speck of dirt to be seen—and how well-mannered its students. "Good morning, Sir," they would inquire politely, "How are you?" JPC was also a new school, in 1991 still a year away from celebrating its tenth anniversary, and thus unconstrained by tradition. But with 2,300 pupils it was already the largest school in the state, and Munn's flair for publicity and promotion had played an important part in its growth.

Cec Munns descended on MLC one morning in 1991. A couple of months later, he was back, bringing with him a retinue of his staff. "They colonized MLC," Stager recalled, "there were John Paul people sitting in for weeks, like pesky relatives from overseas that you couldn't get out of your house."

Adam Smith vividly recalled Munns' visit to his classroom. "Most people would just come in and have a look—they'd talk to the kids about what was going on, and that was it," Smith said. "But Cec walked in, looked around at what was happening, then pretty much cornered me. He started firing specific questions—How does this work, What are the kids doing, When do they do this?—really making me justify what we were doing. At first I was taken aback, but on reflection he asked more critical questions and was far more demanding than anybody else who visited the class."

Deeply impressed by what he had seen, Munns quickly made up his mind that John Paul College needed a laptop program of its own. "I realized immediately that it had to be done," he declared later, "if the education we offered kids who were going to move into the twenty-first century as adults was going to be relevant to their needs."

Instituting such a change would not, he knew, be easy. "Educationalists are a conservative mob," Munns asserted, "indeed, we're reactionary. We're certainly not known for our ability to be innovative, dynamic, outward-looking. And there's no greater pain to the conservative human body than the pain of a new idea. It's more comfortable to teach kids as they were taught in the nineteenth century than as they should be taught, for the twenty-first century.'"

Munns was not a man to do things by half measures. "We decided that it had to be a complete immersion program, there was absolutely no degree of option. At John Paul College, there would be no place to hide—it would be modern technology spread across the whole curriculum, and all staff members would have to be part of it." To spearhead the charge, he poached Adam Smith from MLC to direct the integration of technology into the curriculum.

But though the laptop program would cover the whole school, John Paul College did not rush headlong into the implementation. Munns was determined not to repeat what he saw as a mistake that Loader had made.

"David didn't include, as part of his planning, a very thorough public relations campaign. It had to convince not only his staff, but also his parents and the whole community, that if they didn't do this, they would be negligent. Learning with laptops was an opportunity you couldn't afford not to give your kids. So we had a two-year lead time, from 1991 through 1993. In addition to a very intensive in-service program to skill our teachers, one of the biggest things we carried out was to make sure that we talked to our parents consistently. And on our planning committee we put a parent who was a computer expert, and who we gauged could have been a problem if he wasn't sold on the idea. So we had to sell him first, and then he could sell to our other parents.

"Now by the time we got to the stage of saying, It's on, it's starting next year, this is what it's going to cost you, and this is how you get your computer, I think that if we'd called if off at that stage, we'd have had a revolution on our hands because the parents were so sold on the situation."

◆   ◆   ◆

When Peter Crawley opened his newspaper in 1990 and saw the picture of MLC girls walking down the street clutching their laptops, his first reaction was one of outrage. Putting computers into the hands of fifth grade children—how ridiculous! "This is an absolutely appalling piece of marketing," he spluttered to his wife. Then he put the paper away and forgot about it.

Or rather, tried to. But the image kept gnawing away at him, until eventually Crawley was forced to concede that personalized computers for kids might not be such a bad idea after all. What finally convinced him of the power of the computer was his own experience with them as an English teacher.

Crawley styled himself as a "deconstructuralist" of language. "I like to rip text apart," he explained, "find the qualifying ideas, and reconstruct it. I would work with kids on a few lines of text on a blackboard, just hammering away at it for a couple of periods, rebuilding it into something better And of course, that's basically wordprocessing. And it just struck me that so much of what I did as my passion in the classroom would be so advantaged by having this power in a much more usable form in the hands of the kids."

Crawley taught twelfth-grade English, a level at which students are required to refine their work through several drafts. In 1992 he told his students that henceforth he would only accept wordprocessed submissions. This was a bluff (not all the kids had access to a computer) but nonetheless, the standard of work improved dramatically.

That year, Crawley was appointed principal of Trinity Grammar, a second-tier independent boys' school located just around the corner from MLC. He arrived at Trinity determined to replicate MLC's laptop program. Winning support for the idea was not difficult. MLC had broken the ice; many families who sent their daughters to MLC also had sons at Trinity. With the recent advent of Microsoft's *Windows*, parents were rapidly realizing that the computer was no longer a geeks-only gimmick but an essential ingredient of any conceivable work environment of the future. They were an easy sell.

At the same time, however, Crawley's goals were fundamentally different from those of David Loader. One glance was sufficient to tell you that Crawley was at heart a very conservative educator. His blonde hair was neatly groomed and he dressed in the uniform of business—dark-blue blazer, striped shirt, sober tie. In his mid 30s at the time of his appointment, he was ambitious and seemed exceptionally sure of himself.

Whereas Loader wanted use laptops to transform education, Crawley merely wanted to apply modern tools to traditional activities, to train students for the real world. He liked Loader's concept of personalized computers, the idea that ownership brought about deeper and more committed use of the technology. But learning to program Logo-style was no part of his agenda. For him, programming was "a time-consuming, pernickety little activity that a few children get a lot out of but, for the majority, it brushes over them and it's a pain in the butt." In addition to which, programming also required a huge commitment from staff in terms of preparation.

Crawley preferred software that was acceptable to the business community. "I wanted to use software that parents were using at work," he said, "I didn't want children to come home and find dad or mum would look over their shoulder and say, O you're using an *educational* software package." For him the word "educational" as applied to software was synonymous with "second rate." Educational software had had twenty years to prove itself in the marketplace and had failed, Crawley felt, because it was not much good. What he wanted to get into the hands of the kids was the applications software that business used. That meant Microsoft.

Trinity became the first school to adopt *Microsoft Office* as its core software. The majority of schools implementing laptop programs would follow Trinity's approach in preference to that of MLC. And this choice would have, as we shall see in Part 4, momentous consequences.

Using the software that business used did not mean using it the same way. Crawley was at pains to point out that his philosophy for equipping every student with a laptop was not about training young people in vocational skills. It was about enhancing the quality of their thinking.

◆   ◆   ◆

Another school to begin a laptop program in 1994 was Kilvington, a Baptist school for girls. The principal there was Di Fleming, an old friend of David Loader, who had previously been in charge of implementing the laptop program at MLC's middle school. Kilvington was a much smaller school than MLC, which made it easier to implement change there. Like Cec Munns, Fleming decided not to bring in computers on a year-by-year basis but to go for total immersion. It was risky stuff, but it was a risk she felt was worth taking. Enrolments were way down and the school was on the verge of closing. To lead the initiative, Fleming persuaded Adam Smith to return from John Paul College.

(In May 1995, Toshiba flew the three principals—Crawley, Fleming, and Munns, plus Bruce Dixon—to Tokyo. The Japanese company asked them to make suggestions as to how its machines could be improved as educational tools. This was remarkable in that it was probably the first time that educators had been asked for their opinions about hardware. Of course, to make an educational machine economically feasible, the market would have to grow to a certain size. At the time of writing, it has still not reached that scale. None of the suggestions made on that occasion was implemented.)

That year, 1994, thanks in part to conferences run by Dixon designed to spread the good word, (and, according to a cynical Gary Stager, a growing awareness among principals that they could get their picture in the paper—ie, free publicity for their school—merely by standing next to a student with a computer), the trickle became a stream. Several other independent schools launched laptop programs. They included Geelong Grammar, the most prestigious school in Australia, whose alumni included media mogul Rupert Murdoch and Britain's Prince Charles.[4]

As a result, the number of Australian students participating in one-to-one laptop programs climbed above 10,000. But the most significant new entrant in

1994 was not an elite private school. Frankston High was a 1,400-student public school located in a small bayside town just south of Melbourne.

Frankston started its first laptop class in seventh grade using donated computers. The next two years, the school ran three laptop classes with the parents paying for the machines. And this was remarkable because Frankston High was not a school for the children of the well-off. The socio-economic demographics of the town of Frankston were very much middle to lower. In such a place, parents do not spend thousands of dollars for something unless they think it will have real benefits for their children.

By 1998, half the kids in the year-seven intake were going into laptop classes. The implications were clear. If Frankston High could have a laptop program, so too could almost any school in the developed world. The only remaining issue was how to ensure equity of access, so that all kids could have their own machines.

◆   ◆   ◆

The driving force behind the laptop initiative at Frankston was the school's principal, Ken Rowe. A tall, bearded, powerfully-built man, Rowe in his schooldays had been captain of athletics. Like Bruce Dixon, he was a country boy who had come down to a boarding school in Melbourne to finish his education. Rowe would never forget the gap in the quality of education between the big city and the bush. As principal of a small-town public high school what drove him was a commitment to provide the same level of education as the private schools in the city. And if delivering on that commitment meant rocking the state education department's boat, then so be it.

In 1992 Frankston's principal visited MLC. "I had a look, spoke to a few kids there, and they just won me over. I mean, they talked so naturally about the computer, they referred to it as their educational tool, it wasn't any gimmicky thing." Rowe left MLC feeling excited. "I could see where it was all going. And I told my parents here that if we don't incorporate technology in our education, and we don't develop certain competencies with these kids, we're educating for redundancy, they won't fit into the new world of work. And that was obvious at David's school, when I saw where these kids were going."

---

4.   In 1965, Charles was sent for a year to Timbertops, Geelong Grammar's remote campus in the Victorian Alps.

As it happened, the Australian Council for Educational Research wanted to do an evaluation of a laptop program and was keen to use a government school. Frankston High was selected as the guinea pig. For the evaluation, the school received 25 laptops, chipping in its own funds to buy computers for teachers. Rowe called a PTA meeting to ask whether anyone would like to participate in the program: 119 families and 41 staff said they would. A seventh grade class and half a dozen teachers were selected.

By the end of 1995, the first year of the laptop program at Frankston, the feedback from the teachers was that they felt privileged to taking part. Computers were rejuvenating their teaching, offering them a whole new space in which there was room to grow. The kids and their parents also reacted positively. The following year, the school had a waiting list of 90.

To illustrate the change in the style of learning taking place at his school, Rowe liked to tell the story of how he went into a laptop class one day and asked the kids, "Who's best at *PowerPoint*? I asked. That's Helen, they replied. Who knows how to do e-mail? That's Mary. Who's the best person to show you round the Web. That's Tom. And so it went, around the class, Who's the best at spreadsheets? O so-and-so's the best. Then I said, How about Mr Angus? (the whizbang teacher in charge of the school's information technology department). And they said, O he knows a bit about it, but he's not the expert."

Rowe himself was happy to let kids be the expert. In 1997 he recruited his own computer mentor, an eighth-grader who showed the principal how to do things. "His name's Jordan, and he walks my office at recess and says How are you going Mr Rowe, you want a hand with anything? And I'll say, Look, come in tomorrow, I really want you to show me how to do something." Such public reliance from the top person not only gave the kid a kick, it also sent a powerful message to the school's staff. It let them know that it was all right to go into the classroom not knowing everything.

"And that's what David Loader is talking about, the classroom has changed," Rowe said. "You're not filling empty vessels, it's us as a team—we've got a problem, we've got to construct our own learning with the tool we've got and the problem we've got. Now, if you take the enormous imagination that the kids have, and give them a powerful tool like the computer, y'know, teachers have to hang on to their hats—I mean, Hell, what's going on here?"

That was a question American educators would soon be asking themselves as they encountered at first hand the remarkable developments in Australian classrooms. And this first generation of laptop principals would play an important role in taking back the message about computers in schools whence it had come, twenty years earlier.

But in addition to the high-profile principals, and Bruce Dixon working tirelessly behind the scenes to deliver better learning outcomes, there was at least one more actor who would play a key part in effecting the transition, and spreading the good word: one of the pioneer laptop teachers, Adam Smith.

23

INSTITUTIONALIZING CHANGE

Remember *tamagotchi*? The fad for virtual pets that in 1997 enslaved millions of pre-teens throughout the developed world? Conceived and first launched in Japan, *tamagotchi* were handheld electronic toys. On their tiny liquid crystal display screens, a chick would hatch. Fed properly, played with, and given regular doses of medication, the virtual creature would grow and thrive. Left unattended too long, it would wither and die of starvation, leaving behind (in the Japanese version) a tiny gravestone, or (in the US one) ascending to heaven accompanied by an angel.

At Kilvington Baptist Girls' Grammar School in Melbourne, staff regarded *tamagotchi* as a nuisance because they distracted the students. The girls were forever ducking under the desks to feed their pets, which led to the toys being banned from school. This gave Adam Smith, reckoned by many to be the most brilliant of the first generation of laptop teachers, a golden opportunity. He got the eleven-year-olds in his sixth-grade class to program their own virtual pets on their laptops.

"I didn't really ever know how these *tamagotchi* things worked," Smith said, "so I relied on the kids explaining to me what this thing needed to do. We spent a few lessons building an initial model using *MicroWorlds* [multimedia version of *LogoWriter*], and then they just took it away and expanded on it."

Expanded on it is putting it mildly. The kids threw themselves into inventing virtual pets with a bewildering variety of behaviors and characteristics. When Smith walked into class in the morning, the girls would insist on showing him the latest things their digital creations could do. Some had programmed random pets, so that each time you clicked the "hatch" button, a different creature would pop out. In addition to feeding, the girls had their pets taking showers (and drying themselves afterwards with a towel), reading books, phoning each other, going to school to get educated (after which the fatigued pets invariably had to go on vacation), and playing games against their owners (the altruistic creatures were somehow always happier when the girls won).

"It was an instance of the kids picking up on something and getting engaged in it," Smith said, "enjoying the learning even though some of the concepts were really difficult for them to understand." For example, the underlying math required to get the thing working was hard. It included some algebra, not a normal component of the sixth-grade curriculum.

"More important, programming the pets to have their own behaviors required the kids to reflect on what behavior is. For many of them, it was the first time they had stopped to look at what pets *were* and what they did. It really was a meaningful learning experience." Six months later, long after the fad for *tamagotchi* had faded, Smith was still getting e-mail from the girls saying how much they'd loved doing the virtual pets project in class.

Virtual pets had been an opportunistic one-off. The following year, Smith came up with a more structured way to unleash his students' creativity, this time with a class of fifth-grade kids. The project, to build an ecological model, was part of an environmental topic.

Smith began by setting up the situation. "First of all the students were given a role, as scientists. They'd just returned from a planet called Zilog where they'd observed these life forms—something that looked like a plant, and another thing that looked like an animal. It appeared that the two things had been living in harmony, that there was an ecosystem which was quite well balanced, because obviously these animals and plants had been there for many thousands of years. The kids' brief was to describe this to other scientists.

"They were just starting to get into *MicroWorlds*, learning a little bit about programming. So we decided to build a model to explain what they had observed. We started building the basic parts of the model together, then the students took it from there and developed their own models from that starting point. What they built was a simulation; there was a mathematical algorithm running the model, which to me was the interesting part."

In order to build the algorithm, Smith explained, "the kids first had to theorize how the parts of the system might be inter-relating." Then, through successive attempts, they could build increasingly complex models. They moved between the abstract representation, the computer code, and the concrete representation of the system's behavior over time, the output of the program. The idea was that through this process, they would develop their theory and gain some lasting understanding of the concept being studied.

The kids modelled a plant called "Plantus" that would grow out of the ground, randomly, across the environment (the screen of their laptop). They made sure that they could control how quickly the plant replicated itself. Then the students built an animal called "Animus" that would run around eating these plants. Here, too, they ensured that they could also control the speed at which the animal moved, and at which it ate.

"Of course, there was a lot of fun just creating these plants and seeing the little animal running around and gobbling them up. The students recognized that if the animal ate too many of the plants—it was a bit like a goldfish, that was the briefing, it didn't have the common sense to stop eating—then it would basically explode from over-eating. If the creature didn't eat enough, it would die from starvation.

"So, in terms of building the model, the students started trying to control how fast the plants were reproducing themselves, and how quickly the animal was running around eating the plants, and trying to balance the system. It proved to be a real challenge, because of course they could alter the size of their plants, and all sorts of different variables. And the interesting part came when, in trying to balance the system, they had to go back and control those variables and work out how they could provide themselves with control over more variables.

"And what eventuated out of this, on about the third or fourth lesson, was that we had the kids almost turning it into a game. They were trying to see how long they could sustain an environment, with the little animal running around until eventually it died either from starvation or over-eating.

"So, on the last time we were working with these particular models, we turned it into a competition. We gave the girls about half an hour to fine-tune their models. Then, on the count of Ready, Set, Go! they all started their animals and plants replicating. And we timed them to see who had the longest-running environment.

"Initially, of course, you got thirty of these things running around. And as soon as I said Go, some kids went O No! because their animal had died almost before getting out of the starting blocks. But then the other models started, and after ten minutes we had five or six other kids whose animals had died off, and those kids started to take sides with other groups, cheering for them. So then we had two kids sitting next to every computer cheering. And finally we were down to two or three computers left, and of course groups huddling around each of these kids' machines. And then down to the last two—one of them lasted around 25 minutes, until the thing finally did implode.

"At that stage, as a teacher, you've got to try to decide whether to regroup and try to extrapolate and try to get them to apply what they've been thinking about back to the core concept. But the kids seemed so happy that I just let them go off—I felt that the real object had been achieved and that the extrapolation could be left to another day.

"Most of them, if you'd walked in and asked What are you doing? they would have said Playing a game. And I think that the really interesting thing here is, if you were to look at what was actually happening on any of these screens compared to what you would see on any commercial video game, it would look so clunky and so average. And yet you've got kids jumping up and down and screaming at the top of their lungs, and running from computer to computer to see whose animal is still alive. And that has to send us a really strong message about the ownership the kids feel when they're actually able to build and create their own models and systems."

It was a wonderful lesson, too good for an individual teacher to keep to himself. But how to put it, and other good computer-based lessons, into the hands—or, more accurately, onto the computers—of other teachers and students? That was the problem which Smith set out to solve.

◆   ◆   ◆

Adam Smith's mother was a junior school teacher. Her son grew up thinking that he would not follow in her footsteps. For reasons that he could no longer fully remember, he changed his mind. In the early 1980s, in his mid teens, Smith caught the microcomputer bug, staying up all night programming on a tiny computer with 1K of memory plugged into a black and white TV.

He wrote games for his siblings and friends, who would spend days playing them. "It was only later I realized that this was probably the most powerful learning I had done to that point," Smith recalled. "It was authentic, self-motivated, self-directed, and rewarding." The high point for the young hacker came when a computer magazine published one of his programs. Smith used the prize money to buy more memory for his machine.

By the time he reached teacher training college in Melbourne, however, the infatuation had long since passed. Nor was Smith's interest revived by the college's introductory courses in educational computing, which for him consisted of the most boring sort of stuff. "It just seemed fragmented and not underpinned by a philosophy or meaningful direction as to what this would mean for us as teachers."

For one course, *Mindstorms* was required reading. This was exciting, but there was no follow-up. Smith had learned Logo during his teens. For a programming assignment, while most of his fellow-students were drawing stick figures and trucks, Smith set himself the challenge of coding a kaleidoscope. It turned out to be some of the most complex programming he had ever done, and Smith was pretty pleased with the result. He was not so happy with the five out of ten mark it received. When Smith approached the lecturer for an explanation, she told him that his program didn't work. It turned out that she had not been able to follow his instructions on how to load and run it. They loaded the program together, it worked, the lecturer thought it was pretty, and upgraded his mark to nine out of ten.

Until that time, computing had been a fun thing for Smith, one which had empowered him. Now, what had previously been pleasure was being pre-packaged and fed to him as "education". "I wasn't playing the game," he recalled ruefully, adding "I could have drawn a great truck." The education establishment didn't recognize him, nor did it seem to care about the enthusiasm he had for computing.

By late 1990, when he interviewed at Methodist Ladies' College for his second job as a teacher, the 24-year-old Smith was not a computer user, did not even own a machine. But though computers were no longer important to him personally, he still knew far more about them than most people. And he was very interested in the study of learning and cognitive science.

In a few weeks, the students from MLC's first laptop classes would be moving up to sixth grade. The junior school desperately needed computer-savvy teachers who could walk in and take up where Steve Costa and his team had left off. But finding elementary school teachers who knew something—anything!—about computers turned out to be extremely hard.

Now, as if in answer to their prayers, here was this dashing, raven-haired young man with his confident, slightly amused manner. He seemed to know all about computers. Even better, when the interviewers told him that Smith would be teaching girls who each had their own laptop, he didn't seem in the slightest bit fazed. Nor was he bothered by the prospect of having to learn how to use the software for this new computer before school started. Heaving a sigh of relief, they more or less offered him the job on the spot.

During his first few months teaching at MLC, Smith continued to maintain that he had no particular interest in computers and technology. They were not what mattered to him. Soon, however, he realized that the way the kids in his laptop class were learning was profoundly different from anything he had encountered before.

"They would be doing some programming, then they would run into problems, which they would solve by talking to each other. Or, they would spend half an hour trying to work it out themselves. They were putting their hands up, not because they couldn't do something, but because they had found ways to make it work and wanted to share what they'd learned."

In a traditional class, not much time is spent constructing knowledge. At the beginning of the class, the teacher explains a concept, then the kids consolidate it through some sort of practice, or ask for help if they don't get it. In Smith's class, by contrast, the kids were acting more like scientists or researchers. "There would still be a need to come together as a group and share a concept, but often class time was about everyone trying to make something work. Hence, what stopped the class was a discovery or a new contention."

Smith had a hunch, though he had no formal research to back it up, that the students were able to transfer their coping skills and approach to problem-solving from one subject area to another. (The very thing that Pea and Kurland had tried to prove almost ten years earlier at Bank Street College.) "So if the students couldn't do a math problem, they would have strategies, or they would try and find lateral ways to go about looking for solutions, and be relying on themselves a little bit more."

Probably this was a combination of confidence and strategy. "The key thing was that the kids expected to understand—the answer came from understanding the process or system, rather than carrying out a sequence of steps. They were getting used to grappling with the ideas, working things out for themselves, and becoming confident and resilient in this fuzzy place.

"In old, transmission-style education it was a case of I know, I tell you, now you should know; either you do or you don't, and if you don't, you come back and ask me again. In this new, constructivist-style, relatively young kids were spending more of their time working things out for themselves, or in collaboration with their peers." This was not entirely without guidance. "We provided a scaffold but the kids built their buildings, and each was different. For them, the motivation—and what was valued by us as a whole—was not so much the right answer (arrived at by following the steps), but the process of working something out and understanding how it worked."

After a year of teaching at MLC, Smith was a believer. As far as he was concerned, "the nature of what was happening in the class had changed fundamentally. Suddenly, I couldn't imagine teaching without laptops."

At the end of 1991, the second year of the program, Costa rounded up the junior school teachers and told them they had to write a rationale for using laptops in their classrooms. The group sat around talking about how the kids became more autonomous in the way they worked, more creative, how their thinking skills improved, how even kids who struggled were still gaining a lot of satisfaction in what they were doing—the list of benefits went on and on.

The discussion took about an hour. At the end of it Smith realized much to his surprise that, although they had all been talking about how learning was transformed as a result of using computers, nobody had actually mentioned the words "computer" or "technology" or any of the technical aspects of computers in the classroom. "And that's when it really dawned on me that we were achieving some of the long-held goals for education."

◆   ◆   ◆

In his third and final year at MLC, Smith moved up to the middle school. There, his role was to help staff in ninth grade cope with their first year of laptop classes. These teachers were, he was dismayed to discover, not exactly enthusiastic about the prospect.

In the early days of the program, the first people to pick up laptops had been volunteers. Back then, there had been plenty of excitement, plus lots of pats on the back for doing a wonderful job just for using computers in your classroom. By 1993, however, the fourth year of the program, the thrill was well and truly gone. Laptops were reaching teachers many of whom, so far from being volunteers, had up until this point actively been avoiding using computers. These recalcitrants were now having to embrace the machines whether they liked it or not. Laptops were fast becoming standard equipment at the school; everybody in the lower grades was using them. For the laggards, however, there were no kudos in adopting computers. Nobody was going to bring the press or visiting dignitaries into *their* classrooms to see what they were doing.

Smith's challenge at MLC was thus to build bridges for teachers who were not enamored with the technology. He had to help them cross from where they were, to where the school needed them to be. Or perhaps staircases would be a better metaphor than bridges, given how much of an uphill climb for some teachers using laptops seemed to be.

It could be rewarding, though. Some of the most critical adopters turned into the best users. "Many of them really care about their kids and what they teach, and—rightfully—they won't use a computer until they see a good reason for doing so." Smith enjoyed having to argue with the skeptics and justify his point of view. "The onus was on me to show the value of the learning technology. If they met me half-way, and at least tried some of the ideas, then I was pleased. I never pretended to be an expert in their subject areas—I needed their expertise and their criticisms to ensure that what we did end up trying in the classroom was sound."

In 1994 Smith moved to John Paul College in Queensland as director of curriculum technology. As we saw in the previous chapter, that school had adopted a policy of total immersion: from the outset, all teachers were required to use laptops in their classes. But many were not sure what to do with the machines. Most of the available software seemed to be aimed at business rather than education. The teachers often found it hard to see how the computer could be used at a tool to create opportunities for learning. Smith's job was to sit down with groups of these teachers and figure out how the machines could best be used in their subject.

His greatest success at the College came in an unexpected area. Jenny Moon was a music teacher who taught composition as an elective subject starting in ninth grade. When Smith encountered her, Moon was terrified of technology, literally too scared to turn the computer on. Previously, the kids had composed their music the traditional way, writing it down on paper with no idea of how it would sound when played. Now Smith showed Moon a software package that connected a laptop directly to a synthesizer keyboard. It enabled the kids to compose by playing their music into the computer, then listening to the playback over headphones. The software automatically took care of writing the score, freeing the students to experiment with different instruments and combinations of instruments, and acoustic environments.

In practice, what this meant was that the students were able to extend themselves a lot further. It was particularly good for the less-gifted students, who achieved a lot more success once they could actually hear what they were doing. The technology brought to the fore talents that might otherwise have gone unrecognized. In her first batch of ninth graders, Moon had one student who was a good but not outstanding musician. By the time he left in year twelve, this student was composing pieces for full orchestra, one of which won him second place in a nationwide competition for young composers.

From having been totally computer illiterate, Moon was now no longer able to imagine teaching without the computer. For Smith, having kids make high-level choices about which instruments to use because they had the ability to listen to any number of different combinations, something that would be inconceivable without the technology, represented an undeniable demonstration of the power of the computer.

But despite such powerful demonstrations, the technology was not being adopted consistently across the school. In eighth-grade science, for example, two of the school's science teachers were doing fantastic things, while the other eight were doing absolutely nothing. How to pick up the initiative of the enthusiasts, and drop it into the classrooms of the others? Smith wondered. How to tell these laggards, Here's that thing that So-and-So did well, he collected and analyzed the data in this way: Take it and use it, or do something better, but don't do nothing?

At other laptop schools, the pattern was the same. Every school had two or three enthusiastic volunteers who did brilliant stuff with the computers in the first couple of years. Then, around the third or fourth year, the program seemed to hit a speed-bump and lose momentum.

Schools were spending tons of money on putting in infrastructure—the computers, wiring, networks, and all the rest of it. But few teachers were able to figure out meaningful things to do with the hardware. As a result, all too often, not much happened. Soon laptop schools started to feel the pinch from parents who had paid thousands of dollars for a machine. "How come my kid's not using it much?" they wanted to know, "all she's doing is some wordprocessing."

Smith saw that there was an urgent need to identify teachers who had managed to think up good uses for computers in their classrooms, and to share those ideas with other teachers. In other words, some way of institutionalizing the change process.

"What became obvious to me," he said, "was that we needed models and examples of good practice. What was also clear was that we needed a method of distributing these examples directly to teachers and students in a very easy way, and of bringing down those technological overheads."

Having worked at three of the pioneer laptop schools, Smith was exceptionally well-placed to know teachers who were producing good stuff. At the same time, the mid nineties saw the rise of a wonderful new channel for the distribution of content, in the shape of the World Wide Web. The two came together in his mind to form an idea.

In essence, the idea was to assemble a library of tried-and-tested curriculum-based activities—such as Smith's own ecological model—that teachers could download from the Web. That way, instead of spending hours planning (and only getting half an hour of lesson time out of their efforts), teachers would simply access the website where the library was located. There, they would spend a few minutes looking around, find an activity that might fit their requirements, then download it ready for use in the classroom.

To go with the idea was a business model. For a small additional investment, schools could take out a subscription that would give all their teachers access to the library.

◆   ◆   ◆

Smith was not destined to remain a classroom teacher forever. "Some people can teach for 30 years and still have the energy to do it every day," he said. "I just couldn't do that, go in and look at the same four walls—I live for change." Now came his first big change: moving from teaching to a new career as CEO of an Internet-based startup.

Formed in 1997, the company was originally known as Mathetix, after "mathetics", a term Seymour Papert coined in *Mindstorms*, meaning "having to do with learning". Later, the fledgling firm changed its name to SchoolKiT, the name of its flagship product. The company adopted constructionism as its basic philosophy. "A lot of the things that we've learned with laptops were about open-ended software that lets kids explore and create," Smith explained. "They start with a blank screen that allows them to build their own information products, as opposed to consuming other people's." As, for example, in the case of the virtual pets.

In its first year in Melbourne, the start-up consisted essentially of Smith and his older brother Mark, a professional programmer. In time-honored entrepreneurial fashion, Mark sold his house and lived on his savings as he worked without salary. Bruce Dixon acted as mentor to the brothers. "Bruce seemed to enjoy discussing the educational imperatives," Smith recalled, "and unlike most people, seemed to think we could make a go of it."

They could. In 1998, to provide some much-needed seed funding, the Smiths sold Toshiba an exclusive one-year license. That year, the first commercial version of SchoolKiT shipped to Australian schools as standard software on thousands of Toshiba laptops.

By that stage, the company had identified a number of key developers, teachers with experience in using the technology who could supply them with tried-and-tested lesson modules. "If we have a secret," Smith said, "it is that our stuff is developed by teachers and it works in a classroom—it's nitty-gritty reality, and people like that." By harvesting ideas in this way—and paying the developers for their efforts—SchoolKiT's library was growing at the rate of twenty modules a month. In 1998, the library contained around 200 activities; by 2002, it had over 650.

◆   ◆   ◆

As it turned out, the main market for SchoolKiT would not be Australia, but the United States. In 1997, Smith previewed a prototype of the product at a laptop schools conference in Atlanta, Georgia. This early version only had nine activities, but it seemed like everyone wanted to buy it.

The same year, Smith showed SchoolKiT to participants in a pilot project for teachers in Washington state. Based on constructivist principals, this grassroots initiative aimed to integrate computers into the curriculum. As we shall see in Chapter 27, the teachers loved SchoolKiT. Since local support could not be provided from Melbourne, in 1998 the change-loving Smith and his brother moved across the Pacific to Seattle and set up shop there.

The first year, SchoolKiT worked with teachers at 30 Washington schools, the next 180, then 450, the total rising finally over a thousand. In addition, the company was working with a further two thousand schools across the United States.

The lessons about learning with computers that had been pioneered in Australian schools were taking root all over America. How this remarkable transition occurred is the subject of Part Four.

PART IV
BOOMERANG

24

SERVING TEA TO THE AUSTRALIANS

The sleepy little town of Snohomish, Washington, is dominated by its lumber yard. A gigantic conveyor belt clanks and judders as it hauls up huge tree trunks, newly denuded of bark and branches, depositing them ready to be sawn up into two-by-fours. Originally a farming community, Snohomish is now a bedroom town, most of its residents working either in Seattle, fifteen miles to the south, or Everett, six miles to the north. It's a conservative sort of place, with a population—mostly white—of around 8,000.

On the outskirts of Snohomish is the town school, Emerson Elementary, the oldest (built in 1955) of nine elementary schools in the local school district. Emerson Elementary is a low-slung building with a huge sloping roof. On overcast, blustery November days, a stiff breeze bangs the rope of the flags—the Stars & Stripes above the green banner of Washington State—against their pole. At recess, well-wrapped-up kids play out front in an outdoor basketball court, a huge barn-like structure with a roof but no walls that says much about the rigors of the local climate. (Coastal Washington is one of the wettest places in the United States). Above the school entrance, the movable letters on a cinema-style marquee read "Welcome to Emerson Elementary, a good place to learn"

On one such November day in 1995 the principal of Emerson Elementary, Maureen Cornwell, a passionate, voluble woman in her late forties who wore her straight, flaxen hair cut short, received a call summoning her to the district superintendent's office. It was not a good time for local educators. The district had recently failed its levies, which in Washington State account for some twenty percent of school budgets. On the ballot, in addition to the general maintenance and operation levy, residents had also voted down an individual technology levy. That meant the school would not be able to increase the number of computers it owned beyond the current, miserable level of one per classroom.

When the unexpected summons came, Cornwell was going through the agonizing process of cutting back programs. "O my God, what have I done wrong?" she remembered thinking. In case she couldn't think of a response to whatever the problem turned out to be, as backup, Cornwell took along her assistant principal. "So we go over there, and they tell me, Guess what, Maureen—you're going to Australia!"

Thus began what Cornwell would later call "the most exciting thing" she had been involved with in her 30-year career as an educator. It would lead to lowly Emerson Elementary becoming one of America's first wave of laptop schools.

◆   ◆   ◆

The chain of events that culminated in Cornwell's unanticipated invitation began back in February of that year. Tammy Morrison, an intense, well-organized young woman who worked for Microsoft's Education Customer Unit, happened to be in Sydney on a tour of the company's Asia-Pacific subsidiaries. A local executive, an ex-teacher, told Morrison that she and her boss should take the opportunity to fly down to Melbourne to check out what schools there were doing with laptops and Microsoft products. The pair contacted Bruce Dixon, whose company Computelec was a Microsoft reseller. Dixon arranged for them to visit two schools, Methodist Ladies' College and Trinity Grammar.

The visit to MLC did not go well. The laptop program there was then in its fifth year and a certain arrogance had set in at the College, at least among some of its staff. They seemed to think that the two women had come to sell them software rather than to see what the school was doing with computers. The hosts used the opportunity to lecture their American visitors. They told them how Microsoft would have to modify its products to be acceptable at their school. David Loader was not at MLC that day. Dixon subsequently managed to organize a meeting with Loader at a cafe in the city but this, too, went badly.

At Trinity Grammar, which was just beginning the second year of its laptop program, it was a very different story. The school had been under the impression that it was someone from Microsoft's Melbourne office who was coming to see them. The hosts got a shock when they heard American accents. No special arrangements for the visitors had been made. Trinity principal Peter Crawley recalled that "everything was done on an ad-hoc basis of Who's doing something after recess?"

The Microsoft executives were eventually ushered into a fifth-grade classroom. "It was a very enlightening experience," Morrison recalled. "We were expecting to see kids using *Office*—that's why they told us we were going down there—and we saw that. But the really moving thing was what was happening in that class-room, the level of activity.

"It was loud, it was collaborative, the kids were excited, they were working hard, it was all of these things that were not about using the software but about the environment that was created, with every child having their own laptop and of being empowered to do their own learning—which made it a different learn-ing experience for them. It was obvious at the time that there was a huge differ-ence between what we'd seen in most US classrooms and what we saw at Trinity." The comparison was one that Morrison was well qualified to make. She had been working in educational technology for six years, at IBM prior to joining Microsoft.

The key thing, the visitors soon realized, was saturation. With saturation, the technology became transparent. It could then really be used as a tool. "So we knew we had stumbled across something that was very innovative and amazing," Morrison said, "but we didn't know what to do with it, or how to think about it." So she did the sensible thing, and called for a second opinion.

Morrison contacted John Sabol, a senior Microsoft executive who she knew had the luxury—rare among a company of workaholics—of having the freedom to think about whatever he wanted. Sabol was a sort of vice president without portfolio, someone whose loosely-defined job description was to be anywhere in the world where something interesting was happening. Morrison knew that what Sabol had recently chosen to concern himself with was schools and kids, and how, through education, Microsoft might contribute to society. "So when this opportunity arose, I called John and booked him a plane ticket."

◆   ◆   ◆

Though his business card gave John Sabol's job title as "Assistant to the Chair-man", *consigliore* would be closer to the mark. In 1984, after more than twenty years working at IBM, the Seattle-born, Harvard-educated Sabol jumped ship and joined Microsoft. There, Sabol was just in time to "carry Bill's briefcase," as he said, with characteristic modesty, in the make-or-break tussle between Microsoft and his former employer for control over the operating systems of per-sonal computers. This was the defining moment in the software firm's history: Big Blue's bluff was called; Microsoft's future dominance assured. No doubt Gates found Sabol's insights into IBM-think at this crucial time invaluable.

In 1995, Sabol was nearing retirement age. His white hair and beaky nose gave him the look of a wise owl. Sabol would sit in meetings not saying anything, apparently miles away. Then, suddenly, he would interject with a question that cut straight to the heart of the matter, or a comment that kicked the discussion up to the next level. Sabol was a strategic thinker, a man who could get things done, but whose preferred mode was very much to operate behind-the-scenes.

Sabol dated his keen interest in education back to a visit he had made to a school in Tucson, Arizona, in about 1993. This middle school had around 350 students, each of whom was equipped with a high-end desktop computer, courtesy of a grant from Compaq. "It was a lower socio-economic area and the kids in these classes were sixth-to eight-graders," he recalled. "They were using the most advanced Microsoft *Office* software in completely amazing ways."

Sabol was stunned that such young kids could use the software so effectively. Moreover, "it seemed to be doing amazing things for their self-esteem, they were collaborating a lot more, getting their various projects done on the computer—there were a lot of positive aspects to it. But the technology was all given to them, and you can't do that very many times. And of course, we all know that you can't afford one computer for every student."

In other words, the program was not replicable. Then, at Tammy Morrison's urging, Sabol went to Australia. There, he discovered a model for ubiquitous computing that actually seemed to work.

At the Arizona school, *Office* had been the only software on the computers. The philosophy of the principal there was that he didn't want anything on the machines that would take away the teachers' responsibility to teach. He didn't want the computers used as teaching machines, he wanted them to be used as tools exactly the way they were in business. And the principal didn't want any changes to the curriculum, he wanted these tools to be an enhancement to the curriculum. When Sabol met Peter Crawley in Melbourne, he discovered that Trinity Grammar's principal had independently formed the exact same philosophy. "That's what triggered my intense interest in the subject," Sabol said.

As it happened, the day Sabol and Morrison visited Trinity, the school was having one of its regular evenings for parents of future laptop kids. Accepting the invitation to attend, the visitors were astonished by the parents' enthusiasm for the program. "Sitting on either side of us were two absolutely maniacal parents who were telling us about how great it was to have the opportunity to send their kids to a school where they had this level of technology available," Sabol recalled. "We were both just totally amazed at how convinced these parents were." At John Paul College, it was the same thing. "I want my grandson to attend this school", said Sabol as he came away. "But I can't send him to Australia, so we're going to have to do something about that."

The pivotal moment came one afternoon chatting with Bruce Dixon in a Melbourne coffee shop. "This idea [one kid one computer] is all very well," Sabol said, "but there's no way it can happen in public schools in the US because of the equity issue." Dixon replied, "Look, we have an equity issue in schools here, too. Getting this much money for hardware isn't easy, but these parents want it for their kids. There are cases where parents can't afford it, but you can solve that by philanthropic contributions or whatever. And this is a sufficiently big idea that people will actually work hard to make it happen."

Sabol was intrigued by Dixon's contention that it would be possible to have a computer for every student in US schools also. Back in Seattle, immediately after disembarking, he slotted a quarter into an airport payphone and called one of his favorite public school people, Mark Mitrovich, superintendent of the Peninsula School District, in Gig Harbor, near Tacoma. "I said, Hey, there are these schools in Australia where every kid has their own laptop, and the way the schools do it is they have the parents buy or rent these things. Of course, in a public school, you'd have an equity issue, but could you solve it, could this kind of program work in public schools in the US? And Mark said, Of course it could—come down and we'll explain exactly how."

When Sabol arrived, Mitrovich divulged that his district had been unable to pass its school bond issues in its last four attempts, and was as a result essentially broke. But schools there were still able to offer an athletics program, by charging students two hundred dollars per sport per season. Of course, there were families who couldn't afford that. The solution was for the school foundation to take their names and find ways to get the money to enable students to participate. "We'll use that same technique," Mitrovich told Sabol, "and every kid will have a laptop."

Armed with this simplistic notion, Sabol went to see his boss, Bill Gates. "There's an amazing formula here that might actually allow laptop programs to work in US public schools," he told Microsoft's chairman. Gates was intrigued, but wondered whether it would be possible to get the money, in the form of scholarships or whatever, to make up the difference. Sabol pointed out that the Australians were making it work. The meeting concluded with the pair agreeing that the idea was worth exploring further. The best way to explore further, Sabol suggested, would be to fly some American educators down to Australia to figure out how the Australians' model worked.

When top management at Microsoft says Go, things tend to happen quickly. Within six business days of getting the green light, Sabol had picked ten independent-minded teachers, technology directors, and superintendents from half a dozen schools and school districts, mostly in the Seattle area. Four of them were public school districts, including Snohomish and Peninsula, chosen in part because they had financial difficulties, the other two were the private schools that Gates (Lakeside) and his wife Melinda had attended (Ursuline Academy in Dallas). Sabol secured visas and in some cases passports for the educators—for several of them, this would be their first trip overseas—booked round-trip, business-class tickets, and they were gone. The trip took place over the Thanksgiving holiday in the US, springtime Down Under.

◆   ◆   ◆

Maureen Cornwell had to keep pinching herself to make sure that what was happening was real. "I was just sort of overwhelmed by it all," she recalled. At the time Cornwell had been an educator for almost 25 years, in large schools mostly, making decisions that she thought were in the best interests of kids. Although Cornwell regarded herself as a good leader and a good administrator, she was a self-confessed technological illiterate who hardly even used a computer, other than to email people within her district.

It thus came as a great relief to Cornwell to discover that she could take another person with her. She chose Kelly Starr, a teacher who had taught fifth and sixth grades at Emerson Elementary for 11 years. Starr, then aged 37, was in charge of the planning team, the hub from which emanated pragmatic decisions about the future of the school. In addition to being an excellent teacher, she also seemed to have some understanding of computers.

In fact, by her own admission, Starr was not then a huge proponent of educational computing. Prior to going to Australia, she had never really seen what technology could do for student learning. What Starr did know, all too well, was what a struggle it had been just to get one computer into her classroom. Emerson Elementary had recently taken out a $40,000 loan to equip each of the school's classrooms with a single desktop machine.

"That was the vision of the time," Starr said. "The arrival of the desktop to my classroom seemed to be the end of the vision. The lack of training and the impossible task of using one computer for student learning often meant the computer was only used by students when all of their other work was finished."[1] Though drawn to the open-endedness of the computer, especially with games and simulations like *The Oregon Trail*, she had seen nothing to compel her to invest any time in learning about technology.

Starr was about to be confronted with a radically different reality: schools where every student had their own laptop all the time. And, even more incredible, where it was the parents, not the schools, who paid for them.

The trip began with a hitch. In their haste to get the ball rolling, Sabol and Morrison had overlooked the fact that, time-wise, the west coast of the United States lags the better part of a day behind the eastern states of Australia. Which meant that, following their arduous 23-hour flight from Seattle—changing planes in San Francisco and Sydney—there was no rest day for the party to recover. It was Monday morning when, exhausted and jet-lagged, the educators staggered off the plane in Melbourne. No sooner had they checked in at their hotel than they were whisked off for a daylong visit to Trinity Grammar.

"I can remember going up to my room and taking a shower, and my bags didn't come up," Cornwell said. "What happened was everybody else got a bus, and I was late, so I ended up having to go in a taxi separately. And I remember thinking, O my Lord, am I creating a problem for the group here?"

In addition to Trinity, on their whirlwind seven-day trip, the Americans also visited Kilvington in Melbourne, John Paul College in Brisbane, ending up at another Trinity, Trinity Anglican School in the northern Queensland resort of Cairns. Following Tammy Morrison's unfortunate experience there earlier in the year, MLC did not feature on the group's itinerary.

When they walked into their first classroom at Trinity Grammar, the visitors were simply blown away by what they beheld. For Starr, seeing every student having a computer was "a huge, mindboggling experience, because that was so different to anything we had going on in the US at that time. It was really pretty phenomenal that every child had access to one machine that they had control over, and that they didn't necessarily have to follow set steps, like Click here and Go there—everything they were doing, they were designing and creating themselves."

Presentations were typically formal and well prepared. "Each school visit brought us students anxiously awaiting our arrival", Starr wrote, "to share their personal stories of how this laptop was making learning more fun, more interesting, sometimes harder, sometimes easier."[2] "When asked if they would be willing

---

1.   Transforming Learning: An Anthology of Miracles in Technology-Rich Classrooms, ed Jenny Little & Bruce Dixon, Kids Technology Foundation, Melbourne, 2000, p103

2.   Ibid, p100

to give up their laptops, there was always that resounding NO!" On encountering such enthusiasm, Starr was initially skeptical. Was it really worth all the effort, expense, and anxiety, she wondered, to make learning fun and—maybe—more interesting?

But when she had the opportunity to sit and talk with the kids and ask them questions, her skepticism soon wore off. "The thing that did stick with me was the fact that when I started asking them about the learning and what they were doing, they really could articulate what their learning was about, what the objective was, and what they hoped to accomplish with it."

Starr also talked with teachers who saw their roles as educators changing. "They shared stories of students' interest in learning increasing....I talked with parents who said that [having a laptop] was the best thing that had ever happened in their child's education, and that they thought it would make a huge difference for their child's future."

Were these stories too good to be true? Or was there some exaggeration in the descriptions? Starr reckoned there probably was. What couldn't be exaggerated, however, was what she witnessed outside the organized visits and prepared presentations.

"I saw students taking pride in their work as they described the activity. They were able to explain what they were learning and why they were creating it within their tool of choice." It seemed the learning was much more student-focused when each child had a tool that allowed for the differences between them. In her capacity as leader of the planning committee at Emerson Elementary, looking for ways to improve student learning, Starr had often visited other schools. Now, in Australia, she saw learning personalized for far more students than she had ever seen anywhere else.

The Australian educators Starr met did not attempt to disguise the difficulties of implementing a laptop program. They talked frankly about their problems, sharing "the anxiety that bringing laptops into the classroom can generate. They shared their fears of not knowing enough about computers, not being adequately prepared in how to integrate this tool into the curriculum, or not having enough support at the administrative level."

But the teachers also told Starr that the difficulties were worth enduring for the results that laptop programs produced. Their students were now able to create knowledge more effectively from their activities and projects. At Trinity Grammar, for example, the visitors saw how boys were able to take the same set of data and rework it into several different forms, such as tables, charts, and graphs. The final product was a narrative description which showed that, because of all the data manipulation they had been able to do, in a reasonable amount of time, they fully understood the concept.

Students at laptop schools seemed to have moved away from simply being passive receptors of information towards having more control over how they learned, setting the stage for how they might continue to learn in the future. Starr came away from the one-week fact-finding trip a true believer. "My life was changed forever", she wrote.

Nor was Starr the only one to be profoundly affected by what she saw. Maureen Cornwell described what she had experienced as like being "knocked over the head with a hammer." At first, Cornwell had felt like she was setting out on a mission, to see whether laptop programs would work in US public education in general, and at her school in particular. As the trip progressed, however, Cornwell was overcome by her perception of the gap between what she was seeing and the norm in US schools.

"So the mission was no longer What was going to happen in my school, it was My God, what am I going to do for our country? I was so concerned that we were so far behind in my little section of the world, which I knew to be typical of what was going on across the United States. We were not giving our kids what they deserved to have—access to technology."

As the group sat around collecting their thoughts at the debriefing session after their visit to the final school on their itinerary, Cornwell summed up her feelings. "Guys—you know what's going to happen if we don't do this?" she told her colleagues. "Our kids are going to be serving tea to the Australians!"

◆　　　◆　　　◆

Cornwell and Starr spent the long flight back to Seattle rehearsing what they had seen and discussing how they were going to replicate it. "We knew that we had to go home and begin talking to any person or group who would listen to us about this possibility of having a parent-purchased laptop computer in a public school setting," Cornwell said. "And so, as we sat and talked, that was what was going through my mind: Over my dead body, I'm not going to be the one stopping this—of course we're going to make this work, we've got to get every kid access, and we're going to figure our how.

"All the things that were necessary to make it work we had available to us. The part that was different for us was that, in public education, we're supposed to be able to provide everything for kids. Parents are paying taxes to support public schools, they're not directly buying an expensive piece of equipment that their kids would be using."

A particular concern for Cornwell at this time was her awareness of the need for the US to compete in the global marketplace. "We can't be competitive if other countries in the world are ahead of us," she said, "like they are—all you have to do is read the news to see that we're importing people all the time to do the jobs because we don't have the skills." Herself a mother, with two sons then aged 18 and 21, Cornwell wanted her children to be able to muster everything that would allow them to function in the world of business. Her sons did have computer skills, but she knew that they had acquired them themselves, they had not learned them in school.

For a technological illiterate like Cornwell, someone for whom dealing with change had always been difficult, taking the decision to go ahead with setting up a laptop program was really scary. At the same time, she was nothing if not determined. In her office hung a manifesto which might have been her personal motto. It read: "If it is to be, it is up to me."

Snohomish was far from being an affluent community. About a third of Emerson Elementary's 390 students qualified for free and reduced-price lunches, an indication that their parents were struggling financially. Nonetheless, by the Spring of 1996, by dint of calling them all individually, explaining why laptops were important, and soliciting their participation—"Have you considered this? We really think that for your child, this might be something that's going to help them be successful"—Cornwell had managed to sign up 75 families of kids at her school for the program.

In her ardor, there were almost no lengths to which she would not go. The parents of one little girl came to Cornwell for help. They wanted to take out a loan to buy a laptop, but they had poor credit. Cornwell ran through all the different options with them. Finally, they told her that they were trying to get the girl's grandpa to help—would she be willing to call Wisconsin and persuade grandpa to be the signer on the loan? Cornwell told them "Hey, I'd do anything if you think it's going to make a difference. But I do think we ought to send grandpa some materials first, because I'm so passionate I could overwhelm him, especially over the phone." (A package of information was sent to Wisconsin, grandpa made the decision, and the little girl got her laptop.)

When the school year started that September, Emerson Elementary began its first two—multi-age fifth-and sixth-grade—laptop classes, taught by Kelly Starr and another teacher. Six other schools in the district also ran laptop classes. (We shall return to look at what happened in the Snohomish School District in more detail in Chapter 26.)

After the trip Down Under John Sabol and his wife took off for a week's camping vacation. When he got back to Seattle in December, Sabol called Cornwell. "Maureen had already been talking to the local computer suppliers, she had purchased her own laptop, and she was negotiating with this supplier to get the program working in her school. I said to her, Gee, Maureen, shouldn't you really think hard about whether you want to try this? And again she laid it on me: 'If we don't do this program, my kids are going to be serving tea to the Australians.'"

Cornwell's near-maniacal determination to make things happen for her kids came as a revelation to Sabol. "It was my first real insight into how dedicated, how energetic, how smart, how pragmatic teachers are," he said. "Of all the things I've done in my professional career," Sabol continued, "working with teachers like Maureen Cornwell has to be the most exciting."

Sabol went straight to Microsoft's top man. "Based on what I've seen," he told Gates, "this program can work." The decision was made to invest heavily in understanding how US schools could implement laptop programs. The question was now, How to get the word out to the education community? Early in the New Year, Sabol rang Bruce Dixon and asked him, If you were going to do this, how would you do it? "You've got to run a conference," Dixon replied.

25

NO BOTTOM TO THE PAGE

Anthony Amato was angry. It was late March 1996, and the superintendent of New York City Community School District 6 had been summarily dispatched all the way across country to this cockamamie conference in Seattle. Amato knew nothing other than that boss had told him to go find out what this laptop business was all about. The flight to Seattle was horrible, there were weather delays en route and, as a result, Amato was late getting to the hotel where the conference was being held. He was not in the best of moods when he arrived, just in time for the screening of a video made at Trinity Grammar in Melbourne the previous year. It showed Australian kids dressed in neat olive-green uniforms using Microsoft spreadsheets on their laptop computers.

"Here was this beautiful school with well-manicured children talking in prim [sic] English accents," recalled Amato, whose district spanned some of the roughest neighborhoods in Harlem. "God knows what would happen if our kids walked down the streets with notebook computers under their arms," he thought grimly to himself.[1]

That night, in a phone call to his wife, the 48-year-old Puerto-Rican native vented his spleen. The notion of laptops for every kid just seemed so irrelevant to his district. "This is crazy," Amato fumed, "more than ninety percent of our kids live in poverty!" But even as he fulminated, the superintendent began to have second thoughts. He spent a sleepless night, tossing and turning, going over the issues in his head.

The former principal of a Bronx middle school, Amato was an ambitious man, a born fixer who, had he not been running a school district, could equally well have been a dockside union boss. He had made a career out of taking on challenges that other people had given up as lost causes. Next morning Amato came down to breakfast determined that, whatever it took, he would figure out a way

---

1. Neil Gross, "Mindshare Is a Terrible Thing to Waste", Business Week, 5 May 1997

to provide laptops for his kids. "I don't know how," the superintendent vowed, "but we'll do it."

Amato was not the only convert at that first Microsoft-sponsored conference. Of the 90-odd schools represented there, 52 would commit to setting up laptop programs the following September. Within three years, some 60,000 students at 500 schools across the United States would be learning on their own laptops in direct emulation of the Australian model. By the turn of the century, there would be at least 1,000 US schools with 150,000 laptop students and teachers.

The 240 attendees at the Seattle conference had not been selected at random. Microsoft's Tammy Morrison and John Sabol had gone about setting things up carefully. To get a reality check before proceeding, they consulted senior educators in several states. In New York, they met for an hour with Amato's boss, Rudy Crew, then Chancellor of the City's public school system and a former schools chief from Tacoma, Washington. "We talked to him for about ten minutes," Morrison recalled, "then he spent the next fifty minutes telling us why this had to happen." Everywhere the pair went, educators told them the same thing: This laptop program is exactly what we want, they said.

Morrison sent out exploratory letters to a hundred educators in both public and private school sectors. These were key individuals she had identified by asking Microsoft people working in education, school leaders whose vision of education was focused on the future, who had a track record of success (and whose districts used PCs rather than Macs). "I thought maybe twenty would reply," Morrison said. In the event, she received about three hundred responses. Thus emboldened, Morrison went ahead with planning for the conference. It was, she felt, "an opportunity to make something amazing happen in the US education system."

It was also an extremely risky thing in career terms for an ambitious young woman like Morrison to undertake. But her belief in what she was doing, her sense that she was doing the right thing, was such that she was willing to put her career in jeopardy. Over the next few years, to get the initiative off the ground, Morrison would break all the rules, behaving in a most un-Microsoft-like fashion to get what needed to be done. And all the while, behind the scenes, Sabol would use his clout on her behalf.

◆　　◆　　◆

At short notice, to tell their stories, five Australians were flown to the US. The team comprised Melbourne principals Peter Crawley and Di Fleming, teacher-cum-curriculum-director Adam Smith, professional development specialist Greg Butler, and team leader Bruce Dixon. Dixon acted as MC throughout the three-day conference, which was held beneath the chandeliers in the ballroom of Seattle's luxury Four Seasons Hotel.

The proceedings kicked off with a presentation from Crawley. Dressed in blazer, button-down collar, and striped school tie, Crawley looked every inch the conservative headmaster. He came across as a reassuringly mainstream figure. The ideal evangelist, in short, for a radical new idea.

To a highly skeptical audience of American educators Crawley described in his presentation the dramatic developments that had taken place at his school, Trinity Grammar, over the past two years since the adoption of laptops there. His delivery was dry, lucid, and serious, which made his occasional rhetorical flourishes all the more effective.

"Our children were wonderful," he told them, "the directions they took were just amazing—they pushed our curriculum development at a rate far faster than my leadership within the school could ever have imagined possible." Then, his pace quickening slightly, Crawley continued. "They came to school and said Did we know? And we didn't. And they came to school and said We've discovered. And we had no idea it was there."

Crawley talked of the bemusement in being principal at a laptop school. "All I do now is an awful lot of nodding in agreement to people who generate the ideas, and say That's fascinating, isn't incredible what you're able to do? And I say that over and over again."

During the Q & A session that followed, Crawley was asked whether there had been any research done on using laptops to take standardized tests? It was a question that over the years, in the seemingly endless debate over the effectiveness of computers in the classroom, would come up time and again. On this first occasion, somewhat taken aback, Crawley replied, "In Australia, we speak fairly disparagingly about standardized testing." His audience erupted into loud applause.

Crawley proceeded to address the evaluation issue in a roundabout way, by giving his personal perspective. "You spend time standing at the back in the classroom," he said, "you watch and you listen, and you cannot help but see a difference. It electrifies you—the first time I looked at the laptops in operation at our school, I came out absolutely tingling with excitement about what I saw in the classroom and what I felt." Judging by the enthusiasm with which Crawley delivered this last line, the sensation was still fresh in his mind.

Over the course of the three days, the speakers covered every aspect of laptop programs in Australia, telling real stories about the implementations in their schools. "We talked about getting parents on side, getting kids on side, getting staff on side," Di Fleming recalled, "professional development models, the hardware, the software, how to give financial access to kids, and the social justice aspects."

They also put on demonstrations. Adam Smith showed how open-ended constructionist environments like *The Geometer's Sketchpad* and *MicroWorlds* were used on laptops in Australian classrooms. One example that stuck in people's minds was a simple *LogoWriter* program. It had been written a few years earlier by a fourteen-year-old girl called Joanne in a ninth-grade math/science class at MLC.

The program began with a white dot in the center of an otherwise completely black screen. For a while—long enough for the audience to start getting restless—nothing happened. Then a second dot appeared, followed by another agonizing pause, at which point many people were no doubt thinking that something had gone wrong with the presentation, and starting to feel sorry for the presenter. Then two dots become four, shortly afterwards eight, until finally Bang! the dots multiplied rapidly until they filled the entire screen. The program concluded by displaying the words: "You're dead".

Smith then explained that the object of the exercise had been to model the exponential growth of bacteria in the human body. The power of the demonstration was undeniable: this dynamic, computer-generated representation was so obviously much more meaningful than a static curve drawn on a piece of graph paper.

"It was an amazing three days," Tammy Morrison recalled, "people were so unhappy, sitting listening to the Australians, and at us for thinking that something pioneered in Australian private schools could work in US public schools....It was a very emotional thing, and an intellectual challenge."

In particular, it took awhile for leery American educators to get their minds around the paradigm shift that lay at the heart of the Australian experience. Namely, that schools did not have to provide the hardware. Parents could be persuaded to purchase the laptops, thus freeing schools to invest in infrastructure and teacher training. And alternative revenue streams, like non-profit school foundations, could be set up to help kids get a laptop whose parents who could not otherwise afford one.

"It sounds wonderful," attendees mused as they listened to the presentations on the first day of the conference, "what these Australians in their nice little private schools with their nice little school uniforms are doing—but who can do it here?" In 1996 the idea of every student having a laptop still seemed like science fiction. By the second day, however, veteran public school superintendents like Tony Amato, and Herman Gaither of Beaufort County, South Carolina, and Walt Buster of Clovis, California, and Charlie Rhyan of Shelby County, Ohio, were beginning to scratch their heads. All four had independently reached the same conclusion. "We can't afford to do this," they told themselves, "but we can't afford not to do it, either."

◆   ◆   ◆

In Harlem, Amato began by taking an understandably cautious approach, starting with just 18 kids in one fifth-grade class. The superintendent was adamant that he wouldn't expand the program unless he saw the laptops having a positive impact on learning outcomes. Amato didn't have to think too hard about where to locate his first laptop class. Mott Hall was the jewel of District 6, a middle school that consistently ranks close to the top in New York City. Housed in a former convent, a graceful brick building on the edge of the City College campus near the northern tip of Manhattan, Mott Hall is a magnet school that accepts only talented kids. The school's 425 fourth-through-eighth-graders are mostly the children of immigrants from Spanish-speaking countries, predominantly the Dominican Republic.

Almost two thirds of Mott Hall's students are eligible for free and reduced-price lunches, which effectively means that their parents are poor. Nonetheless, when they heard that their kids had been selected to participate in the pilot laptop class at Mott Hall, the parents were thrilled. They immediately recognized that owning a computer would give their kids a leg up, even though it would mean that they themselves would have to sacrifice in order to pay for the machines. Amato arranged a three-year lease under which the district would pay half the cost of $58 a month, with the parents contributing the other half. To protect their investment, the parents got together to organize safety brigades to escort the kids to and from their homes and the school buses. The system worked—that first year, not a single computer was stolen.

Though she confessed that the laptop program added a lot of extra stress to her life, Mott Hall principal Mirian Acosta-Sing was from the outset a strong supporter. She saw in the program a wonderful opportunity to bridge what people in 1996 were beginning to call the "digital divide", between the children of rich and poor parents. Those on the wrong side of that divide were disproportionately African-American, Hispanic, and female.[2] If minority students and girls were to have a future in the twenty-first century, Acosta-Sing believed, then they needed technology skills.

Janice Gordon, the daughter of Jamaican immigrants, was chosen as the teacher of that first fifth-grade class. Though she herself was not exactly computer literate, the charismatic Gordon accepted the challenge with alacrity. Soon after the computers arrived that November, she began to experience the characteristic phenomena of computer-rich classrooms.

The children quickly took to their laptops, giving them pet names. Jose, a shy, bespectacled student who had previously struggled to fit in with his classmates, became a valued member of the community on account of his ability to solve technical problems. The kids wrote far more than before; they also wrote better. Mark, a student Gordon had taught the previous year, had failed every subject. He was frustrated because his handwriting was illegible and he would constantly omit letters from words. Now, equipped with a laptop, Mark no longer had to think about his handwriting or dropping letters because he had a wordprocessor and a spellchecker. As a result, his self-esteem had risen appreciably. "I know that I can show you what is in my head now," he told his teacher, "because I don't have to worry about what it will look like on paper."

Gordon discovered the value of cooperative learning, instituting a policy of "ask three [other students] before me" [the teacher].[3] "My expectations for the children and their perceptions of what they can achieve have changed," she said.[4] The attendance rate in her classroom reached almost 100 percent.

At the end of the trial year, progress at Mott Hall was so substantial that Amato decided to expand the program. Over the next few years, Acosta-Sing and her staff added classes and grade levels. By Fall 1999, every student in the school owned a laptop. That year, there were 4,500 laptops in District 6 schools. The superintendent predicted—overconfidently, as it turned out—that laptop computers would be on the desks of most American students within five years. "I'd put my reputation on it in minute," he enthused to a reporter from *Time* magazine.[5]

---

2. The term "digital divide" between information haves and have-nots was first used in a 1995 Merkle Foundation study by James Katz

3. *Transforming Learning: An Anthology of Miracles in Technology-Rich Classrooms*, ed Jenny Little & Bruce Dixon, Kids Technology Foundation, Melbourne, 2000, p63

4. Microsoft press release, 4 March 1998

5. Romesh Ratnesar, "Learning by Laptop", *Time*, 2 March 1998, Vol 151, No 8

(In April 1999, Amato left District 6 to become superintendent of public schools Hartford, Connecticut. There, too, he would initiate a laptop program. Gordon moved to Hartford to serve as program coordinator. In February 2003, Amato moved to yet another daunting job, as superintendent of New Orleans public schools.)

◆   ◆   ◆

"Who'd give a sixth-grader a laptop? Someone who can't even button his shirt?" Herman Gaither summarized his initial skepticism about the laptop concept. "What a dumb idea!" Then, pausing for dramatic effect, he added, "It's a dumb idea until you watch it work."

Gaither's district, Beaufort County, lies at the southern tip of the triangle that forms the state of South Carolina. Beaufort—pronounced "Bewfert"—is famous for its sandy beaches and historic antebellum houses. Each year such attractions draw thousands of tourists to the area. Ocean breezes and a balmy climate have also made the Palmetto State a haven for retirees. But the State is not exactly known for taking the lead. "The last time South Carolina was first was when we seceded from the Union," (in 1860, following Lincoln's election), Gaither observed dryly.

The superintendent had been in public education for 35 years when he and his director of technology, Anne Carver, flew to Seattle in March 1996. There, they discovered that laptops appeared to have the potential to change the way kids learned. Gaither had been looking for a way to create greater motivation and participation for kids in the public school system. Now it seemed he had found one.

Gaither began Beaufort's laptop program by targeting 250 sixth graders. Three middle schools were chosen for the experiment. The support of the principals and 25 teachers was solicited and obtained. In May, letters were sent out to parents asking whether they would be willing to participate in a pilot program. The response was enthusiastic: it seemed like everyone wanted a chance for their children to join in the computer age.

So far, so good. Now came the difficult part—how to ensure equality of access for all students? Beaufort County is unusual in that its students come from a wide variety of backgrounds, encompassing farming communities, military bases, Hilton Head residents, and rural natives, spread across a district of 24 schools and eighty-plus islands. The county was home to some of the wealthiest and some of the poorest families in the southeast; the digital divide in microcosm. Just over half of the 16,000 students in the district qualified for free and reduced-price lunch. "It was absolutely crucial that we did not separate children by economic status," Gaither said, "that we did not create a new class of haves and have-nots."[6]

As it happened, just the previous year Beaufort had passed a $10 million bond issue for technology. In a district where 73 percent of people do not have a child in school—all those retirement communities—local voters were unlikely to approve hundreds of thousands of dollars more for laptops. Another source of funding would have to be found.

The answer, for Beaufort County, was to form a non-profit foundation to raise money privately to subsidize the purchase of the laptops. Happily, the community was strongly committed to public education. The foundation solicited funds from local businesses, community groups, churches, and individuals. Dollar by dollar, the money was raised.

The school foundation purchased the laptops, then leased them to parents. Contributions were made on a sliding scale, based on ability to pay. The idea was that even a partial payment would ensure parents and students had a vested interest in the program. Families of students on free and reduced-price lunches would pay just $10 a month. "For some of our families even $10 a month is significant," Gaither said, "but it's not impossible if the family is interested in the child's education."

For the first three years of the program, a formal evaluation was conducted by researchers from the University of South Carolina.[7] They found that kids with laptops did better on standardized achievement tests than kids without the machines. In terms of improved academic performance, the computers had their biggest impact on African-American males, the group which had traditionally been least successful in school.

By the year 2000, the number of kids in Beaufort schools equipped with laptops had risen from 250 to 2,500. In five years, reckoned Gaither, who was himself African-American, fewer than five machines had been stolen. To be sure, some of his teachers were still resisting having computers in the classroom. But Gaither had come up with a policy designed to encourage participation in the program: "Feed the rabbits, and starve the snails."

---

6. "Laptop Schools in Action", Microsoft press release, 10 April 1997
7. www.beaufort.k12.sc.us/district/evalreport3.htm

◆   ◆   ◆

Walt Buster was in his office at Clovis Unified School District when Tammy Morrison of Microsoft called. Morrison had grown up in the Central Valley of California, her parents still lived in the Fresno area, and she had always been intrigued by Clovis's can-do attitude. Would Buster like to come to Seattle to take a look at some recent developments from Australia in using computers in the classroom? Buster told her No, he wasn't interested in participating in some promotional junket aimed at persuading him to buy more computers. Morrison had to work hard to convince Clovis's newly-appointed superintendent that this was a for-real deal.

Buster ended up going to Seattle. There, he soon became enamored with the idea that it was possible for all young people—not just the affluent, but also the disadvantaged—to have access to powerful learning tools.

Buster had long been interested in applying technology to education. It made him angry that almost any business you walked into, no matter how poor its performance, would have so much more in the way of technology than his schools did. At his former district in Sonoma County, north of San Francisco, Buster had established a technology high school on the campus at Sonoma State University.

When headhunters called to ask if he would be interested in relocating to the Central Valley, Buster replied "Gee, I dunno—it's awfully hot in Fresno." But regardless of the rigors of its climate, the area also had its attractions. "Clovis is a place that for some reason had never adopted the cynicism of many school districts," Buster said. "It was a culture that had always assumed that people were going to work together, and that there were good intentions." Clovis had no teachers' union, which meant there was none of the rancor that, in Buster's experience, often soured relationships between staff and management. At Clovis Unified School District, the attitude was positive; the focus firmly on the students.

Clovis is a small, suburban satellite of Fresno. The town reminded at least one visitor of Mayberry, the fictitious setting for the Andy Griffith Show, the 1960s TV sitcom. It was "an old-fashioned type of community in which people can walk through the downtown after dark without fear, in which the school dress code prohibits hair longer than mid-collar."

Clovis was slightly better-off than some parts of Fresno but, compared to the Northern Californian school districts where Buster had spent most of his career, the Central Valley—California's agricultural heartland—was a relatively poor region. Some 30 percent of the 34,000 students in the district's 35 schools were on free and reduced-price lunches. Though the majority of students were Anglo-American, Clovis also had some schools that were largely Hispanic and southeast Asian—Cambodians, Laotians, and Hmong. "These disadvantaged young people needed to have more stimulation, more powerful learning tools," Buster said. "And I had some principals at schools that were traditionally low-achieving who said Whatever it takes to get our kids to grade level."

Buster decided to begin the laptop program in Clovis by focusing on middle school, grades seven and eight. "We thought within those grades was where kids were falling behind, where we were losing students at risk, minority students, when they went from being a self-contained classroom to a compartmentalized schedule." To make sure every student was involved, Academic Block, a two-hour class which met daily, covering the subject areas of reading, language arts, and history/social science was targeted.

Parents at the district's three middle schools were offered the opportunity to buy a laptop for their kids. Unlike Beaufort, Clovis did not get involved with fundraising, or providing low-interest loans. Parents who bought laptops for their children did so outright or made monthly payments to repay privately-arranged financing. In September 1996, 94 seventh-grade students brought their computers to school. In addition, instead of devising a low-interest payment scheme for everyone, the district itself bought 200 laptop computers, enough to put half a dozen machines in every seventh-grade class. With 35 students to a class, these "mixed" classrooms provided one computer for every five or six kids.

Although Clovis did not ask the local community for help in funding the program, community support was still crucial because the district was spending public money on these school-owned machines for the mixed classrooms. The superintendent was the laptop program's number-one champion, pouring effort into drumming up support. He saw his primary role not as implementor, but as protector. "Walt Buster is everywhere," said his director of technology, Chuck Philips, around this time. "He's in the Rotary Clubs, the downtown associations, and other civic groups. He's always encouraging visitors from the community to come see what we're doing with laptops. And he brings teachers with him to the downtown meetings to talk about what's happening in their classes. That's been crucial to community support for our investment in this program."

Having at least some of the parents buy into the program proved the right way to go. When the district subsequently opened a new high school for students who were mostly very poor, the principal talked Buster into providing all the laptops. "Huge mistake," Buster recalled, "the program didn't work nearly as well when it became just like an entitlement that came with the school. It worked much better when the young people bought into the concept. That was what was so powerful about the program.... It takes some public relations time on the part of the superintendent and the board to explain why you're doing this, but it was certainly worth the effort."

The most appreciative parents were the most needy. At reception night, when Philips would take the laptops out of the boxes and pass them out to the students, many parents would be in tears. "They just could not believe that their young people had this, and that the school district had helped them," Buster said. In the seven years he was at Clovis, Buster could not recall having had a single complaint about the laptops from parents. For their part, the students were very respectful of their machines: "we didn't have any trouble with loss or vandalism."

The kids were astonished that adults were placing so much trust in them. As at Beaufort, the impact was greatest on students who were from underprivileged homes, or had learning disabilities, or had been reluctant learners. The laptops seemed to make them more interested and attentive. They became proud of their work: Buster liked to tell the story of one Cambodian-American youngster who, when asked why he wrote much more on the computer than he had done on paper, replied "Well, there's no bottom to the page now."

Such memorable moments did not happen of their own accord. They were nurtured by what Buster called "this incredible cadre of technology teachers. They gained such respect for their own teaching, and became experts in an area where they were highly regarded by their peers, and people in industry. I saw their stature as educators change so dramatically that I was just extraordinarily proud of their accomplishments."

One such teacher was Karen Ward, who taught Academic Block to eighth graders at Alta Sierra Intermediate in Clovis. Her first laptop year found her teaching this same curriculum with one class of laptop students and one traditional class. "My first big personal lesson using technology was of a practical nature," she wrote. "Although I had spent the summer practicing on my new laptop, my students had spent an entire year involved in the program before they came to me, and their knowledge of the computer's functions...was broader than mine."[8]

Ward felt uncomfortable with the fact that the students consistently knew more than she did, but she was determined to catch up. "I spent hours in the evening working on my laptop, acquiring new skills, designing lessons and activities that I knew my students could connect with. Of course my students were

---

8.   Transforming Learning, pp169,170

practicing and playing [too]. Soon I found that the old saying, 'The faster I run the behinder I get' was particularly true for me. I was frustrated and definitely out of my teacher comfort zone. When students would ask me questions about the laptop, I would have a hard time answering them. Finally one day a young man by the name of Russell pulled me aside and offered to tutor me in the use of the laptop. I put my teacher pride aside and took him up on his offer. I also decided that a more drastic course of action was required, and eventually I began to release some of my control over the learning culture in my room."

One instance of letting go was the Technology Show and Tell session that Ward ran every Friday. "It was some of the most valuable technology time I would spend with my students that entire year. They were thrilled with the opportunity to become the teachers, and I was thrilled to learn so much in such a short amount of time....I found that I not only learned from my students, but it was fun to see them show off their abilities to one another. I also experienced firsthand the difference between a technology learning culture and the traditional classroom environment. Generally, my laptop students stayed connected longer with what they were learning and tasks assigned. They asked one another for help, sought one another's opinions, and were more concerned with their final products. The difference between the two classes was very apparent, and I knew I wanted the same environment for all my students."

Ward would get her wish. By the time Buster retired as superintendent in 2002, almost 9,000 of Clovis's students—about a quarter of the student body—would be carrying laptops. Tammy Morrison loved to tell about the day her dad was driving to work early one morning along a country road—one lane, no sidewalks—when he passed this little boy on the side of the road waiting by himself for the school bus, "and he was crouched over on the curb working on his laptop."

◆   ◆   ◆

During that first year—1996–97—Microsoft worked with the pilot schools to support their laptop initiatives. The corporation kept a reasonably low profile. Other than a video taken at Mott Hall that was used in corporate TV ads, and a subsequent visit to the school by Bill Gates, Microsoft made little attempt to exploit its involvement in laptop programs for publicity purposes.

Morrison and Sabol were careful not to make the mistake that other technology companies had made in the past, of underwriting the entire cost of pilot programs. "Our two goals were to make sure that anything we did would enable the model to be replicable and sustainable long-term," said Morrison. That meant the corporation would not pay for the laptops, but it would provide support in areas like professional development, investing in the training of teachers in the use of the technology.

The other important commitment that Microsoft made was to put on a series of annual conferences. These were designed to spread the message to new schools and to give educators a forum where they could gather, to work out issues related to one-to-one computing.

Somewhere during this first year, the initiative acquired a name: Anytime Anywhere Learning. The conference at which the program was formally launched was held in Atlanta, Georgia, in April 1997. Before preparations commenced, however, Morrison and Sabol began to have second thoughts about moving forward. Was it the right thing to do? By letting this vision out of the bag, would they be creating an even bigger chasm between the haves and have-nots? To put their minds at rest, the dynamic duo went to consult Theodore Sizer.

An emeritus professor at Brown University, Sizer is widely regarded as the leading voice of contemporary American progressive education. In response to their enquiry, Sizer told them that what they intended to do would not widen the digital divide. Rather, they would be changing the culture so that it would no longer be possible to ignore the gap in access to technology, and making it the responsibility of the public to narrow that gap. Reassured, the pair decided to proceed with the launch.

In Atlanta, representatives from 28 of the original 52 schools—including Tony Amato, Herman Gaither, and Walt Buster—met again to share their experiences from their new laptop programs with 450 representatives from schools in 48 states. The Australians were also there, but this time they took a back seat. Peter Crawley confessed his amazement at the progress the Americans had made in twelve months. "I sat at the back of the room most of the time," he said, "admiring how fast they'd got control of the agenda, how far they'd pushed it, pursued it, and how much success they were having."

American educators told how the Australian program had been seamlessly transferred across the Pacific. "Good teaching and learning practices are not tied to geography and culture or people and personalities," asserted Charlie Rhyan, superintendent of the small rural school district of Anna in Shelby County, Ohio, "they are universal. We implemented the model the Australians showed us at our middle school—after proper training—in a positive, productive, and very exciting fashion."

"I've been in education thirty-one years", Rhyan continued, "and this concept is the only one I have experienced that is truly transformational in nature. The staff and students are growing and learning in ways we had only dreamed about." Many of the examples presented at the conference in Atlanta mirrored the ones that the Australians had given the previous year in Seattle. But this was now an American story and American educators told it their way.

In that first year, replicability had been achieved. Now the challenge was long-term sustainability. And this, as the experience of two Washington State schools shows, would be far easier to achieve in the private sector than the public. Narrowing the digital divide was never going to be easy.

26

A TALE OF TWO SCHOOLS

Of the half-dozen implementations of laptop programs that began in 1996 in Washington State following the initial exposure to the Australian experience, two stood out. One was Emerson Elementary in Snohomish where, as we have seen, Maureen Cornwell was doing her level best to replicate what she had encountered Down Under. The other was Forest Ridge School of the Sacred Heart. At this Catholic girls' school, the driving force was its dynamic headmistress, Sister Suzanne Cooke. At their respective schools, both Cooke and Cornwell strove to transform learning through the use of laptops. But for Cooke at a private school with the freedom to make her own choices, it was always going to be easier than for Cornwell who, almost from the outset, had to battle an unsympathetic public school bureaucracy.

Forest Ridge is located in Bellevue, east of Seattle across Lake Washington. Its elevated location gives the school a fine view of the skyscrapers of downtown Seattle. Bellevue (population: 110,000) is a mixed suburb that contains both an immigrant community and a wealthy high end. Forest Ridge caters to students in grades 5 through 12. The school's parents are mostly middle-income, in many cases both working—like at MLC—to ensure that they can afford the annual tuition of around $12,000. That's pretty steep for a Catholic school, but not nearly as high as fees at nearby non-religious private schools like Lakeside (where Bill Gates went). Many parents work in the high-tech industry, whether at Microsoft, whose headquarters are just up the road in Redmond, or some other software company, or Boeing. About a quarter of the school's 375 students are on financial aid, receiving assistance from the school.

Nuns are not exactly known for enthusiastically embracing radical new ideas. But then Suzanne Cooke is not your conventional nun. A New Yorker, she is bright and quick to catch on to things. At Forest Ridge, she was a risk-taker, someone who made things happen and the school an exciting place at which to work. Like David Loader, she was always encouraging her staff to stretch them-

286

selves. At one faculty meeting, Cooke read out a parable about a school of fish. Some fish just swam around in the safe parts of the pond, while others jumped willingly into uncharted waters. She used the story as an illustration of the necessity of having the courage to go forward into the unknown. At the same time, it sent a clear message to her staff that they needed to get on board—or find someplace else to work.

Cooke's salient physical feature is a pair of big brown eyes. They could look steely or seductive, depending on the situation. She has a warm and humorous nature which draws people to her. The headmistress of Forest Ridge was always accessible to her staff. She had a phenomenal memory, knew people by name, and could recall minute details about everyone. Students and their families sensed that she cared about each of them individually. Cooke is highly articulate, which makes her an effective public speaker. She is also a good listener. Talking with her, you felt you had her undivided attention.

When Suzanne Cooke first came to Forest Ridge in 1990, the school had just 16 computers, all of them—to use her word—"ancient". The new principal arrived in the Northwest knowing next to nothing about technology. She soon realized that it could not be ignored. Computers were obviously important for her students' future, and she set out to discover how they could be factored into learning.

As one way of bringing herself up to speed, Cooke organized a monthly breakfast. "I invited any parent who had anything to do with the field—hardware or software, I didn't care—so that I could understand what was going on." What grabbed her attention in particular was application software. "My Gosh!" she thought, "This is just incredible, we've got to get this into the classroom!" But Cooke didn't have a lot of teachers who understood what she wanted to do. "So I had to sort of regroup and figure out How do I get them to understand that we've got to embrace this for the sake of the girls?" A large part of the solution to her problem was the arrival of Janet Graeber at Forest Ridge in 1991, to take up a position as curriculum technology person.

A decade earlier Graeber had been in the vanguard of US teachers who recognized the educational potential of computers. At Stone Ridge County Day School of the Sacred Heart in Bethesda, Maryland, she persuaded her principal to buy an Apple II for her kindergarten class. Already a card-carrying constructivist, Graeber attended a workshop given by Seymour Papert and his graduate students at the Children's Museum in Washington, DC. They gave her a copy of Logo. Moving to the Sacred Heart School in San Francisco in 1982, Graeber built a technology program for the kindergarten through eighth-grade students there that was based on Logo and application tools such as wordprocessors and spread-sheets.

Graeber counted herself fortunate to have worked throughout her career for administrators who were prepared to support her experiments with changed learning environments. In this regard Suzanne Cooke would be no exception. Shortly after she arrived at Forest Ridge, at Cooke's request, Graeber formulated a vision of technology for the school. In part it read: "Excellence in education on the eve of the twenty-first century presupposes that technology is seamlessly inte-grated throughout the curriculum. We believe that constant and consistent access by the individual learner to the learning tool of her era strengthens her evolution as a critical thinker, thereby ensuring her success for the future."

The school began its attempt to provide constant and consistent access by building computer laboratories. First a Macintosh lab, then a PC lab, then satel-lite labs—classrooms dotted around the campus where English or math was taught were each equipped with five or six desktop computers. If you had planned ahead carefully and happened to be in one of those classrooms that had computers when an idea was triggered, it was wonderful. But if you were some-where else—Forest Ridge is laid out in a cluster of six separate buildings—you couldn't take advantage of the moment. And that was a big frustration, because, as the prophet Papert had said, "discovery cannot be a setup, invention cannot be scheduled." Another source of frustration was that, although many of the girls had computers at home, the software they used at school was not always compat-ible. So students would bring a disk home intending to continue their work there, only to find that they could not.

By the time Cooke and Graeber went to hear the Australians tell their story at the Seattle conference, the headmistress was already convinced in her heart that what they were doing at Forest Ridge wasn't working, didn't make sense any more. Computer labs, having half-a-dozen desktops here and there, "I knew that neither of those models allowed the students to use the technology at the ideal moment, when the learning was occurring", Cooke said. "No matter how clever or talented the teacher was, you always ended up creating something that was slightly artificial. So that something had to be more immediate."

As soon as Cooke saw the video that Microsoft had made of laptop classes at Melbourne's Trinity Grammar—the same one that had so enraged Tony Amato—she knew immediately: "That was it—the intimacy of the student's rela-tionship, having her own laptop allowed the learner to be independent, focused, and ready to learn." And, whereas there was a world of difference between Trinity

Grammar and Harlem's Mott Hall, Forest Ridge was, like Trinity, a private school. At private schools, there is very little bureaucracy.

The decision to introduce laptops at Forest Ridge was quickly taken. The plan was to start in the first year with two grades, seventh and ninth.

For all their independence, private schools tend to be very sensitive about tuition costs. By March 1996, parents at Forest Ridge had already signed contracts for their daughters to return to the school the following Fall. Now Cooke faced the tricky task of telling parents that in addition to tuition of $10,000, they were going to have to fork out a further $2,000 for a laptop.

To make the pill easier to swallow, Graeber resorted to a tried and tested strategy—using students to argue the case. At the introductory meeting to explain the program, she had some of her ninth graders speak to the parents about what difference they thought that having their own laptops would make to how they went about their learning.

(Though only the seventh and ninth graders were required to have laptops that first year, about two-thirds of the tenth graders also purchased them, including the students who had made the pitch to parents. A year later, when Graeber looked back on the girls' predictions, she found it remarkable how many were starting to come true.)

The parents were not easily won over. At the introductory meeting one of them challenged Cooke, citing the example of Lakeside. The most prestigious private school in the Seattle area—which was after all *Bill's* old school—had vowed, despite having sent a representative on the trip to Australia, never to implement a laptop program. "That was a big blow to our parents," Cooke recalled. "They worried, What was this tiny little convent school with this nun thinking? How could we do this?"

To her rescue came John Sabol, who was at the meeting to help argue the case for computers. "Forest Ridge is ready," he assured the doubting Thomases, "and the other schools are not." In the event, only a couple of parents decided to withdraw their daughters. (Graeber would have a big chuckle when in 2001, Lakeside finally decided to implement a mandatory laptop program of its own, and even then, only after raucous debate.)

Though Forest Ridge was a private school, it was certainly not flush with cash. In fact, when the laptop program commenced, the school was still working to retire the debt on one of its buildings. Every decision had to be made very carefully in terms of what would be the financial impact on the parents and the overall impact on the school. "Forest Ridge was poor," Cooke insisted, "we were really struggling, we had a huge deficit, and our enrolment was down. In those initial stages, there was a huge risk involved because if we had failed…it sounds melodramatic to say that the school might have closed, but it is factual that life was not assured."

In addition to the laptops themselves, the program would also incur additional costs. The school's textbook budget almost doubled: it was felt that you could not ask a young woman to carry a laptop computer as well as all her science, math, literature, and history books. So the girls kept their textbooks at home and the school purchased an additional set of books that stayed in the classroom. Another essential additional expense was a technical support person hired to maintain the laptops.

Cooke did her best to ease the transition to the new learning style for staff. She told her teachers they had three years to figure out how to integrate the technology into the curriculum in order to enhance learning outcomes. At the same time, Cooke gave them the tools and took away all issues about money. The principal handed out laptops to all her staff, and made funds available to pay for Internet access, so that they could log on at home as well as at school. She also provided staff with professional development classes in their free periods.

In this highly supportive environment, the teachers had to make it up as they went along. "We felt it was important to demonstrate to our faculty that they were experts in their field," Cooke said. "So anytime anybody did anything incredibly successful with the girls, and the learning was just unbelievable, we would highlight that at a faculty meeting, and move from the idea that there were only a few naturally technologically literate teachers, to the idea that all of us were capable of being this way."

Forest Ridge's staff consisted of the usual mix of early adopters, middle-of-the-roaders, and outright resisters. Amongst the latter category was a religion teacher who told Graeber in no uncertain terms that she felt that computers did not belong in her classroom and had no plans to use them. Within two years, this same teacher had become one of the most enthusiastic users of the technology, employing PowerPoint slide shows to illuminate some of the more complicated ideas from the Bible.

When Cooke was challenged to produce evidence of the laptop program's efficacy, she often cited the example of Christine Burton. "Christine's a really lovely girl," she said, "an OK student, well-rounded, but she wasn't as a youngster one of those people that stands out, is president of the class or whatever." Christine had been frustrated by the lack of access to computers at Forest Ridge. "I would just get started and then it was time to stop," she recalled. "I would have to wait for another day to finish my work."

Christine was one of the students Graeber used to sell the laptops to the high school parents. Following the introduction of laptops, a remarkable change took place in Christine's learning as her horizons broadened beyond the four walls of the classroom. "Having constant access to this technology had exposed me to new tools for doing my work, for collaborating with my peers, and for accessing information," she said. "I am no longer restricted to just a physical location. Rather, I move around in a global classroom."[1]

As the word about what was going on at Forest Ridge got out, some other private schools in the Northwest decided to investigate the potential of laptops. Forest Ridge was invited to give presentations. For these occasions, the school always brought along girls like Christine to talk about their experiences. "It matters more what's happening to you as learners," Cooke told the girls, "than what I think as headmistress." One time, the venue was an independent elementary school where the parents were angry because they did not want the school administration to go ahead with a laptop program.

The presentation involved demonstrating *The Geometer's Sketchpad*. Christine described why all the students loved the program because of its interactive nature and its capacity to help them understand the concepts behind geometry. But it had been several months since Christine had last used *Sketchpad*, and when she looked at this proof, Christine realized that she had forgotten how to arrive at it. But she was unfazed, and in a few seconds it all came flooding back to her.

Cooke was amazed. "She could *see* it, and that was really my first time of realizing that this generation is ninety-five percent visual learners. And to be hearing, learning, experiencing the concepts while you're seeing them on the screen, in this case geometry, does reinforce mastery of concept, so that they can be recalled and applied to a new situation." For Cooke, it was undeniable proof that laptop learning really worked.

Later, Christine went as part of an exchange program to another Sacred Heart school, in Newton, Massachusetts, taking her laptop with her. A teacher there asked Christine what she thought she was doing, causing a disruption, bringing a computer into class? And Christine replied, respectfully but firmly, that one of the objects of the exchange program was to see how Sacred Heart education happened in other parts of the country, "and at our Sacred Heart school," she said, "this is how we learn." The following month, Christine was asked to conduct a

---

1.   Transforming Learning: An Anthology of Miracles in Technology-Rich Classrooms, ed Jenny Little & Bruce Dixon, Kids Technology Foundation, Melbourne, 2000, p138

meeting for all of the faculty, and then for the parents. The school subsequently implemented a laptop program.

In 1998, Suzanne Cooke left Forest Ridge, to take over the reins at Carrollton, another Sacred Heart school, in Miami, Florida. Since her arrival it, too, has become a laptop school. For Cooke, laptops were the most powerful tool for learning she had come across in twenty years as an educator. They were, she was convinced, "the most hopeful thing in education."

Despite her absence, Forest Ridge has continued to forge ahead with its new style of learning. These days, staff and students there make intensive use of the school's computer network. Some faculty sign on in the evenings to answer student questions regarding homework. Others use the microphone on their laptops to dictate comments on each student's work, attaching the audio comments to the work as part of the review. Still others have created online discussion groups to broaden dialog about literature themes. The school recently launched a long-term research project to study the effects of acid rain on three continents. It involves seven other Sacred Heart schools located in Australia, Canada, and Europe.

In Fall 2002, Forest Ridge experienced some problems with its wireless network and upgrades to its laptop system. Unable to do their work or engage in learning was highly frustrating for both faculty and students. To Janet Graeber, their frustration was an indicator of that attitudes at the school to teaching and learning had been permanently transformed. "No-one was interested in returning to the traditional classroom," she said. "Our educational culture has changed."

◆   ◆   ◆

Forest Ridge was one of four pioneer sites chosen for an evaluation of laptop schools conducted during the 1997–98 school year. The other three were Cincinnati County Day School, generally regarded as one of the most successful of the first wave of laptop implementations, plus two public school districts. These were Clovis Unified School District, which we looked at in the previous chapter, and Federal Way School District in Washington, whose enthusiastic young superintendent, Tom Vander Ark, would later become executive director for education at the Bill & Melinda Gates Foundation.

The evaluation was conducted on behalf of Microsoft and Toshiba by Rockman et al, an independent research consultancy based in San Francisco. The firm's founder and guiding light, Saul Rockman, was a veteran experimental psychologist whose involvement with research on learning had begun in the late

1960s. Back then, he had examined the impact that television programs like *Sesame Street* had on children (work which included the famous photographic studies of eyeball movements). In the early 1980s, Rockman moved into computers, working for Apple and helping the US Department of Education formulate technology policy. He got involved with Microsoft via an old friend. "He said, They need somebody who's skeptical," the puckish Rockman recalled, "and I said, I'm skeptical!'

The sponsors gave Rockman a free hand to look at what happened when students had full-time access to laptop computers both in school and at home. The evaluation was the most thorough study that had ever been conducted on the effect of computers on learning. Rockman and his associates surveyed 144 teachers and 450 students (including a comparison group of non-laptop students). Among other things, they shadowed students—seventh and tenth graders—following them around for 48 days, noting when and how they used their laptops.

It turned out that seventh-graders with full-time access used their computers as much in a day as non-laptop students used them in a week. The tenth-graders used their laptops in school more than two hours per day, almost ten times as much as non-laptop students. More importantly, the kids used their computers for work they were accomplishing in school, not for games or chat or surfing the Net.

Rockman's results, published in October 1998 under the title *Powerful Tools for Schooling*, provided a stunning confirmation of everything the Australians had experienced, as well as a resounding endorsement of laptop learning.[2] The study showed that, as far as the students were concerned, they participated in more project-based work, and produced better projects; they did more and better writing (based on standardized tests), and more presentations; they did more independent learning, and also more collaborative work. From the staff point of view, teachers became facilitators; they spent less time lecturing and more time consulting and counselling; they became students and also did more collaboration with other teachers.

Rockman, a self-styled "affectionate cynic", confessed himself completely won over. "I've been looking at [educational uses of technology] for a long time now," he said, "and I really do believe that laptop classrooms are involved in some of the most dramatic shifts in education compared to any other innovations that I've seen." In particular, Rockman was impressed by the ownership implicit in the

---

2.   Rockman et al, Powerful Tools for Schooling, <www.rockman.com>, San Francisco, October 1998

programs of the computer, and by extension the learning. "Ownership is an extraordinarily powerful aspect," he said.

"What the laptop programs have shown," Rockman concluded, "is that you can shift the power. And that has been very difficult for education. If you look at the difference between independent schools and public schools, and how they adapted, in independent schools [like Forest Ridge], the headmistress says, Teachers, you are all going to be teaching laptop classes next year; [whereas] in a public school, it's Well, which of you want to volunteer to teach laptops? It's a very different environment."

Very different indeed. But for Maureen Cornwell at Emerson Elementary just twenty or so miles up the road from Forest Ridge, the real problem was not short-age of volunteer teachers or parents, or even money, but lack of vision from local leadership. As Cornwell herself said, "If you're going to have a laptop program be successful in a district, you need the superintendent and the school board to think that it's the best thing going."

◆   ◆   ◆

That first year in Snohomish, the original idea had been to do laptops at just at one school. Emerson Elementary was chosen to demonstrate a commitment to fairness, because it was the school with the highest proportion of students on free and reduced-price lunches in the district. But the more Maureen Cornwell and her teacher Kelly Starr raved about what they had seen in Australia, the more other schools wanted to join in, too. Especially when it became apparent that the state would provide money to buy technology.

"The program suddenly snowballed like crazy," Cornwell said. "We had other schools wanting to do this, and so we ended up making the decision that they could get involved, which with hindsight probably was a mistake. We tried to go too big too soon, and people didn't have the vision—they just thought they were missing something."

In Spring 1996 parent nights were held at each of the nine elementary schools in the Snohomish district. Getting parents excited was the easiest part. Starr was amazed at how many parents stood up when given the opportunity to invest in their children's education. "In the first year, there were seven schools involved," Starr said, "and each school had at least one or two classrooms of twenty five or more students in the program, and these parents were all volunteers." All in all, 268 laptop kids.

Arranging financing for the laptops proved more difficult. Initially, the district spent a lot of time and money setting up a scheme under which it would lease the computers itself. Coming up with a scheme that met the requirements of state law was a challenge. So was working with a leasing company inexperienced in public sector education. Ultimately, the district switched to a low-interest bank loan, bought the computers outright, then rented them to parents. Monthly payments of $58 were collected by the district's business manager. That meant if parents reneged on their payments, the district was liable for the debt. In retrospect, this arrangement turned out to be a bad idea.

Snohomish also worked out affordable insurance. This was not the case elsewhere in the state. For example, the Seattle School District had managed to find the money for 170 laptops. Then, deeming insurance too expensive, the district did not allow the kids to take their computers home, thus negating one of the most important aspects of laptop learning.

The Snohomish School District superintendent, Ginny Tresvant, while not actively against the laptop program, was not exactly a fan, either. The real support in Snohomish came from Kathy Klock, the district's newly-appointed director of curriculum, instruction, and assessment. The Australian approach matched Klock's own philosophy of how computers should be used in the classroom. When the principal of Emerson Elementary came back from her trip brimming with excitement about laptop learning, Klock was quick to rally round.

The first year at Snohomish everything went remarkably well. The teachers had been hastily trained over the summer. There was little or nothing out there for them to follow, no pattern or curriculum and so, as at Forest Ridge, they had to make it up as they went along. Australian experts—Adam Smith and Greg Butler—came by a couple of times to give professional development workshops, but that was the extent of the in-service training. Being at separate schools made it hard for the teachers to get together to swap ideas. They met as a group only once a month.

There were the usual infrastructure issues, like how to deal with machine repair. In this area, the parents provided phenomenal backup. They became activists, forming their own support club. "The parents were willing to do anything that needed to be done to make this work," Starr recalled.

In the second year—1997-'98—the program expanded. The number of laptop kids more than doubled, to 630. Schools offered additional classes, Emerson Elementary leading the way with three mixed fifth-and sixth-grade classrooms. Cornwell tried to set up the laptop classes just like any others, including in them all kinds of kids. About a third were on free and reduced-price lunches, others had behavioral problems or special requirements. As elsewhere, it was often these challenged and disadvantaged students who seemed to gain most out of the program.

But during the second year a serious problem emerged. Some of the sixth graders from the laptop program moved up into middle schools. There, they were grouped in mixed classes with other kids who did not have laptops, a further complication being that students had to rotate between different classrooms.

Snohomish's secondary schools had never bought into the laptop program. "Once they got the technology from all that money that had come via the state, they didn't care anymore," Cornwell said. "They didn't want to do anything like this program, they didn't want to be held accountable, they didn't have the vision, they didn't understand what was being talked about; it was just too much work, and it was too hard to keep those kids together that had that background, to schedule them into six periods or whatever." This failure to connect placed an additional burden on Cornwell. Now she had to convince her community that the laptop program was going to be worthwhile for their kids on a one-or two-year basis only.

The third year, 1998–99, enrolments in laptop classes continued to grow, to a total of 740. Then disaster struck. Snohomish had long been living beyond its means. The district ended its financial year with a deficit of about $650,000. Local law said that school districts must not fall into debt. Tresvant was forced resign. An interim superintendent was appointed by the state to clear up the mess. Cuts to the budget had to made, and quick. The laptop program presented an obvious target.

Some parents had reneged on repaying loans for the laptops, forcing the district to make up the difference. Word spread that the program was responsible for almost half the district's debt. (In fact, it later transpired that the laptops were only a very small drain on resources.) The new superintendent was a man called Jack Thompson who had been brought out of retirement to do the job. He had no understanding what the laptop program was about, nor did he take the time to talk to any of the teachers or principals involved in it. All Thompson knew was that there was this program which was costing the district money in a precarious financial situation. He decided to "sunset" the laptops.

Cornwell was left out on a limb. That summer Kathy Klock, her most ardent supporter at the district, had quit the education department to set up a new teacher training initiative for the Gates Foundation (which we shall examine in the next chapter). Klock's replacement as curriculum director was not supportive of technology. Cornwell's best teacher, Kelly Starr, having that year won the

Milken Foundation's prestigious Educator Award, was spending more and more of her time out of the classroom, working with Greg Butler on professional development activities.

Her two closest confidantes gone, Cornwell was alone and vulnerable. Sometimes it felt like the whole world was against her. "It's so stressful," she lamented, "stressful and exhausting, because instead of my superintendents supporting me, I'm having to argue with them." But Maureen Cornwell is nothing if not a battler—she was not about to let the bureaucrats kill off her precious program. Over the next five years, she fought Thompson and his successor tooth and nail to keep providing laptop learning for the kids at her school.

Though at the district level the laptop program had officially been "sunsetted", Thompson relented sufficiently to allow Cornwell to continue to run the program at her school, on a volunteer basis. But she was obliged to promise that the program would not cost Snohomish a penny. There would be no technical support from the district office. The kids owned the machines and it would be up to their parents to get the machines fixed if they broke down.

Before allowing her to proceed, Thompson also insisted that Cornwell address all administrators in the district, to explain to her peers why she should be allowed to continue running the laptop program. This put the principals at the other elementary schools in a difficult position. Though they themselves were not committed to the program, they had teachers who wanted to continue with the laptops. In addition to which, there were many parents who were loath to see the laptop program die. Reluctantly, two other principals agreed to allow the program to continue at their schools. This arrangement lasted for a year. By 2000–01, Cornwell was the only one running a laptop program in Snohomish. By then she had been diagnosed with breast cancer.

Perhaps because they knew Cornwell was sick, the district bureaucrats let her continue running laptop classes for a further year. "They didn't want to get me upset, because I had cancer," she recalled. "They knew how passionate I was about this program and how hard I had worked for it. I was in the middle of chemotherapy, so they weren't going to come and tell me I couldn't have this program, because they've seen me, y'know, cry and get mad and all kinds of things about it."

To make matters even worse, Thompson's replacement as superintendent was a strong believer that labs were the best way to provide students with access to computers. Though she knew full well that he had already decided to can her program, Cornwell refused to accept his decision. "I would always say Why can't I keep doing this?" And the bureaucrats would tell her, Well, it's probably because you haven't been listening. There was no more money to continue, they said.

But in fact there *was* money—a grant of $200,000 from the Gates Foundation to Snohomish buy laptop computers. Cornwell got on the phone to John Sabol, told him what was happening, and how the district was trying to get rid of the program. Eventually, she broke down in tears of rage and frustration. Sabol responded soothingly, telling her that she was the only one still doing a laptop program in local public schools, that she was an important leader, and that she had done a lot and should be proud of her accomplishments. Then he contacted Kathy Klock at the Gates Foundation. Klock made it clear to the district that $70,000 of the grant was earmarked for Maureen Cornwell at Emerson Elementary.

The superintendent wanted Cornwell to instal a computer lab at her school. Cornwell refused, instead using the money to buy what she called "a laptop lab"—thirty computers on carts that could be rolled around the school as required. The laptop lab she knew was never going to be as good as a proper laptop classroom, but at least it would help her teachers see what the possibilities of laptops were. And it would give her kids more access than they otherwise would have.

In 2001, after 31 years in public education, Cornwell was eligible to retire. But the principal chose to stay on because she knew her school was getting the laptop lab, and she wanted to make sure that it worked OK. Initially, the lab was parked in the library, where the librarian taught all the 390-some kids at Emerson Elementary the basics of how to use the laptops. "So I'm not just touching a couple of classrooms by it," Cornwell said, "they're all getting touched."

Not that Cornwell had given up the idea of laptop classes. In 2002 Snohomish appointed a new superintendent who said his role was to support the principals in his district. "Sometime this year he's going to be in my building," Cornwell said, "and I fully intend to show him what's going on with technology. I'm going to have him see the laptop class in operation, and then I'm going to revisit the whole idea of having me bring the laptop program back."

When that day came, Emerson Elementary would be ready. Cornwell had made a point of preparing her staff. She had five teachers that could teach laptop classes. There had of course been no money from the district to pay for this professional development. The teachers had been trained through the Teacher Leadership Project, the program set up by Kathy Klock and funded by the Gates Foundation.

For her part, though in emotional terms the experience had cost her dearly, Cornwell had no regrets about her involvement as a pioneer of laptop learning in public school education. "When I look back on this as an old person in my rocking chair," she said, "I'm going to feel good about this, because it was significant, and I was part of it."

27

ACROSS THE GREAT DIVIDE

Melinda French Gates, though very bright (high school valedictorian at Ursuline Academy, Dallas; degree in computer science from Duke University) and married to the world's richest man, struck most people who met her as unassuming and down-to-earth. Since her retirement from Microsoft, and especially after the birth of her first child, Jennifer, in April 1996, Melinda had taken an active interest in education, girls' education in particular.

In 1997 Melinda was appointed by the governor of Washington State to co-chair a state commission on early learning. At her local parochial school in Belle-vue, she was active on the parent-teacher committee. When the school authorities began to explore whether technology fit in with their educational objectives, it was only natural that they should turn for guidance to Melinda Gates. Equally, given that hers was a Catholic girls' school, and there was this other Catholic girls' school in Bellevue called Forest Ridge that was getting all this publicity because of its new laptop program, it made sense that Melinda should contact the school's headmistress, Suzanne Cooke, whom she had met previously a couple of times. Melinda asked Cooke if she could visit her school, preferably anonymously, and Cooke immediately agreed.

So Melinda came to Forest Ridge, and Cooke walked around with her, explaining what was going on. On one point Cooke was particularly insistent: "Don't do anything if you don't want to invest in your teachers," she said. "Maybe that'll take a year, but that's the most important thing." Intrigued, Melinda asked Cooke to tell her more about the teachers at Forest Ridge. And Cooke explained the approach—free computers and Internet access plus plenty of professional development—that the school had taken with the teachers in its laptop program. The headmistress firmly believed that this investment in her staff was the reason why the program had been so effective with the girls. Then Cooke had Melinda talk with some of the teachers. As well as enthusiasts like Janet

Graeber, they included resisters who had initially opposed Cooke, but who had now come round to embracing the laptop program.

Shortly afterwards, Melinda's friend John Sabol introduced her to Kathy Klock of the Snohomish School District. Melinda also visited Snohomish. Her visit initiated a series of discussions between the two women. Melinda asked Klock to start a project to train teachers in the State of Washington in the use of computers in the classroom. Funding would come from the newly-established Gates family foundation.

In this informal manner began the Teacher Leadership Project, arguably the most successful attempt to address the problems that educators—public school educators in particular—face in trying to come to terms with technology. And in the process, turn them into better teachers.

◆   ◆   ◆

Behind her conservative appearance and measured, quietly-spoken demeanor, Kathy Klock hid a highly determined, forward-looking nature. To achieve her goals, Klock moved in subtle ways. "Kathy knows where she wants you to go," said a former colleague," and she just has this wonderful way of getting you to come round to her way of thinking, and making you think that it's your idea".

Klock's keen interest in how technology could be used in education dated back to the beginning of the personal computer era. When she returned to teaching after being home a long time raising her children, Klock took a course in using computers. "At that time, what they were teaching teachers to do was programming," Klock recalled. She was fascinated.

In the early 1980s, computers could still be purchased in kit form. The Klock family built a Heathkit micro, a primitive machine, but programmable. Writing simple assembly-language programs for it was hard fun—time-consuming but ultimately enormously satisfying.

At the Washington State middle school where she taught, as soon as she had the chance, Klock brought computers into her classroom. In addition to two Apple IIe's, her students also had access to a computer lab down the hall. Klock thus experienced at first hand the frustration of trying to ensure that all her students got equal and sufficient access to these limited resources.

"We had a technology class where the students would go for maybe ten weeks to the computer lab," she explained. "In the classroom, the kids were assigned a computer in language arts class which they could have for the whole week. So you had like two kids and they didn't have access very often, but they could get a start on their work, then continue it when the computer lab was free. For a good part of the day the lab was open, and students could be in there so long as we had some other people there. I tried to get parent volunteers to help me out, so my students could go back and forth to the lab, because I had to be partly there and partly in my room so that we could use those computers there."

To help solve the monitoring problem, Klock turned for assistance to students who were already computer experts. In September, at the start of the school year, she put an advertisement on the bulletin board. A couple of kids applied for the job. It was not until the following April that Klock learned that one of the experts she had recruited had previously had major behavioral problems. "And I had no clue, because the other kids had to go to that student any time they had difficulty with the computers, because I was busy with all the other kids in the class. And that really worked out well, because it was a new niche for him, and he had recognition by the other students."

Such experiences stimulated Klock's interest in what happened to students' learning when they had access to computers. As a teacher, Klock was a progressive, committed to inquiry-based instruction. Though at this time not aware of Seymour Papert by name, she wholeheartedly believed in the constructionist approach he advocated.

Klock subsequently moved from teaching into administration. At Snohomish School District, she served as a central office administrator in charge of curriculum, instruction, and assessment. In October 1995, soon after her arrival at Snohomish, Klock attended the seminal meeting at which John Sabol and Tammy Morrison of Microsoft proposed sending educators on a feasibility study to look at Australian laptop schools. Klock recommended that the people who went should not be administrators like herself, but principals and teachers, because they were closer to the classroom and the kids. In the case of Snohomish, that meant Maureen Cornwell and Kelly Starr

As a newcomer to the district, it would have been hard for Klock to move her technology agenda forward by herself. But in Maureen Cornwell she had found an enthusiastic ally. On Cornwell's return, Klock was excited by what she heard. The open-ended, child-driven Australian approach seemed to match her philosophy of how computers should be used in the classroom. If each student could somehow have his or her own computer, then the technology could truly be used for learning. Students could begin to manipulate the computer, taking control of their learning, instead of being forced to follow a program that told them what to do.

Klock became heavily involved getting the laptop program off the ground at Snohomish. That first year, 1996-'97, some individual success stories emerged, notably at Emerson Elementary, Maureen Cornwell's school. To Klock's dismay, however, it soon became clear that in general the program wasn't working, and moreover could not be sustained. The leap from having hardly any technology to a one-to-one ratio was just too radical a change. Most teachers didn't have the skills to take advantage of the opportunity. They needed training, but in the public system securing the funding to pay for that training was simply not possible.

Klock saw that there was a desperate need build understanding of how computers could be used. And, having built that understanding, a mechanism for spreading it throughout the school system. She also saw that, in order to succeed, such an initiative had to be teacher-driven. Since leadership in technology in public education was not going to come from the top, where in a politically charged environment, elections could make or break superintendents and school boards, it would have to come from the grassroots, from the teachers themselves. Hence the title, Teacher Leadership Project.

Teachers leading teachers was not an entirely new idea. As a model Klock drew on the National Writing Project, a professional development initiative which began in 1974 at the University of California, Berkeley. The goal of this highly successful initiative was to improve student writing by improving the teaching of writing. It was firmly based on the belief that teachers are key to education reform, and that teachers make the best teachers of other teachers.

This grassroots approach was to become one of the most powerful aspects of the Teacher Leadership Project. "It almost gives you goose bumps when you watch it," one of the project's organizers commented. "The teachers up in front instructing at our meetings are fresh out of the classroom, just like the rest of the teachers. And they're just true witnesses and testimony to it; they're the ones revising the curriculum, and doing all the training."

◆　　◆　　◆

Klock invited a few like-minded educators—including Kelly Starr and Mike Hyland from Emerson Elementary, and Suzanne Cooke and Janet Graeber from Forest Ridge—to help her plan the project. Together, they mapped out what they thought educators needed to know. The goal was to design a program that teachers would take ownership of. The authors reasoned that, if the teachers loved it, they would go back and infect their local schools with their enthusiasm, serving as catalysts to bring about the change in culture that needed to occur.

The Teacher Leadership Project commenced in the summer of 1997 with 27 teachers drawn from schools around the State of Washington. The participants came mostly from public schools, but there were also a few from private schools, an unusual mixing of perspectives that sometimes opened new avenues to understanding. All were self-starters, never-take-no-for-an-answer pioneers like Becky Firth, a language arts teacher from the Burlington-Edison school district in north Washington. Before each new session, an inner group that included Klock, Starr, and Graeber held planning meetings.

The teachers all taught fifth, sixth, or seventh grade. This was partly because it was felt that these grades were where technology could bring the greatest educational benefits, and partly for pragmatic reasons. The state had recently implemented some basic academic standards. "We wanted to focus on whether technology would be able to meet those standards," Klock said bluntly, "because unless it does, then we shouldn't be using it."

When teachers go to conferences and workshops, all too often they are expected to eat junk food and sleep four to a room. The teachers in this first group, and its two successors, spent five days at Semiahmoo, a beautifully-appointed resort located near the Canadian border on the site of a historic salmon-packing cannery. Putting the teachers up in such a luxurious setting, with good food and facilities and their own rooms, was a sign. For once in their long-suffering lives, educators were being taken seriously and treated like professionals.

The teachers rose to the gesture. They put in 14-hour days learning together how to use the computers, and working out ways of integrating technology into the classroom. Through discussion they also became able to articulate clearly what they believed about technology and learning. This intensive experience forged a long-lasting camaraderie and spirit of community. As follow-up, the teachers came back during the school year for three weekends, an extra six days for a total of eleven days' training in all.

Each teacher participating in the project was issued with a laptop. At the same time, the organizers recognized that it was not yet financially realistic to expect that every kid in the state could have his or her own computer. As a compromise, the project provided each participating teacher with a $9,000 grant to buy eight or nine desktop computers, enough to produce a ratio of one computer for every four students. (In addition, each of their classrooms was equipped with a presentation device—a data projector—and a printer.)

Though not ideal, 1-to-4 was a significant improvement over Washington's statewide ratio of one computer for every 14 students. It was a way of bridging the great divide that separated the technology-rich from the technology-poor.

And, as Klock pointed out, "you cannot have eight computers in a classroom and ignore them." It was interesting, she thought, to watch what happened between teacher and student when there were all these computers, "the change in the classroom, how it becomes a real learning environment, because the teachers are learning, too."

For many teachers, viewing themselves as learners was a big change. "We used to think, Well you finish school and you quit [learning]", Klock said. "For some teachers, it's hard to get past the idea that they are now learners in a classroom with their students, and at times the students are the teachers....So the teachers have to begin to think, it's OK, I'm a learner, too, and get excited about learning. And that happens—you see teachers 15, 20, even 30 years into teaching get excited about learning. It's not an age thing, you'll find teachers of any age group eager to do technology; in our first group, we had one woman who was very close to retirement."

The teaching was based on applications software, much of it donated by Microsoft. But from the very beginning SchoolKiT, the library of tried-and-tested classroom lesson modules distilled from the hard-won experience of Australian teachers, was a central component of the project. Melinda Gates came to watch Adam Smith's initial presentation and herself gave SchoolKiT the nod. The project purchased a subscription to the software and Smith's company set up a special website for Washington that tied SchoolKiT activities to the State's learning standards.

Giving the teachers SchoolKiT opened up a whole range of activities that they could access quickly then adapt for use in their own classrooms. It provided curriculum, a crucial piece that had been missing in previous attempts to implement technology in the classroom. SchoolKiT also functioned as ongoing professional development. It gave teachers models that they could draw on in discovering what was possible with technology across different content areas and using different applications.

In time, many graduates of the project would go on to create new modules for SchoolKiT. Two of the core participants in the Teacher Leadership Project, Kelly Starr and Mike Hyland, both formerly of Emerson Elementary, would subsequently join the fledgling firm.

In its use of constructionist, start-with-an-open-ended-platform-and-have-kids-build-stuff-and-make-it-up-for-themselves, the Teacher Leadership Project was thus philosophically very similar to the laptop programs. "We're really promoting use of the computer as a learning tool," Klock said.

◆   ◆   ◆

As we have seen, funding for the Teacher Leadership Project came from what is now known as the Bill & Melinda Gates Foundation. Education had not been one of the Foundation's original concerns. Following in the footsteps of the great Scottish industrial philanthropist Andrew Carnegie, the Microsoft founder's family initially chose to support public libraries. The Gates Library Foundation was formed in June 1997, with a commitment to purchase computers for public library patrons and to provide technical training and support for library staff in low-income communities.

At the end of the Teacher Leadership Project's first year, 1997-'98 the Gates family pronounced itself satisfied with the results. In July 1998, Klock left Snohomish School District to run the program, becoming the first fulltime education person at what would shortly become the world's largest foundation. Since the Foundation then had no facilities of its own, she set up shop in a tiny office above a pizza parlor in Redmond.

Following the success of the pilot year, in its second year, the Teacher Leadership Project grew to accommodate 157 teachers. For the most part, these were people recommended by the initial 27 graduates, some of whom served as instructors that summer. The next year, 1999, the program expanded to 250 teachers, selected this time via an application process.

Klock ran the Teacher Leadership Project for its first three years. Towards the end of that time she decided that, if the program was good enough to train a few hundred teachers a year, then it should be good enough to train a thousand teachers. Klock approached Wayne Sweeney, an assistant superintendent at one of the state's educational service districts who had shown outstanding vision. In 2000 Klock handed over supervision to Northwest ESD 189, which ran the project for a further three years, at an annual cost to the Foundation of $15 million.

In 2001, Becky Firth, one of the project's original graduates, took over as director. By that time, the Teacher Leadership Project had generated a tremendous amount of interest in the state. In 2002-'03, the project's final year, five thousand teachers applied for the thousand slots that were available.

Having demonstrated what was possible when you put a lot of computers in the classroom, the Gates Foundation decided it was time to move on. With a vastly increased budget, it withdrew from hands-on projects, opting instead to work through existing organizations. "Whole school change" became the Foundation's new watchword; that is, breaking up huge high schools into more manageable units, restoring the human element. In this new program, technology was no longer heavily emphasized: it was just one of seven attributes which the Foundation felt that any self-respecting school should have.

By the time it officially ended in 2003, the Teacher Leadership Project had trained 3,908 teachers. They had come from over half the schools in Washington State. A huge cohort had formed of teachers, all of whom had undergone the same experience. They could speak the same language and understood what true integration of technology into the curriculum looked like. As a result, the influence of the project was beginning to be widely felt.

The explicit intention had been to take teachers and turn them into leaders. Many of the project's graduates were no longer in their classrooms. They had moved out to positions were they could influence more teachers. Some had been scouted by other school districts. A high percentage had gone on to leadership positions in the state, as technology coordinators or even principals.

The project's scope extended well beyond Washington. Its graduates gave seminars and workshops for schools in 18 states. In 2002, the Gates Foundation began funding pilot teacher leadership projects in Michigan and Mississippi. That year, the project received an award from the National Staff Development Council, for exemplary use of technology in training teachers.

Though the Teacher Leadership Project would no longer receive Gates Foundation funding for mass training in Washington, the word was it would continue to operate, albeit on a smaller scale. "We're out surfing," Firth felt, "right at the crest where we're ready to go down and make the run." School districts were coming to her asking to train their staff. "We've got a great project," she said, "we know that it works, we know that it's successful, and we know that it's making a difference."

That difference was much greater than just knowing how to use the computers. "Our graduates are more aware of state educational requirements, and of good teaching. We're really teaching them to be better teachers, we're teaching them about better lesson design, we're teaching them to be more intentional about what they're teaching, their classrooms are definitely more project-based, they're working with their kids on high-level thinking skills, and those kinds of things."

Perhaps the ultimate compliment came from the assistant superintendent for professional development in Washington State's education department. On leaving a meeting held by the project in the state capital, Olympia, she commented,

"I thought I was coming to see technology, but that's not what this is about at all—it's about good teaching practice and good classroom instruction."

◆   ◆   ◆

Not everyone was as sanguine as Firth. As its official evaluator, Seattle Pacific University professor of education Jeff Fouts followed the Teacher Leadership Project closely.[1] "We've been in I don't know how many classrooms, interviewing teachers and looking at the nature of the lessons they do and so forth," Fouts said. His conclusion: "the training takes—actually makes a difference—in about half of the teachers, and in about a fourth it probably made them better teachers, but they haven't quite made the whole transition. And in the other fourth, within a short period of time, you would never know that they had had the training, it just didn't gel with them for whatever reason."

Fouts was not inclined to be critical of the backsliders. "One of the reasons why the success rate was not higher than it has been," he explained, "was that the schools were unable, unwilling, or didn't understand the importance [of technology]. For whatever reason, they didn't follow through on their commitments to keep the computers running, to provide the technical assistance, so some of the teachers just plain gave up. If things don't run smoothly after a while, you just say, Forget it."

To the best of Fouts's knowledge, there was not a single district in the state of Washington where all of the schools were on board. "Some are, to varying degrees—y'know, they have technology, and they all have Internet access and that type of thing, but the degree to which it's really transformed teaching in all the schools…it's just a long, drawn-out process in which, at any point, because of budget problems or union problems, whatever, they can say, No, I'm not doing it, or, I don't believe in it."

◆   ◆   ◆

In addition to being the last year of the Teacher Leadership Project, 2002 was also the swansong of Microsoft's Anytime Anywhere Learning program. In the US, the program had been picked up by over 1,000 schools (although it was unclear the extent to which schools—especially public schools—had managed to achieve long-term sustainability) reaching some 200,000 students. The program

---

1.   See, for example, <www.esd189.org/tlp/images/tlp2002report.pdf>

had also been exported, most notably to England, where in 2000 Bill Gates launched an initiative that in its first year included 28 schools. Other countries with participating schools included Canada, South Africa, and Belgium.

Following the initial bash in Seattle in 1996, Microsoft ran a further six Anytime Anywhere Learning conferences. As the location Atlanta, Dallas, and Philadelphia alternated with Seattle. The final conference was held in March 2002 in Boston. At that last conference, Bruce Dixon was there, as he had been at the first, still passionately advocating the substantive changes in classroom practice that one-to-one computing could bring about.

There were several reasons why the Anytime Anywhere Learning program seemed to have lost its impetus. Some schools, notably small independent or private schools like Forest Ridge, were going from strength to strength. But in the public sector, with a few exceptions like Clovis and Beaufort, school districts were finding it hard to sustain a laptop program over the long term. The cost was still too high and the provision of adequate infrastructure, especially technical support, remained a major problem.

At the same time, there were now so many more computers around. Educational technology was no longer regarded as such a big deal. After all, had not schools made enormous investments in hardware? Did not most of them have computer labs and Internet connections? The fact that teachers were still not being trained in how to use that hardware seemed somehow to escape most people.

Like any living organism, as Papert had observed, the education system is very good at defending itself against foreign bodies. Tiny germs like Anytime Anywhere Learning and the Teacher Leadership Project seemed to have triggered an immune reaction whose purpose was to digest, assimilate, and, if possible, neutralize the intruder.

"Those programs came along at a time when people were wondering, is technology a good thing for the schools, is it something that schools ought to be doing?" Jeff Fouts said. "And they basically provided the answer, Yes. It's hard now to envisage schools not preparing kids—Who would want to send their kids to a school where technology is not part of the life there at some point? It'd be like sending them to a school without paper and pencils, it's just become so important that it's not questioned any more. The question is teaching kids how to use technology, to make it a tool, and to have the technology become an integral part of the learning process."

By the early years of the new century, the issue of computers in the classroom seemed to have receded in the consciousness of most Americans. Except, that is, in the State of Maine. In September 2002, describing it as "the largest and most ambitious educational technology program in American history", the state began issuing laptop computers to all 17,000 seventh-graders in its public school system. And it was no coincidence that Maine just happened to be the home of Seymour Papert who, 30 years earlier, had prophesied that such an outcome would come to pass.

28

THE LEARNING STATE

Seymour Papert had been living in Maine for about five years when one day in 1998, out of the blue, he received an invitation to lunch with the Governor, Angus King. The venue was the Blaine House, the stately white Victorian mansion that serves as the Governor's official residence in Augusta, Maine's pint-sized [population: 18,560] state capital.

In his adopted state, where he and his third wife, the Russian scholar Suzanne Massey, had taken up residence in the picturesque coastal village of Blue Hill, Papert had long since been making his presence felt. Although now aged 70 and nominally retired, he continued active across a range of education-related projects. Papert had been teaching experimental classes of teenage school dropouts, turning them with the aid of computers into successful learners, talking to teachers at meetings about his ideas, and writing articles for Maine newspapers.

The Governor summoned Papert to share his table because he wanted to sound out this conveniently local world authority on computers in the classroom on an idea that he had had. "Wouldn't it be an achievement," an enthusiastic King asked Papert, "if, instead of having one computer for every six kids in Maine, we could have one computer for every three kids?" Papert looked at King, and in his inimitable style—respectful but insistent—he replied: "No, no, no, Governor—it's not about ratios, it's about making technology available to all of the children, and their teachers, all of the time. The power is in one-to-one, that's where the qualitative change takes place."

It was one of those conversations, King recalled, "that you have and sort of file away." A couple of years later, while suffering through a soporific session at a national governors' meeting, King had a revelation. He had been going to these meetings, which take place two or three times annually, for half-a-dozen years. "Two things suddenly hit me," King said, "A: all governors—and by extension legislators and other public officials—are chasing the same thing, which is prosperity and opportunity for their people. And B: they're all *doing* the same thing—everybody is doing tax cuts, regulatory streamlining, all of the same investments in R&D, in education, educational standards, learning results.

"I realized that it was an echo chamber—we were all saying the same thing. And as a business person, it suddenly hit me that Maine is never going to get ahead by doing the same thing that everybody else is doing. There's an old saying in business: you don't get ahead of the competition by keeping up." The insight was crystal clear: unless King did something new and different, Maine would remain trapped in the lowest third of states in per capita income.

As it happened, the Governor had just been informed that new state budget projections pointed to a one-time surplus of almost a hundred million dollars. He was trying to think up worthy options for spending this unprecedented windfall. Whatever it was, King wanted it to be something big.

"I found it frustrating that most of what we do around here is incremental, at-the-margins stuff," he explained. "You get a little more money, you put a little more money into fixing roofs; you fix a few more roads, you do a hundred miles of roads instead of 88 miles. We decided that this was a kind of once-in-a-lifetime chance to do something transformational instead of incremental."

King summoned Papert for another lunch. Once again, Papert explained the concept of one-to-one computing. This time, he also went into detail on how it could be done, how the state could afford to implement it. "So here we were with extra money and Seymour's vision, and the idea was really a natural," King recalled. "To try to do something different, something that no-one else was doing on the scale we were proposing, that could leapfrog us in terms of the opportunities available to our people, and put Maine in a position of national leadership."

On 2 March 2000, during his annual State of the State speech, the Governor announced his bold new initiative. Entitled "From Lunchboxes to Laptops", the program promised, beginning in 2002, to provide every seventh-grader in Maine with an Internet-ready portable computer. Within six years, every student in the state above the sixth grade would have a laptop which would be theirs to keep. That would mean giving out a total of approximately 20,000 computers each year—17,000 to students and 3,000 to teachers. To pay for the laptops, an endowment fund would be established using a one-time appropriation of $50 million from the state's budget surplus.

"I view this as the best opportunity for a relatively poor state to transform itself in a reasonable period of time in order to provide greater opportunity to its citizens," King proclaimed. "I want Maine to have the most digitally literate society on earth."[1]

The immediate response to this bombshell, the writer and Maine resident Nicholson Baker recalled, "was a general wave of incredulous consternation".

◆   ◆   ◆

Angus King was that rare thing in American politics, an independent. Indeed, until the election of Jesse Ventura in 1998, he was the only independent governor in the US. King had swept to power four years earlier, riding a tidal wave of voter discontent over the partisan tactics of local politicians. A graduate of Dartmouth College, King originally worked as a lawyer. He was known to the public via a long stint hosting a show on Maine's public broadcasting network.

In 1989, aged 43, King founded his own firm, Northeast Energy Management. There, he discovered the power of technology. Since the company couldn't afford to hire a lot of people, it had to do more with less. So King bought computers. Technology became the company's core, enabling it to compete with established rivals. When he came to office, King drew on this experience to modernize Maine's antiquated computer systems, introducing email to the state government and increasing its efficiency—eg, by making all interactions with citizens possible via the Internet—many times over.

As Governor, King soon demonstrated an ability to reach out and connect with the citizens of the Pine Tree State. Tall, lean, and handsome with a full head of strawberry-blonde hair and matching mustache, he cut a dashing figure. King whizzed around the state on his motorcycle, often stopping for a chat with local folks. People invariably referred to their Governor as "Angus". He made Mainers feel good about themselves. They liked his eccentric sense of humor, as exemplified by the mechanical wooden moose he kept on his desk that dispensed M&Ms, from its rear end.

King was exceptionally articulate, with a folksy way with words. He liked to quote sports stars, all-time ice hockey great Wayne Gretzky being a favorite source. "I think Wayne Gretzky had it right when he said you miss 100 percent of the shots you do not take," King said, in reference to the laptop initiative. "It is much better to fail than to not try in the first place." The Governor's charisma and his desire to confront difficult problems did much to secure him statewide

---

1.   "King Unveils Bold Plan to Provide Portable Computers to Maine Students", Press Release, 2 March 2000

See also "A Governor Would Give Every Student a Laptop", *New York Times*, 3 March 2000

support. In 1998 King was re-elected by one of the largest margins of victory in Maine's history.

Undoubtedly the trickiest challenge confronting King as Governor was the disappearance of jobs. Maine is a state that historically has depended largely on its natural resources—trees, paper and wood products, potatoes, fish, and of course, lobsters. Even tourism is a natural-resource-based industry. The issue was that all these industries are in decline, or if not in decline, because of technology, employing fewer people.

How to attract new, high-tech jobs to Maine? Image is a big part of the problem. Maine bills itself as Vacationland, a place to holiday in and eat lobster, not a place to do business. The laptop program was an opportunity to change that backwoods image. The day after King made his historic announcement, in a speech in Silicon Valley, President Clinton mentioned Maine's technology initiative, calling it "an amazing thing."[2] "I guarantee, that's the first time in the history of Silicon Valley that the terms 'Maine', 'amazing', and 'technology' have been used in the same sentence," King commented wryly.

The Governor saw his job as a leader as "to try to look out into the future, see what's necessary, then equip my people with whatever it is." (As Wayne Gretzky put it, in explaining how he scored so many goals, "I skate to where the puck is going to be, not where it is.") Whatever it would turn out to be, there were two things about the future of which King was certain. "One is that it involves education, and more of it; and the second is that it involves technology." When King talked to businesses looking for a place to establish new facilities, they told him that the most important thing for them was not cheap land or tax breaks, but qualified people.

It seemed to the Governor that Maine, with its manageable size—a population of just 1.2 million people, 210,000 kids—was small enough to attempt something like the laptop project on a statewide basis. Papert urged King to enshrine the change by decreeing that "Vacationland" be replaced on car license plates with "The Learning State".

◆   ◆   ◆

King's proposal was at first an extremely generalized idea, without any concrete implementation plans. Initial reaction to it was strongly negative. A vocal rabble of naysayers arose. Nobody could recall an issue in Maine that precipitated

---

2.   <www.privacy2000.org/archives/POTUS_3-3-00_Aspen_Institute_speech.htm>

in such a short time so much public outcry—editorials, op-ed pieces, columns, letters to the editor, as well as discussion on radio talk shows, Internet websites, chat rooms and other such forums.[3]

The response came as a surprise to King, who prided himself on his ability to read Mainers. Some branded his proposal as merely "flashy and fun" at a time when there was a $200 million backlog of school repair projects—serious things like leaky roofs, crumbling walls, obsolete heating systems—demanding attention. Others suggested that King was more interested in his personal legacy than the critical needs of young people.

Seventh-graders were too immature, too irresponsible to be trusted with such expensive equipment. The laptops would be lost, dropped, or stolen. Students already had access to technology, in the shape of computer labs. (If a young hockey player was going to get into the NHL, King shot back, he'd need more than an hour's ice time each week.) Many critics resorted to the time-honored protest against any educational innovation: "my grand-daddy didn't have one…". Someone actually wrote a letter to the paper suggesting that if the governor wanted to do something for the children of Maine, he should buy them all a good pair of winter boots.

King was hit by a barrage of hostile emails. "Dear Governor," read a typical one, "This is the stupidest idea any politician has ever had—what have you been smoking?" One of King's favorites went "Dear Governor: If you want to help the kids in our town, give them each a chainsaw." He wrote back saying, "At least you understand it's a tool! The difference is the tool you want to give them maxes out at fifteen bucks an hour, the tool I want to give them maxes out at Bill Gates." Perhaps the most poignant message read: "Dear Governor: We are a poor state—let someone else lead." He responded, "Yes, and we will stay a poor state unless we lead."

King felt that he had made his biggest strategic error in the press conference held immediately after the laptop announcement. A local reporter asked him "Will the schools own the machines, or the kids?" Not having given the matter much thought, King answered, "the kids". That turned out to be politically disastrous: henceforth the program came to be known as "Governor King's Laptop Giveaway." The idea of *giving* these valuable machines to kids seemed to really offend a lot of people. The state legislature subsequently modified the draft program to say that the schools would own the machines, like library books. It would

---

3.   See, for example, the articles collected at <www.papert.com/articles/laptops/ laptops_master.html>

be up to individual schools to decide whether, and under what circumstances, the machines would leave the premises. (In the end, about half of them would allow students to take their machines home.)

Papert was called in to give a talk to a meeting of the state legislature. There, he ran into a solid wall of opposition from angry representatives. "It was one of the worst days of my life," Papert recalled. It took almost a month for details of the plan to emerge and the misinformation to recede. To inform the discussion, the Governor made available on his website studies from laptop programs, like the one Saul Rockman had conducted on Anytime Anywhere Learning schools.[4]

As late as mid-April, not a single legislator had agreed to support the plan. The state appropriations committee turned it down by a vote of ten to one. Then, as a result of the outpouring of discussion, public opinion and support from lawmakers shifted dramatically. The tide turned to such an extent that the final budget, signed on April 27, included $30 million in funding for a compromise plan that was closer to King's original proposal that anyone had thought possible just two weeks earlier.

By June 2000 legislators who still opposed the plan were losing confidence. King managed to win a further concession. A 17-person task force would be set up to look into learning technology and recommend specific uses, half nominated by the legislature, the other half by the governor himself.

At the same time, to bolster support, instead of talking about the laptops and the proposal, the governor adopted a new strategy. King had argued in favor of laptops till he was blue in the face. Now he was tired of arguing. He told legislators and other interested parties that, if they wanted to know whether computers were beneficial to education, then there were a couple places in the state where they could go and see them in action.

One was Piscataquis Community Middle School in the rural mill town of Guilford which, by happy chance, had recently begun an independent laptop program of its own. The other was a demonstration project in Portland at the Maine Youth Center, a prison for juvenile offenders where Seymour Papert and his colleagues were achieving dramatic results.

◆   ◆   ◆

Maine divides into two halves. The southern half of the state is relatively well populated and growing, with a wide variety of industries and a reasonable tech-

---

4.   <www.state.me.us/education/technology/laptops.htm>

nology base and infrastructure. The northern half, by contrast, is extremely rural, fairly poor, and rapidly losing population, with an economy for the most part based on traditional industries. Piscataquis County falls north of the divide. By population, it is the smallest county in Maine. It has about four people per square mile, the lowest density of any county east of the Mississippi. Piscataquis also has the lowest per capita income in the state.

Located on the Piscataquis River, Guilford [population: 1,531] is about 50 miles northwest of Bangor on the map. The town is pretty much in the middle of nowhere. Crystal Priest, the teacher who led the laptop program at Piscataquis Community Middle School, lives just north of Guilford. "If you go out my back door," she said, "you cross two roads in the first five miles then there's nothing but pine woods until you hit Canada, about 300 miles north." There wasn't much in Guilford for any kid with a shred of ambition. Priest was unusual in that, unlike the vast majority of students in her graduating class who grew up in the area, she was one of the very few who left to get a college education then managed to make it back to work in her chosen field.

Piscataquis Community Middle School was a new school. Opened in the Fall of 1994, the school initially served around 280 kids in grades five through eight. At the time, Piscataquis Community was considered a model of high tech. "That meant that all the teachers had a phone and a computer on their desk, and that we had a computer lab with a network consisting of a file server, an email server, and two laser printers," Priest explained. But no connection to the Internet, nor to any of the other schools in the district.

Priest and a colleague started teaching computer applications classes, one period a week, for all the kids in the school. "We took the approach that the computer was a tool to get work done and taught the students how to use the tool to do real work," she said. But by 1998, both teachers and students felt frustrated. "We were doing a good job teaching the kids to use the tools to do work, but then they couldn't access the tools to get their work done." So the teachers applied for a Teacher Literacy Challenge Grant, federal funding offered on a competitive basis. They used the $35,000 grant they won to purchase 17 Apple iBook laptops. In the school year beginning September 1999, the teachers shared out the computers between the school's eighth graders.

Within a few short months, the characteristic laptop phenomena were manifesting. "Students were using their machines to organize themselves," Priest recalled. "Students and teachers were communicating via email, frequently. Students would read something in a textbook, or hear something in a class discussion and then go onto their iBook to find out more about the topic. They would then starting bringing the info that they found back into class and start asking questions. It really changed the classroom delivery from lecture mode to more of a dialog or discussion. Students became active participants in the classroom for a change. When I checked out the machines, kids were working on their own projects, doing things that had nothing to do with their classwork, but they were interested in something, so they were pursuing it. We started a clay animation unit, among other projects. Students were allowed to express themselves, in a variety of ways. For a lot of our kids, the virtual field trips on the Internet really constituted the first time they had ever 'been anywhere'. Considering that most of our students had never been beyond Bangor, Maine, this was a phenomenon in itself."

The fact that a laptop program could be seen to be working out in the sticks in backwoods Guilford, at Piscataquis, which was one of the bottom ten schools in the state in terms of per-pupil spending, and where over sixty percent of the students were on free and reduced-price lunches, gave the Governor the ammunition he needed to get his statewide laptop project off the ground. One of King's frequent comments during the time when he was getting blasted with criticisms about his proposal was "Don't listen to me, see it for yourself, go to Guilford—ask for Crystal."

All kinds of people made the trek: state legislators, business people, teachers and school administrators from around the state, plus a wide assortment of media—TV, radio, newspapers, magazines. Other visitors included Seymour Papert and Kathy Klock. On Klock's recommendation, the Gates Foundation would subsequently donate a million dollars to fund training for teachers at nine demonstration sites in Maine, including Piscataquis. One in each region of the state, these schools would begin using laptops in February 2002, six months ahead of the statewide rollout.

For Piscataquis, there would also be a unexpected bonus. As a result of hearing King speak about laptops, Guilford of Maine, a local manufacturer of panel fabrics for offices, stepped up with a donation of $100,000. This enabled the school to buy 120 more iBooks. In September 2000, all its eighth graders were issued with the laptops, seventh-graders had 3:1 access, while fifth-and sixth-graders had to share a classroom's worth of laptops between them. Priest commented that it was interesting to watch the "almost cut-throat competition" on Monday mornings among fifth-and sixth-grade teachers vying for the limited number of iBooks.

◆   ◆   ◆

Prior to his laptop initiative, the single achievement that Angus King was most proud of was his record in revamping Maine's prison system. In addition to renovating dilapidated facilities, the Governor had also initiated rehabilitation programs. Thus, when in 1998 Amnesty International and the American Correctional Association criticized as excessive the state's treatment of the 200-odd juveniles incarcerated at the Maine Youth Center in Portland, King was quick to take action. The standard school system having manifestly failed these kids, the Governor decided to try a different approach. One again, he turned for advice to his favorite educational guru, Seymour Papert.

(By coincidence, aware that Papert had been having success teaching teenage high school dropouts, authorities at the Youth Center had independently written to the professor to solicit his help. But, thinking that "youth center" meant some kind of boy's club, he had dismissed their request.)

Papert responded to King with a proposal for a radical restructuring of education at the Youth Center. It would become a learning environment that was as different as possible from the traditional school model. "We'll throw everything out," he said, "there'll be no grades, no standard curriculum—we'll try to build something on a sort of *tabula rasa*." The Center would also serve as a place to try out ideas for learning activities that most schools were too conservative to try. It would generate examples of how technology could be used that would then be adopted by the public school system.

King gave the plan the go-ahead. The teachers Papert recruited included David Cavallo from MIT and Gary Stager, now a professor of education at Pepperdine University, whom we last met conducting professional development workshops in Australia. Maine's Commissioner of Education, Duke Albanese, freed them from having to meet the state's curriculum requirements and, beginning in September 1999, they were off.

"We had the kids for five interrupted hours," Stager recalled. "There was one computer per child, it was based on projects, multi-age [13 to 21], interdisciplinary. The goal was to acquaint or reacquaint these at-risk students with the joy and power of learning." Officially, this alternative classroom in the state prison for teens was known as the Constructionist Learning Laboratory. But because there were invariably pieces of Lego scattered all over the place, the kids soon started calling it the Lego Lab.

At any given time, about a dozen students would be in the Lab. More than half were labelled "special ed". Most hadn't been near a school since seventh grade, and didn't know anyone who had. Conveying to them the notion of a project was hard. It was only after the teachers had been working with the kids for some time that they discovered the answer. Visitors would come by the Youth Center nearly every day. The students would have to drop everything to show what they were doing. They became really good at demonstrating their work. What the kids chose to share was stuff that they had been working on for a long time, things that meant a lot to them. So "a project" became, by definition, something that you wanted to share with others. Happily, that coincided with one of Papert's definitions of constructionism, which is that knowledge should be shareable.

Some of the projects were extraordinary. For the first time in their lives, the kids were able to have authentic intellectual experiences. One 15-year-old boy who was classified as illiterate built a vending machine that charged higher prices for cold drinks as the temperature rose (an idea that Coca Cola was reportedly toying with at the time). Programmed by computer, actuated by heat, touch, and rotation sensors, and driven by motors that made parts go back and forth, it was an incredible feat of engineering. Other kids built luggage sorters, phonographs, temperature plotters, outcomes with which many second-year university engineering students would have been happy.

A particularly popular theme was building motorized vehicles to climb ramps. One girl experimented with putting sandpaper on the ramp to increase the friction. When she found the grade of sandpaper that seemed to work best with her vehicle, she decided to look at the tread of its tires and the surface of the sandpaper under a digital microscope. She printed out images of each at the same magnification level. When she compared them she discovered that the texture of the wheel and the surface were very similar—it was like teeth meshing in a gear. Result: a profound understanding of how friction worked.

For many visitors, seeing what kids in the most challenged student body in the state were capable of came as a revelation. One such was the Commissioner of Education himself. Before he came to the Youth Center Albanese had tentatively believed in the potential of computers to transform learning. Now, thanks to the incredible case studies he saw there, it all became much more concrete for him. "What Seymour has done with a different approach, using technology, motivating learners, just dramatically discounts the notion that all children can't learn," Albanese said. Whenever he encountered teachers, principals, or superintendents who doubted the power of technology, Albanese would urge them to go and watch what the juveniles were accomplishing with Papert at the Center.

As part of their research into learning technology members of the Task Force on the Maine Learning Technology Endowment visited the Center. In January 2001, the task force delivered its final report. Not surprisingly, given that Papert was a member, its recommendation was to proceed with Governor King's proposal.

"We know that computer technology in schools—*learning technology*—done the right way can provide...tremendous boosts to teaching and learning", the report concluded. "Hundreds of individual schools nationally and internationally have piloted 'anytime, anywhere" learning technology, putting portable computers into the hands of students. Results are universally positive. Mistakes have been made, and those we can learn from. Others have tinkered, but Maine can be first...".[5] [emphasis in the original]

◆   ◆   ◆

Among the mistakes that Maine would be able to learn from were those made by Henrico County School District in suburban Richmond, Virginia. In May 2001, Henrico County superintendent Mark Edwards announced, out of the blue, the purchase 23,000 Apple iBook laptop computers, one for every high school and middle school student and teacher in the district.[6] This was significant for two reasons. First, because it was the largest order for computers ever placed by a school district; and second, because the district was able to fund the $18.6 million, four-year deal to lease the machines with its operating budget. Henrico thus demonstrated, for the first time, that it was possible to pay for a laptop program out of existing recurrent funding.

Having pioneered a new model for funding, however, the district seemed determined to go it alone in other respects, too. Henrico officials showed no sign of having looked at laptop programs underway elsewhere. With 18,000 desktop machines already in place, the district was, after all, technologically sophisticated. Staff there were performing a number of their administrative functions, such as

---

5. "Teaching and Learning for Tomorrow: A Learning Technology Plan for Maine's Future", Final Report on the Maine Learning Technology Endowment, January 2001, p7

6. Rebecca S. Weiner, "School District Buys 23,000 Laptops", *New York Times*, 8 May 2001

grading and attendance, via computer. And, whereas most previous laptop programs had used PCs, Henrico had opted for Macs. Who could teach them anything?

Hubris led Henrico to make some unfortunate decisions. Like rushing the introduction of the machines, allowing only five months between initial announcement and distribution of computers, not enough time for crucial preparations, in particular teacher training. Like *giving* the computers to the students, the only cost to parents being $50 for insurance to cover, theft, loss, and damage, thus taking away the ownership component which had proved so important in previous programs. And above all, like issuing the first batch of computers to *high school* students, rather than elementary and middle school kids, as had been the norm elsewhere, and imposing no restrictions on their use. This was asking for trouble.

The 11,800-odd teenagers at Henrico's eight high schools received their iBooks in September 2001. By December, 50 to 60 students had already been disciplined for using their computers to download pornography. In January 2002, the national media had a field day when two Henrico 16-year-olds were suspended from school after being caught hacking into a teacher's computer, attempting to change their grades. Police were called in to investigate the matter.

In addition, it appeared that there was a good deal of surreptitious playing of games going on in class. The lion's share bandwidth on the school's network was being eaten up by students trading music and movies. "[The laptop]'s basically just a $1,200 CD player and a Game Boy," one blasé student told visitors.

In February 2002, these embarrassing incidents and the resultant bad publicity forced the district to call in all the computers for a refit. School technicians "scrubbed" hard drives to remove offending material, stripped out class-disturbing features such as file-sharing and instant messaging, and inserted filters to restrict network access to school-approved areas only.

All of this was directly relevant to Maine. Especially after the Governor signed a $37.2 million four-year deal in December 2001 to lease 36,000 wireless iBooks from Apple. "We saw some cautionary things in Henrico," said Yellow Light Breen, a spokesman for the state's education department, "but certainly we learned from their experience, both good and bad." The department worked closely with Apple to ensure that computers would be used for learning, not entertainment. "I was not going to be the governor who brought 36,000 Game Boys to Maine," King said. In addition, students and parents would be required to promise in writing to adhere to the state's acceptable-use policy.

Conservative activists urged that Virginia's "lapflop" program was proof that the Maine legislature should pull the plug on the controversial plan. Supporters countered by pointing to the success of the Guilford project, and how thorough teacher training and clear, well-enforced rules on student conduct seemed to be working there.

That Spring, two thousand computers were distributed to the State's other eight "exploration" sites. Public response at these schools was extraordinarily positive. Funding for professional development from the Gates Foundation kicked in. King spent an afternoon with the teachers at the training program. "If you people screw this up," the Governor joked as he left, "I'll find you and kill you!"

Then in April, just when momentum behind the laptop initiative seemed unstoppable, disaster struck. Tax returns indicated that the state was heading for a budget deficit of at least $200 million, perhaps double that. A special session of the state legislature was convened to deal with the shortfall. The legislature had previously cut the laptop plan back from $30 million to $25. Now some legislators advocated breaking the contract with Apple. They asked the Attorney General's office to determine what would be the state's liability if it did.

In a desperate bid to save his plan, King proposed a further trimming, to $15 million. The new, bare-bones version of the program would no longer have an endowment to guarantee perpetuity. It would now be dependent on annual appropriations, something that the Governor had previously resisted. The gutted program was left with just enough money to equip seventh and eight grades for four years (on the assumption that machines lasted that long). Beyond that, Lunchboxes to Laptops would have to prove its worth.

◆   ◆   ◆

In August 2002, to launch the historic initiative, a conference entitled "Laptops, Learners, and Powerful Ideas" was held just outside Bangor, at the University of Maine. (Co-organizer Gary Stager had wanted to call the conference "Mainestorms", a play on the title of Papert's best-known book, but wiser counsels prevailed.) Chaired by Papert himself, the conference was in large part a celebration of the achievements of the pioneers in the field. Alan Kay was there, talking of his first meeting with Papert back in 1968, seeing children programming computers.

"I thought then that was the best idea that anybody had ever had for computers," Kay said, "and I still do: What could be greater than to be able to help many more children go off to thinking about many more things in the most advanced way?" He demonstrated his pride and joy, Squeak, a powerful "idea processor for children of all ages", inspired by Papert and directly descended from Logo.

The conference functioned as a kind of gathering of the laptop clan. The Australians were there in force. They included David Loader, the first laptop school principal, Steve Costa, the first laptop class teacher, Bruce Dixon, the behind-the-scenes implementor who made it all happen, and Gary Stager who by this time was more or less an honorary Australian. Clothilde Fonseca was also on hand to regale the audience with remarkable stories about the impact computers had had on education throughout Costa Rica. The only no-show at the conference, oddly enough, was Angus King himself (though he did manage to confer his blessing via video hookup). His presence was required elsewhere, hosting the eighth annual Great Taste of Maine Lobster Governor's Tasting, outside the Blaine House in Augusta. Such are the imperatives of state politics.

Last-minute efforts by Maine's legislators to block funding for the laptop program failed. The rollout of 17,000-plus laptops to every seventh-grader in Maine's 239 middle schools—urban and rural, rich and poor—went ahead as planned. There were inevitably some initial glitches but, after six months, the word was that at most schools the program was going well. But as the state wrestled to come to terms with a billion-dollar budget deficit, the question of whether it would be able to sustain the program remained moot. Crystal Priest, for one was convinced that it would. "Personally," she said, "I think the legislators are going to have a hard time taking the machines out of the kids' hands."

King, too, had no doubt that his laptop program was going to work. Or that, once the concept was proven, other states would quickly follow Maine's lead. "Governors are an immensely competitive bunch," he said, "and if something is really happening and making an impact in a given state, it's going spread across the country very fast because they're not going to want to fall behind, they're going to want to be involved. We've already had three or four states that are taking an interest. If I were governor of another state, I'd be sitting back and watching how this works...."

CONCLUSION

On 8 January 2003 Angus King left office, packing his wife and two younger children into an RV and heading off for a much-anticipated tour of the United States. King left feeling confident that Maine's laptop program would survive and prosper without him. His successor as Governor had come out in favor of the project. As a parting gift, King contributed $100,000 of his own money to help pay for home Internet access for middle school students in the State.

Elsewhere, other pioneering laptop leaders were likewise no longer in place. Superintendents like Walter Buster and Charlie Rhyan had retired. Boosters like Tammy Morrison and Kathy Klock had moved on to other things.

By the middle of the first decade of the new century, it seemed computers were no longer the priority for education that they had been in the 1990s. The idea of the need to integrate technology into the curriculum, as opposed to teaching it as a separate subject, was now increasingly well understood. There was even a movement away from fixed computer laboratories towards carts of laptops that could be wheeled around from classroom to classroom, like at Emerson Elementary. But in a time of huge budget deficits, there was still precious little money available for professional development of teachers at the state level.

New pressures were pushing the mass adoption of laptops. In Florida, a class-size amendment passed by voters in November 2002 obliged the state to find thousands of extra classrooms. Rather than build new schools, a local teachers' union leader suggested that the state could save money by converting 1,680 existing computer labs to classrooms and giving laptops to all 644,000 high school students in the state. Governor Jeb Bush said the idea "could be a win-win."[1]

At the same time, the price of laptops and notebooks continued to drop, by on average around $100 a year. Massive over-investment in production capacity had prompted savage competition between manufacturers of liquid crystal displays, the laptop's single most expensive component. The semiconductor industry's move from eight-inch to twelve-inch wafers promised to reduce the cost of chips by forty percent over five years.

---

1.   Matthew Pinzur, "Teachers leader pushes laptops to free up labs for class space", *Miami Herald*, 11 Feb 2003

As production volumes increased, and with education no longer the market of last resort (especially with states contemplating banding together to get bulk discounts), it seemed reasonable to predict that full-function laptops costing around $500 would be available by around 2007. In addition, the rapid spread of wireless networks, a technology that could have been invented with education in mind, meant that schools no longer had to invest in expensive wiring, thus reducing the cost of installation. The tipping point seemed nigh.

Schools were discovering, belatedly, that computers could reduce the administrative load on teachers. Marking attendance electronically was merely the most obvious example of this ability. Paradoxically, however, at a time when businesses were stressing the need to become less hierarchical and more entrepreneurial, schools seemed to be moving in the opposite direction. In many districts, standardization and ever-increasing micro-management were the order of the day.

There seemed no limit to America's obsession with testing and test scores, or to the eagerness of politicians to exploit voters' fears in this regard. By definition conservative, parents allowed themselves to be persuaded that higher test scores equalled better education. But parents also want the best for their children. Some were beginning to demand that their kids should be better prepared for the twenty-first century workplace, and that more emphasis be put on fostering creativity, autonomy, persistence, and risk-taking. Unfortunately there was no way to get inside kids heads to measure these things, and failing that, no way for politicians to promote themselves based on delivering such eminently desirable outcomes.

◆   ◆   ◆

In Australia, too, changes had taken place. David Loader had long since left Methodist Ladies' College. He resigned unexpectedly in 1997 after 18 years as principal, moving on to head Wesley College, one of Australia's most prestigious schools. On his departure from MLC, at a hastily-organized gathering over morning tea, Loader was invited to speak to the staff. He managed only a few words before breaking down in tears.

In retrospect, Loader did not see the introduction of laptops as his greatest achievement at MLC. For him, a more significant educational statement, which occurred around the same time as the computer initiative, was the purchase of a farm on which the school built several houses for ninth-grade girls to live in during a residential semester. But in both cases—laptops and residentials—the message was the same: "we no longer have faith that the classroom can solve the educational question."

Certainly not the classroom in its traditional form, with students all sitting in rows facing front. In 1997, Loader's final year at the school, the year-eight building at MLC was completely refurbished. Significant features of the new design were fewer classrooms, large open areas suited to group work, bench desks with network connections for independent learning, tiered seating to serve as an amphitheater or conversation pit, mobile furniture units to create smaller spaces or alcoves, and walls that curved.

The building, felt David Dimsey, MLC's original computer teacher, embodied the school's commitment to a flexible new philosophy of learning. It was what he called the third step in computing. "The first step is to get the laptop computers in place," Dimsey explained, "the second step is you actually develop computing that suits that way of working"—like longer lesson times, allowing the kids to work independently, instead of having them all do the same thing at the same time like they always used to.

"The third step is you start knocking down the walls, changing the physical space of the school to reflect the different ways that the students work. I think if you embrace the philosophy and commit yourselves to putting it into practice as a school, as an organization, then that happens—rooms are not in the right size or shape to do what you want to do. And it's that commitment to bricks and mortar that convinces me that MLC is still ahead of most other schools who are doing this."

After Loader's departure, MLC continued to promote new and more flexible styles of learning. For example, the school devoted a lot of resources developing online learning. "We do things like tailor individual activities to individual students," explained Silvia Guidara, who headed the school's online learning team. "For example, at the moment, the year-seven English coordinator has developed a unit where she's created a lesson, but she's identified different learning preferences, or abilities, or styles of student. Through the online learning system, she could have a class of thirty students and deliver thirty different lessons tailor-made for those students without having to disrupt the class.

"Our research shows that students who don't find school such a great experience, and who have struggled in the past, do pretty well in this style of learning. Students who were normally quiet in class and wouldn't say anything communicate a lot more in the online discussions. Online forums, from year-seven immersion French to year-twelve media, have proved to be really productive learning tools, where students will say more because they're writing, or they'll say it in a different way, and it's terrific for our English-as-a-second-language students.

"The other thing online is doing, with the wireless network, is that it's changing our physical learning environment—if you're online, do you need to be in rows? We were able to do it so that students were in different classes in different parts of the school, but they were operating in online groups. And it allowed students to work with different teachers. So where classes were blocked on the same time, we'd email the students and say, you can work here, here, or here, just email us and tell us which teacher you're with. In one unit, on *To Kill a Mockingbird*, we had teachers who were online as experts, so you could ask a politics expert about American politics or a history expert about history, so the students had more teachers available."

◆   ◆   ◆

In 2003, Irene Grasso was one of the few teachers still left at MLC who had been involved with the laptop program since its inception, thirteen years earlier. Now, looking back, Grasso thought that "one of the big changes is that there is no longer a guru." The technology had become so deeply ingrained in the school's culture, that there was no longer any need for a charismatic leader to show the way.

Grasso would sometimes take visitors around the school. She would start out intending to bring them to see someone like Silvia Guidara, someone she knew would do something incredible in their classroom. Invariably, however, "I get waylaid along the way, because as I walk down the corridor, we pass other classes, people I hadn't realized are doing really exciting things, and I get drawn into a commerce classroom or a politics classroom where they're looking up the police website and checking for gender bias and all sorts of things, things I hadn't even thought of, and often staff that none of us knew were doing anything really exciting. The visitors are impressed, and the teacher thinks, Doesn't everybody do this? And of course the reality is that they don't; but in this community, they do."

Grasso was glad to have worked with extraordinary individuals like David Loader, Liddy Nevile, and Gary Stager, and to have participated in the excitement of the early days, when they were doing groundbreaking things. Ultimately, however, as she said, the reason why MLC's laptop program flourished, why people continued with it, was because the program worked for the students. "If it didn't work for kids," Grasso emphasized, "teachers wouldn't be doing it. Teachers are really critical of anything that's a fad. So while a charismatic leader might help you with a fad for a few years, the fact that [the laptop program] is still going is because it works for kids."

◆　　　◆　　　◆

Overall in Victoria, the state in which MLC and most of the pioneering laptop schools were located, the picture was not encouraging. Some independent schools seemed to be resting on their laurels, imagining that by giving their students laptop computers, their job was finished, as opposed to just beginning. In the public sector, the state government had issued laptop computers to all its 37,000-plus teachers. This initiative was originally proposed by the indefatigable Bruce Dixon (the government showing its gratitude by refusing to allow Dixon's company to bid for the contract to supply the machines). But the grand gesture having been made, there was little in the way of follow-up in terms of educating the teachers to use the machines or encouraging their use in the classroom. Laptop ownership in public schools remained the exception rather than the rule.

To judge by coverage in the Melbourne-based media, the laptop revolution might never have happened. Instead of celebrating the world-leading work happening in some Victorian classrooms, local newspapers mostly preferred to run critical articles ("jury still out on computers in schools"; "PCs a health risk to pupils"; "laptops get mixed report") many of them reprinted from overseas sources. Australia's notorious "tall poppy syndrome" required that anyone aspiring to rise above the pack must be cut down to size. At the same time, there was a prevailing egalitarian ideology. By insisting on laptops for their pupils independent schools were acting in an elitist manner, hence could be ignored because beyond the ideological pale.

But as in the US, the trend towards every kid having a computer was not slowing down, it was if anything accelerating. The challenge, as Bruce Dixon saw it, was to make sure that all those computers had some impact on learning. That meant bringing down the barriers to change, foremost among which was teaching practice. "How do you get a teacher to decide that it's worthwhile taking the risk to change what they're doing, to implement technology to produce better outcomes for kids?" Dixon asked. His answer as ever was, by identifying success models, then spreading the good word about them through the medium of conferences.

Since 1994 Dixon had been running annual conferences for educators under the banner Expanding Learning Horizons. At these meetings, teachers got to together to share ideas, feel good about themselves, and build a sense of community. Then, duly inspired, they would go back to their classrooms and do good things. This was all very well at the individual teacher level, but such conferences did not provide enough substance to produce sustainable change in teaching practice.

Dixon's goal was now to provide the means of bringing about significant changes in teaching within entire departments and, ideally, schools. To this end, he conceived a new initiative called the Technology, Teaching and Learning Institute, which because too risky for his company he funded out of his own pocket. The idea was to bring in from around the world top experts in various subjects—science, math, the humanities—who were used to working in "technology-rich environments" (meaning classrooms with lots of computers, but not necessarily laptops). These experts would give intensive, ten-hour workshops over five days to small groups of experienced teachers.

Dixon ran the first Institute in 2002. His biggest problem was finding people capable of leading the sessions. It seemed that there were only a handful of teachers in the world with sufficient experience of technology. Most, like Tom Seidenberg of Phillips Exeter Academy in New Hampshire, Nils Ahbel of Deerfield Academy in Massachusetts, and Gloria Barrett of the School of Science & Mathematics in Durham, North Carolina, came from the US. It pained Dixon to admit that, for all the experience with laptops that Australian schools had had, of the 21 teachers who would lead the sessions at the 2003 Institute in Melbourne, only about one third were Australian.

Dixon hoped that, in future years, being a session leader at a Technology, Teaching & Learning Institute would become something to which ambitious teachers would aspire. It would be an acknowledgement from the teacher's peer group that he or she had something worth sharing.

The Institute was merely one phase of Dixon's ongoing campaign to bring about substantive change. A second phase was SchoolTech, another annual conference, this time in recognition of the ongoing headache of how to provide adequate technical support in schools. Here, Dixon set the bar at what he called "Internet cafe" standard.

This was derived from his experience using an Internet cafe on London's Oxford Street. "It had 250 machines, not a human being present, and you buy a tag from a slot machine. On average, there are of the order of a hundred-odd people a week on each computer, 24 hours a day, therefore not caring anything about the machine. I went there five times, never saw one machine with a Do Not Use sign on it. So how come we can run these sorts of facilities, make them work, but you put them in a school, and you spend your life being told, The network's down, or, The computer doesn't work? Because we're crap at doing it, and we don't set standards."

These days, physical repairs to computers are typically done by the vendor under contract. But schools still need people to support what's happening in the classrooms. Specifically, one or two technicians to do software diagnostics and interface with the vendor. In addition, a manager to run the network, set high standards, and make sure that they are maintained. The idea behind SchoolTech is to improve the quality of these people. Dixon reckoned that the conference could have a significant effect within five years.

After technicians, Dixon's next target was school business managers, the people responsible for the financial side of laptop programs. "They've loomed as the big thorns in the side," he said. "Business managers have a problem when such large expenditures come into play, hence start to intervene in the decision-making process, sometimes making decisions based on financial considerations rather than educational ones."

It would take him another few years, but eventually Dixon reckoned he would reach all the decision makers, anyone who presented a barrier. Ultimately, the change process was very complicated one. Transforming learning was not something that was going to happen overnight. "Just because we're able to equip kids with laptops," he said, "that doesn't mean we've succeeded. We haven't even got to first base, we've only just put the first batter up."

◆   ◆   ◆

"[T]he reality is sobering," wrote three US researchers in a report published in August 2002. "[T]o a first-order approximation, the effect of the computing technology over the past 25 years on primary and secondary education has been *zero.*"[2] There is, indeed, a very long way still to go.

In almost all other walks of life, computers have long since been accepted as indispensable. In schools, however, it is still possible to argue that technology is causing a crisis, one that actually imperils learning. Alas, there is no shortage of examples of the misuse of computers in the classroom that can be advanced as evidence in support of that argument. But that doesn't mean the baby should be thrown out along with the bath water.

---

2.   Cathleen Norris, Elliot Soloway, and Terry Sullivan, "Examining 25 Years of Technology in US Education", Communications of the ACM, August 2002, Vol. 45, No.8

In most schools, most students spend at best only a few hours a week using a computer—a tool that other sectors of society regard as essential to their functioning—and even then often for trivial ends. To be sure, many kids do acquire fluency in the technology, but typically they do it outside of school, with no particular intellectual aim in mind. In many classrooms their computer skills are still not welcome, indeed are actively discouraged.

At the same time, it is hard to conceive of a future in which a portable computer is *not* part of every schoolchild's standard equipment. Perhaps the balance will only tip when a new generation of techno-savvy teachers who have themselves grown up with computers begins to ripple up through the school system. In the meantime, however, the average age of teachers in most Western countries continues to climb, especially in subjects like maths and science, where computers are most effective intellect-boosting tools.

So what about the students caught in the gap between the receding and oncoming tides? Do these kids have the right to be educated "in the medium of their own time"? Of course they do. The question is not whether, but when. We cannot afford to dither any longer. Parents, teachers, principals, administrators, politicians, employers, journalists—we must all work together to transform learning, for the sake of our children and their future.

ACKNOWLEDGEMENTS

James Joyce once said that it was a wonderful experience to live with a book. Having lived with this one for almost half a dozen years now, I think I know what he meant. Joyce was talking about fiction, and the sheer pleasure he derived from writing. The great thing about non-fiction is that, in addition to writing, you also get to go places and meet people.

This book has taken me from Melbourne to Cambridge, Massachusetts; Hanover, New Hampshire; New York City; San Francisco, Palo Alto, and Glendale, California; Seattle, Washington; Bangor, Maine; and of course, Tokyo. Along the way I have met many extraordinary individuals, some of whom have turned into friends. I thank all of them for giving me their time, telling me their stories and, in some cases, reading and commenting on draft versions of my chapters.

Seymour Papert and Pat Suppes were particularly generous, allowing me to interview them repeatedly. David Loader was extraordinarily open, among other things letting me follow him around for several days. Adam Smith was always ready to discuss things, guiding me through historical and contemporary issues. Above all, I am grateful to Bruce Dixon for keeping me up to date on developments, for introducing me to all the right people, and for the inspiration of his example.

Angelos Agalianos very kindly sent me a copy of his PhD thesis, A Cultural Studies Analysis of Logo in Education, which was an invaluable reference for my chapters on Papert's work at MIT.

The cover photo of David Loader and the girls of the first laptop class at MLC is used by courtesy of The Herald & Weekly Times Ltd.

Every writer needs a good librarian. In my case, I was truly fortunate in being able to rely on Alison Daams of Hume-Moonee Valley Library. No matter how recondite the reference, Alison was always able to track it down for me.

During the long years of research, whenever there was a setback or I needed reassurance that I was doing something worthwhile, I was always able to count on sympathy, support and good guidance from two loyal friends: my mentor, Victor

McElheny, and my guardian angel, Michael Bessie, to whom this book is dedicated.

Melbourne, March 2003

ABOUT THE AUTHOR

Bob Johnstone has been writing about technology's impact on society for 20 years. During that time Johnstone was a correspondent for many magazines, including *New Scientist, Far Eastern Economic Review,* and *Wired.* His first book, *We Were Burning: Japanese Entrepreneurs and the Forging of the Electronic Age,* was published in 1998.

Index

0-595-65897-0

Printed in the United States
1308100001B/235

9 780595 658978